"With a brilliantly plotted and perfectly paced novel, ~~~~~ Scott McDaniel once again captures her readers from the first page and doesn't let go until the very end. Irresistibly set in the glittering world of the 1920s, this second-chance romance satisfies on every level."

—Rebekah Millet, award-winning author of *Julia Monroe Begins Again*

"If glittering, heart-stopping romantic suspense is your genre, then you don't need to look any further than this masterpiece from Rachel Scott McDaniel. *The Dreams We Knew* is nothing short of a reader's dream. Incredible mystery is suspensefully woven through a swoon-worthy romance with well-placed threads of faith and second chances. The interspersed flashbacks offer an amazing point of view, supplying clues, redemption, and clarity, and helping readers deliciously unravel this story clue by clue. The history and attention to detail is the cherry on top that allows this book to truly shine and come alive, giving readers the experience of a lifetime."

—Tasha, @the_clean_read_book_club

"I loved this romantic mystery. The second-chance romance was sweet, and Kent and Delvina's banter and chemistry provided a level of intimacy that allowed them to reconnect and grow together. I loved how the mystery tied together to supply all the answers, even though it kept me guessing until the end. The fast pace made for an engaging read that was full of heart, finding the truth, and falling in love."

—Cait Goodey, book reviewer on GoodeyReads (@goodeyreads)

"Rachel Scott McDaniel's exquisite storytelling in *The Dreams We Knew* delivers a story brimming with mystery, romance, and captivating characters, all wrapped in a quick-paced adventure you can't put down.

Every page of this intriguing story proves why McDaniel is the very best in her genre!"
—Natalie Walters, award-winning author of *Better Watch Out* and the SNAP Agency series

"Rachel Scott McDaniel sweeps readers away to the 1920s with this dazzling novel of mystery, second chances, danger, and romance! McDaniel brings a mystery that both feels cozy and had me on the edge of my seat. Readers won't want to miss this story."
—Hannah, @modernmissgranger

THE
DREAMS
WE KNEW

Books by Rachel Scott McDaniel

Walking on Hidden Wings
The Dreams We Knew
Something Borrowed: A Historical Romance Collection

RACHEL SCOTT McDANIEL

THE
DREAMS
WE KNEW

A NOVEL of the ROARING TWENTIES

KREGEL
PUBLICATIONS

Library of Congress Cataloging-in-Publication Data
Names: McDaniel, Rachel Scott, author.
Title: The dreams we knew : a novel of the roaring twenties / Rachel Scott
    McDaniel.
Description: Grand Rapids, MI : Kregel Publications, 2025.
Identifiers: LCCN 2024034651 (print) | LCCN 2024034652 (ebook)
Subjects: LCGFT: Detective and mystery fiction. | Novels.
Classification: LCC PS3613.C38576 D74 2025 (print) | LCC PS3613.
    C38576 (ebook) | DDC 813/.6—dc23/eng/20240802
LC record available at https://lccn.loc.gov/2024034651
LC ebook record available at https://lccn.loc.gov/2024034652

ISBN 978-0-8254-4814-0, print
ISBN 978-0-8254-7094-3, epub
ISBN 978-0-8254-6993-0, Kindle

Printed in the United States of America
25 26 27 28 29 30 31 32 33 34 / 5 4 3 2 1

Here's to those branded the misfits and outcasts. I see you. I carry that same brand—a mark I once felt grounded me with shame but since have accepted as my wings. Soar to new heights, friends.

Chapter 1

Delvina Salvastano Kline
October 1924

MY CHANEL EVENING FROCK HAD conspired with the darkness to cloak me, but the approaching dawn would soon betray my trespassing presence. Daybreak whispered a ghostly chant across the expanse of abandoned warehouses. Without the shadows to cling to, I pressed my back against the soot-crusted walls of the fifth structure I'd searched in as many hours. The coarse stucco snagged the expensive silk, reminding me of the horrid party I'd subtly invaded in order to wheedle the information that brought me here.

Though maybe the drunk butler I'd chatted with at the posh speakeasy had led me wrong. I'd thought it'd all been a lost cause until about three in the morning. His fourth glass of scotch had unhinged his jaw and loosened his tongue, but that didn't mean he'd provided the right location. One could never tell where loyalties lay. Especially when it came to Jules Dempsey and his bootlegging empire. The recently sacked butler of the Dempsey estate was too deep into his cups to be certain. Though he wasn't so far gone not to recognize I was siphoning information.

And with the hours stripping away, I couldn't afford a mistake. A life depended on my accuracy.

The faint yet sour smell of corn mash in the air betrayed the presence of a nearby still. But I wasn't traipsing around the outskirts of New York City to sniff out a moonshine operation.

I was here on behalf of Judge VanKirk. Hopefully, His Honor would keep his end of the bargain and stall the verdict of the case against Dempsey until I could recover the judge's fifteen-year-old daughter from the mobster's cronies.

If I could find her.

I set my sights on the grime-laden structure before me, keeping alert for any movement other than the skittering of rodents. The lower windows were blackened with soot, but one sweeping gaze of the angled skylights closer to the rooftop revealed the truth. Those glass panes were significantly less grimy, meaning the ones at eye level had been purposefully darkened.

Someone didn't want trespassers peeking inside. Maybe because those seedy walls housed Judge VanKirk's daughter. Kidnapping the presiding judge's child in an effort to get him to throw out the case against the notorious crime boss was a cruel but effective tactic.

The harried father couldn't rely on the corrupt police to recover his only offspring, so he'd turned to me. And I had to deliver the girl before court resumed—otherwise the judge would no doubt rule in Dempsey's favor, marring the integrity of his legendary iron gavel.

Ignoring the slight pinch of my little toes in these satin slippers, I dashed toward the ladder affixed to the side of the warehouse, which led to a narrow landing on the second story.

I wound my purse strap tight on my wrist and climbed the dew-slicked rungs. I clambered over the ledge, my silk stockings catching on the rusty railing, and settled my feet on the puddle-dotted surface.

After freeing my purse from my wrist, I withdrew my revolver. A thigh holster sounded reasonable in theory, but the blasted thing had a habit of slipping down my leg with the weight of my weapon. Clearly a man's design.

Besides, I needed my bag for my lockpicks, which I'd had to employ several times this morning in search of the fair-haired Marianne VanKirk.

The shuffle of footsteps reached my ears, and I whirled on my heel, aim at the ready. An unexpected view of wavy black hair coupled with an easygoing smile—more fit on a *Variety* ad than on a shifty rooftop— greeted me.

"Kent Brisbane." I feigned indifference, as if that name hadn't haunted me. "I wouldn't suppose you fancied getting shot today." Ignoring my pounding pulse, I offered a practiced smile. "Because my Colt almost left its lead calling card between your ribs." I lowered my revolver and noticed his own was clutched in his right hand.

"What a nice keepsake." That voice. It was just as smooth and deep as I remembered. "One that'd hit very close to my heart."

I didn't want to talk about his heart. Or mine, for that matter. I'd come here to do a job. Question now, what was *he* doing here? Our paths hadn't crossed in four years, intentional on my part. And though there was a time I'd once trusted him implicitly, I wasn't certain now. Crime lords and bootleggers had bloated bank accounts controlling most of New York City. For all I knew, Kent could be on Dempsey's payroll. If so, I might indeed have to shoot him if things turned aggressive. Not the most pleasant thought, considering the man had once been my husband.

His gaze took me in, a serious note darkening his gray eyes before masking any hint of emotion with that easy breeziness I'd known so well. The scar on the upper corner of his mouth made his smile lopsided, which only added to his charm. "I don't suppose you brought a change of clothes? With that kind of dress"—he stepped toward me and playfully flicked the bow on my shoulder—"you're bound to attract attention and ruin my cover."

He implied he was working on a case, which had me easing my grip on my gun. Though I knew better than to lower my guard. One could never tell with Kent. I'd fooled myself into thinking I'd understood him, only to be betrayed before the ink had dried on our marriage license. I didn't have time to unearth the buried hurt. Any other day I could wallow in fuzzy memories about one poor life choice that had led to a terrible marriage, but not now. A young girl depended on me.

So I pushed back the rising disgust of my former husband's presence and reclaimed my composure, albeit a bit shaky. "Who hired you, Brisbane?"

"Same man who employed you. Judge VanKirk." He slid his hand into his coat pocket and withdrew his cigarette case, which never stocked nicotine sticks. But what it did hold? Secrets. He'd stash his notes from current cases within that little silver-plated box. He cracked it open and withdrew a picture, flashing it my direction.

Marianne VanKirk. The same photo was in my purse.

This shouldn't surprise me. Though His Honor was also a family friend, he'd expressed doubt in hiring a detective who also happened to be a woman. The thought that my gender alone gave him misgivings rankled me. Hadn't I proved myself in the Big Dante case back in Pittsburgh? I'd been the one who'd exposed the high-ranked police officer leading a double life as a mobster. With such a victory also came a tragic loss. Something my brain couldn't touch on at present. That case gained national attention, but all it took was one glimpse of my pleated skirt and pomaded lips, and I was reduced to my *proper place*.

Hosting social gatherings that would make my mother proud held as much appeal as embroidering enough pillows to fill all Hemswick Manor's parlors, something Mother had always threatened when I was a child if I didn't behave. Which had been often.

"Sure it's nothing personal, Vinny." He tucked the photo back into the case and slipped it in his pocket, all while keeping his gaze on me. "His Honor may not know of your competency. He only wants his daughter back."

Once again my pride had gotten the best of me. It was only logical the judge would worry about his child and therefore do all he could to secure her safety. Even if it meant employing more detectives. I would go to extreme lengths to protect those I loved. In fact, I had. Which was why I was back in New York in the first place. I checked my watch pin—7:45. Court resumed in a little over an hour. "Who gave you this location? Do you know for certain she's here?" I silently congratulated myself for carrying on a civil conversation, keeping any emotion from my voice.

"Turns out Dempsey's chauffeur likes to flip the cards. I trounced him in poker." He raised his hands in a show of surrender, but his rogue smile revealed how amused he was by my narrowed eyes. "I used my powers for good. Saved the man from explaining to his wife why he'd lost several hundred bucks, by giving me information instead. He provided me with this address." He peered at me from beneath dark lashes. "As for Miss Marianne, I was just about to take a gander through those skylights. Perhaps you'd like to go sightseeing with me." He offered me his arm, as if we were strolling Central Park and not spying through glass smattered with bird droppings.

The man could charm a teetotaler to guzzle moonshine, but I knew the likes of Kent Brisbane. Fell too hard and too fast, only to regret it. I ignored his mock gallantry and brushed past him toward the skylights. "Have you encountered any of Dempsey's men?" I asked in a hushed tone over my shoulder.

"No. You?"

"Not yet. But no doubt this warehouse is crawling with them." I hoped I was wrong. If a legion of armed brutes awaited us, I wasn't sure how to safely rescue Marianne.

"I'm guessing not." He moved close, and the hair prickled on my neck. "The fewer men aware of this hideout, the fewer chances of a location leak. Besides, how many goons are needed to guard a defenseless girl?"

We crouched the last few steps before reaching the glass. The row of panes slanted on an inclined section of the roof. Kent tested its sturdiness by putting his weight on the weathered boards, all the while holding the metal railing to his left. Once proven he wouldn't plunge through the splintery planks to his death, he leaned onto the roof, rising just enough to glimpse through the glass. A muscle leaped in his jaw.

"How bad is it?" Fifteen men? Twenty?

"I can't see." He glanced over. "Just below us appears to be a landing, but it's stuffed with crates."

"Is there space enough for us to get in?"

"Barely. Maybe for one of us." And his tone specifically meant he referenced himself. Evidenced by him fishing his pocketknife from his trouser pocket and using the tip of the blade to unscrew the fasteners in the metal strip securing the glass.

"There's no way I'm letting you take control of this case."

His hand stilled, and he glanced over, the early morning light shimmering in his eyes, making them appear as silver pools. "We're going to get real cozy then. You know . . ." His grin took on a wicked twist. "There are other ways to get close to me. You only have to ask."

I'd always assumed our first interaction after our wrecked marriage would be bitter and accusing, though I supposed after nearly four years, the hostile edges had been worn down. Kent was now as he'd always been. As if we hadn't a disastrous history between us. Meanwhile, I put on a decent air of indifference, but my insides hummed with chaotic energy.

When I didn't reply to his teasing, he only shrugged and finished unfastening the window. With careful handling, I helped him remove the glass pane from its spot without a sound. I peeked inside the hole. Kent hadn't exaggerated—there was room for one breathing body, and judging by the narrow space, Kent's broad shoulders wouldn't fit. "I'll go first and clear the way for you."

As if realizing it to be the best option, he nodded. "The exposed sill is shaky. Any extra strain and it could make a clean break from the wood. I'll lower you down."

Hating to be at his mercy, I studied the warped frame and had to concede. Better to stay clear of anything that could come crashing onto the landing. I wrapped my purse tight around my wrist and drew in a fortifying breath. I moved as near to the opening as possible.

"Ready?" The warmth of Kent's body encircled me as he cupped my elbows.

His chest lightly pressed into my back. The gentle fall breeze sent traces of his cologne my way, surging unbidden memories of those early moments of marriage, taking my mind to places I'd rather not revisit. Especially now, when I needed to keep my wits about me.

I scooted back, letting him take the brunt of my weight. He held me with ease. As I lowered, his firm grip slid to my wrists. The tips of my toes brushed the dusty floor, and I glanced up at his serious expression. For all the charm and flirty remarks, Kent would always take his job—which right now included my safety—seriously. I nodded, and he released me to find my footing, which proved simple enough.

I took inventory of my surroundings. Tall pillars of crates surrounded me. Thankfully, the stack to my right was low enough that I could see over it. The glare from the skylights didn't help my vision any, but a stairway appeared to be on the far left. Maybe I could slide the boxes back, giving a clear route to the steps. Though perhaps I should climb over the crates rather than risk the scraping noise against the concrete. This level didn't go all the way across the space. The narrow glimpse of a railing told me the center of this warehouse was wide open, which improved our chances of scouting Marianne but also increased our risk of being spotted. I inhaled a deep breath, my mind sorting through possible strategies.

A masculine voice cut through the silence. "Boss says to stay put until further notice."

While I couldn't see the man, the location of his voice seemed below and to the left. "That includes sneakin' out to see your dame."

"You got this under control." A lower snarl marked that at least two brutes were on guard. "No one knows we're here. 'Sides, I don't wanna be round when you kill the kid. My conscience is sensitive like that."

His droll tone ignited fire in my veins. They weren't going to let her go, no matter if Judge VanKirk threw the trial or not.

I had to get to her.

"What's going on?" Kent whispered from above.

I held up a finger to my lips, and his brow wrinkled.

"You make me stay and do all the dirty work, then I'm taking half your cut," the man snapped.

"Suits me. Small price to see my girl. I'll catch ya tonight at the Thirsty Trough."

A speakeasy on Rum Row.

The click of footsteps was followed by the closing of a door.

I didn't have time to clear the space. Kent needed down before he got spotted. I motioned him with a clipped jerk of my head and mouthed, *Now.*

Sensing the urgency, he climbed down. I flattened myself against the crate, but Kent was pressed flush against me, his face too near to mine. "What's happening?" His hushed words tickled my neck.

"It seems there's only one goon left. But we need to act. He's going to kill her." I didn't wait for him to follow but hoisted myself over the crate, relieved to see a clearing that indeed led to a stairway. I eased back onto my feet but kept low.

Kent trailed behind. "Let's get closer."

Still crouching, I moved behind a crate positioned close to the railing. I held my breath and peeked around it, zeroing in on the ground floor.

There she was.

Marianne sat tied to a chair in a shadowed corner. She'd been gagged, her youthful complexion as pale gray as the cement blocks behind her. A man stood guard by the door, a good twenty feet from his prisoner.

I eased back to the safety of the crate and lifted on my tiptoes to Kent's ear. "She's here. In the far corner."

"And the crony?"

"By the door." Which neither of us could glimpse without easing into the brute's view again. That included getting a clear shot at him. Though I didn't want to take out the guard if we didn't have to. I scanned the area, an idea forming. "See that shelf?" I pointed to the line of wooden barrels. That particular shelf was suspended on each side by ropes. "The door is almost directly beneath the edge of the left side."

"We can create a diversion with the barrels."

Which was actually a good idea. Partly. "Give me your knife." I wiggled my fingers impatiently.

He reluctantly handed it over. "What are you going to—"

"Just be ready to nab the girl." Then I was on the move. Slinking into the shadows toward the other edge of the landing. Kent hissed my name, though I wouldn't look back. We were running out of time.

I pressed my back to the wall and rounded the corner of the open landing. I was directly above the barrels. The ropes were knotted just below me. I flattened on my stomach and reached over the ledge. Problem was, the top of my body was visible. If the goon happened to glance up, I'd be spotted. So I'd better be quick. I locked the pocketknife in place and eyed the blade. Kent kept it sharp.

With quiet movements, I worked at cutting the rope holding the left side of the shelf. It felt like an eternity but could only have been a minute. Finally the rope snapped. The shelf hitched lower, sending the barrels careening off the side.

The guard yelled.

I launched to my feet and moved to snatch a better view.

The guard scrambled for safety, but a barrel collided with his shoulder, knocking him to the dusty floor. Another barrel fell, landing atop the man's leg, his anguished moan following. No doubt a break.

As soon as he was immobilized, Kent dashed down the stairway, his gun drawn.

"You get her," Kent yelled as he sprinted toward the gunman, who grappled for his weapon. But Kent moved with speed and finesse, quickly grabbing the thug's gun and apprehending him.

I rushed down toward Marianne. Tears filled her stricken eyes.

"You're safe now." Still holding Brisbane's knife, I severed the gag so she could breathe better. I made quick work of the rest of the bindings and tossed them to Kent.

He tied up Marianne's captor with the ropes that had once bound her.

I helped the young girl to her feet. The poor thing trembled all over. Wrapping my arm around her, I held her to my side. My Duesenberg was parked only two blocks away, but we still had to drive to the courthouse. One quick glance at my watch told me we had time. "Let's take you to your father."

Chapter 2

"I NEED ANOTHER MAN."

I nearly spewed my coffee at my sixty-year-old mother's remark. Well, *adoptive* mother, but truly the only maternal figure I'd known. "What? Why on earth do you need a man?"

My adoptive father, Harvey Kline, had passed away two months ago. Which had been the motivating factor of my returning to the city. If it were up to me, I'd remain in Pittsburgh with my biological sister, Kate, but Mother seemed to be floundering since Father had passed. So her casual statement seemed outside of the ridiculous.

The thin lines framing her narrow mouth deepened with her soft smile. "I do believe you weren't listening again."

And that one sentence made me feel like I was six instead of twenty-six. But Mother had been right. I was thinking about yesterday's case. The palpable relief on Judge VanKirk's face when Marianne entered the courtroom. The look of doom in Dempsey's expression. And the sound of justice when the gavel struck. Dempsey and the thug who'd had a bad encounter with the barrels were both behind bars. Judge VanKirk had sent the authorities he'd trusted most to the Thirsty Trough to collect the other goon responsible for Marianne's kidnapping.

His Honor had compensated us most generously, though I let an unsuspecting Kent have the bulk of it. I didn't take on cases for the wages. I had problems enough with the surplus of money I'd inherited not only from my adopted father but also from my biological one. The funds from the latter weighed considerably on my conscience, since my birth father had once been a leading crime boss in Pittsburgh.

After I'd discovered the truth about my parentage, I'd assumed my birth parents continued to reside in Italy. However, over a year ago, my path unexpectedly crossed with that of Hugo Salvastano—my birth father. I was doing undercover work in Pittsburgh, gathering evidence against the notorious crime boss Big Dante, which led me to Hugo. He and Big Dante had been rivals. Apparently Hugo had come to the States from Italy after my birth mother had died. He also revealed that I had a younger sister, Kate, who'd recently sailed to America. Of course, I'd gained all this knowledge before everything had turned for the worse. As far as family trees went, mine had tangled roots and several shaky limbs.

The tabloids had fun with that tidbit—"Kline Family Heiress Also a Mobster's Daughter." Cartoon artists drew sketches of me having two names on my birth certificate. One being Kline, the other Salvastano. Yet no one seemed to care that I'd lost both my fathers—the one responsible for my birth, the other for my upbringing—in the span of four months. Or that I'd been in the throes of grief.

No, status didn't allow the luxury of privacy. I'd had my fill of the press invading every aspect of my life. But despite my penchant to seclude myself, Mother needed me. So here I was.

"I'm sorry. I've a lot on my mind lately." And I wouldn't even begin to contemplate the shock of seeing my former husband on a filthy rooftop. Four years. I'd had four years to dislodge Kent Brisbane from my mind, purge all the memories, but one glance at those smoky eyes and it had all come flooding back.

Worst of all, I couldn't breathe a word. Since Mother, along with the rest of the world, had no idea I'd ever married. And subsequently divorced.

I frowned into my empty coffee cup.

"Quite all right, dear. I don't mind repeating myself." She took a dainty sip of tea. "The dinner party tomorrow evening. Mr. Montague can't attend, so our numbers will be off. I need another gentleman to balance dinner."

Mother hadn't flicked an eyelash when I'd told her I wanted to join the workforce and be a private investigator. Those two permissions alone were complete miracles, especially with the elevated status of the Kline family. But one conventional morsel Mother stubbornly kept on her etiquette plate was the formality of dinner. I had to dress formally every evening, no matter if it was a party or just the two of us.

I knew better than to argue with her on this front. Though with all the events she'd been hosting lately, I wasn't quite certain if these parties were to fill the void of her grief or a slight bit of matchmaking on her part.

I leaned forward. "What about Mr. Crawford?" The fellow was at least ninety. And while most people my age wouldn't bother engaging in conversation with such an antiquated person, I found his stories from when he'd fought in the Civil War fascinating.

"No, child. He's been nervous about accepting invites since Mrs. Welch's passing."

"Mrs. Welch?" Living in the upper echelon of families in New York City, a myriad of names were tossed at me. I usually was able to remember them, but I didn't recall Welch.

"She just returned from spending years abroad. She survived decades in Guam only to return to the States and pass." Her lips pressed into a thin line, and a touch of color drained from her already pale complexion. Her voice dropped to almost a whisper. "The sleeping sickness."

Oh.

If there was any case I wished I could solve, the dreaded sleeping sickness would be it. Just so Mother could have some peace of mind. The illness was a mystery. Doctors couldn't identify how people contracted it, nor how to cure it. The cases were so sporadic—some would fall into deep sleep only to wake up a few days later, while others slipped into a coma and never wakened.

The doorbell sounded, and Mother jolted. Ever since the press had gotten wind of my birth father being the one and only Hugo Salvastano, we'd hardly had a moment's peace. So while Mother had been grieving her late husband, she also had to deal with the persistent attention of journalists. She'd come a long way from the shattered widow with fragile nerves, but little reminders of that difficult time cropped up now and then.

She took a calming breath and said, "The *Times* suspects the sleeping disease is getting worse. The death toll is rising."

"You shouldn't read that. It only breeds fear." Growing up, Elizabeth Kline had never cracked open a newspaper, complaining a woman had to share her husband with a slab of paper at breakfast, so often had Father read *The New York Times* at the head of the table. When he'd passed, she'd taken up reading that publication, making me wonder if it was an effort to remain close to him.

After discovering the truth about my adoption in my early twenties, my father had ordered me to lie regarding the specifics of our family dynamics, forcing me to pretend I'd been aware of my birth story all my life. He hadn't wanted the newshounds catching scent of anything amiss and howling about the rising discord among the prestigious Klines. I'd done as commanded, but in my defiance, I'd altered the details with each recounting of the story, such as changing the age I'd sailed to America or inventing memories of my time in Italy. Needless to say, Father and I had had a strained relationship. Though I was angry, I was grateful we'd completely reconciled in those final moments before he'd slipped into eternity. I'd forced myself to remain at his side, witness his passing. Unlike when I'd run away from my birth father, refusing to watch him scrape in his last breath.

Mother opened her mouth to speak but was interrupted by our butler, Jamison. "Mr. Kent Brisbane to see Miss Kline, madam."

I squeezed the handle of my coffee cup. What was he doing here? I didn't want to have an audience with him with Mother present. Who knew what he'd say. A sliver of guilt always pricked from keeping my marriage from my parents, but it wouldn't do any good to confess now. I'd learned from that painful time and refused to allow Kent Brisbane any room in my heart since that day I'd seen him at the station. So no,

I wouldn't be discussing my failed marriage with my only remaining parent. She'd been through enough these past months. "Take him to the front parlor please, Jamison." He nodded and left the room.

A humming noise pulled my attention to Mother.

"Kent Brisbane. He's the gentleman you used to seek out at parties those years ago." She lifted a knowing brow. "The same who worked with you on the VanKirk case."

I couldn't refute the first claim—though I'd no idea how Mother uncovered that information—but that last bit I could address. "I didn't work with him." In the end, I supposed I had. It hadn't been intentional. The man had just happened to be there.

"The *Times* says otherwise."

That preposterous article sensationalized everything about the VanKirk kidnapping, including a romantic pairing between Kent and myself. If they only knew. "You really need to take up reading novels," I shot back with a forced smile as I set my coffee cup on the tray and stood. I didn't want Kent to get bored and wander in here. Because one glance from Mother at the handsome detective and—

"That's it." She pressed her palms together in an exuberant move, making her appear years younger. "Your gentleman will make up my number."

Bad idea. "Oh no, Mother. He's not my gentleman." Not anymore. "You really—"

"I can always join you and extend the invitation?" She moved to stand.

I softly patted her shoulder. "Fine. You win. I'll invite him. But I can't guarantee he'll come." Because I intended to do my best to discourage him. With one more gentle squeeze to her shoulder, I went downstairs to the formal sitting room.

Upon hearing me enter, Kent stood from the chair he'd been seated on and removed his hat. Very mannerly, but I knew better.

"Why are you here, Brisbane?"

Anyone else might be offended at my bluntness, but he smiled, as if what I'd said had been entirely charming. "Because you wanted me here." He winked and waited for me to sit down on the sofa before re-claiming his seat. "Your little plan worked."

"Did one of those barrels land on you as well?"

"No, I'm perfectly in my right mind. Though I have to say, I'm touched by your eagerness to see me again."

I folded my arms and leaned back. "And you call yourself a detective. You're not reading my cues correctly. You're mistaking annoyance for *eagerness.*"

"Of course, most women would subtly take my handkerchief." He kept his amused gaze on me, as if I hadn't countered his words. "Or some other token to lure me back for a visit. Not you though."

"Not me. I can say with all adamance—not me."

"No, Vinny, you're the first woman to swipe my weapon."

Oh, that. "Is this your absurd way of asking for your knife back?" I'd forgotten I'd stashed it in my purse after I'd sliced Marianne's ropes. It'd also slipped my mind just how important that knife was to him, though I didn't know why. Kent didn't have a habit of opening up to people, me especially.

"You say absurd . . . I say accurate." He slid his hand behind the lapel of his jacket and withdrew an envelope. "And there's the other matter, of course."

"Please tell me whatever's in your hand has nothing to do with those foolish rag articles." It would be just like Kent to flaunt that article in my face as a silly joke. "Reporters should consult the facts before printing slander. Whoever coined the phrase 'Sleuthing Sweethearts' needed to provide antacid coupons beside their column."

"Though it all was true a few years ago." Something entered his eyes, softening those crinkly corners, reminding me of things I wanted to forget.

So much had been left unsaid. It was almost as if the secrets swirled between us, sliding across my skin and settling on my lips, daring me to mention what I'd held captive for so long. But I didn't want to bring up what I'd seen that day any more than I expected Kent would want to dive into why he'd behaved as such.

"Don't you think it's finally time to discuss what happened between us?"

Or maybe I was wrong.

"Why you left?"

I bristled. "Because you left first."

"It's because I was—"

"On a case. Yes, I know." But *he* didn't know what I'd discovered about his sudden disappearance. "Now's not the time, Kent."

His jaw tightened for a fraction of a second before giving a tight nod. "I came regarding this." He waved the envelope. "This, my sleuthing sweetheart, is more than my share. I'm returning it to you."

So he'd come to return the extra cash from yesterday's case. "It doesn't matter."

"To me it does. You earned this wage, so you should take it." He dropped the envelope on the table next to the sofa. Instead of returning to his seat, he lowered beside me. "But I will take my pocketknife."

"It's not here."

Something flickered across his features—panic maybe?—but then he schooled his expression into that of casual interest. "Did you lose it?"

"No, it's at my flat."

This made his head rear back. "I thought you lived here at Hemswick Manor."

Most believed that. And it was nice to have my flat remain a secret. Though I doubted it would stay so for long. "I moved back to the city for Mother's sake, but I live . . ." No. I wasn't about to tell him about my flat at Park Towers. "Somewhere else."

The corners of his mouth crept up at my almost blunder. He knew I'd nearly slipped my address but reconsidered. I wouldn't apologize for it. I'd fallen for his charms before, and it left me with nothing but heartache and a soul full of secrets. Distance from Kent Brisbane was equally as important as oxygen. Which was why I needed to find a way around my obligation to invite him to dinner tomorrow.

Jamison entered the parlor holding a silver platter with an envelope centered on it. I spotted Mother's handwriting and shoved down the urge to snatch the paper from the tray.

He extended his arm toward Kent. "For you, sir."

Kent lifted his brows but took the envelope. He eased out the card, his eyes widening so briefly I nearly missed it. I didn't need to see the smile cresting his lips to know what it was. "It seems Mrs. Kline has invited me to her dinner party tomorrow."

How swiftly Mother had drawn up that card. I waited for Jamison to leave, then said, "You don't have to come."

"And deny you the opportunity to see me in a tux?" His voice lowered. "I recall you do prefer me in formal wear. Like the day we met, Vinny." His gaze dropped to my right hand, and I knew without a doubt what scenario he referred to.

"You're ridiculous, Kenny." I tacked on the last part solely to annoy him. It worked. For his nose wrinkled, as if someone had stuffed rotten fish in the sofa cushions.

"Kenny and Vinny. Sounds chummy."

"We're not chums," I said hotly.

"Then you don't have to call me that."

"For some reason, you feel at liberty to use my nickname. Thought I'd do the same."

"Yes, but yours is a shortened form of Delvina. Kent's already one syllable. There's no need for a diminutive."

Were we seriously arguing over nicknames? And I found it ironic he quoted rules when he'd proven the first to break them. "Kenny is a lot nicer than other things I could call you."

"Tell you what." The sparkle in his eyes told me whatever rolled out of his smirking mouth next would likely crush my last nerve. "I'll let you call me Kenny any time you desperately need me."

The gall of this man.

He couldn't have picked a more infuriating turn of phrase. Because I'd determined never to need him a day in my life ever again. Something he obviously knew. "Well, I don't *desperately need* your company tomorrow." I flicked the invitation in his hand. "So feel free to disregard."

"Mrs. Kline was gracious enough to include the likes of me." He grinned, but something in his voice made me pause. Kent Brisbane wasn't upper class. And judging by the brief glimmer of surprise on his face when he'd first opened the invitation, I could tell he was mildly shocked to receive one. "Please tell your mother I'm honored to accept."

I had an entire twenty-four hours to build up my defenses. "Fine. I'll bring your beloved pocketknife to the dinner party." Then hopefully we could return to our mutual avoidance of each other.

His smile only widened, as if he could hear my thoughts. I braced myself for another offhanded quip, but instead he stood, and his expression shifted, not quite somber but assuredly not playful. "I'm sorry about what happened to Mr. Kline and Mr. Salvastano."

My gut clenched. My fathers. One dead from illness, the other from a bullet . . . and my failings. "Thank you" was all I could say. Which was more than I gave most people.

He set his hat on his head with charming finesse. "Till tomorrow."

But I couldn't let him leave, not without asking the question that hovered between us. "Kent?"

He paused at the door, refacing me. "Yes?"

"That case. The one that consumed your attention." The one that had driven a wedge between us. "Did you find what you were looking for?"

His gaze swept my face, searching. For what I could never know. Kent was difficult to read. He turned back toward the exit, and I assumed he was going to leave without answering. At last he murmured, "Not yet."

Then he was gone.

Chapter 3

Kent Brisbane
1920 (four years earlier)

I SHOULD'VE NEVER COME TONIGHT.

The blinding amount of chandeliers in the ballroom didn't strain my vision as much as the brightly falsified smiles. All aimed at me. I knew their intention. I'd observed enough of humanity to realize where I belonged, or rather didn't belong—and this evening's grand ball topped the proverbial list.

I'd come here to show support of Warren Hayes, a close friend who'd recently rejoined society after his father's passing. I respected the man but questioned his social calendar. This wasn't exactly the best choice of events to attend, especially if he was in search of a bride. Not to say there weren't enough ladies in attendance. On the contrary. The female gender dominated the populous. And they all had their hungry eyes on my friend. Matrimony wasn't for the weak.

Which was why I'd ducked outside onto the terrace for some much-needed space from the vultures. Warren could fend for himself for a spell. I strolled into a garden ornamented with statues and even taller hedges. Which only meant I needed to be careful not to happen upon an embracing couple. Lawn lanterns were strategically placed about, giving the area a dim glow. The strains of the orchestra floated out the fancy doors into the crisp fall air. New York in the fall had never been my favorite. It only served as a warning of winter. I hated winter.

But perhaps I should soak in these moments when the bitter wind didn't assault my face.

"Don't you dare touch me."

Speaking of assault. A woman's clipped voice sounded not too far from me. Her tone, while in command, put my feet in motion.

"No one would know." Decidedly male. "It will be our secret."

I moved along the path leading to a secluded alcove, but not before I heard the unmistakable sound of fist meeting flesh. If that man hit—

"I won't tell a soul," the woman said. "I'll let your face speak for me."

The man cursed, rushing past as I rounded the corner and nearly clipping my shoulder. His head was tucked, his hand shielding his eyes, preventing me from getting a decent look at the swine.

A young woman emerged a second later, looking immaculate, as if she hadn't just decked a gentleman. I couldn't tame a smile. "And here I rushed over to come to your aid."

Her gaze met mine, and she stopped. "But you have." She plucked my handkerchief from my front pocket and dabbed the corner of her mouth. "His sloppy advances ruined my lip pomade."

She wasn't the least bit shaken up, as if she fought off gentlemen at every event. Though judging by her beauty, she probably did. There wasn't anything delicate about the woman before me. By the sharp angle of her bobbed dark hair, high cut of her cheekbones, and firm set of her mouth, there appeared no softness to her. Even her bare arms poking out of her fashionable gown were lean and toned. I imagined the same went for her legs, but I wasn't about to ogle the woman after she'd just pummeled a man for behaving ungentlemanly.

"Glad I could be of service to you. Or at least, my handkerchief."

"You're new." She assessed me. "You haven't been warned of me yet."

"Or I may have been warned. I'm not one to hedge my bets." My gaze dropped to her hands, and I raised a brow. "Though I didn't bring my sparring gloves."

She raised a brow in return. "Do you have any intention of accosting me?"

"No."

"Then you're safe." Her brow lowered. "Though in a way, I'm not. I should've returned to the ballroom ahead of Mr. Marlone to curb any excuses he'll no doubt prattle. Not that anyone would trust a thing I say."

"Whyever not?" I watched her toy with the edges of my handkerchief. "I can vouch for you."

This made her full lips curl into a smile. "Oh, believe me, you wouldn't want to chance that. Don't risk your reputation for only a D class."

"You're a debutante?"

She appeared slightly older than the standard eighteen-year-old. But I wasn't a good judge on that sort of thing. Because if I were, I wouldn't have labeled this woman a D. It was a foolish and cruel system, the rating for debbies. Another stupid facet of this sphere I loathed. At every onset of the season, the press attributed each debbie with a grade from A to D. Those with the highest ranks were supposedly best for matrimony. A prize so to speak. Stupid.

"No, not this year." She held out my handkerchief, but I shook my head, letting her keep it. "But once a D always a D. Which is fine by me."

"Some of my favorite adjectives begin with D."

"Such as?"

"Devastating."

Her head tipped back with a laugh, highlighting the graceful column of her throat. But I'd noticed something else—a birthmark stretched across the bottom of her neck. The angled collar of her gown almost framed the patch of pale red skin, as if she purposefully showcased it, making a statement. Which only served to intrigue me more. Because the swells delighted in perfection, striving to appear flawless. Covering up any blemish. Not that I considered her birthmark a flaw. Quite the opposite, but I could only imagine the grief she had to endure because this layer of society possessed a warped view of perfection.

"Devastating is a stretch, but I'll allow it. I needed that bit of cheering up."

I gave a slight bow. "Like I said before, I'm at your service, Miss . . ."

"Delvina Kline."

I'd heard of the family name. Harvey Kline was a financial tycoon. So Delvina was not only beautiful but wealthy. No idea who would punish her with such an insulting grade, though I did know the low ranking had branded her, secluded her even. Higher-rated debbies wouldn't associate with the lower, all in fear of falling from their elevated status. This also meant the gentlemen wouldn't even ask her to dance—such a thing would be a mark against them.

Her gaze drifted to the terrace, and a small sigh escaped her lips. "The gossip has certainly spread already. I'm sure it's being painted as my fault. As always." She shrugged, as if deciding not to care, and glanced my way. "Don't pity me. I'm used to this sort of thing."

"Sounds very . . ." Deplorable. Unjust. "Confining."

She agreed. "This kind of life is."

"I wouldn't know." Because it didn't matter if she were an A, D, or even Z. Miss Delvina Kline was out of my league.

Her head tilted in question.

"I'm here as a bodyguard of sorts for Warren Hayes." It was a test of mine to gauge reactions. I'd just mentioned my extremely rich friend who owned a newspaper empire, and she had no response. No subtle arch of her brow or sparkle of interest in her onyx eyes. Nothing. In all honesty, it almost seemed as if her attention waned. As if millionaires bored her. I was beginning to like Delvina Kline. "He's the toast of the evening, though I doubt he'd use your tactic to ward off attention."

She glanced at her knuckles. "I don't usually make a practice of it either."

One thing her lower rank would attract? The scoundrels. Because the public eye wasn't focused on her, no one would notice these vile encounters. Men like Mr. Marlone should be held accountable. "Would you care to dance?"

She shook her head. "I can't return to the ballroom. I should probably wait out here until my parents fetch me. Father will be in a mood when he finds out, but he'll get over it. He always does."

"Even if you were protecting yourself?" It wasn't difficult to imagine. The upper crust hated scandal. They often placed appeasing the masses over defending their own family.

"No, he'll probably be upset about that, but wouldn't approve of my method. Though it was necessary." She winced, as if reliving the moment, making my jaw lock.

Just how far had the cad gone? "Well, I didn't mean to dance in the ballroom, but right here." I held out my hand. "I'd rather you leave this garden with a better memory than you started with."

This made her brows jump, but then a small smile graced her lips. "That's a sweet gesture."

"Then I ask you to keep that impression of me, because I'm bound to say something stupid if we keep talking."

Amusement lit her eyes. "You don't appear witless."

"I blame my present company." I hooked my gaze on hers. "I can't control my words around a beautiful woman."

"As long as you can control everything else."

"On that, you have my word. You're safe with me."

"Good. Then you have my permission to be a shameless flirt."

"I'm obliged."

"This is the part where you tell me your name."

I smiled. "Kent Brisbane."

"Very glad to meet you, Mr. Brisbane." She held out her hand, and I bowed over it.

This close, I noticed slight swelling on her knuckles. The aftermath of her delivering justice. I swiped my thumb tenderly over her fingers, careful not to be too forward but letting her know she had an ally.

Then with an ease as if we'd rendezvoused a thousand times in the stillness of the garden, she stepped into my arms, and we danced.

● ● ●

Another thing the upper elites didn't experience was rising Monday morning and heading to an office the size of a matchbox in a sketchy area of Manhattan. Not that I was complaining. I wasn't afraid of the rough parts of this city. I'd grown up in it. Slept on the icy walks. Battled for every meal.

Those trips down memory lane weren't exactly welcome. Especially when said lane was littered with mildewed crates, rotted food, and vagrants who'd pry the last crumb of bread from your fingers.

It was eerie how certain smells could be recalled with perfect clarity. I shook my head and summoned the enticing fragrance that had wrapped around me last evening in the garden. Delvina Kline. I'd held the woman for two minutes, maybe less, but it might as well had been for hours, considering the impression it left.

I turned the corner, moving to the alley that led to my tiny office, and stopped in my tracks. A line of people stood outside my door. For a private detective agency that struggled to gain a couple cases a month, this was . . . unusual.

Also unusual? Every person in line—there had to be at least fifteen—all held a copy of a newspaper. Warren Hayes's, to be exact.

I didn't recognize any of them, which made it easy for me to casually join the end of the line.

The woman in front of me took one glance over her narrow shoulder and sniffed. "Another one."

"Indeed," I answered in a friendly tone. "Wouldn't want to miss out." I had no idea on what, but it seemed like the right thing to say, for she turned fully toward me.

Dark brows lowered over deep-set eyes. "Well, ya ain't goin' to get a cut of my share."

"Wouldn't dream of it, madam." Now my curiosity heightened. Share of what? All I had in that office was a rickety typewriter and a hand-me-down desk from Warren. Oh, and a telephone that cost me a small fortune to keep connected. "I'm sure there's enough to go around."

She scoffed. "Two hundred dollars? Split 'mong all these people? We be lucky if they don't turn us all out."

I nearly choked. "I don't believe it's that much money." I didn't even know what was going on, but I was certain of one thing—if I had two hundred dollars to spare, I'd put it in rent for a better office.

"Shows what ya know." Her chapped hands opened the paper with a flourish, and she pointed at the advertisement section. "Right 'ere." I leaned over slightly and read the inked words.

Information Wanted
In search of any person with the knowledge of a woman named Kit Mason who gave her child up to the Manhattan Children's Home in 1898. Reward $200. Visit 103 Parson Ln.

This was Warren's doing. I was going to pummel him. This was why I didn't trust people with sensitive information. My information. I had no misgivings he intended to pay the reward money, but I also was aware that probably every one of these people conjured up a pretty story to fool me. At least Warren hadn't listed my name. My agency and name weren't even painted on the door. Why? Because I'd hoped to have leased a better place by now. And since I'd had more rats than people accosting my door, 99 percent of Manhattan didn't know I rented this place, a fact I'd once bemoaned but now was grateful for.

I skimmed the varying faces in line. They all had that look. I didn't even know how to describe it. Growing up on the streets had granted me the skills necessary to survive, and one of them was judging the intentions of those around me. I casually walked up to the door, as if interested in reading the sign I knew was absent, feeling the scrutiny of those now behind me.

I made a show of rubbing my jaw. "Whoever it is must've found the information she needed," I said to no one, but also everyone. "Why else would she leave us waiting like this?"

"She?" The first person in line wore an oversized trench coat and a curious expression. "How'd you know a lady's behind this?" He shook his newspaper.

"The ad doesn't specify." I shrugged. "But in my experience, it's a lady that always kept me waiting." I coupled that with a good-natured wink, and those around me chuckled. Just the inlet I needed.

I spent the next several minutes talking with the waiters and easily deduced that not one of them had any worthwhile information. Not all were trying to deceive—a few knew of people who'd given up their children—but none were the right woman.

In the end, I left. Not bothering to open my office. I wouldn't get a scrap of work done over the next few days, maybe weeks, thanks to this ad. I couldn't even get mad at Warren. He was only trying to help. He was the only person besides myself that knew this mystery had remained unsolved from my birth. The most important case I'd ever had was the one that meant the most. And the one that could cost me everything. Finding her.

Finding my mother.

Chapter 4

Delvina
1924

I SWEPT THE RIGHT SIDE of my bobbed corkscrew curls with a shiny hair comb and gave myself another once-over in the cheval mirror in my childhood bedroom. The décolletage of the silver satin gown plunged deeper than I remembered, but it would have to do. I only kept a handful of dresses here for the few occasions I was stranded at Hemswick, last night being one of them. I'd stayed upon Mother's insistence. It had stormed all last evening, and she was uneasy about my safety should I venture to my flat. She'd truly no idea the danger involved in my line of work.

I hadn't the heart to tell her that only two days ago I'd climbed the dew-slicked rungs of a tall warehouse in an evening gown or had draped half my body over a dusty landing just above a ruthless gunman. She'd never asked for the details of my work, so I rarely offered them. But knowing her fear of thunderstorms, I couldn't leave last night. Or today, since the storms continued, only to let up an hour ago. Which meant I hadn't retrieved Brisbane's knife, securing yet another time I'd be forced to meet with him. It was a series of unfortunate events that served to fuel my frustration.

I shot a glance at Mother's maid, an ally. "Who's on tonight's guest list?" Besides my former husband.

Flossie's gaze met mine in the reflection. "Mrs. Kline still keeps mum with you about her guests, does she?" The older woman chuckled, making the magazine she held bob in tandem with her shaking shoulders. "It's your fault, you know? All those dinner parties you skipped. You were the queen of excuses back then."

No, not a queen. I'd been more like the court jester. My marriage had been one cruel joke, and Mother had been on a matchmaking rampage shortly after I'd realized what a fool I'd been. Of course, she hadn't known, so I could hardly blame her for being annoyed at my constant refusal to attend her dinner parties consisting of eligible bachelors and their parents. Since then she'd kept quiet about her guest list.

"Be nice or I'll make you be a proper lady's maid." I knew my threat held no weight. Flossie was more than willing to help me dress for the evening. I was the one who'd told her to sit and browse the latest edition of *Vogue*. Mother had insisted I had a maid during my brief stay. Another old-fashioned stance she clung to.

Flossie made a humming noise of indifference as she turned a page. "She invited Mr. Stratton."

I grabbed my lip pomade and popped open the lid. "The banker with the questionable amount of ear hair?" He had to be at least seventy.

"No. His son. Much less ear hair and much more your age. Your mother discovered his favorite meal to help encourage things."

Ah, Wallace Stratton. A dandified gent if I ever saw one. Well, I wasn't about to encourage him in anything. I only hoped Mother wouldn't draw me into too many awkward conversations with the man. I had a feeling most of my evening would be monitoring Kent, ensuring he behaved. I knew he wanted his knife, but the warm glint in his eye yesterday betrayed he had another motive. And if that motive was to squeal about our short-lived marriage, I might have to gag him with a napkin.

"But I overheard your mother telling Cook that Mr. Stratton is bringing a date," Flossie continued, yanking me from my not-so-gentle schemes of silencing my former husband.

"Good." I brushed some crimson tint on my lips, tossing a wink at a frowning Flossie. She was as bad as Mother when it came to finding me a fellow. "That's one more potential suitor out of Mother's grasp."

"But perhaps we can give his date some competition, huh?" Flossie lifted the magazine and pointed to the page featuring an elegant woman in a sophisticated pose directly above a shoe wax ad. "Look at this model. Her hair is parted at the side, with a dramatic sweep practically over her eye."

I appreciated the latest fashion trends as much as the next girl, but a style that involved partial blindness was where I drew the line. "No thank you. I've grown accustomed to using both eyes," I said dryly. "And I don't want to enter into a flirt contest for Wallace Stratton's affections."

She stood and tossed the magazine onto the side table. "Just saying, my dear." Her spindly fingers tugged my neckline even lower. "You have to hook them before you can reel them in."

"Are you speaking of salmon or men? Because I prefer the first over the second."

"I just don't want you to end up lonely." Though she tried her best to hide it, her eyes held a tinge of sadness, making me wonder if she was sharing from experience.

"I know, Flossie. And I'm grateful you care." I placed my hand on her narrow shoulder. "I may not say it often, but I'm glad you're in my life." I didn't open up to most.

To the world, I was the bohemian adopted child of a wealthy family. My manners might seem cold, but only to those who hadn't taken the time or interest to concern themselves on my behalf. Though Flossie was different. She'd taken me in. Held my hand as Mother had hugged me tight that awful night of my debut, when society had accepted the general speculation about my birth—despite the fact that my adoption had yet to be exposed—and refused to accept me. Three-quarters of the guests hadn't bothered to show, despite my father's position in their society. Even after my birth father had been revealed, Flossie had been there just as much as Mother.

"Even if you're trying to make me look scandalous." With a smile I adjusted my gown so I wouldn't appear to offer the guests an extra serving of cleavage with their dinner.

She drew me in for a hug. "Get on with you now. The guests should be here soon."

My stomach dipped. I'd been to hundreds of Mother's dinner parties over the years—this one should be no different. With that thought, I snatched my elbow-length gloves from the vanity tray, gave Flossie a parting smile, and left the room.

I wasn't surprised to find Mother already in the reception hall, but she wasn't alone. Kent stood beside her, engaging her in conversation. He flashed her a smile and said something to which my dear, prim mother playfully swatted his arm with her handkerchief. I quietly observed their exchange, but as if sensing my presence, Kent glanced over. Any traces of amusement from chatting with Mother drained from his expression, and . . . something else replaced it.

I could blame the heat in his gaze on the cut of my gown, but his eyes hadn't roamed my form. No, they fixed on my face with an intensity I'd glimpsed before but had forgotten all about.

I didn't like the sudden pinch in my chest as I approached. I couldn't let him make me feel. Make me remember. So I hardened my heart to his reaction and adopted a disinterested expression, which now shoved that familiar glint, a subtle teasing, into his eyes.

"Delvina." Mother air-kissed both sides of my face, as if she hadn't seen me in weeks rather than a couple of hours ago. "I believe you know our guest, Mr. Brisbane."

I knew him more intimately than she understood. He did look resplendent in a tux, which I would never confess because it would only add more weight to his heavy ego. "Good evening." I spoke in the same droll tone I reserved for these events and extended my gloved hand.

He bowed over it. "Always a pleasure, Delvina." His fingers gently tightened around mine before releasing them, leaving a tingling of fire in the wake.

"What good turn of events for the rain to hold for tonight's dinner. I was certain the side streets would flood." Mother placed a hand on my arm, smiling at me. "I'm so happy I could convince you to remain at Hemswick."

Kent flicked a speaking glance my way, as if telling me he read the situation perfectly—if I hadn't returned home, I hadn't retrieved his knife. He aimed a soft smile at Mother. "I'm certain it was a comfort to have your daughter with you."

The butler crossed the room, and Mother halted him with a question, leaving me alone with the detective and his infuriating smirk.

I nailed him with a glare. "I know what you're thinking."

His gaze roved over me, purposefully this time. "Couldn't possibly."

I rolled my eyes. "I didn't contrive to stay here in hopes of being unable to get your silly knife."

He shrugged. "It's okay to confess if you did. I always appreciate some good old-fashioned flattery."

"I'll pass." The doorbell rang, pulling my attention for a second. I returned my focus to Kent, only to find him watching me. "Mother's afraid of storms. I couldn't leave her."

"Admirable of you." The sincerity in his tone raised my suspicion. "I'll just have to come to your flat sometime this week."

"Oh no you won't." The rest of my refusal was cut short at the sight of another familiar gentleman. *She didn't.* "I can't believe she did this."

"Did what?" Kent followed my line of sight. "Your mother invited His Honor."

Judge VanKirk and his daughter, Marianne, stood next to Mother. Now I wished I could have persuaded her to let me approve the guest list. The VanKirks had just survived a traumatic experience, and Mother was chatting about the weather.

I moved to greet them. "Judge, how kind of you to come this evening. Especially after the week you had." I threw in the last part for Mother's benefit.

Marianne perked. "Oh, I'm afraid I was the one who's been intrusive. I just had to come and thank you. Thank you both." The young girl bounced on her heels, waving Kent over. "I telephoned your mother, and she extended the invitation. I hope you and your husband don't mind."

I almost choked on my own breath. "I'm not . . . we're not . . ." One glance at Kent's lax expression told me he was uninterested in fixing the error. Same with Mother. I cut a look at the judge, who wore an amused smile. Apparently, he was only concerned about upholding the truth in the courtroom and not Mother's reception hall. I wasn't as inclined. "I'm relieved to find you looking so well, Miss VanKirk, but I must clarify. Mr. Brisbane and I aren't married." Anymore. "The papers got it wrong."

Rather than being dissuaded, her gaze took on a dreamy quality. "Then when you do set a date, you must have Father officiate the ceremony."

The judge nodded along, a conspiratorial gleam in his eyes. "It's the least I can do for the two of you."

Mother grinned delightedly, as if she'd tutored Judge VanKirk in her devious ways of matchmaking.

I made the unfortunate error of glancing at Kent. His gaze lit on me, and my gut clenched. Surely he wouldn't reveal the truth. Wouldn't uncork our bottled secrets. I stepped forward. "On that score—"

"Maybe we should give it a go."

My eyes slid shut at my former husband's words. Everything was a game to him. Or a joke. He'd wanted to discuss our failed marriage yesterday, and this—this!—was one reason why I'd refused. Nothing would be accomplished by rehashing the past, especially when Kent could only be serious for a handful of moments out of the day.

While I battled for a neutral expression, Marianne clasped her hands in front of her, her grin wide and brilliant. "Oh, that would be the berries."

Enough was enough. "Pardon us a moment." I grasped Kent's wrist and dragged him along to a secluded corner.

His lips twitched, and I pulled in another breath, for composure's sake. It didn't help. "We're not a couple."

"I'm aware." He bent his head toward mine. "There's no harm in letting the girl believe so. She's been through enough."

I adjusted my glove with a light scoff. "Marianne just survived a kidnapping. I'm certain she could handle having her romantic hopes disillusioned." I glanced at the VanKirks, grateful more guests had arrived.

Mother, ever the dutiful hostess, flitted about introducing everyone. But it seemed I'd lost my opportunity to rectify everything, thanks to Kent.

Over the next five minutes, I greeted our neighbors Mrs. Ida Elliot and her son, Edward. Two years younger than myself, Edward was the sole heir to the Elliot fortune and an overall decent gent. Ida was in her midforties and still retained that youthful glow. She was often over at Hemswick, probably more than me. The woman could be tiresome at times with her incessant rambling, but she was a good friend to Mother.

I exchanged a few polite remarks with our neighbors, then welcomed Dr. Otis Ewing, who'd entered the reception hall just before Wallace Stratton and his date.

My gaze hooked on the tall brunette dressed in a stunning black gown with gold lace accents. She seemed familiar. As if I'd recently seen her. There was a sophistication to her beauty, but Wallace always had a gorgeous woman on his arm.

The couple approached Mother and me, and I wondered why the man was here. I, of course, had known the motive behind Mother's invitation, but what induced such a man about town to accept? What lure did a boring dinner party have?

Wallace set a hand on his date's back. "Allow me to introduce Miss Adele Thayer."

The woman gracefully dipped her head, her dark brown hair styled in a fashionable bob, sliding against her cheek.

It hit me. "Thank you for coming, Miss Thayer. Though I confess to seeing you only moments ago."

Her brow rumpled in confusion.

I smiled. "In this month's *Vogue* issue." It had taken me a second to fathom the woman standing before me was the same that Flossie had pointed out on that page from the magazine. "My maid was encouraging me to style my hair like yours in the photo."

Her scarlet lips eased into a warm smile, but before she could utter a word, Wallace spoke, "She's the bee's knees, isn't she? Her dedication to the fashion world is nothing but inspiring." He smiled at her adoringly. "I've taken it upon myself to acquire clients for her for fashion consults. She's getting so popular, I may expand my agency in order to utilize her talents."

Ah, that explained his eagerness to attend tonight. Either his bank-mogul father refused to finance the venture, leaving Wallace to solicit funds from wealthy families, or he was here to drum up more business, preying upon women who might need an updated wardrobe but had no fashion sense. I also noticed how he'd deliberately omitted just what kind of *agency* he spearheaded. The upper class wasn't exactly accepting of the modeling profession.

"I don't believe Miss Kline would benefit from any tips I could offer." Miss Thayer's voice was soft, but not in a timid way. "I couldn't improve her appearance if I tried. You're simply stunning." She seemed like someone who knew exactly which words to say to flatter the hostess, but her tone wasn't oily or forced. However, she did seem somewhat distracted by something behind me.

One subtle glance told me exactly what caught her attention. Or rather who. Kent. Sure, the man was handsome, but it was more than that. There was this roguish mystery about him that appealed to most women. Though from personal experience, the air of secrets that lured me to Kent had proven to be the very thing that pushed me away.

The butler announced dinner, and Mother was so pleased to have enough gentlemen to escort the ladies. Of course, she paired me with Kent. The ten of us were seated, I on the opposite end from Mother, with Brisbane to my right and Edward Elliot to my left. By design, I was certain. No doubt Mother had originally seated Wallace beside me but exchanged his seat upon learning of his date.

The meal progressed smoothly. Kent said only two annoying things to me, but mostly behaved himself. Mother kept a tight rein on the conversation, the topics including Mrs. Elliot's support of Dr. Ewing's recent lectures. Mrs. Elliot's paternal side of the family were major catalysts in the medical world, and so she took great interest in the subject. Miss Thayer chatted with me about the theater, and we discovered we'd both attended the opening night of *The Widow's Triumph*, a well-developed but underrated show.

"That was good of you, Delvina," Edward Elliot said quietly, as if for my ears only. "Rescuing Miss VanKirk like you did."

It hadn't only been me. Kent had a major hand in the success of the case.

"Look at His Honor." Edward pointed his fork at him. "I've never seen the old codger smile so much. He must be relieved to have his daughter back." His head tilted in thoughtfulness. "Must be nice to have a father that cares."

The late Mr. Reginald Elliot had passed away a few years ago. I understood the absence of a parent. My birth father had been a nonexistent figure for most of my life—it was only within those last several months before his passing that our relationship had established. And while Mr. Elliot may have been the head of the household, he'd never shown any interest in his wife or his son. He'd preferred to live at his country estate, only returning to the city once a month. If that. Edward didn't seem to expect an answer, so I didn't offer one.

"Do you think there's any hope for an old woman such as myself?" I overheard Edward's mother asking Miss Thayer. "When I stopped wearing my mourning gowns, I realized my wardrobe was positively outdated."

Miss Thayer dabbed her mouth with a napkin, then opened her mouth to speak.

But Wallace cut her off. "I'm certain Miss Thayer can assist you. Why, she helped Mrs. Welch just last month and . . . What's the matter? Have I misspoken?"

The room had fallen silent at his remark. The only three who hadn't a solemn look on their faces were Kent, Wallace, and Miss Thayer. Even Mother, who usually remained calm and poised, was flustered. And I knew why.

I leaned forward and adopted a soft tone for Mother's sake. "I regret to tell you that Mrs. Welch passed away not too long ago."

Miss Thayer dropped her fork, then fumbled to retrieve it, almost spilling her water. "Please forgive me. I had no idea." She reclaimed her silverware and regarded the table with an apologetic look. "What happened?"

This time Dr. Ewing spoke up. "Sleeping disease. Nasty business, that." He shook his head with a sigh. "Continues to elude us. There's no common symptom among those it preys upon."

My gaze flickered to Mother, who'd grown paler the more the doctor spoke. I needed to steer this conversation back to something boring and less panic inducing for Mother. "The weather—"

"One minute a person would be just fine." The doctor ignored my diversion tactic. "And the next they're unawakenable and on their way to the pearly gates. Now take Mrs. Welch's case. I attended her and—"

"We're all saddened by Mrs. Welch's passing," Kent chimed in. "Perhaps just like the Spanish flu, all this will pass and be behind us. Then we can move on to more pleasant views life can offer us." His eyes met mine, meaning in his gaze. He had to have caught onto Mother's distress, because I'd bet every dollar I'd ever earned sleuthing he had no idea who Mrs. Welch was.

Sadly, his interruption was short lived.

"Well, I, for one, am shocked." Miss Thayer shook her head. "She seemed in such good health when I'd last seen her. Telling me stories of her life in Guam and of interesting events she witnessed during her time before that." Her gaze drifted to Brisbane, as it had on numerous occasions, though this time her lower lip slightly pouted, as if trying to present herself pitiable while also alluring.

But Kent's attention was on Mother, distracting her with a question about the soup. I had to admit my heart softened a tad at his care. He knew how much she meant to me. But I couldn't return to that young girl who'd impulsively thrown herself at Kent Brisbane. No, once I returned his knife, we'd go our separate ways. Again.

Chapter 5

"Do you have a husband who'll sign for you?"

After last night's dinner party, my patience tank was drained empty. I didn't bother schooling my features, simply because this landlord doubled as an expensive-cigar-smoking toff. "Are you saying that even though I have more than enough funds to purchase this office"—I swept my hand, gesturing to the ample space I hoped to call mine—"you refuse to sell because I'm not married?" The gleaming parquet floors, large picture windows, and wall-to-wall shelving were perfect for me.

Mr. Groves stroked his narrow mustache, a knowing glint in his eyes. He'd found a loophole and was clinging to it for all its worth. "It's more of a safety net for me, you understand."

"I don't understand. My money is just as good as anyone else's." Such had been my argument for the past fifteen minutes. But the man wouldn't budge.

After a bit of a staring match, he finally broke eye contact and tugged his waistcoat with a haughty sniff. "I'll think about it."

He wasn't fooling me. He wouldn't consider anything. I'd arranged this appointment with his secretary, who must not have relayed my name. Because once I'd arrived here and given this man my card, I noticed a definite shift in his attitude.

His tone held traces of disgust, and I understood the true hesitation on his part. No doubt it was less that I was a woman and more of who my birth father was. Or perhaps a combination. Being the child of a notorious mobster had its setbacks. The manhunt for Hugo

Salvastano had been nationwide, since most of the country suspected he'd slaughtered his two brothers along with a police commissioner and then gone into hiding. My cracking the case behind it all and establishing my father's innocence—on that score at least—had gained me credibility in the private detective world, but not so much in the eye of respectable society.

Mr. Groves's narrowed gaze and suspicious glances all but told me I wasn't welcome here. It wasn't only him. This was the seventh office building I'd been to since moving back to Manhattan.

If I wanted a prime location for my detective agency, I would need a miracle. Thankfully, God didn't hold my name or my parentage against me. At least that was what my sister, Kate, had said. We'd just met several months ago through our connection with Hugo, but Kate warmed to me as if we'd known each other all our lives. She had struggled with the knowledge of our birth father having been a known criminal and explained to me how her faith helped her through. My heart begged me to yield, to place my trust in someone besides myself. Even though I knew I wasn't strong enough, I couldn't. Not yet. I'd experienced too much betrayal from those important to me to fully surrender to another ever again. But even in my skepticism, I could see the Almighty's hand in impossible situations. Such was the case with Marianne VanKirk. Hmm. Maybe I could ask His Honor for a recommendation to obtain an office, but then again, I hated asking for favors.

I exited the building and walked toward my flat. I should be grateful the owner of Park Towers hadn't snubbed my offer for the penthouse flat. Of course, that had been Mother's doing. She played bridge with the owner's wife. Thankfully, not all of society was against me.

I glanced at my watch pin. I was cutting it close. I wasn't far from my apartment building, which had been the sole reason I'd wanted that office. But I knew better than to keep Kent Brisbane waiting. How he'd retrieved my telephone exchange, I could only guess. Yes, he was an excellent detective, but I suspected my own mother had been his informant. He'd rung me up only moments before my appointment, asking if he could meet me at my flat, since he was visiting someone at Park Towers today.

Which was why I needed to hurry. My plan was to already be inside, pocketknife in hand, when he rang the bell. I couldn't have him trailing me inside my flat and waiting as I retrieved it. So I picked up my pace, only to stumble to a halt.

Police cars. An ambulance. And a sizable crowd huddled on the narrow strip of lawn in front of the regal-looking complex.

What was going on?

I moved with purpose, reaching the outskirts of the throng, spotting the neighboring tenant, Mrs. Flanders. If anyone knew what was happening, it'd be the resident busybody.

I sidled up next to her. "What's all the fuss about?"

Had there been a raid? Had Park Towers been moonlighting as a luxury complex all the while selling moonshine out of the cellar? Silly notion, but nothing surprised me anymore. Though if that were the case, why the ambulance?

Mrs. Flanders waved a handkerchief in front of her in clipped motions. "It's dreadful. So young. So tragic for things to wind up this way."

"What are you talking about?"

"If I had known, I would've reached out more. Such a shame. She had so much to live for."

"Who?"

"The young girl who lives in 317." She buried her face into the handkerchief and then blew her nose. "Well, I should say *lived*. Poor girl ended things last night. They found her this morning."

Horrible. "Who was she?" Having recently moved in, I didn't know many tenants.

The older woman's sobs continued, and she was led away by a younger lady who kept muttering, "Don't make a scene, Auntie."

I scanned the uniformed men, searching for any recognizable faces. But a group of fellows in bulky overcoats shifted in front of me, blocking my view. No matter. I knew exactly the right person who'd give me answers. The maintenance man, Paulo. I rushed to the side of the building, the ground still soft and soggy from last night's round of thunderstorms. I turned the corner, colliding into something.

Rather, someone.

Kent.

His hands shot out, steadying me. I'd completely forgotten about our meeting. His mouth quirked, and I could only imagine what flirty remark would tumble from his lips.

Instead he looked into my eyes, and all pretense vanished. "What's the matter?"

I jerked a thumb over my shoulder. "Someone died. Apparently a suicide."

His brows lowered. "That's tough."

I agreed. There was a tangible somberness that seemed to thicken the air. "I didn't know her. I don't think I'd ever stepped foot on the third floor. But—"

"Third floor." His eyes took on a sudden intensity. "Do you know what flat number?"

"317."

He turned aside and muttered something under his breath. The hard planes of his face and sharpness in his gaze made my stomach dip.

"You knew her?" I asked.

"So did you." His lips parted with a heavy exhale. "It's Adele Thayer."

I blinked. Miss Thayer. Wallace Stratton's date. The up-and-coming model and fashion consultant lived in Park Towers? The building had seven floors and many residents, so it wasn't surprising I hadn't run into her.

What was surprising? That she'd taken her own life. I'd just seen her a week ago. What had transpired between then and now that would cause her to take such a drastic action? My mind ventured back to that evening at Hemswick. She'd seemed somewhat distracted at first, not unusual though, considering she was a guest in an unfamiliar house with complete strangers. She'd soon found her footing, even to the point of exhibiting a flirtatious attitude around Kent.

"No." I shook my head. It didn't make sense.

"No what?" Kent tilted his head. "I'm certain that's her flat number."

"And just how do you know where she lives?" Understanding dawned, and my stomach knotted. "Wait. Was she your other *appointment*?"

He opened his mouth to speak, but the answer was already in his eyes.

"Never mind. It doesn't matter now." I brushed past him, needing away.

"Vinny, wait," he called after me, but I kept moving.

It shouldn't have shocked me that Kent would visit Miss Thayer. She was stunning and had definitely made her interest in him known. Plus, it wasn't as if Kent and I were anything to each other anymore. He was free to romance any woman he chose.

And that was that. I wouldn't spend any more time on the matter, especially since this situation was more pressing. Because Miss Thayer was gone, and something was off about the entire thing.

So while Kent endeavored to keep pace with me, I flagged down someone I hadn't seen since my early cases as a private detective. "Officer Burkett."

The police detective glanced over. He'd been conversing with Mr. Paddy, the apartment complex manager, but now the uniformed man approached me. I cut a look to my left. Kent had caught up with me. Whatever it was he intended to say would have to wait because Matthew Burkett stood before me.

"Delvina." His blue eyes drifted to Kent, then back to me. "What are you doing here?"

"I live here." I motioned to the building.

Out of my peripheral I caught Kent slipping away a few feet, giving us some privacy. But I suspected he remained within earshot. The man was just as interested in this information as I was. Perhaps more.

I blew out a breath and turned my attention back to Officer Burkett. "I want to ask you about the deceased."

The policeman held up a hand, as if to refuse, but I wouldn't take no. "Adele Thayer was at my mother's dinner party last Saturday evening."

His eyes slightly widened. "Really? How did she seem?"

"Somewhat distracted, but nothing abnormal. How'd she die?"

He exhaled. "Anyone but you, and I'd say take a hike. But I know your persistence." His tone was part fondness, part exasperation. No doubt he recalled our first interactions from years back. He'd fallen in bad graces among the elite when he'd accidentally mistaken someone from the upper class as a person of interest in one of his cases. Though he'd apologized, the man he'd offended had called for his badge. I'd been able to smooth things out. Well, more like my father had, since the accusing man had been one of his business associates.

I politely smiled. "You're right. I'll find out another way, so it's best to hear it from you."

Another sigh. "It was a bullet wound. Died instantly, if you're concerned about your friend suffering."

My gut clenched. "I don't think she did it."

"Delvina." He eased closer, voice low. "It's an open-and-shut case."

"But if—"

"Look. I got to get this ambulance out of here. There's no foul play. Her right hand was curled around a revolver. Doesn't get any clearer than that."

"So you found powder marks on her right hand?"

He gave my arm a gentle squeeze, as if I were a four-year-old needing placating. "Let it go, Delvina."

"Matt, if you'd just listen—"

But he was already walking away, disappearing into the crowd.

The New York Police Department was swamped with cases. This one was easy for them to wrap up, and they wouldn't look into it any further. Which was frustrating.

"What did you find out?" Brisbane's low voice floated over my shoulder.

A few thoughts sprang to mind, but one took precedence. I glanced at my watch pin. Earlier I purposed to seek out Paulo, but it would've been a fruitless endeavor because no doubt he'd already left.

"Look over there," someone called.

My gaze tracked the voice to the hub of scribblers with press badges shoved into their narrow hat bands. Their nosy faces swung our direction, and I wanted to vanish. The press? When had they arrived? Though I knew most cub reporters lounged at hospitals and police stations in order to follow the patrol cars to the scene.

Either way, we'd been spotted.

"Miss Kline. Mr. Brisbane. Are you investigating Miss Thayer's death together?" And what seemed like a thousand questions followed.

"Come on." I clasped Kent's wrist and stalked away at a brisk pace, dragging him with me. It was obvious I couldn't head inside Park Towers. I couldn't have reporters following me and discovering where I lived.

Kent looked pointedly at my hand around his cuff and then at me. "This is becoming a habit with you." He referenced the moment in the reception hall at Hemswick when I'd tugged him to the secluded corner to scold him.

"I can't leave you unsupervised with the newshounds."

His brows rose in silent inquiry.

"You could leak the word about our past."

"I could." A challenge entered his eyes as he drew his arm closer to his side, bringing me nearer, almost daring me to pull away. His head dipped to mine, the brim of his hat almost skimming my forehead. "But I wouldn't."

I held his gaze, but the closeness was getting to me, so I released him and put a respectable distance between us.

But Kent wasn't having it. He closed the gap, our sides nearly brushing. "Really, Vinny. I know things between us weren't perfect, but give me more credit."

I didn't respond. Things hadn't been perfect, and there was a reason. But I wasn't about to go into what I'd glimpsed that day at Penn Station. Instead I moved down the block. Then another. Surprisingly, Kent kept quiet.

My thoughts went back to Adele Thayer. She had been murdered. Questions piled like cinder blocks on my chest, compressing. Who killed her? Why?

We paused on the corner, waiting for traffic to slow, and he glanced at me. "Not that I don't enjoy a good romp through the city, but where exactly are we going?"

"Twelfth Street."

"Any particular reason?" He casually strolled alongside me. "I'd been hoping to return to my office at one point today."

I tried not to let jealousy sink in as we crossed the street. Kent had his own agency, and unlike when I'd first met him, his office now was in a great location. "You're free to return. It's not like I want you with me. I only wanted you away from the press."

"I can't imagine peeling myself away when you sweet-talk me like that." He was back to his charming self, though it was a front. He was bothered by the model's death just as I was.

But how close had Kent been to Adele Thayer? I'd just assumed he hadn't met her before last Saturday. Their relationship could very well have been established long before. "How did you know where Miss Thayer lived?"

He looked me straight in the eye, as if he had nothing to hide, but I knew better than to blindly trust. "She telephoned me the other day and asked if I could meet her."

"Indeed. You certainly make the rounds, don't you?" I kept my voice light, though it took some effort. "Was your little rendezvous supposed to happen before or after you met with me?"

"I'm not so sure I like your tone."

"There's nothing wrong with it."

"There's obvious insinuation in it." He watched me from beneath dark lashes. "To answer your question, after. My appointment with Miss Thayer was after yours."

"What kind of appointment was it?" Okay, that sounded better in my head than on my lips.

"The professional kind." His gaze strayed to the road. "She said she'd explain when I got there."

Of course she did. "I can't believe you fell for that."

He slowed his pace, his scowl making his scar more pronounced. "For what?"

"Nothing." Though it was pointless to hash this out now. Poor Adele Thayer had been killed. It didn't matter what her motives were with Kent. "Did you know her before last Saturday?"

"No."

He answered without hesitation, but I wasn't sure if I believed him. Once upon a time I had, and it hadn't turned out well for either of us. My time of questioning ran out because we arrived at our destination. "Here we are."

Kent's eyes squinted as he took in the restaurant. "John's?"

"The chicken parmigiana is excellent here."

"So I've heard. I've also heard it was the very meal Umberto Valenti ate just before he was shot dead"—he pointed down to the sidewalk— "probably right where we're standing."

He wasn't wrong. John's Italian restaurant was a hotbed for mobsters and bootleggers. A few summers ago, the future crime boss of the Valenti empire had been gunned down by a rival gang. But there was a valid reason to be here. I reached for the door, but Kent beat me to it.

He darted a glance inside, then to me. "You sure you want to go in there?"

I patted his cheek. "I'll keep you safe, Brisbane." I heard his amused snort as I brushed past him into the cozy restaurant. I inhaled the addicting scent of garlic and fresh bread, my gaze alert. And true to routine, Paulo sat in the back booth, garbed in his maintenance uniform, his head bent over a large plate of spaghetti.

With a nod to the head waiter, I weaved through the tables, approaching Paulo, former Pittsburgh bootlegger and current janitor of Park Towers. Brisbane followed at a close pace, by the sound of his steps.

Paulo's hooded gaze lifted to meet mine, his thick lips curling into a half smile. "The house special is good today."

I shook my head at his burgundy-colored glass. "House special" was code for their in-house wine, which they made in the basement. John's might have the best manicotti, but it was also a notorious speakeasy. "I thought you were cutting back." The manager at Park Towers, Mr. Paddy, probably wouldn't appreciate his employee drinking on lunch break.

He heaved a sigh. "Needed it after the morning I had."

"That's why I'm here." I knew Paulo always took lunch at John's on Wednesdays, when the special was spaghetti and meatballs. Everything about Paulo seemed slouched, from his curled shoulders to his sagging jowls. Even his eyelids drooped lower today. "Sorry you had a rough morning. And I suspect it has to do with flat 317."

He took a long sip of his drink, then wiped his mouth with the back of his hand. "Been a long time since I've seen that . . . kind of scenario." He gestured for me to sit, then his gaze cut to Brisbane and hardened. "He on the level?" Paulo wasn't one to hand over his trust.

"As far as I know."

The answer seemed enough for Paulo, for he gave Brisbane a nod and extended his hand. "Paulo Valducci."

Brisbane leaned forward and secured the handshake. "Kent Brisbane."

"Have a seat. I only have a few minutes left." As if remembering his narrowing window, he shoveled more spaghetti into his mouth.

"I hate to ask this, but I want to talk about what happened in 317. Did you see Miss Thayer?"

Paulo pushed a meatball about his plate, then stabbed it with his fork. "Yeah. Had to let the cleaning lady in."

This caught my attention. "The cleaning ladies have keys."

"Not for 317. The Thayer dame hired an outside service. I always have to let the lady in at ten a.m. on Tuesday, Wednesday, and Saturday. I let her in this morning. Just two steps down the hall and I heard her scream."

So the cleaning lady found the body. "Then what happened?" I noticed Brisbane idly toying with the edge of a discarded menu, seemingly disinterested, but I knew better.

Paulo's cheeks puffed with a held-in belch. "I ran back into the room to see what the fuss was about and saw Miss Thayer on the floor. It was too late to help."

"The police called it a suicide."

"Looked like it." He bit off a chunk of bread.

"I heard her right hand held a revolver. Was that how you found her?" He nodded.

Good. So the body hadn't been moved upon discovery until the time Detective Burkett arrived. "Anything else catch your attention?"

"Not really. The maid fainted, but can't blame the dame."

I gentled my voice. "In your professional opinion, how long was she dead?"

He gave me a look that told me he didn't want to go into it.

"I know you left all that behind, but a window is all I need."

He wiped the corners of his red-stained mouth with a napkin and tossed it on the table.

"It's important or I wouldn't ask."

"She died last night at nine fifty-five."

My face slacked before I could control it. I knew he could tell me a window, but the precise moment?

He caught my surprise and shrugged a beefy shoulder. "Didn't have to use my *expertise*. Her clock pin busted when she fell on the floor. That was the time."

"Could it have been tampered with?" This from Kent.

So I'd been right. He'd been paying close attention. And he must not be buying the suicide claim either.

Paulo's expression turned thoughtful as he brushed breadcrumbs from his overgrown mustache. "No, I don't think so. The pin was under the body, barely peeking out. And Miss Thayer wasn't moved, according to my experience with such things."

"Well done, Paulo." I slipped a wad of cash across the table.

"No, Vinny." His jowls flapped with his adamant refusal. "You did enough getting me this job." He plucked at his uniform.

I grinned at him and nudged Brisbane to stand so I could scoot out of the booth. "This"—I tapped the cash—"is for your missus. A consolation prize for having to clean up after you." I pointed to his shirt, where some spaghetti strands had failed to reach his mouth, striping his shirt with sauce.

He chuckled heartily. "That she does. Looks like I'll be avoiding Paddy for the rest of day or else I'd be getting an earful."

I was certain the head manager of the complex had more to deal with today than his janitor's stained uniform. "Oh, and Paulo? Do you remember the cleaning lady's name? The one who fainted."

He squinted, as if it helped bring clarity. "Rosalie something."

After thanking Paulo and Brisbane offering a polite "nice to meet you," we headed back onto Twelfth Street.

"You're one fascinating woman, Vinny." He spoke first. "One second you're chums with the police inspector and the next with a man such as Paulo." He lowered his voice. "I'm assuming the tactful way of throwing around phrases like 'experience' and 'expertise' regarding a dead body doesn't mean he was a doctor."

"Far from it." I lowered my voice. "I met him in Pittsburgh while working a case. He was a rumrunner for a territory that rivaled my birth father's. He wasn't too far up the crime chain, never harmed anyone, but I know he's seen his share of gruesome. He admitted to me he wanted out of that life, and so I got him the job here in the city."

His gaze lit with . . . something. Respect, maybe? As if I passed some sort of test. Which sounded silly, but his reaction made me wonder more about him. Though I'd once shared his name, he remained a mystery to me. I knew his background was humble but had no idea of his upbringing or family. No clue, really, how he'd spent the past four years. How many sweethearts he'd charmed. And while my thoughts were on that nauseating subject, what about his meeting with Miss Thayer? He'd acted as if he had no idea why she'd invited him.

"I was at Warren Hayes's townhouse."

Brisbane's voice cut through my thoughts. "Pardon?"

His lips quirked. "Just relaying I have a solid alibi for my whereabouts yesterday. I attended a dinner party at the Hayeses' residence. Was there from seven until about eleven, then hailed a cab home."

Warren Hayes and his wife had been linked to a sensationalized scandal a couple of years ago. Warren had faked his own death in order to uncover the person wanting him dead. His wife, Geneva, had even been a suspect for a while. Together the two had traveled rural New York as barnstormers, looking for the person behind his plane crash. And while their adventure seemed fascinating, I was currently concerned with Kent's motives. "Why are you telling me this?"

"Paulo said Miss Thayer died at nine fifty-five. I was on the other side of New York, being bored out of my mind by the relentless chatter of an eligible heiress and her mother." His elbow nudged mine. "Hopefully, that will acquit me of suspicion in your eyes."

I adopted a cool tone. "Suspicion?"

"You're not one to blindly trust—"

"Whose fault is that?"

"Unless you have concrete proof about something," he continued, as if I hadn't launched an accusing question. His nonchalant expression shifted, his gray eyes softening. "Though I hope, Vinny, you realize that you don't always have to be so brave."

My thoughts clouded as I tried to pick apart what he meant. How were trust and courage the same? Several years ago I'd collided with a street preacher as I was navigating through the pedestrian traffic on Fifth Avenue. When I'd apologized for causing him to drop his box of Bibles, the scraggly old man had looked me dead in the eye and said, "It takes strength to lean on God, young lady. If you stubbornly remain on your own two feet, you'll wind up falling."

I'd never forgotten.

Was I stubborn? Perhaps. But life had made me this way. I'd rather fall on my own than get pushed down by others. It was easier for me to look out for myself. Though I wasn't about to venture into this discussion with my former spouse. "Why would you need to prove your where-abouts?" I tilted my head. "You heard Detective Burkett. He said it was a suicide."

He paused on the corner, his eyes taking on a serious quality, like those moments while rescuing Miss VanKirk. "Come on, Vinny. You and I both know it was murder."

I did know. But I wanted to hear his reasoning, so I motioned for him to continue.

"Detective Burkett said her right hand gripped a gun."

I lowered my voice. "He did say that."

"But we both saw Miss Thayer fumble her fork at your mother's dinner party."

Ah, he had noticed as well. "I remember that moment vividly."

"I thought you would." His eyes sparked. "Which means you saw her reach for said fork and why it makes suicide unlikely."

I nodded. "Because she was left-handed."

Chapter 6 ————————————————————————————————

MY FAITH IN THE LOCAL authorities had never ranked high on the trust meter, but now whatever favorable opinion I'd had sank to the bottom. I'd contacted Detective Burkett, relaying the theory of a staged suicide, even bringing out the point about Adele Thayer being left-handed.

"She could be ambidextrous, Vinny." He'd sounded very sure of himself. "The case is closed. Let it go."

I'd been dismissed. Just like with Mr. Groves yesterday. Yes, it'd been a different circumstance, but I couldn't help the nagging frustration at being tossed aside once again.

So there I sat at a desk in my not-an-office flat, typing out an invoice for another client, whose case I'd resolved a few weeks back but hadn't gotten around to billing. Not that I charged much. I tucked the invoice inside an envelope and set it aside to be mailed even as a knock sounded on my door. I paused. The in-house cleaning service shouldn't be here for another hour. Mother was at brunch with friends. And that was the extent of people I ever expected at my door.

Unless . . . it was Kent wanting to retrieve his silly pocketknife.

Yesterday we'd parted ways after talking to Paulo, Kent claiming he had pressing matters at his office but assuring me he'd be in touch. It almost seemed he intentionally delayed getting his blade back in order to see me again, but that would be absurd. After that awful day four years ago, I'd gone out of my way to avoid him. As for Kent? He'd never attempted to contact me. No romantic pursuit trying to win back my affection or arduous plea for me to return to him. Nothing. Which reinforced my belief that he'd never truly wanted to marry me in the first place. That I'd talked him into it, and his condition at the time had made it so simple, only for him to have second thoughts shortly after.

Because if he'd cared, why hadn't he tried to explain what had happened? Why he'd abandoned me?

And here I was, mulling over the past while someone continued to knock. With a sigh I made my way to the foyer and opened the door.

"Are you Miss Salvastano Kline?" A petite woman with a thin face shadowed by a faded hat stood in the hall.

Usually people knew me by my adopted surname, so for this woman to include my given one had me alert. "Yes. I am."

"Good." Her shoulders sagged. "Mr. Valducci told me to come here. Said you be fair."

Ah, that made sense. If Paulo had mentioned me, she'd refer to me by the Salvastano name because that was how he addressed me. Though I hadn't any clue what she meant by calling me fair. "And you are?"

"I came 'cause I wanna hire you." Her hands shot out, as if I were going to slam the door in her face. "Please hear me out before ya be sayin' no."

"Why would I refuse you?" Other than she pointedly hadn't given me her name.

"Because several detectives gave me the boot."

So I was the last resort. I was used to this sort of thing, though it never helped my pride any. "Come in." I opened the door wider and stepped back.

She continued wringing her hands, and judging by her chapped knuckles and callused fingers, she did manual labor. Her frock had been patched in some spots, and it hung on her narrow shoulders, making me believe the dress had originally belonged to someone heartier. Or she'd lost a considerable amount of weight.

As soon as we moved to the parlor, she launched into her petition. "I wanna hire you to find out who killed Miss Adele Thayer. She didn't do herself in. Someone else did. I know it."

So not everyone bought the suicide theory the authorities were clinging to. Interesting. But how was this woman connected to Adele Thayer? From her outdated frock to the coarse edge of her speech, it was obvious she wasn't living among the swells. "I want to hear your thoughts, but first will you tell me your name and how you knew Miss Thayer?"

"Rosalie Adams." Her thin lips pulled into a sheepish smile, telling me she'd purposefully ignored my first request for her name. No doubt she'd wanted to say her piece, since she'd expected a refusal. "She hired me to clean her flat. She was a good person. Always kind."

Ah, Ms. Adams was the cleaning lady who'd discovered the body. The maid whom Paulo had said fainted.

"Such a good payin' job. Another one lost." She shook her head, then muttered, "Two times now. My rotten luck."

My chest twisted. I'd always wanted to live independent of the Kline fortune—such was my motivation for becoming a detective. That and to prove something to myself after my broken marriage. But even if I'd failed, I had the security of my inheritance to fall back on. It didn't seem the case with Ms. Adams. I knew of households always looking for domestic help, and I'd offer to put in a good word for Ms. Adams, but I needed to know her better first. "You think the police misjudged the situation regarding Miss Thayer?"

She frowned. "Miss Thayer wouldn't have done that. Not her. Only that morning she be rattling off all the excitin' parties she be goin' to this month. She always be goin' here and there. So full of life." But then her face tightened, her eyes darkening. "It just seems too much of a coincidence, ya know?"

"What does?"

"That Miss Thayer and him be arguin' in her flat, then next time I see her she's dead."

"Who was the man? Did you get a good look at him?"

At this, her entire frame grew rigid, and for some reason, I couldn't see this woman fainting, like Paulo had told me. Had she been faking? My suspicious mind never took things at face value.

"Mr. Stratton. He was fumin'."

Oh. That threw things into a different light.

"Wallace Stratton?"

She nodded. "A pompous man. He be usin' Miss Thayer. Her beauty and fashion smarts."

"What did they fight about?"

"I be in the other room gettin' her laundry. I didn't hear it all. But what I did hear sent my blood to chillin'." She visibly shivered. "I'll never forget. He be sayin', 'If you don't do as I ask, you'll be sorry.'"

Not exactly a detailed threat, but one nonetheless.

Her gaze dropped to her scuffed shoes. "I wanna see justice done, but . . ." She rubbed her arm. "I can't be payin' much." She then offered a payment far below the standard rate for this type of service. I could see why the other detectives hadn't wanted to waste their time, especially when the authorities had closed the case.

"You specified that you were Miss Thayer's cleaning lady, but do you have experience baking?"

Her brow bent, clearly not expecting this turn of conversation. "Yes, miss."

"Can you bake cannoli? I haven't had any for a long while."

"I can. Learned when I was a girl. My mother's papa be Italian. He owned a bakery."

"My papa did too." Then my birth father promptly had become a mob boss, but some details were better left unsaid. Though considering how she'd called me by both surnames—Salvastano Kline—she might be aware of the Salvastano family's less-than-stellar reputation. "Maybe we can make a compromise. You bake me some cannoli, and we'll call things even."

Her head tilted, eyes squinting. "Are you foolin'?"

"Not at all." I realized I often came across gruff, so I softened my words with a small smile. "I'm already invested in this case. But I need to know a few things. Have a seat, Ms. Adams." I gestured to the plush wingback chair I'd recently acquired from Chippendale. Given her reluctance, she knew it was an expensive piece, but I motioned again with an encouraging smile. Once she sat, I swiped my notepad from the desk and flipped it open. "This may seem odd to you, but it's important—have you ever seen Miss Thayer use her right hand for anything?"

Her forehead rippled in confusion. "No. Always this hand." She wiggled her left fingers. "It was one of the first things I be noticin' about her. Bein' raised Catholic, I know about how it . . . looks."

I caught her undertones. I'd heard stories of nuns slapping wrists with rulers if a student wrote with a left hand. Even in my circles, using the left hand wasn't exactly welcome. This made me suspect that while Adele Thayer was sophisticated and stylish, she wasn't from the elite sphere. But with Ms. Adams's confirmation that her employer only used her left hand, it tossed Detective Bartlett's ambidextrous theory out the window. "That clears one thing up, Ms. Adams. Thank you."

She offered a gracious smile.

"Next question. I'm assuming you were there on Tuesday, the day she died, since you said she argued with Mr. Stratton."

She nodded.

"What time were you at her flat?"

"The usual. Ten in the morning to noon."

I jotted that down. "Did you see anything suspicious?"

"No."

"What about Miss Thayer's mood? How was she?"

"Fine." She shrugged. "Then Mr. Stratton came, and she be mad."

So the suave Wallace Stratton had made Miss Thayer angry. For what reason? "Was anyone else coming to the flat? Or had she any other appointments that day?"

"She did." Ms. Adams ran her hands along the armrests, back and forth slowly. "She didn't say who."

"I see." I scribbled down *Unknown Appointment.* "I need to find a way to get inside her flat and look around." Paulo maybe? I hated to ask any extra favors of him. But—

"I've a key." Her hand slipped into her pocket. "You can have it." She held it out, but I didn't take it.

"I was under the impression that you didn't have access to Miss Thayer's flat. That Paulo always would let you in."

Her weathered cheeks stained red. "I took it after I found her. When Mr. Valducci left the room, I took the key from her bag."

Warning bells sounded. So the maid had no qualms about digging into a dead lady's bag. And I configured just how she did so. "You faked fainting, didn't you? It was a ruse." Because once Paulo had fled for help, she was free to search the room and, apparently, take the key.

She gave an apologetic nod.

This woman was more deceptive than I'd thought. What else had she been lying about? "Ms. Adams." I held her gaze. "For me to take on this case, I need you to be entirely truthful with me. If I suspect you're not, I'll end our agreement."

Her fingers curled around the armrests, her face pinching with remorse. "I know it be wrong. But I had to take it. She didn't do that. Couldn't have done that. Someone else did that to her. I wanted to prove it in case the police wouldn't listen." She blew out a heavy breath. "And he didn't."

"Who didn't?"

"The detective. He told me it be suicide. But I know someone killed her. So I took the key. To see if anythin' be taken. She had a lot of jewelry."

"So you took the key to investigate yourself. You wanted to find proof that someone had another motive for harming Miss Thayer." I watched her nod. "Was any of her jewelry missing?"

Her shoulders curled forward. "No."

"Was anything of value taken?"

She shook her head.

I took a second to process, my silence only making Ms. Adams squirm.

She set the key on the table beside me and looked at me imploringly. "It don't matter if nothing be taken. Someone killed her. Will you help?"

I wasn't entirely convinced Ms. Adams was being truthful, but I had to agree that foul play was involved. Miss Thayer had been murdered, and my curiosity was growing by the second. The model's killer was still on the loose and no doubt wouldn't want me poking around, but the risk of trouble had never stopped me before. "I'll see what I can do."

• • •

The hinges on Miss Thayer's door screeched louder than I'd expected, but thankfully the third-floor hallway was empty, making my entrance into flat 317 simple. I had a feeling that would be the only easy facet about this search. I had no idea what I was hunting for or what was relevant—nevertheless, my skin hummed with the thrill of it all.

I locked the door behind me and took a deep breath. Time to get to work. Her flat was a smaller version of mine. The narrow foyer expanded into a tiled hall. Off to the left was the parlor, which seemed the perfect place to start.

I stepped inside the very room where Adele Thayer had been murdered. The space had been scrubbed clean, as if the awful incident never occurred, but I could sense the subtle tremors of death.

The drapes had been pulled, but thankfully a slice of daylight pushed through the edges. By the window, a Victrola sat on a stand, and adjacent to that, a bookshelf burdened with records and books. No, not books. Magazines. I flipped through several, hoping I could find a note or message of some kind, but nothing. I moved on to the writing desk in the other corner.

The wooden surface was spotless, so I searched the two drawers. The top one held paper, pencils, and scissors. The bottom held absolutely nothing. I'd hoped to find at least a calendar or a planner.

I continued my search, going through the dining room, bathroom, and front closet, finding nothing noteworthy. I saved the bedroom, in the back area of the flat, for last.

This was my least favorite part of the investigation. Being a private person, I'd never grown comfortable invading the intimate details of someone's life, such as their bedroom. But often this approach led to more significant findings.

Miss Thayer's room had been decorated in shades of gold and pink. I browsed her vanity table, crowded with cosmetics and perfumes. An ashtray that hadn't been emptied sat among the beauty products. A small dresser box sat in front of the mirror. The top was a painted garden scene framed with gilded edges. I opened the lid and studied the jewelry—a few gold necklaces and a decent strand of pearls, but the rest was paste. What caught my attention was the stub of some sort of paper poking out of a small gap between the box and the crimson velvet lining. I carefully slid it free. A subway ticket.

Odd.

The city transit had done away with tickets over four years ago. Which meant Miss Thayer had held on to this one for some particular reason. Why? What significance did this hold?

Nothing on it stood out as different. The wording—*City of New York Board of Transportation New York City Transit System*—all matched what I remembered it to look like.

I tucked the ticket into my bag and moved to her closet. Her gowns were hung and organized, nothing as chaotic as her vanity tray. It showed she took top care when it came to her clothes. Nothing jumped out at me there or anywhere else in the room. That bothered me. No photographs. No personal tokens. It only prompted my curiosity to check into her background. I moved to the dresser, and the faint screech of door hinges met my ears.

My gut lurched.

Someone had entered Miss Thayer's flat.

Being in the rear area, I couldn't make a run for it, and the only other exit was the window. I didn't feel like launching myself out from three stories high, so I ducked into the closet. I tried to tug the door closed, but it wouldn't shut all the way.

I huddled into the line of clothes, the base of my skull pressing into the row bar. With quick movements, I pulled my Colt from my bag, just in time to hear heavy footfalls approach and the bedroom door yawn open.

Unlike the hall, the bedroom was carpeted, so I didn't know where the person stood. The narrow gap in the door darkened. A flash of a suitcoat sleeve, a large hand holding something. I shifted slightly for a better view out the door.

A cigarette case. But gold plated with detailed scrolling, not silver like Brisbane's. So it wasn't Kent on the other side. This was the first time since our strange reunion I actually wished it were him. My grip tightened on my revolver.

Through the narrow gap I watched the hand flick open the case. The distinct sound of a striking match. Then silence. I considered pushing the door open, knocking the intruder, but too soon he stepped away. I listened, keeping my senses alert. He could return at any second and open the door, but the scrape of wood told me he was across the room, no doubt in the dresser.

Blast!

I should've searched there first. Because from the rustling sound and the masculine exhale of relief, whoever it was had found what he'd been looking for. I leaned closer to the door, making out the swish of trousers, then the click of heels fading down the hallway. He was leaving, but I didn't release my breath until I heard the blessed squeal of door hinges signifying his exit.

I waited a few minutes before stepping out of the closet, the lingering cigarette smoke the only residue of the man's presence. I went straight to the dresser, searching for any clues he might have left behind.

Nothing.

Who was he? My mind went back to the cigarette case. Did Wallace Stratton smoke? Did Miss Thayer have another beau? I'd immediately dismissed Kent, but what did I truly know of him? He could have several cigarette cases. Though why would he be in Miss Thayer's apartment?

There was only one way to truly scratch him off the list. I hustled back to my flat and telephoned his office. The operator connected us.

"Hello, Kent?"

"Vinny." I heard a smile in his voice, and I couldn't help but breathe deeper.

If Kent had been in Miss Thayer's flat, there'd be no way for him to return across town that quickly. But now I needed to think of a reason why I'd call him. "I'm going to be in your section of town tomorrow." As of now. "So I'll drop off your knife if you're free."

"I always make time for my former wives."

"You have more than one?" It was possible. Nothing he did surprised me. Though I didn't like the tiny lurch in my stomach. I'd no claim to him anymore. I didn't *want* any claim to him. I'd cut Kent Brisbane from my heart four years ago—the rest of my body needed to fall in line.

"No, only you hold that particular distinction, Knuckles." He didn't wait for me to scold him about the nickname. "What time do you figure for tomorrow?"

I had no idea. "In the afternoon?"

"I'll be here." A slight pause. "Vinny, I want to tell you that Wallace Stratton hired me to look into Adele Thayer's case."

That was unexpected. Had it been Wallace Stratton in her flat? Maybe he hadn't been doing anything suspicious but retrieving something for Kent. "He didn't believe the suicide theory either, then?"

"No. He told me she never owned a gun because she hates them."

I clenched the telephone tighter. "Did he relay that to the police?"

"Yes, but they told him the case was—"

"Closed. Yeah, I know. It's a favorite phrase of theirs." I debated what to say next. He had been forthcoming about Wallace hiring him. I didn't want to tell him I'd been hired to investigate Miss Thayer's death as well, but there was a good chance our paths would cross. "I was asked to look into the case too."

"By Stratton?" It was no wonder his mind went there, considering the judge had asked us both to find his daughter.

"No, someone else." And that was all the information I'd leak. "Do me a favor, Kent?"

"I'm listening."

"Don't tell Wallace Stratton I'm on the case." Because I intended to visit him and didn't want him on his guard.

He was quiet for a stretch, and I prepared myself for one of his sarcastic quips. But instead his deep voice rumbled, "Your secret's safe with me."

My heart jumped. He'd spoken those words to me before. It was that remark all those years ago that had led us on a path I tried hard to forget but lately was all I remembered.

Chapter 7

Kent
1920

"I SHOULD LEAVE YOU ON your own tonight, old man." Such was my greeting to Warren when I joined him in his posh automobile. "After that stunt you pulled with the news ad." I sent him a fierce glare, to which he responded with a good-natured shrug as he gripped the steering wheel.

Warren had dispensed of his chauffeur of late, wanting to drive his new Rolls Royce himself. The man wasn't your typical millionaire. He flew airplanes, turned his nose up at caviar, and meddled in his best friend's affairs instead of being self-consumed.

"Thought it was worth a shot." He was entirely unrepentant. "If it's the two hundred dollars that has you grumpy, I intend to pay that."

I frowned. "You know how I feel about charity."

"I do." He glanced over briefly. "Which was why I put the ad in the paper to begin with. I knew you wouldn't agree to it."

And he'd have been right. The only way to find my mother was through my own channels. I should've never told him about my life-long investigation. I knew he'd only wanted to help, which lessened my annoyance.

"Anything come of it?"

"I got a few weeks' vacation, since my office was flooded with reward hunters."

"I've been saying you needed to take a break." He seemed pleased with himself.

"So where are you dragging me tonight? I don't think I have the forbearance for a vaudeville show." People parading about the stage singing and dancing? No thank you.

Warren had telephoned only an hour ago informing me he was attending a society event and would be bored out of his mind, so he wanted to include me in the misery. He was thoughtful that way.

"A dinner party at the St. Clairs'," he said.

My curiosity spiked. "Vincent St. Clair, the tobacco tycoon?"

"The very one."

I adjusted my cuff link. "Should be an interesting night."

His brows lowered. "Doubt it."

"You don't know?"

"Know what? That I'll have to spend the evening dodging the advances of brazen females?"

"I offer my condolences. How awful it is to be wealthy and pursued by beautiful women." I ignored his scowl and continued, "Vincent St. Clair is known to have separate rooms for card games."

He shrugged but kept his gaze ahead. "Most dinner parties do."

"Yes, but for tame rounds of cards. St. Clair holds poker tournaments." Which was considered shameful among the higher set. "At least that's what I've heard."

He leveled me with a knowing look. "Then all I can say is, behave yourself."

"That's quite general. Perhaps you can narrow it down," I shot back. "Behave myself with the women, with holding my tongue around the stuffy old guys, or from emptying the men's coffers in cards?"

"All of the above."

"I'll try." Of course, I wouldn't do any of those things, but I did have a reputation when it came to poker. It seemed Warren hadn't taken my reformation seriously. "You realize I gave up gambling?"

His dark expression was indeed skeptical, but it was true nonetheless. Poker was a blend of mind games and dumb luck. The latter

I couldn't control, but the former I'd found myself pretty decent at. Growing up as I had, masking emotion came relatively easy. Though I'd noticed how a man could get addicted to the thrill of the risk, and I never wanted to let my livelihood hang on the turn of one card. So I'd stopped playing for money.

"I promised you I'd be a better man, didn't I?"

"There's only one way to get there, my friend." He reached into his pocket and retrieved exactly what I suspected—his New Testament. Without pulling his eyes from the road, he shoved it into my hand. "Keep it. Read it."

I understood what a treasure the book was to him. Which was a clever move on his part, for he knew I wouldn't be careless with this copy. The Hayes family had given me many Bibles over the years, and Warren believed I'd lost each copy. But I hadn't. I'd simply returned them all to the family's expansive library. "I can't accept this, old man. It was your dad's."

"I have a few more of his. Besides, he'd be overjoyed knowing his favorite heathen now has his New Testament."

I laughed. Peter Hayes had been a powerful man who'd been generous and blunt in equal measure. He'd offered me a job, yes. But he'd also purchased for me, a thirteen-year-old at the time, quality clothes and shoes. For a kid who'd never owned a new pair of shoes, they were as valuable as a chest of gold. Me being stubborn, though, I wouldn't accept charity, so Mr. Hayes had told me I was to accompany them to church on Sundays and help Warren reorganize the library. That was, after Mrs. Hayes taught me to read. I owed that family a lot. So I could do nothing but take the gift.

"Thank you." I pocketed it with a bit more emotion than I was used to.

The St. Clair residence wasn't on Billionaire's Row but in the Upper East Side of Manhattan—the hub of old-money New Yorkers. When Warren introduced me as a friend, Mr. and Mrs. St. Clair, who appeared in their early sixties, greeted me with an air of reserved curiosity. Vincent St. Clair didn't have the oily look so notable in a compulsive gambler, which made me wonder if the gossip had been exaggerated.

Slippery things, rumors were. I did expect to see a card room, but not a gambling den like the whispers about town had implied. Warren and I had conversed easily with the older couple, but a few more guests joined our small circle, and as always, the topic shifted to the Great War.

Mrs. St. Clair smiled at me. "In what capacity did you serve, Mr. Brisbane?"

I pretended as though I hadn't heard, which wasn't much of a stretch, considering the orchestra started playing a lively song. I didn't expect much help from my friend either. Warren disliked chatting about the Great War as much as I did. Though I wasn't certain why. He'd at least done his part as an aviator instructor, and when the fighting had ended, Warren had gotten a government biplane as a souvenir. Not many could boast of having their own flying machine.

Warren's gaze fixed on something just beyond my shoulder, and he stiffened. "Pardon us, Mrs. St. Clair," he said smoothly, but I could detect a hint of anxiousness in his tone. "We don't intend to overtake your attention. Thank you kindly for the invitation this evening."

Warren rushed to the card room like a mouse fleeing a housecat. "I spotted Polly Harsten. This year's prestige debbie. Did you know she slipped her handkerchief into my suit pocket the last time I saw her?"

"Strongly perfumed, I would wager." Women were strange.

"You wager correctly. It's best to scram before she sinks her manicured claws into me."

I tried not to chuckle at my friend's panic and kept pace with him as we moved through the ballroom as a show of appearance. Warren nodded at some guests, while my gaze swerved in search of a tall dark-haired beauty with a mean right hook.

"Sorry about that conversation in the receiving line," Warren said as we entered a hall cluttered with gilded sconces and fancy portraits. "They were only trying to be polite."

I thought back to what he referenced. "You mean Mrs. St. Clair's curiosity about my serving?"

"It seems all people talk about is the war and the Spanish flu." He pointed to a set of rooms to his right. "I know you purposely ignored her."

"Call me insensitive, but I'd rather not shock the delicate Mrs. St. Clair by revealing the gruesome details about my feet." More like the numbed tissue on my soles, which had kept me from fighting. "Remember, most only tolerate me because I'm your friend." Which was a kinder way of saying they wouldn't invite a guy who'd grown up on the streets. Whose body bore the marks of frostbite. "And only became your friend because of Geneva Ashcroft."

"Ah, so that's who you're looking so earnestly for," Warren surmised as we entered the card room. "Doubt she'll be here. Not that I know her to point her out. I've yet to attend the same event as the Ashcrofts. That family only goes to gatherings with a stocked guest list of governors and senators. Maybe a former president or two."

I wasn't looking for Geneva Ashcroft, but I'd allow my friend to think so. I was highly indebted to the young woman. It was she who'd spotted me over a decade ago shining shoes outside the barber shop, when a toff knocked me about for accidentally spilling polish. She'd taken action and exposed the cruelty to the Hayeses' newspaper. It was through her detailed letter that Warren had found me, and his father offered me a job. Warren and I had been friends ever since. I jest in calling him "old man," but only because he'd always acted as such, behaving as if he were twenty years older than me rather than twenty days.

Such was my musing as we chose our seats with two other fellows who appeared in between games. The card tables each had chips divided up to each player. But unlike the gambling dens, these chips had no monetary value.

Warren browsed the table with an amused smirk, as if I'd be disappointed. I wasn't. I didn't have any intention of gambling anymore.

"Good thing this is a friendly game," the gentleman across from me said decidedly. "I heard about you." He wagged his cigar at me. "And about your high-stakes rake-ins."

He no doubt referred to the game in which I'd won a hunting cabin on several acres of property. The man I'd won it from was the same who'd continually seek me out at the poker pit on Kingston Avenue. I never understood why he'd always return to my table knowing he hadn't beaten me once. "All in the past," I replied with a shrug. My gaze drifted in a show of indifference, and that was when I saw her.

Delvina Kline. She was in the adjoining card room, standing by a table near the connecting door.

I never considered myself to be the kind of sap who lost his breath at the sight of an intriguing woman, but the lack of oxygen in my chest said otherwise. Her mink hair slid against her jaw like a curtain of silk. She wore a black flowy number with another scooped neckline, putting her birthmark on display. An act of defiance if I ever saw one. I liked her even more for it.

"Brisbane?" Warren's humor-laced tone pulled my attention back to the table. "Did you hear anything we said?"

I shook my head. "Sorry, fellas. You're a whole lot less interesting."

They all turned to see who I referenced. The guy to my left let out a low whistle, his mustache so waxed stiff that it didn't twitch with the movement. "She's pretty, but she's trouble."

"Best keep away from her. Rebellious, that one." The man with his mouth curled around a cigar started shuffling the deck. "What does she think she's doing invading the men's rooms? Scandalous."

He talked as if Miss Kline strolled through the gentlemen's lounge at the club. Yet as the man yammered on, I watched as she spoke with an older fellow seated at the table closest to her. She held out a watch, which made the man's silver brows spike high. He searched his pockets vigorously, as if confirming what he'd lost with an incredulous shake of the head. He took the watch, then grasped both of her hands in his, obviously thanking her for returning it. In the two scenarios where I'd been privileged to witness her, one she'd defended herself against a louse's advances and next she'd returned an expensive watch to an old man. Yeah. Scandalous indeed.

Warren also watched her with curiosity. "I've been gone from society for a while. I don't remember her."

She was difficult to forget. At least for me. I still recalled the feel of her in my arms. The alluring scent of her perfume. I couldn't name the fragrance—I only knew it was the enticing sort of concoction that turned a man's brain to mush. Speaking of brains, from our short interlude in the garden, it was clear the woman was sharp. I appreciated a beautiful form, like every guy, but give me a lady with clever wit and I was a goner.

The mustached mister across from me responded to Warren. "She's the only child of the Kline family. The few men that aren't intimidated by her won't dare go near her. Too many rumors."

This caught my interest. "Rumors?"

A glint entered his eyes. "Pedigree is important among *our* sort."

He aimed that jab at me. I brushed it off. I knew I was an outcast here, but the peculiar part was he'd implied Miss Kline was as well. Pedigree? She was the daughter of a high-society family.

Before he could expound or insult any further, Miss Kline straightened and locked her gaze on me from the other room. The men around me noticed as well, for the conversation muted, only to begin again about the upcoming game. Now Miss Kline moved into this room, her gait smooth and confident, her chin held high, as if challenging anyone to question her presence here. She glided up to our table. Warren and I stood on ceremony, but the other two men remained seated.

I narrowed my gaze, but Miss Kline didn't seem to mind, her disinterested expression conveying she'd expected their slight.

"Mr. Brisbane." She dipped her chin and held out her hand. "I was wondering if I could speak to you for a moment?"

I bowed over her fingers, while the two men still perched in their chairs frowned, disapproval pinching their faces. I never bothered to address slights directed at me, but their demeaning behavior toward a lady ignited something in me. Miss Kline seemed to sense my agitation, for her gaze lit on me, and understanding passed between us.

Realizing I hadn't answered her, I offered a smile. "Certainly, Miss Kline."

I accompanied her to the hall, where only a few guests meandered, but none close enough to catch our conversation.

Her mouth tipped in a smile. "You're a difficult man to track down."

I masked my surprise as she continued.

"I went to your office, only to find it locked up."

She'd gone to my office? In that questionable area of the city? As soon as I saved more funds, I was relocating. More so, had it not been for that blasted newspaper ad, she would've been able to contact me. I couldn't even explain. Only Warren knew about my search for my mother, and I regretted even telling him. "I'm sorry for your trouble."

"I have a case for you."

My spirits sank. Though I didn't know why else she'd seek me out. I wasn't foolish enough to think I'd left any impression on her a few weeks back. It was just another dance for her. But no matter how my masculine pride took a hit, I knew better than to refuse the work. Especially if she'd gone out of her way to recommend me to someone. "What kind of case, Miss Kline?"

"It's Delvina." She smiled, then lifted her brows, as if waiting.

I nodded. "Call me Kent."

She continued to study me. Had I misspoken? I tried to keep up with high-society manners, but their silly rules changed like the wind. "Did I say something wrong?"

"Not yet."

"Pardon?"

A smile lifted her lips. "I thought for certain you'd spout off a flirty remark." She spoke as if we'd conversed a hundred times instead of once.

"I promised my friend I'd behave tonight."

"How gallant."

"I have my moments." I leaned forward, unable to help myself. "But they're short-lived, Knuckles." I glanced pointedly at her hand, so dainty looking in her black gloves, but I knew the truth.

Her lips puckered, as if she was going to shush me, but then her mouth collapsed into a resigned smile. "I suppose I deserve that."

"That wasn't an insult, and there's certainly nothing to be ashamed about," I corrected. "My only regret was being a second too late. I would've enjoyed seeing you deck the fellow."

She relaxed at my teasing, her shoulders lowering, drawing my attention to her birthmark. The light from the hall sconces shimmered across her collarbone, highlighting the rosy hues of her skin.

"Quit gawking at my birthmark."

"I was admiring it. There's a difference."

She eyed me, as if unsure. "Entire gossip columns have been devoted to the 'Kline Daughter's Unfortunate Blemish.'" Her hand swept through the air, as if displaying a headline.

"They're idiots."

"They said to cover it up."

"I say flaunt it like a diamond necklace."

"You're serious, aren't you?"

I'd never use the word *delicate* to describe Delvina Kline, but her tone edged on the fragile side, reminding me of a willow branch—for while it mostly danced with the strong wind, sometimes it snapped.

"Very much. It's fascinating, just like the rest of you."

"So much for behaving yourself." She laughed. "That was the flirtiest line I've ever heard."

I only shrugged. Because while I'd been accused of being fluent in the language of flattery, I'd been entirely honest. I found this woman remarkable.

"Now for the real reason I wanted to speak with you." Her expression tightened. "I want to hire you. I need answers regarding my parentage." She didn't hesitate. Didn't cower. She spoke the words evenly without a hitch, but her eyes darkened, making me realize she was troubled.

"I thought Mr. and Mrs. Kline were your parents?"

"They are. But"—she glanced about, then lowered her voice. "People have said things. I know I shouldn't believe gossip, but I want to be certain there isn't any truth to it."

I thought back to moments ago when the fellow had remarked about Delvina's pedigree. "Tell me, what you do know about your birth?"

"My parents were along in years and had been wanting a child for a while. Their escape to Italy seemed a last resort. Father getting away from the city for a while would help. My parents ended up staying in Florence for a bit. That's where I was born. Then when famine struck, they brought me to America."

"And why don't you believe that story?"

"I want to believe them, but there's just something inside me. I can't even explain it." Her eyes met mine. "Will you help me?"

Oh, the irony of someone hiring me to search for the truth about their birth when I'd been unsuccessful for years regarding my own. "If by chance you were given up, it would be easier to trace the details about your birth here in the States. But overseas? It makes it almost impossible to know unless I had contacts in Italy or would investigate there myself." Which I couldn't. Though I hated disappointing her. "And with it being so long ago."

"It wasn't *that* long ago." She arched her brows, as if I'd just called her elderly.

I chuckled, which didn't assuage her. "I meant no offense. But anything over twenty years and in another country altogether, it would be difficult to trace."

Her gaze lowered, as if processing my words, then snapped to mine. "Then teach me."

"Teach you?"

"Yes. School me on how you'd go about finding answers. And if I was able to sail to Italy, I would know how to conduct a search."

She made it sound as if she might hop onto a steamer ship next week. Maybe she would. But there was no way I could teach her. The detecting world seemed intriguing to an outsider, but it had its drawbacks. The informants, for one. I'd grown up on the streets. I had contacts. Some were decent, while others were unsavory. Delvina Kline might be spirited, but she seemed innocent. Then there was the element of risk—you never knew if you'd stumble into danger. Often there were reasons—usually dark—why things were kept secret. But her deep-brown eyes glittered with determination. She'd set out to get answers with or without my help. "My line of work is dangerous. It's not the kind of job for—"

Her eyes narrowed, as if suspecting I'd say something demeaning about her gender.

"—someone inexperienced."

Her grin sparked. "Well, it's a good thing you're experienced and can teach me. I wouldn't need any defense lessons. I already know how to handle and shoot a gun. And you're already aware that I can box."

I choke-coughed, which amused her.

She tossed another breezy smile. "I've made a habit of seeking people out and asking them to teach me. Like Helen Hildreth, the lady pugilist."

If this woman told me she'd designed a flying machine similar to Warren's that would take her to the moon, I'd believe her. I'd heard of Ms. Hildreth. She'd defeated a man in the boxing ring several years ago. The police had broken up the fight, but if I remembered correctly, the young woman had knocked the stuffing out of the gentleman. Which now made sense as to why Ms. Kline had been unafraid to defend herself against that idiot who'd accosted her when we first met.

"I don't expect my lessons to be free—I'll pay you," she put in, misinterpreting my stunned silence.

I shook my head. "I don't want your money." Which was probably foolish on my part. I could use the cash, but accepting payment from her felt wrong.

Her eyes widened even as her head tilted, her bobbed hair grazing her shoulder. "But I have lots of it."

"Keep it."

"Then what else do you want from me?" Her gaze turned leery, and why wouldn't it, considering how I'd found her a few weeks ago?

"Nothing. I'll give you some pointers at no charge."

"Truly? That's generous of you."

"Save the praise." I waved her off. "I've never taught anyone before. I may be a flop at it and the whole endeavor a complete waste of your time."

"I highly doubt that." I wasn't prepared for the touch of admiration in her eyes. "Oh, and would you please not mention this to anyone? People already talk about me enough as it is."

I smiled. "Your secret's safe with me."

Chapter 8 —————————————————————————————

Delvina
1924

I OPENED THE DOOR DIRECTLY beneath a sign reading *Stratton Modeling Agency* and stepped inside. If any high-society matron spotted me entering this building, I'd be ostracized even more than I was. Such a thing as modeling wasn't openly accepted. Not yet, at least. I'd noticed Wallace had been careful at Mother's dinner party, addressing the fashion-consulting side of his agency rather than the modeling. Wise move on his part, since most of the uppers considered it vulgar. But with the leading department stores staging fashion shows to flaunt their latest lines, models had recently been more in demand. So it only made sense to have an agency that could connect the businesses with appropriate talent.

The space was decked out in *le style moderne*. The carpet held various shades of gold in geometric patterns, the walls sleek black with fan-shaped sconces placed about. I removed my gloves, thankful to be out of the cold. Late October in New York was the precursor to winter, and this morning held a frosty bite in the air. But one glance at the young secretary seated behind the desk told me the atmosphere inside could prove just as icy.

She pushed her wire-framed spectacles up her nose, regarding me with a scowl. "Are you here for the country-club fashion shoot?" Her huff stirred the brown ringlets framing her face. "We were told you'd be blond. Mr. Stratton specifically asked for a blond model."

Well, that answered my question about Wallace's intention on continuing the agency now that his prized model was gone. "I'm not here for—"

"Ah, finally," a masculine voice exclaimed from the other side of the room. "We've been expecting you." The man was about two inches shorter than my five foot nine, but he'd scrutinized me as if I were but a speck beneath a microscope, his auburn hair gleaming with too much pomade. He must've approved of what he saw, for his smile unleashed. "Perfection! We'd summoned a blond from our records but"—he stepped back, his amber gaze inching over my frame yet again—"you've got good lines. I can work with a form like yours. Go back and get outfitted in the pale pink sports frock."

I didn't quite appreciate how his eyes roved my body, and made sure my tone conveyed it. "I am not a model for this agency."

His smile vanished. "Are you from John Powers's group?" His voice smoothed deeper. "He may have been the first to open his doors, but we've been steadily growing. We have plans of branching out once the idea catches on."

As of now, New York City was the primary hub for modeling. Sure, there was enough work if one wanted to live overseas in Paris. But in America, the modeling profession didn't exist outside the city limits.

"Our models have been sought after."

Have been? Was his use of present-perfect tense, rather than simply *are*, a slip of the tongue, or was he thinking of Adele Thayer? She'd been their top model, appearing in all the fashion magazines. This was the open door I hoped for.

"I've heard about your recent loss of Miss Thayer. She was a charming woman." The comment sounded shallow, but I'd hardly known her. Plus my wording was intentional, to gauge the gentleman's reaction.

But he hadn't much of one. He only nodded. "She will be missed." His voice didn't contain any hint of sadness or . . . anything. As if his remark was merely the standard response. The complete lack of emotion only fueled my curiosity about Adele Thayer.

I tucked my gloves into my coat pocket and offered a bland smile. "I apologize for the misunderstanding, but I'm not a model. I'm here to see Wallace Stratton, if he's available."

He blinked, as if processing what I'd said, then with a flick of his hand, he dismissed me. "I'm a photographer. Appointment taking is beneath me." Faster than a finger snap, he pivoted and fled the room, leaving me with the cranky secretary.

"Mr. Stratton stepped out." But before she could point to the exit, the door flung open and Wallace stepped inside, his expression sullen.

His gaze connected with mine, and his rapid strides halted. "Miss Kline." Surprise edged his voice, along with wariness. Hopefully, Kent had kept his word and hadn't informed his client I was also investigating Adele Thayer's death. "To what do we owe this honor?"

I could've sworn the secretary snorted at the word *honor*, confirmed by Wallace's reproving glance in her direction.

I adopted a friendly smile. "I was close by and remembered your kind invitation to visit your agency." I made a show of glancing around. "Unless it's a bad time."

"Not at all. I'm glad to see you again." Yet the sag in his spine and the slow shuffling of his feet toward me conveyed the opposite. Dark circles hung beneath dull gray eyes. Gone were the wide smiles and energy from Mother's dinner party. Before me stood a man deep in grief. Was he mourning the loss of Miss Thayer or the loss of revenue she'd brought this place? Perhaps his distress was the result of something more sinister. According to Ms. Adams, Wallace had threatened Miss Thayer during an argument. Could he have followed through with his words? If so, then why would he hire Kent to investigate her death?

I shot a discreet look at the secretary, who was clearly eavesdropping, then refaced Wallace. "I'm sorry about Miss Thayer."

He pressed his lips together with a tight nod. "It's been . . . difficult without her."

The man could be a decent actor, but the pain-pinched lines fanning from his sorrowful gaze seemed genuine. Though I'd been fooled before. "Do you have a moment to talk?"

Another nod. "Please forgive me. I've barely been functioning since the news of Adele's death." He motioned for me to follow and then opened the second door that led down a narrow hallway. "I wanted to close the agency for a while, but there are contracts we can't get out of. Otherwise, we'd lose our business to the other agency."

I suspected the other agency was John Powers's. "That's understandable."

He held the door open for me to enter, and I stepped into a large office. The space was decorated similarly to the lobby, but with one exception—a large portrait of Miss Thayer hung on the wall behind his desk. She'd been posed in a sparkly evening gown, her face tilting upward, as if staring into the heavens. The gilded frame was situated between some artsy sconces, but the effect seemed more like a shrine rather than an agency featuring their top model. Was Wallace Stratton in love with or obsessed with Adele Thayer?

He sat behind his desk, his dark hair sliding over his forehead. "What did you want to discuss?"

I paused until I had his full attention. "You mentioned at Mother's dinner party about inviting investors for your agency. Can you tell me more about it?"

A spark lit his eyes, and his expression shifted. The grief-stricken beau seemed to fade, and the businessman emerged. He folded his hands on the desk, regarding me. "What would you like to know?"

"If someone were to invest, what return would they have?"

He launched into a spiel about the percentage of such and such and a share of this and that. I only halfway listened because I marveled at the transformation. Only a few moments ago, he'd lamented about having to keep the agency open, as if it were a burden, but now his impassioned delivery made me think otherwise.

Though maybe I was being cynical. Perhaps he felt continuing this business venture would be a way of preserving Miss Thayer's legacy. I couldn't be certain, but once his monologue ended, I wondered if he'd even paused to take a breath.

I leaned forward, keeping eye contact. "This might seem insensitive, but from a business standpoint it needs addressed."

He held out his hands, as if he'd nothing to hide. "By all means, ask."

"From what you said at Hemswick, I understand that Miss Thayer brought in a lot of revenue for the agency. Not only with her modeling contracts but with her fashion consults. Will her passing negatively affect the agency?"

He took his time considering, then exhaled. "I'd be lying if I said her death wasn't a hit to our income. Several designers wanted her to model their new line, but where we made the most was the consults. We charged more than five hundred dollars an appointment."

"Five hundred?" Just to suggest the right way a gown would fit or the perfect color for someone's complexion?

He shrugged. "Irene Castle would charge a thousand for dance instruction. Thing is, people paid it without question. They want to look their best, and Adele had a great success rate. You should see our schedule."

That was *exactly* what I wanted to see. "Truly? I find it difficult to believe someone, even in our sphere, would pay such an exorbitant amount. Especially when leading department stores such as Macy's and Saks have fashion advisers as well."

His head reared, as if I'd said something dirty. "Those stores have employees who give tips to increase their sales. Adele taught clients how to wear clothes and what cut flattered them the most. As for the schedule, I keep it right here. It never leaves my office." He dug into his drawer and tugged out a book. "See for yourself."

Ah, there we had it. Her schedule. I feigned skepticism about clients paying such an exorbitant fee, but really, I did believe it. Society enjoyed indulgence on every level. Some women among our class would gladly waste their husband's wealth in the name of style.

I flipped out the black leather calendar, browsing the dates until my gaze landed on the day she'd died. It was blank. Hadn't Ms. Adams said she had an appointment that day? Maybe it was personal. I flipped back to the previous week and scanned the list of businesses, probably for modeling shoots. And one name was Beatrice Reinholt. I knew her. She'd been a debutante the year after me, and a bit on the vicious side. I'd speak to her only if necessary. I flipped back a few weeks prior and recognized names of notable society women. I endeavored to commit them to memory. I spotted Maude Welch, the woman who'd recently passed from sleeping sickness. I recalled Miss Thayer speaking about her at dinner and how it had distressed Mother.

Kent's face flashed into my mind. It had been kind of him to distract Mother, even while Miss Thayer had been trying to steal his attention. This brought another question—how faithful had she been to Wallace? He would've been blind to not see how his sweetheart had worked to snag Kent's eye, and yet he'd hired this same man to investigate her death? Something didn't add up.

As I flipped through the pages searching for reoccurring names or events, the secretary swept in and asked Wallace a question about that afternoon's meeting. I reached the end of the entries, nothing leaping out at me. "You were right." I handed him back the planner. "Miss Thayer was indeed successful at attracting clients."

His gaze narrowed at my wording, which had been intentional. I needed to gauge his response.

But the secretary, who'd just huffed a humorless laugh, spoke first. "I see you're checking Miss Thayer's *office* schedule. I figure she didn't log all her trips beyond Eighth Avenue Station."

The subway. My mind went back to the ticket I'd found in Miss Thayer's room and why she even had it, since the transit now used coins. What was I missing? Before I could ask the secretary what she'd meant, she gave me a clipped look, then sashayed out.

Whatever the young woman intended, it didn't seem to have any effect on Wallace, as if his mind had been somewhere else. Finally, his gaze cleared, and he offered a polite smile. "Are there any other questions you have for me, Miss Kline?"

"No. You've been very informative."

He nodded with a smile. "Good. I hope you'll consider investing with us."

I stood, and he did as well. "Again, please accept my condolences. And I truly hope you and Miss Thayer were able to reconcile before she passed."

His eyes darted to mine. "Reconcile? I don't understand what you mean."

I gave a commiserating smile. "I apologize, but I live in the same building as Miss Thayer, and word has got out that you two argued the day she died."

His face hardened, then melted into a defeated expression. "We did. It was a silly disagreement."

"What about?"

He frowned. I was testing his limits, but I wasn't sure when an opportunity would arise to question him again. "She was going over her planner. We argued about the appointment she had that afternoon. Like I said, foolish on my part."

"But Miss Thayer didn't have an appointment." I nodded toward the planner resting on his desktop. "At least according to that calendar." Never mind that Ms. Adams had already confirmed Miss Thayer was to meet someone.

He blinked. "Did I say that afternoon? I meant the previous day. Sorry. The days just seem to blend together."

"I see." And I could see very clearly that Wallace Stratton had lied. Because there wasn't an appointment the day before either. Up until now I couldn't find a motive for him to kill Miss Thayer. If anything, her death hurt the agency. But his last words revealed he was hiding something.

On my way out, the secretary hardly spared me a glance as she brushed past to another room. My gaze fell to her desk, then the morning newspaper beside the telephone.

The headline made me falter to a stop.

I read it again, ensuring I wasn't mistaken. Of all the things I'd expected in this strange city, this particular instance had never crossed my mind.

This changed everything.

I snatched the paper and headed to see Kent Brisbane, who, according to this article, was still my husband.

Chapter 9 ————————————————————————————————

I WAS NO LONGER THE woman with two last names, for I currently possessed three—Delvina Salvastano Kline Brisbane. It was laughable, if not for my world caving in on me.

All because I'd placed my trust in a swindler. A fraud who'd moonlighted as a divorce lawyer. Back then he'd taken me for a small fortune, but that was nothing compared to the punishment he currently inflicted.

At least the article hadn't been explicit about who the swindler's victims had been—otherwise I'd be forced into yet another uncomfortable conversation, only this time with Mother. No, the newspaper only printed the bogus divorce lawyer's name and his lengthy list of fraudulent infractions. However, it was enough information for me to grasp one aspect with perfect clarity.

I was still married.

I blew out a shaky breath. All this time. For four years I'd been Kent's wife without realizing. What if he had remarried? Once I'd cut Kent from my heart, it was best just to keep it empty. My effort to remain callous to romance had served me well to this point. But Kent could've found another bride, and if he had, he would've unknowingly committed bigamy. Even now he could very well have a sweetheart who hoped to soon be the next Mrs. Brisbane.

A familiar ache rattled my chest.

I normally wasn't a coward. If something frightened me, I'd rather charge the terror than dash away. I'd danced with death more times than I'd done the Charleston. Unflustered, calm. No, danger I could handle.

This however? Standing in front of Brisbane Private Investigative Agency, with Kent's knife tucked in my purse and the incriminating newspaper in my white-knuckled grasp, I wanted to ditch my extra-high Louis heels and make a break for it.

But Kent should be told.

Though what was I even to say? *Sorry to inconvenience you, but I'm still your wife?*

I bit my lip, refusing to acknowledge its trembling. I couldn't change the past any more than I could've persuaded Kent to confide in me during that crucial time.

There must be a way to resolve this. I was nothing if not intuitive.

With renewed determination, I tucked the newspaper beneath my arm and curled my hand around the brass doorknob. I'd never been to this office. The one Kent had occupied before we were married had been in a rough area. Now it appeared he'd done well for himself, because this spot was in an enviable location in Manhattan.

I opened the door and was greeted by . . . no one. The empty foyer consisted of a coatrack and a three-legged table against the wall. No front desk and, thankfully, no snooty secretary like the one from the modeling agency. My stomach lurched at the thought of Kent employing a young woman to assist him, and I didn't like my body's reaction. Kent could spend his time with whomever he chose. I was just out of sorts, that was all.

"Leave the mail on the table, Joe," Kent called from a room off to the left, which I suspected was his office.

Apparently he believed me to be the postman delivering letters. But what I was about to deliver was news that changed everything.

The few paces to Kent's door seemed to stretch a mile. I could do this. I had to do this. I pushed back my shoulders, straightened my spine, and took the final step to the entrance of his office.

But I wasn't prepared for the sight. Kent had shed his jacket, his shirtsleeves rolled past his elbows, his right hand holding a feather duster. A frilly apron wrapped his large frame, making him look adorably ridiculous. I clung to this light moment as much as my next breath and leaned against the doorjamb. He was oblivious to my presence. "For a private detective, you aren't aware of your surroundings."

His gaze swung to me. If he was surprised, he didn't show it. He was the best at schooling his features, making his expressions unreadable. A wonderful quality for a detective, not so much for a husband. He lowered the duster, a smile lifting his lips. "I disagree." He moved closer. "I'm more aware of you than you realize."

The deep rasp of his voice sent chills along my skin. He always had a way of turning things around. But I held the advantage. I wasn't the one wearing a lace-trimmed apron. I touched the haphazard bow at his side. "This is a nice look for you."

His gaze dipped to my fingers, still toying with the edges, then slowly crept to my face. "This belongs to Edith."

My hand fell away, and I retreated a step. It was as I suspected. "Your sweetheart?" I asked, though my throat was unnaturally tight, making my voice sound rougher than usual.

"My cleaning lady. She left a few weeks back. No word or anything." His eyes met mine. "That seems to be my bad luck. Women leaving with not even a goodbye."

Delivered with such finesse and charm, no one but me would ever imagine how cutting the remark was. Though I wouldn't rise to his baiting words. I could easily remind him that he'd abandoned me first and hadn't pursued me when I'd responded by leaving, but it didn't matter now. Because we'd other things to discuss.

"I know of someone who needs work. I can get you her information if you'd like."

He shrugged out of the apron and shoved both it and the duster into a cabinet. "It's challenging to replace help. I've got a lot of sensitive files in this room."

I understood. It was difficult to find someone trustworthy in our line of work. "I don't know her too well." Moreover, I couldn't exactly praise Ms. Adams's honesty, considering she feigned fainting to steal a dead woman's flat key. "Her name's Rosalie Adams. She used to clean for Miss Thayer."

His brow edged slightly north. "Ah, now I'm sorting the pieces together. Was she the one who hired you for the Thayer case?"

"She was in a tight spot."

His features softened. "A couple of detectives at my club mentioned her."

Mentioned her? I bet they'd been making a joke of her. "She told me she got turned away by other agencies. Did she ask you?"

He shook his head. "No. From what I gather, she only visited Harrison and Cleary."

I fought rolling my eyes. Those two agencies' fees were expensive. More money than the services they rendered. I wouldn't think Kent the type to refuse Ms. Adams, but it cheered me to know he was innocent in the matter.

It was time to address what I'd truly come here for, but first things first. I dug out his knife. "Not even a scratch."

He took it from my hand, his fingers lingering on my mine longer than necessary. "Thank you, Vinny."

I nodded even as my focus snagged on an open letter on the edge of his desk, a tarnished key atop it. Curiosity was either friend or foe, and today it proved the latter, because the swirling, feminine script had me snatching the paper with my free hand, the key plunking on the scarred wood. "What's that?" Before he could respond, I read aloud,

Kent Brisbane
    I missed you today. So I left this key here. When I return, I'll explain.
    Ettie

It seemed Kent had his fair share of admirers. I glared, waving the page as if I were presenting evidence in a case against him. Which I sort of was. "What, so women just stuff their flat keys under your door?"

If I expected to glimpse any embarrassment on his handsome face,

I'd be disappointed. The man felt no shame. Instead, his lips did this annoying thing most people called a smile. "Jealous, Knuckles?"

"Absolutely not." I huffed and dropped the letter back onto the desk. "There's just a fine line between bold"—I cast a pointed look at the key—"and ludicrous."

He nodded at the letter. "I don't know anyone by that name. That note appeared on my doorstep a month or so back. No one has come to claim it."

"You want me to believe some woman randomly left their flat key?"

He tsked. I hated being tsked at. Something he knew. "Get a closer look. It's too small for a flat."

I peeked around his shoulder at the dulled brass key. Okay, so maybe he was right, but I still was unsure if I trusted him.

"If you truly want to chat about bold women?" He ambled away, a slow saunter, rounding to the other side of his desk. "I remember one who ambushed me with a kiss." He ran his finger along the wood, stopping on the corner. "In my other office, it was right about here." With his pocketknife in one hand, he pointed down with the other to where the supposed crime had been committed.

"Actually, it was a bit to your left." My scowl deepened at his grin. I didn't want to reminisce about that day—or that night.

"Ah, don't look at me like that, Vinny." He erased the gap between us in two strides. "In case you may have forgotten, I enjoyed the ambush kiss and was just as much a willing participant."

Problem was, I'd thought that as well. Yet his later actions proved otherwise.

"Related to that . . ." I cleared my throat.

His eyes lit up, as if awaiting my suggestion to re-create that particular moment.

"I found out not long ago that you're unknowingly *still* a participant." I braced my free hand on the edge of the desk, the severity of it all hitting me again with renewed strength.

"What do you mean?" Amusement danced on the edges of his mouth. "Are you proposing we—"

"No." Whatever was about to spill out of that smirking mouth demanded an absolute no. In a quick movement, I grabbed the newspaper from under my arm and flicked it open. "This is . . ." I raised the offending morning edition. "Is . . ." The words seemed chained to my tongue.

His brows raised, no doubt at my rare blip of emotion, then those dark slashes seemed to sink in realization. But how could he possibly know? His gaze hardly touched the headline that sent my world off-kilter.

"I didn't get a chance to read the papers yet. Is there another article about us and our supposed romance?"

"In a way." I lowered onto the nearby chair with a shaky exhale.

"I'll talk to Warren about it." All humor fled his face. "Maybe he can convince the other papers to let the matter drop. I didn't realize any link to me would be that distressing to you." He masked it well, but traces of hurt bled through his voice.

"That's not what I meant." This wasn't going well. But what else could I say, except, "Kent, we're still married."

The knife slipped from his grasp, clattering to the floor. But he didn't pay any mind to his beloved blade. No, his gaze fastened on me, the intensity in his eyes almost more than I could bear. "What did you say?"

"Look." I opened the newspaper, pointing to the article above the fold. "The man here." I tapped the grainy picture. "This is Jerry Perkins. The divorce attorney I hired." Which Kent would remember because Perkins had served Kent the petition. "He promised a discreet and quick foreign divorce. Turns out he took my money but never filed. I'm not the only one he duped. He got arrested for fraud and practicing law without a license. He's not even a lawyer." I'd paid him a lump sum, which supposedly paid for the legal process, plus travel and lodging in the Dominican Republic, where he'd allegedly filed our divorce. I doubt he'd even left the States.

"The court certificate?"

"Forged." I winced. "We're not divorced."

The idea of foreign divorces was popular among those who wanted to separate far from the spotlight. Getting a divorce in America was difficult. The couple had to have a legal reason—be it adultery, abuse, or desertion—and even then, they had to present proof in court.

"Though it wasn't as if we had a real marriage anyway."

He jolted, as if I'd slapped him. "I have a license that says otherwise."

He still had that? Why? And why did my heart flip in my chest at this reveal? No matter. A wrinkled piece of paper from Elkton, Maryland, didn't ensure a happily ever after.

"One day." I fought to keep the pain from my tone. "Our marriage lasted only a day, Kent."

"Because things were out of my control."

"What things?" From where I'd stood that afternoon at Penn Station, he'd seemed very much in control. But he didn't know I'd been there, and I wasn't about to offer that information. "Tell me why you left me that afternoon."

Kent stalked toward the only window in the room. He'd just turned his back on me. And that summed up what had happened between us. He'd turned away and refused to let me into his life.

My gaze landed on his desk, more specifically the silver nameplate. *Kent Brisbane P.I.* I'd bought him that. Back when I'd had stars in my eyes and innocence in my heart. That time seemed so long ago. It almost felt as if that young girl charmed by the handsome investigator had been a different person altogether.

"I'll figure it out." My words seemed to bounce off his tense frame.

He'd always carried himself with a sort of languid poise, but now he stood as if made of granite. The only movement was the throbbing tendon on his neck. This news was a shock. Of course he'd be furious. I was more disappointed in myself than anything. I thought I'd moved past the foolishness of my youth, but my mistakes had caught up with me. At that time it'd been one impulsive choice after another. As in my whirlwind marriage to Kent followed by a rushed meeting with a lawyer who'd specialized in discreet divorces. All because I'd been in a state of hurt and confusion over Kent's abandonment. On top of that, I hadn't wanted to disgrace Mother. Though now it seemed I would.

There had to be a way out of this.

I glanced at Kent as he glared out the window, his jaw rigid, along with the rest of him. This wasn't the version of Kent I'd once known. Flirty, sure. Confident, always. But now it seemed he was out of sorts, just like me.

"I'll fix this, Kent." Somehow. "I only ask that you remain quiet about this until I can get things resolved. Then we can go our separate ways like before."

"No." He finally turned toward me. "I won't accept that. Not this time."

What? He refused to stay silent? What would he do? Go to the papers and expose our marriage in some cruel form of revenge? Or . . . was this his way of blackmail? My stomach twisted. He'd been the only one who'd never cared about my money. But people changed—both for good and bad. I retrieved my checkbook and swiped a fountain pen from his desk.

He left his post by the window and approached. "What are you doing?"

"What's it look like? I'm paying you off. How much—"

"Really, Vinny?" Disgust dripped from his tone as he ran a hand through his hair, tousling his dark locks. "You think I want your money?"

I threw the pen back onto his desk with exaggerated flourish. "I don't know what you want." When I faced him again, he was a lot closer, our noses only inches apart.

His eyes flashed. "I thought I made it obvious."

"You never make things obvious. It's always a guessing game with you." Because even now, his scorching gaze tracked my face as if I was the pinnacle of his desire. I knew better. He might flirt and enjoy a tryst as long as it was convenient for him. Commitment and Kent didn't belong in the same sentence. At least not from what I'd experienced.

He leaned closer, his lips brushing my ear. "I suppose I'll have to make myself clearer, wife." Then as if he hadn't just stirred everything in me, he stepped back. "But that will have to wait, because I'm due for an appointment."

I blinked. "Kent, we need to talk about this."

"We will." He grabbed his suit coat from the chair back. "I'm sorry, but I do need to go. Can we discuss this Friday?"

That was two days from now. "Only if you can spare the time in your busy social calendar." Okay, that was unfair. He hadn't the foreknowledge I was going to drop this situation into his lap. He'd only thought I was returning his blade, not upending his entire life. I took a calming breath. "I'm sorry. This has me all flustered."

He nodded, his face softening. "That's why I think it's a good idea to give this a couple of days."

This was where he and I had always been different. I'd rather cut open the entire infected wound and bear the brunt of pain in one fell swoop. Yes, the anguish would be intense, but also short-lived. Kent would rather slice open a bit at a time. Cleanly. Methodically. It was probably healthier that way, but prolonged the pain.

It seemed he'd be that way here. He wanted to process everything. Sift things through. Because behind that nonchalant expression was a man who calculated.

I grabbed his hat from the corner of his desk and held it out to him. "Okay, Kent. We'll go with your way."

Chapter 10

Kent
1920

"THERE." DELVINA SET SOMETHING ON my desk and grinned at me. "Now you're official."

My gaze followed the exaggerated sweep of her hand, as if displaying some priceless artifact. Though what it truly was hit me square in the chest. My name had been etched on a silver plate with the initials *P.I.* It was expensive. Too flashy for a humble office like this. But more than that, it was personal. "You needn't have done this."

Her smile only widened. "You didn't allow me to pay for my lessons. So this"—she tapped the top of the nameplate—"is how I get around your obstinance."

She was just as obstinate as I was. As for the "lessons" she'd referred to, that was somewhat of a stretch. Today marked the sixth time we'd met. While I'd discussed the objectives and tricks of being a private investigator—rambled about different methods—I hadn't quizzed her much about her true intention for wanting to learn the detecting trade or about her parents. Why? Because it had become clear she needed a friend. She'd mentioned she'd been tutored by various people, but she'd never spoken of friends. Which led me to think she hadn't any. But things had been shifting between us, made more obvious by her gift. As a rule, I disliked charity, though the way she currently smiled at me, I'd gladly take anything she handed over, especially if it involved her heart.

"I can't take it back. It's not like I know another Kent Brisbane who's a detective."

Delvina misinterpreted my silence as reluctance. Oh, I was reluctant all right, but not about her gift. About my growing feelings for her that needed stuffed back into the sensible parts of my brain.

The nameplate she'd casually plopped onto my desk would've cost me at least a month's wages. I might flirt with her, but I wasn't an idiot. I knew she wasn't intrigued by me as much as by my profession. The mysteriousness. The adventure behind each case. But once that shiny luster wore off, she'd be left with a man who'd once gotten his meals from garbage bins. My mind was acutely aware of the chasm between us, though the rest of me didn't care one bit. And that was the dangerous part.

"That was thoughtful of you, Delvina." I motioned to the expensive trinket lying on the scarred wood. "Thank you."

"You're welcome." She lowered onto a seat, while I perched on the edge of my desk. "What are we discussing today?"

"We've covered a lot of the general ideas in sleuthing, so today let's go to the specific. Let's discuss your parents."

"I suppose we probably should." She fidgeted with the fancy trim on her dress, then finally met my gaze. "How would I go about finding the truth? Despite the rumors, it seems almost a lost cause."

"Why does the general public believe you're adopted?"

"Because my parents had me late in life. Mother was in her forties. Which isn't unheard of, but she didn't have any other children. Then they moved to Italy for a while and returned with a baby. It looks suspicious."

"I see." I took out my cigarette case and opened it, withdrawing my small notepad.

"Why do you do that?"

"What?

"Carry your notes in a cigarette case?"

"Because it's easy. Most expect men to carry them, and it looks more inconspicuous than hauling around a bulky notepad. When it's open, I can discreetly write." I picked up the small pencil for demonstration's sake. "On your side, it looks like I'm fussing with a cigarette. But I'm jotting something down even as I speak." I pulled the small paper from its home and handed it to her.

"'Delvina Kline is clever and beautiful,'" she read aloud with a roll of her eyes, but a smile touched her lips. "I see your point. You didn't look as though you wrote anything. But doesn't it look odd when you don't retrieve a cigarette?"

I hated to disillusion her and tell her most didn't pay me any mind. "That's when I shrug with disinterest, like I decided not to smoke."

She leaned forward, her onyx eyes shimmering. "So you must also be a bit of an actor in this line of work."

"Sometimes." I slid my case back into my pocket. "Especially if I go undercover assuming a false name."

"Have you done that a lot?"

"Every once in a while." I generally didn't divulge prior or current cases, so I needed to redirect this conversation before she got too nosy. Though it turned out I didn't need to, because her expression shifted, a thoughtfulness knitting her brows.

"My maid told me the milkman's wife has a sister in the theater. I could ask her to give me lessons."

"You can always get a book on the subject."

"I can't learn that way." She moved toward the modest bookcase adjacent to my desk. "I struggle with reading. My concentration drifts. It's been like that since my grammar school days." She wrinkled her nose at the shelves of books, as if the very sight of them disgusted her. "I do better when I'm shown something rather than looking at words on a page."

"Which is why you ask people to teach you. Like asking Ms. Hildreth to train you to box."

She clasped her hands behind her back and lifted her chin. "I've always felt unintelligent because of that, so I determined to have as many people teach me as I can. I can box. A police officer taught me to handle a gun and shoot. I can paint . . ." Another nose crinkle. "But not very well. And I know the parts of an engine for an automobile."

Unintelligent? It seemed like she devoted herself to learning, just not through textbooks. I preferred her way. I wouldn't even have known how to read if not for Warren's mother. "From your impressive display in the garden that day we met, it seems you retain that knowledge."

She shrugged. "The boxing side of my education came early on when one of my father's friends got forward with me after getting some gin in him."

My jaw tightened. I restrained from remarking because I knew I wouldn't be able to keep a nice word on my tongue. I knew that sort of gentleman. I'd polished their shoes while they'd bragged about their conquests. It sickened me. These men were the envy of society, yet they treated women as playthings.

"Nothing occurred, thankfully. Father walked into the room when the man had cornered me, and threw him out. But I didn't like feeling helpless. I never wanted to be in that position again. So I sought out Helen Hildreth." She examined her fist. "I've a decent uppercut too."

"If you don't mind, I'll stay over here, Knuckles."

She beamed at me, but then her grin softened. "I like you, Kent. You're . . ."

"Charming? Ridiculously handsome?"

"You're broke."

If that wasn't a sledgehammer to my ego. "Well, thank you for noticing."

Her head tipped back with a laugh at my dry tone. "Trust me—it's not a bad thing. You don't brag about how much stock you have in some company. Or how your family's wealth could last for generations." She adopted a bored look, as if fortune and grandeur were dull. "They put all their confidence in their money. Take that away, and they're nothing. You're confident regardless. It's admirable."

If she kept talking like that, she'd find herself thoroughly kissed. Which probably wasn't a good idea.

"You have your own agency," she continued. "You have vision. In a way, you're more successful than those filling a ballroom."

She presented the perfect opportunity for a teasing response. Problem was, I couldn't think of one. I couldn't conjure *any* words. Never thought it was possible for a woman to rob me of that ability. But with her eyes shining with regard, I was stripped of my armor. So I settled for a weak "Thank you."

"Now back to business," she announced, as if she hadn't just stolen my sanity. Delvina Kline was a remarkable thief and hadn't any idea of her talent.

I opened my cigarette case, as if glancing over notes instead of taking an extra moment to clear the haze. "Have you ever asked your parents if you were adopted?"

She bit her lip, which only made the blasted thing look plump and inviting. No doubt her parents would object to their daughter being in a detective's office unchaperoned in an unsavory part of the city. After the war, that kind of propriety had seemed to fade, but those in the upper tiers of society still clung to the rules.

She folded her arms and propped herself on the desk beside me. "I asked once, when I first heard the rumor, but Mother only assured me I was her daughter."

"So she said she was your birth mother?"

"No, only that I was her child." She frowned. "Father only huffed and said I shouldn't listen to gossip."

I snapped shut my cigarette case. "Neither answered you directly. Only skirted the question."

"Yes."

"Maybe the best course of action is to ask again."

She angled more toward me. "Really?"

"Sometimes you need to be cunning, but other times the direct route's the most effective."

She seemed to consider this, then her shoulders sank. "I don't know. What if I don't want the answer? I thought I did, but if I happen to be adopted . . . that would only mean all the gossip about me was right.

I'm a misfit." Her eyes darkened with a vulnerability I'd yet to witness in her.

I couldn't offer her answers, but I could offer a distraction from dark thoughts. I slipped my arm around her and gently squeezed her shoulder. "Haven't you heard?"

She peered at me, our faces close. "Heard what?" Her voice was breathless, and I wondered if my touch affected her as her nearness did me.

I dared to get closer, my mouth nearly skimming her ear. "The misfits have all the fun."

She didn't move, but I heard her catch of breath. "They do?"

I eased back. "See for yourself." I moved to grab my hat from the rack, then snatched her coat. "You up for it?"

She hopped up and turned around without a word.

I helped her into her coat. "Aren't you curious where we're going?"

She refaced me, and that sparkle in her eyes would be my undoing. She added to the torture by giving a soft smile. "I trust you."

I almost fumbled my hat. I hadn't expected her to say those three words any more than I could have predicted how they'd pummel my defenses. *I trust you.* I'd think by now she knew my intentions were honorable, considering we'd been alone in my office several times these past weeks. But still, having her trust seemed like a precious gift. Yet also fragile. I hoped I could handle it with the care it deserved.

If Delvina was nervous to walk through this area of town, she hadn't shown it. Daytime was usually safe, but if by chance we crossed paths with a ruffian, I could manage it. I'd done so over a thousand times in my short lifetime.

We turned the final corner, and Delvina slowed her steps, studying the large building. "What is this?"

"It used to be Hayes Publishing until the family purchased that fancy building along Park Row."

"Ah." She continued to inspect everything, as if counting each brick and windowpane. "What's it used for now?"

"Mostly storage. I look after the place for Warren. I come here often."

Warren had wanted to put me on the paper's payroll again, but I'd declined. I'd tend to this humble spot all my days if need be. Because in all senses of the word, this building had been my first home. I led Delvina to the back and unlocked the bolt, opening the door. "It doesn't have electricity, but there's a lot of daylight left. Come on."

She poked her head inside, then met my eyes. "You didn't bring me to this remote abandoned place to kill me or anything? Because I don't feel like dying today." To her credit, she said that string of nonsense in a nonchalant tone.

"You're safe with me." I meant this as a reply to her absurd words, but it came out gentler and more serious than intended.

Delvina, too, seemed surprised, but her rounded gaze softened, even as her hand found mine. "I know I am."

Our fingers laced. We both had gloves on, but the spark of warmth in my chest pulsed hotter with the press of her palm against mine. People in her class looked down their noses at someone like me. Where others rejected, Delvina embraced. It made me want her all the more. I needed to get my head on straight before I said something stupid.

"Ready?" I nodded toward the open door.

"Yes."

I tucked her hand into the crook of my arm, as if we were entering the Ritz-Carlton instead of a dusty building, and led her into the first place I'd ever really felt safe. Instead of carpet, there was ink-stained concrete. Instead of furniture, grime-layered crates. To me though, it was a beautiful sight.

We went through the long hall and down the steps, where the ancient printing press still stood. By the time the Hayeses had bought their new building, this press had become outdated. So they'd purchased all new equipment. The rest of the space had been cleared out, leaving a large, open area that was perfect for what I had planned.

While Delvina was preoccupied looking at the iron beast of a printing press, I wandered briefly to the set of rooms along the back. I could recall the slap of my bare feet against the concrete. The hum of the press. And the swell of belonging. I peered into the last door on the right. It was here that a young Warren had shuffled thirteen-year-old me inside and tossed a blanket and pillow into my hands.

"No one ever comes back here," he'd said with a confident nod. "I'll be back to bring you food."

At first I'd thought it a trap. No one showed kindness, especially to me. But my first and only friend had proven goodness still existed in this cruel world. I'd stayed here until Warren's mother happened upon me, having followed her son out of curiosity of where he'd been escaping to each night after dinner. She'd then welcomed me into her home. Taught me to read. How to be a gentleman.

"What's back here?" Delvina's voice tugged me into the present.

"Just some storage rooms." Rooms that had sheltered me. Kept me dry. Warm. But I couldn't tell her that. She wouldn't understand. Most didn't. The less I revealed to Delvina about my past, the better. "I had to come get these." I reached inside the closet and retrieved what I'd brought her here for.

"Roller skates?" She eyed the wheeled contraptions, a smile teasing her lips. "I thought I told you I didn't feel like dying today."

"I'm wounded you'd think I'd let anything happen." I set down my skates and snagged my handkerchief from my pocket to dust off hers first. "I thought you liked learning new skills."

She met my challenge with a glint in her eyes. "I'm happy to try, but if I break any bones, just know I won't let you forget it." Her threat held no weight, considering the amusement in her voice.

I gathered both pairs of skates. "We can sit there to strap these on." I nodded toward a nearby bench beneath one of the windows, but the usual honey-colored wood looked a sickly gray from collected filth. I set the skates on the ground and shrugged out of my jacket, but before I could spread it on the bench, Delvina plopped down.

"I'm not afraid to get dirty." Her tone was almost a rebuke. "But I appreciate the gesture." She reached for the skate. "So how do these contraptions work? I just step into them?"

I knelt in front of her and removed my gloves. "See these straps? This first one goes around the front of your shoe." I helped secure it for her. "And the second one goes around your ankle. May I?"

She nodded, and I gently tied the strap, securing her foot to the skate. "Now for the other one."

"I wouldn't picture you as the roller-skating type." She shifted so I could assist her. "Where did you get these?"

"They're actually Warren's. He bought them to impress a young lady." I couldn't help the smile creeping onto my face. "Let's just say it didn't turn out as he'd hoped."

She gave a mock gasp of indignation. "You can't end a story like that."

"Like what?" I stood and brushed the grime off my trousers, then lowered beside her to strap on my skates.

"Without any details." She rolled her eyes, as if the answer was obvious. "What happened?"

"He took the girl to Central Park to skate. He tried to show off and wound up in the bushes."

Delvina covered her smiling mouth.

"Maybe that wasn't the best story to tell. I don't want to scare you off." I stood and showed her how to balance. "Skating is easy once you get the hang of it."

While still seated, she moved her feet back and forth on the concrete. "You realize I'll have need of your arm until I know I won't fall and shatter any bones."

"See? My plan is working." I held out my hands to her. "We're not even five minutes here and you already want to touch me."

She playfully swatted at my fingers.

"I've a better idea on how to teach you. Grab both my hands."

She did, and I tugged her to her feet. Her skates shuffled, her eyes widening at the instability.

"I've got you." I tightened my grip. "Now let's skate."

"But you're backward."

"I don't see a problem here." I grinned. "I'll help tow you along all the while enjoying my view."

She good-naturedly shook her head at my remark, and while I was purposefully being over the top, I wasn't entirely joking. I pulled her with me, her skates responding to my momentum. After a few circles around, she relaxed, even smiled.

"Like I said. Nothing to it." I gave her hands a squeeze. "Should we go faster?"

"Don't you dare let go of me."

Her breathy words made my pulse thud faster. I'd obey that command as long as she'd let me. Our skates made tracks in the dust even as Delvina cut a stronger path to my heart. I'd milk this moment for all it was worth. Holding her. Hearing her melodic laugh. Being the recipient of her bright smiles. It made a man forget every purpose but one—to make her happy.

I pumped my legs, increasing our speed. Her grin broke free, and I could only stare. She truly was the most beautiful woman I'd—

She gasped at something behind me.

I looked over my shoulder, and it cost me. My skates went out from under me.

I tried to pull away from Delvina's grip, but she clung tighter. My body smacked the hard ground, the air whooshing from my chest. Delvina landed atop me.

She lifted her head from its spot on my shoulder. Dark brows slanted over distressed eyes. "Are you okay?"

"Nothing broken." I coughed, my lungs still short on oxygen. "You?"

"I'm fine." She exhaled. "Dumb rat." Her gaze darted past me. "It's gone now." Slowly her focus returned to me, her nose accidentally skimming my cheek.

Awareness hit us both. Our bodies tangled together. My arms still around her waist. I could feel the quick rise and fall of her breaths.

She bit her lip, her warmth pressing into me. "We look scandalous."

"That we do."

The shock in her eyes melted away with her laugh, complete with shaking shoulders and snorts. Crashing on roller skates wasn't exactly the *fun* I'd intended, but her unrestrained laughter went straight to my head. I'd never been one to give in to addiction, but Delvina's laugh? I craved it.

She gazed down at me, her sparkling smile drawing my full attention to her perfect lips. I wanted to kiss her, but I wouldn't. No, a woman like her deserved to be romanced in a fairy-tale-like setting. Someplace where moonlight streaked her hair. Or the sunrise glittered in her eyes. Not here on the dirty floor riddled with spiders and rodent droppings. If it were a fairy tale she deserved, I could never be her prince. I had no castle. No so-called kingdom of any kind. I had nothing to offer her. That revelation knocked the air from my chest more than any toppling on skates. But as always, I quirked a breezy smile. "And here I thought *you* would be the first to fall."

She pressed her cheek to my shoulder, and I could've sworn she murmured, "Oh, but I was."

• • •

I returned to my empty flat still thinking of Delvina. After we recovered from the tumble, she dedicated the next hour to mastering the art of skating. While she gained a new skill to add to her list of others, I gained the understanding to never underestimate Delvina Kline.

I'd barely unbuttoned my coat when a knock sounded at my door.

"Telephone for you, Brisbane." It was Billy, my landlord's son.

The owner of the building also ran the cigar shop beneath my flat. Owning a private line to my flat was an expense beyond my means, so I'd cut a deal with my landlord to pay a small fee for the use of his. I rebuttoned my jacket and went downstairs to the shop.

"I have information that might interest you," Warren said the second I picked up the speaker.

I scoffed. "If it's another society event, I'd rather pluck out my eyelashes one by one."

"Someone answered the ad."

I lowered onto a nearby stool. "Dozens have answered, old man."

"But she refuses to take the reward money."

That was new. All the others had been lured by the two hundred dollars. "She?"

A slight pause. "She says she's Kit Mason."

The name of the woman who'd given me up to the children's home. My mother. "Anyone can say that." I didn't want to hope. After a lifetime of searching, this seemed too simple.

"She said something else. She gave me two dates."

"Which are?"

"April 7, 1898, and April 5, 1898."

I drew in a slow breath. The first was the day I'd been taken in by the home, and the second was my birthday. Anyone could get the first one—it was written in public records. But the latter wasn't. The home didn't always list birthdays because of the numerous children given up at various times. It was too difficult to determine when each child was born. My birthday had been scribbled on a piece of paper by Kit herself. A paper I still had.

This could only mean one thing. We'd found my mother.

Chapter 11

Delvina
1924

I'D SPENT MOST OF THE next day following up on leads from the names in Miss Thayer's calendar. I searched for any link between her past clients and the night she'd died, beginning with tracing her clients' whereabouts for that evening. Several had attended the dinner party at the Hayeses' residence, the same event Kent had gone to. The remaining clients had been out of town that entire day. The only name left was Maude Welch, who had passed from the sleeping sickness a month earlier. All my hot leads had fizzled out.

Just to be thorough, I'd spoken with the other residents on Miss Thayer's floor, asking if they'd seen anything or anyone suspicious. None had. Nor had they heard the gunshot. Unsurprising, since the thunderstorm had been particularly loud the evening of her death. The next step should probably be trailing Wallace Stratton. His behavior yesterday had spiked my suspicion. Part of me felt it was necessary to exhaust every angle of the case, while another part of me was simply avoiding Mother.

I felt guilty for leaving her in the dark about my marriage.

I understood that avoiding her would only provoke her questions. Since Father's passing, I'd made a habit of visiting her three to four times a week. So I'd broken down and visited. I sat in her dainty parlor, sipping overly sweet tea and half listening to her chat with Ida Elliot about the problems of today's youth—all while wildly vacillating between utter boredom and panic that Mother would find me out before I formulated a way to tell her about my marriage.

"I have a question for you, dear." Ida peered my way, and I nodded with the distinct trapped sensation that I'd missed something important. "I've been feeling like a bit of a matchmaker."

I resisted the urge to duck cupid's arrow and merely gave Mother a subtle shake of my head in response to her excited glance. I'd once dodged a dozen knives hurled at me from cranky bootleggers when I'd accidentally stumbled upon a still in an abandoned house. I was confident I could deflect anything Ida Elliot threw my way. Though I could venture a guess she intended to involve her son. She'd no doubt noticed Edward speaking with me at Mother's dinner party and decided to renew her campaign. She'd pushed his suit, probably without his knowledge, around the same time I'd first met Kent. But like back then, I held no interest in Edward. Even more so now, considering I was legally married.

"That young man I met here a little over a week ago? Mr. Brisbane, was it? Do you think he'd enjoy dinner at my house? I'd like to introduce him to my nephew's daughter. Oh, she's a sweet young thing."

I stared into my teacup. How would one prevent a pushy busybody from setting up a socialite with one's secret husband? I could almost envision Kent's amused smirk at the absurd situation. Well, at least I'd imagine he would smirk. After yesterday's conversation, I didn't know what the man was thinking. What had that silence meant? Kent had never been the broody sort. So the definite clench of his jaw and stony glint in his eyes caught me off guard. Just how angry had he been? Angry enough to go to the press? Yes, he'd been disgusted about my offering money, and worse, he hadn't promised to remain quiet. My stomach dropped.

Mother cleared her throat, and I realized I'd taken too long to respond to Ida, drawing a curious look from the older woman. I forced a smile. "I'm not certain. I know Mr. Brisbane is busy with a case at present."

She sniffed. "He's truly a detective, then?"

Hadn't she read the papers? Listened to the radio broadcast hour? The news about us and the VanKirk kidnapping had been everywhere. "Yes."

"Then perhaps I shan't introduce." She patted her sleek blond chignon. "I have no idea why I'd thought he was one of us."

My blood sparked with familiar heat. The impressionable years of my youth had been wasted in straining to be accepted. I'd striven to do everything expected of me, but in the end I was still labeled an outcast. And I mean with a literal label of a D rating for my debutante season. It was that year I'd decided the approval I'd craved, thinking it would fulfill me, had actually been depleting. By the time I'd met Kent, I'd given up trying to impress. But it seemed Kent had learned that lesson long before I had, for he cared little what anyone thought of him. And my younger self had found that quality not only refreshing but attractive.

Even now, if Kent were here, he'd easily brush off Mrs. Elliot's pert remark.

But I couldn't. "I don't see how that's a mark against him. I'm a detective as well."

"Yet yours is more of a hobby. Just like my father with medicine. He devoted himself to the study and was a credit to the field," she said wistfully. "Though I would suggest it was more of a passion than a hobby."

I took a slow sip of tea, bracing myself for one of her predictable monologues. She'd always made a point of mentioning her family's contribution to the medical world at least once at every event she attended.

"Why, I was just telling Mrs. Clemens the other day how my knowledge in herbal remedies helped save my distant cousin's phalanges from being amputated. The poor man needed his phalanges if he were to marry."

Mother sputtered.

"Fingers and toes," I quickly put in, before Mother fainted. "That's the scientific term for fingers and toes." During my adolescence, Ida had tutored me on early medicine and ancient practices. I'd found most of it boring, except for the gory parts. Surprisingly, I remembered a lot of what she'd taught me.

Ida nodded in approval. "In his case, it was the fingers. And because of my assistance, he was able to wear his wedding band for the big day."

The woman could've easily said *fingers*, but some people loved embellishing their stories for the sake of sounding intelligent. And for the sake of my sanity, I needed to make my exit. "Excuse me, but I have an appointment I must attend." It was a much-needed meeting with my pillow. I hadn't slept well last night.

"At seven in the evening?" Mother blinked. "It's dark out."

Another tug of guilt. I could tell she was hoping I'd stay, possibly all evening so we could breakfast together. She'd once confided that the mornings were the most difficult for her regarding her grief. "I'll be back in the morning."

She visibly brightened, and I knew I'd made the right choice. I bussed her cheek and savored the sweet escape from Ida Elliot and her snobby ways.

Getting across town took longer than expected, and by the time I reached the floor of my flat, I was ready to collapse onto my bed. But a lone figure hovered in the dim shadows of the hall.

I stepped back, increasing the distance between me and the stranger, and slipped my hand into my bag, ready to withdraw my gun. Having the only set of rooms on this floor, there was no reason for anyone else to be up here. My fingers slid across the cool metal of my weapon.

The mystery guest stepped into the light.

Rosalie Adams.

I exhaled relief and closed my purse. "Good evening, Ms. Adams."

She saw me and perked. "Did ya solve it? Is that dandy Mr. Stratton be arrested?"

I shook my head. "No, not yet."

"Oh." Her shoulders slumped, but then as if remembering her manners, she held out the basket that had been resting in the crook of her elbow. "Here's the cannoli."

"Thank you." My stomach promptly growled. To my relief Ms. Adams was caught up in her own thoughts and hadn't noticed the roar of my obnoxious organ. "I'm sorry I don't have results yet concerning Miss Thayer, but there's something else I'd like to speak to you about. Care to step inside for a moment?"

Surprise lit her face as she nodded. I opened the door, and she followed me to the parlor. I motioned for her to take the Chippendale seat. This time she sat without hesitation.

I set the basket on the end table, then lowered onto the sofa. "I have a possible employment opportunity for you. A fellow detective, Kent Brisbane . . ." I waited for a flash of recognition in her eyes, but thankfully, there wasn't any. This helped confirm Kent had been honest with me about his dealings with Miss Thayer. Because I knew from experience that the maids knew everything. "He's looking for someone to clean his office. His line of work demands someone who's discreet."

Her mouth tightened. "Is he superstitious?"

Odd question. "Not that I know of." Yesterday when I'd visited his office, I'd noticed a New Testament on his desk. He hadn't shown much interest in faith four years ago, but the Bible's weathered state suggested constant use. So with that, coupled with my knowledge of him from four years ago, I could safely say the man wasn't superstitious. "Why do you ask?"

She tugged her gloves, the left, then the right, then the left again. "I just be having rotten luck with clients lately. I don't want Mr. Brisbane to drop dead."

My gut lurched. I realized the remark was absurd, but her blunt words had sharp edges. I supposed most wives would have strong reactions to flippant comments about their husband's sudden death, but the tense chill currently throbbing its way through my body was startling. Perhaps my response could be blamed on fatigue and residual shock from yesterday's events.

It seemed that while Kent wasn't superstitious, Ms. Adams was. Or maybe she was only hesitant after the shock of finding Miss Thayer's body. Understandable. "I can promise you that Mr. Brisbane's not going to drop dead." I watched the tight lines soften around her gray eyes. "Take your time and think about it. If you'd like the chance, go to his office and tell him I sent you." I rattled off the address.

"Thank you. That means a lot." She exhaled and slightly sank into her seat. "Losing Miss Thayer be hurting me in many ways."

I nodded my understanding. "Well, as to that. I was wondering if there's anything else you may have remembered that could help things along."

She shook her head.

I recalled what the stuffy secretary from the Stratton Agency had said. The woman had implied something suspicious about Miss Thayer, but I couldn't pinpoint why. "Does the Eighth Avenue subway line mean anything to you?"

"No. Should it?"

"What about that subway ticket on Miss Thayer's vanity?"

"Oh yes," she said readily, but then her enthusiasm dimmed. "I thought Miss Thayer be holding on to that ticket because it be important to 'er."

I'd had the same thought. The subway ticket had to be significant. Why else had Miss Thayer kept it? The transit had switched to coins once they'd installed the electric turnstiles. What happened in Miss Thayer's life four years ago that made her keep hold of that ticket? Did it involve a lover, perhaps? "Was Miss Thayer seeing anyone else besides Mr. Stratton?"

She hesitated, and I caught it. "I know you don't want to besmirch her character, but it's important to the case that I know everything."

A weary sigh pushed through her thin mouth. "I only saw 'im once. Miss Thayer be in a mood that day he came. He surprised her, I be thinking. 'Cause soon as she opened the door and saw 'im there, she asked me to leave."

"Did you catch his name?"

"No."

That certainly made things more difficult. "What about anything that could identify him? What did he look like?"

"Handsome. His hair"—she motioned to the crown of her head—"be black with a stripe of silver."

That could be half the men in the city. She must've realized how that sounded, for she quickly amended, "It's different. He got a stripe in the front of his hair." She pointed to her own widow's peak.

My blood froze. This wasn't good. There was only one man I knew of with such a distinction.

One of the up-and-coming crime bosses.

Angelo LeRaffa.

• • •

The following morning and well into the day, I'd fulfilled my promise and spent time with Mother. Kent hadn't tried to contact me, and since I refused to mope about my flat and wait for him, I'd then gone to a pool hall.

Swirls of smoke climbed to the rafters as I made my way through the labyrinth of billiard tables, dodging the several cuspidors and rogue cue sticks. Women weren't usually allowed in pool halls, but that didn't deter me.

The general clamor of the joint hushed to a grumbling hum as I perched on one of the stools at the bar. This wasn't a speakeasy. Only a somewhat dingy lounge that offered working-class men a reprieve from the daily grind.

My gaze swung to the hulking form who spearheaded it all. Spider. That was how everyone knew the man because of the webbing of scars on his face. He looked every inch the terrifying menace. Even now his monstrous frame stalked toward me in slow, prowling steps.

"What are you doing here?" His low, gruff voice coupled with his fierce glare could scare the whiskers off grown men.

I grinned. "To see you, ya big oaf." I reached up, up, up and brushed the lint off his massive shoulder. "Have you missed me?"

He huffed a grunt. "You know ladies aren't welcome here."

I rolled my eyes. "Since when did rules stop me?"

He conceded my argument with a twitch of his lips.

"Perhaps I came to put these lounge lizards in their place." I nodded at the closest billiards table. My adoptive father had taught me to play when I was young. It was a game we'd bonded over. Some of my favorite memories had been with a cue stick in hand. My throat grew thick. Grief had no manners. It sneaked up on a person when least expected and ruined a perfectly good mood. I bit back the invading emotion and remembered my purpose for being here. And while I liked to tease Spider, I wasn't here to empty the pockets of his patrons. Though I probably could.

"Don't go bankrupting my customers." Spider folded his massive arms across his chest. "I want them to come back."

I laughed. "You're no fun."

He shrugged, but amusement lit his dark eyes. The dim hanging lamp splayed shadows across his face, making the warped tissue appear more prominent. Where Kent's scar was alluring, Spider's was intimidating. Though it was mostly an act. I'd no doubt the man could probably snap a cue stick with his pinkie finger, but he wasn't as cruel as he posed. Still, I shouldn't test him. He had a business to run, and I was taking up his time.

"I have a question for you." I dug the subway ticket from my purse and tossed it onto the bar counter. "What can you tell me about this?"

"To stay away." He slapped his beefy palm over it, as if shielding it from view.

"From the subway?"

"You don't know what this is?" His lips tipped in a rare smile. "For once I know something the clever Vinny doesn't."

"Har. Har." I nudged the man with my elbow, but he didn't even shift. "What is this?"

"A membership card." He pushed the ticket back into my palm. "To an underground gin joint."

Ah, that was it! I knew it had to be significant. "I'm assuming the speakeasy is accessed through the subway?"

He nodded. "Remember the Fifty-Eighth Street terminal?"

I blinked. "Yes." But that station had been out of use for years. The city had closed it for good five months ago and replaced it with . . . Eighth Ave. The same station Wallace's secretary had mentioned yesterday. Interesting. A gin joint hidden in the abandoned subway line and accessed through Eighth Ave. The secretary must've known Miss Thayer frequented the establishment. Now I was curious if Wallace Stratton had known. "That's an ingenious place for a secret speakeasy." I glanced at the ticket in my hand. "And you can only gain entrance with this?"

"Yeah. Them tickets are scarcer than Napoleon brandy. How'd you come across one?"

"Adele Thayer's flat. Do you recognize the name?"

"Nah." He rubbed his stubbly chin. "Not that I know of."

"She was killed last week." I glanced around and lowered my voice. "I believe she's linked to Angelo LeRaffa?"

He cussed under his breath. "Vinny, he's no good. I haven't heard anything about his connection with this Thayer dame, but I've heard other things. If ya know what I mean."

Probably the same rumors I'd heard. Since discovering my birth father had been a leading crime boss in Pittsburgh, I'd come to understand the inner workings of mob rings. They were cutthroat. Sometimes literally. And from what I understood, LeRaffa was ruthless. "I just need to ask him a few questions. Do you think Miss Thayer met LeRaffa at this gin joint?"

"No doubt. The man owns it."

Had LeRaffa been Miss Thayer's secret lover? Had that relationship been the reason for the feud between Miss Thayer and Wallace Stratton the morning she'd died? "What's the name of this place?"

"The Terminal."

Ah, clever. With a name like that, people could speak about it openly, such as "Meet me at the Terminal" or "The Terminal was busy yesterday," and others overhearing would think nothing of it.

I glanced at Spider. "Open nightly?"

He nodded. "At eleven."

"Anything else I should know?"

"Yeah—don't go near that man."

"I love how protective you are of me." I lifted on my toes and patted his scarred cheek. "Liza made a big teddy bear out of you."

At hearing his wife's name, he visibly softened. Then as if realizing that was my intention, he scowled, pulling a laugh from me.

"It's all right, Spider. If anyone asks, I'll say you've got the meanest mug I've ever seen."

He grunted.

This meeting made me think of the one I'd had with Paulo recently. Society would label these men outcasts, misfits. But to me they were friends. I could only snort at what Ida Elliot would think of the company I keep. It made me want to linger here a bit longer, but I couldn't. "Thank you, Spider. We're even now."

He shook his head. "No, Vinny. We can never be even."

I gave him a warm smile. I'd rescued his wife from being victimized in a brothel. It had been one of my first cases. Liza's sister had hired me, claiming Liza, who'd been a young girl at the time, had disappeared. Thankfully, I'd quickly and easily found her, then entrusted her to a family friend who'd taken Liza on as kitchen help. And that was where she'd met Spider. "Tell her hello for me." I squeezed his elbow and turned to leave.

Spider's grumbling skittered over my shoulder. "Don't forget a flashlight."

Chapter 12

THE CHIC STYLE OF TODAY'S frocks seemed tailored for my profession. The loose-fitting, straight-lined seams allowed easier movement. Something convenient if I ever found myself in a scrape. Which hopefully, tonight I wouldn't.

My heels—again stylish yet sensible—clicked against the cement tunnel. The way the residents embraced underground transit, it would seem as if this means of transportation had been around longer than twenty years. The lateness of the hour meant I wasn't hemmed in by a throng of people, but there were still a decent number of commuters threading Eighth Avenue Station. I put a nickel in the slot and eased through the turnstile, giving me access to the landing. Though tonight I wasn't boarding a train. I planned to find a secret speakeasy.

Over the years, plenty of tunnels had been dug beneath the city, providing ample nooks and crevices perfect for concealing a liquor fountain. The first order of business was to locate the Terminal. The second? To get in without raising suspicion. If I succeeded in both, then I'd search for LeRaffa.

I nodded at a charwoman whose cheekbones bore soot smears and eyes held exhaustion, then I skirted around a group of factory workers laughing loudly while waiting for the incoming train. It was a genius concept to place a speakeasy near an area where people moved about during all hours of the day and night. It wouldn't look at all suspicious.

I wandered toward the section of landing stretching to the closed-down tunnel. At one time, the trains had continued to the Fifty-Eighth Street Station, but the line had been terminated years ago. Though it was only recently that the city had sealed off the tunnel.

I kept my expression curious, as if I were simply meandering over to glimpse the newly bricked barricade. It was obvious this far-off area of the platform had been neglected. Old newspapers, discarded playbills, and other debris littered the dusty cement. The few lamps that hadn't burned out flickered weakly, as if fighting to push away the pressing shadows.

I searched for anything that could be hiding in plain sight. I'd seen my share of speakeasy entrances. Sliding walls in ritzy town houses. Trapdoors in theaters. One particular gin joint—tucked inside an art gallery—was called Display 22 simply because access to the speakeasy was behind the twenty-second exhibit, which was a large painting.

I almost reached the edge of the landing, taking in an abandoned newspaper stand, an overstuffed garbage bin, and a rickety phone booth.

After a few glances over my shoulder, ensuring no one paid me any attention, I slipped inside the booth, unsurprised to find no hanging lamp to light the darkness. Faint traces of perfume twisted into the shadows. Someone had been in here recently. I pulled the curtain along the splintery rod above the door. My presence now even more concealed, I switched on my flashlight. Judging by the mangled candlestick base and detached speaker, whoever visited this booth before me hadn't come to use the telephone.

The interior was more spacious than the cramped boxes clogging Manhattan, making me think this one had been built when the city had first installed the booths more than fifteen years ago. A sign hung by a single nail on the back wall. Faded words listed the calling rates. The fees were outdated. This telephone booth had been out of use for at least a year.

LeRaffa must've bribed just the right person to turn a blind eye to this particular booth. Because why else would it be here, except to camouflage a hidden door?

Now to find said door.

One good stomp told me the ground was solid concrete. No trap-door, leading me even more underground. I skimmed my fingers along the corners, over the walls, searching for an access point. There wasn't one.

My gaze returned to the sign. There wasn't any dust coating its surface. I slid the sign to the left.

Ah, now what do we have here?

Stooping, I shone my light on an odd-shaped hole in the wall. Perhaps there was a latch. Or a button. But I couldn't spot anything. I slid my fingers inside, taking in the different divots and notches.

It needed a key, though not the standard kind—something larger, like the size of a doorknob.

Disappointment coursed through me. I'd thought all that was required was the ticket. But now it seemed those who were granted entrance to the Terminal had also been given some sort of key. Why hadn't Spider told me? Maybe he hadn't known. I studied the shape of the hole again.

I wonder . . .

I wrapped my purse around my wrist and reached for the severed telephone speaker. The dimensions seemed to add up, but there was only one way to tell. Skinny end first, I maneuvered it into the wall.

Click. Click.

A mechanism in the wall caught hold of the speaker. My pulse pumping, I gently turned it as one would a doorknob and gave a slight push.

The wall gave way into . . . the tunnel.

I'd found the Terminal.

Triumph sluicing through me, I slipped through the gap into the ghost subway. I expected to be met with darkness, but the tunnel was well lit, giving me a clear view of the burly man a couple of yards ahead, his hard glare locking on me.

He was stuffed into a ticket-agent uniform. His enormous bulk stretched his jacket to the point that the line of brass buttons hung on for dear life. The man stalked toward me with a scowl that could rival

Spider's for most menacing. This scenario reminded me of a childhood story with a giant troll who guarded a cave entrance and rattled off complicated riddles those wishing to pass must solve.

I knew some speakeasies required patrons to whisper a secret message or code word. I hoped this subway ticket would speak for me. I dug the slip of paper from my purse and held it out with a casual indifference, as if I'd done so a hundred times. My gaze strayed just beyond him. Men capped in fedoras and women in fringed frocks milled about with drinks in hand. Some danced to jivey music from a band huddled together on an open railcar. It was uncanny that barely a stone's throw away, commuters boarded the Eight Avenue line oblivious to this place.

"Looks like a decent crowd tonight."

His hooded gaze roamed over me in a lazy sweep. "The usual," he grumbled, and gave the ticket a thorough inspection. Satisfied, he handed it back and let me pass.

My profession had led me to visit plenty of gin joints over the years, but this one surpassed all in terms of creativity. Three subway cars were situated on the ribbon of rails. The first held the band. The one after it was the bar. All the window glass had been removed for the bartenders to easily hand out drinks and take money from those in line. And what a line it was. A chain of people stretched around the car and snaked through the labyrinth of tables. Those wanting alcohol were yelling things likes "the five-fifteen" or "the ten-oh-six," and I realized the drinks were named after the train schedule. I could imagine flappers outside these walls saying to each other, "Let's go to the Terminal and catch the five fifteen," and none would be the wiser.

The last subway car I suspected to be LeRaffa's office. It was slightly down the rails from the others. I moved at a leisurely pace so I wouldn't draw attention, all the while keeping an eye out for the legendary crime boss. I passed a cluster of cigarette girls parading about half-dressed with trays fully stocked with smoke sticks. The band struck up another lively tune, and as couples raced toward the makeshift dance floor, I approached the last railcar.

One glance through the glass and my heart sank. It was filled with bottles, glasses, and extra chairs. A storage car. So much for that. Since there wasn't anyone here, I rounded the back of the car and climbed the two steps of the shadowed caboose. The dim space would serve as my thinking spot.

I sat on the iron chair, considering my next move. If LeRaffa wasn't here, then how was I to find him? I supposed it was foolish to expect him to be at the Terminal at the exact time I was. This gin joint was just one of his many *projects*. It seemed like I'd be frequenting this place until he surfaced. Not exactly a pleasant thought.

I took in a deep breath and ran a hand along the cool railing. I lifted my gaze and took in the artificial sky held by a series of columns. The dark ceiling was threaded with hanging lamps, designed to resemble a starry night.

It seemed LeRaffa spared no expense. Though I suspected he stole the electricity from the city. How simple it would be to tap into the lines and power this space. I scoffed. "Leave it to LeRaffa," I muttered, "to run an illegal joint and make the city pay for it."

"It is rather clever."

I jumped from my seat and turned toward the masculine voice. A man leaned forward from the veil of shadows. The weak glow from the nearby lamps highlighted strong features.

Angelo LeRaffa.

He took me in as clearly as I did him. He couldn't be much older than me. Early thirties, maybe. Dark eyes glittered within the hard lines of his cheekbones, which angled to a sharp chin. The man was attractive. A fact he certainly was aware of.

He stood and retrieved a cigarette case from his suit pocket. Without pulling his gaze from mine, he opened the gold-plated box and offered me a smoke. I waved him off. He retrieved one for himself, lit it, and shook out the match. "So what brings you to my humble place, Miss Salvastano?"

One thing about being the daughter of a mobster whose disappearance and reemergence had gained national attention, it was hard to remain anonymous. I could've laughed at his wording. Nothing about this underground speakeasy was humble. It practically screamed extravagance. It also didn't slip my notice he'd called me by my birth father's surname. I found it fascinating that people acknowledged me by what they identified with. Those in the upper class always referred to me as Miss Kline, because that name spoke of class and affluence, while those like LeRaffa related to my Salvastano background. Yet I was no longer either of those. And the man whose name I currently shared hadn't bothered to contact me today. Though why I expected him to keep promises was beyond me. He'd already proven himself incapable.

Speaking of poor character traits, I remembered LeRaffa's scandalous reputation with women and casually positioned myself between him and the caboose steps. Something that hadn't escaped his notice, given the slight twitch of his lips. "Mr. LeRaffa." I dipped my head instead of offering my hand. "What brings me here? I was actually looking for you."

He took a drag on his cigarette and flicked the ashes over the railing. "I'm honored."

"I have to admit this place is impressive." I gestured toward the main area of the speakeasy. "And genius too. No one would think to look here after the city sealed up this tunnel." I tilted my head. "Though I suppose if a raid did happen, you'd all be like sitting ducks. Since there's only one way in and out."

"Ah, now you insult my intelligence." He wagged his finger at me and leaned closer. "Strategic exits are important in my field."

Which was a fancy way of saying getaway routes. I knew he'd have another escape plan, most likely several, but any way I could engage him in conversation increased my chances of getting him to speak more openly about Miss Thayer and his connection to her.

"There's a staircase down the rails that leads out the tunnel to the street." He blew out a stream of smoke, regarding me with a dark glint in his eyes. "Thought you'd like to know in case my presence makes you uneasy."

I wasn't scared of him, but I wasn't foolish either. I'd heard rumors he'd crushed men's throats, and while my own neck seemed blemished to most, I'd grown rather accustomed to it.

"Though it's really *me* who should be wary of *you*." His gaze sharpened on me. "You see, I personally approve each membership. I'd remember if a Salvastano wanted entrance to my club." He made a show of stubbing out his cigarette on the railing. "Knowing your versatile background, I'm led to wonder if you're a threat or an ally."

"I doubt anyone could be a threat to you," I countered. "But I gather you're referencing my birth father and his former activities."

"Are you looking to get into the family business?"

"Not interested." Not even a little. Sadly, I'd been asked this question before. Especially since I had connections with those on the not-so-ethical side of the law, like Paulo and Spider. "But since you want to know how I got in, how about we strike a deal?"

He eased closer. "Depends if I like what I get out of the bargain."

That was a bit oily, but I hadn't expected anything less. "I'll tell you how I got inside your booze fortress if you tell me why you were inside Adele Thayer's flat the Thursday after she died."

His lips broke apart with a huff of surprised laughter. I hadn't realized he was the one who'd come in while I was searching the flat until I'd seen the cigarette case. The gold-plated trinket with the detailed scrolling he'd tugged from his pocket moments ago had been the same one I'd glimpsed from my hiding spot in Miss Thayer's closet.

"Next time I need a private detective, I'm hiring you." Flattery might've been an effective redirection tactic on most women, but not me. Thanks to Kent, I was immune to charm. LeRaffa soon realized his failed strategy and shrugged. "Not sure why it matters since the police ruled her death a suicide."

"If it doesn't matter, then why did you take something from her dresser drawer? That seems to me like you don't want anyone seeing what was once in her possession."

He didn't answer.

"I promise to tell you how I got in here if you reveal why you were in Miss Thayer's bedroom."

He folded his arms and leaned against the railing, observing me. "Why's it so shocking? If anything, it's obvious why a man like me would know my way around a beautiful woman's bedroom."

I shook my head. "Fine with me if you choose to be dishonest." I glanced at the ticket in my hand. "That means I can be too."

"You calling me a liar? Not many get away with that kind of mistake." His tone was cool. "I assure you my reputation with—"

I huffed, knowing this was a dangerous move, but I couldn't help myself. "I'm very aware of your *reputation*. But if you're about to dish some vulgar details about a whirlwind romance with Adele Thayer, I'm not buying it." Because unlike what Ms. Adams believed, I was convinced he and Miss Thayer weren't lovers.

He'd no reaction whatsoever to the mention of her name. If they'd ended a tumultuous relationship on a bad note, wouldn't there be hints of disdain? Or if he'd favored her in any way, I'd expect even the slightest touch of regret. Although he didn't seem like the kind of man to grow attached to anyone. I could see him using Miss Thayer for his own pleasure, then discarding her. That was a definite possibility. But I'd already spouted off my assumption and needed to stick by it. "Here." I fished the ticket from my purse and handed it to him. "You can have this back. The ticket was on Miss Thayer's vanity. You should've grabbed it when you were there. Though you seemed in a rush to get something else."

He eased the ticket from my fingers, the brush of thumb swiping across my knuckles making my skin crawl. I'd just relinquished my biggest bargaining chip.

He angled away from me, peering down the tunnel. "Adele owed me money."

I dared not interrupt.

"She wanted away from her old lifestyle and needed help. I pulled some strings and got her what she needed to start over."

Which probably included forged papers. A different name. A shiny new residence in Park Towers perhaps? Maybe a stylish wardrobe?

He'd probably funded everything. Which now made me wonder what life she'd escaped from. "Seems expensive."

"She paid me back." He shrugged. "She wrote the receipt in her own handwriting, and I signed it."

Understanding hit. "And that was what you took from her drawer. The receipt."

The glint in his eyes had dulled. Any amusement he'd derived from this conversation had waned. "Worth the effort to avoid the police. Even if it was ruled a suicide, I don't like people sniffing around asking questions."

The last phrase was a jab at me. "Do you still have the receipt?"

His jaw tightened. "It's in my office." He gestured farther down the tunnel.

And I remembered there had once been a station on Fifty-Eighth Street. He must use the abandoned building as his office. While he may have indicated where his office was, he hadn't extended any invitation to see the receipt. "As much as it's been fun chatting with you, I need to go check on the bar." He peered down at me. "Feel free to stay and enjoy a drink."

I wouldn't. "That's kind of you."

"Think nothing of it. If you ever want to become a real member"—he lifted the ticket with a smirk and gently skimmed it along my arm—"we'll talk."

I didn't even flinch. Men like him took pleasure at causing a reaction. So I gave him none. "I'm obliged," I said dryly, to which he chuckled.

He brushed past me down the steps of the caboose.

"Do you happen to know why Miss Thayer wanted a new life?" I blurted before he dashed fully out of earshot.

He called over his shoulder, "You would too, if your family was linked to the Galleanists."

The Galleanists. An anarchist group rumored to be behind the 1920 Wall Street bombing. A horse-drawn cart filled with TNT had exploded in front of the J. P. Morgan offices, killing thirty-eight New

Yorkers. No one had been taken into custody, but it was commonly suspected that the Galleanists had orchestrated the attack.

I leaned over the railing, about to ask the name of Miss Thayer's family, but LeRaffa was gone.

The crime boss had spun quite the story. I wasn't certain if there were any threads of truth. But I did know I didn't want to linger in this place. So I made my exit. It didn't take me long to return to that dilapidated phone booth and emerge onto the Eight Avenue platform.

Several people meandered about but didn't spare me any notice. The incoming train would take me the opposite direction I needed, so I left the station in hopes to catch a cable car back to Park Towers. I regretted not driving here myself, but this section of town was awful when it came to traffic. And finding a parking spot? Nearly impossible.

The night air had a bite to it, making me wish I'd brought my coat. When I'd readied earlier, I hadn't been certain what I would encounter, so I'd left the bulky thing behind. I hustled down the street, my gaze zipping about for a taxi. I could always jump on the trolley, but it would take me longer to get home.

A door burst open, almost knocking into me. I reeled back even as a man stumbled out of what seemed like an abandoned office building. The figure hunched over, breathing hard.

Kent.

He braced himself on the lamppost, and that's when he caught sight of me. "Hello, wife."

My gaze swung to the door. "What are you doing?"

"I'd love to stay and chat." He grimaced. "But I'm in a bit of a scrape."

I noticed he was favoring his right leg. "What happened?" But I didn't wait for his answer. I crouched down for a better look. His trousers had been gashed, the fabric stained crimson. My heart clenched. "You've been stabbed." I couldn't see the extent of the injury, but I glimpsed enough to know he needed medical attention.

He nodded. "That's not the worst of it. LeRaffa's men are after me."

I flicked a glance at the door. That must've been the strategic exit the crime boss had mentioned. He'd said a staircase led out the tunnel to the street. Kent had climbed flights of steps in his condition. More disturbing, just how much time until LeRaffa's men stormed out this same door?

"Go, Vinny," he rasped. "I don't want you caught up in this." He hobbled away.

No way he'd outrun them.

"I got another idea." I grabbed his hat from his head and peeled back his jacket.

His face drained color by the second. "Darling, now's not the time to be undressing me."

"Work with me, you oaf. You need to look different." I helped him shrug out of his charcoal suitcoat and tossed it—and the hat—into the nearby garbage bin.

I threw his arm over my shoulder and willed for a taxi to magically appear. If it were daytime, it wouldn't be an issue. But after one in the morning, most cabs lingered south of here in the busier parts of Manhattan.

The familiar clanging of the cable car met my ears. I nearly cried in relief. I pulled out two nickels from my purse. "Come on." Bearing most of his weight against me, I tapped into the spike of adrenaline surging my veins. We didn't have much time. The trolley stop was about fifty feet away.

I practically dragged Kent alongside me.

The cable car slowed to a stop and I waved my free arm, hoping the driver would have mercy on us and wait for us. But compassion came second to a punctual trolley schedule, so I pushed harder to get us to the corner.

I glanced over my shoulder. The door Kent had stumbled out of flung open, men in suits filing onto the sidewalk. We reached the trolley doors. My side aching and muscles burning, I pulled Kent up the few steps and deposited the coins. The cable car's doors slid shut. We all but fell onto the bench on the opposite side of the walk where the goons now stood, searching.

He couldn't afford to be seen. Not even through the window.

"Kent. Duck down."

But his face twisted in anguish. The pain overtook his attention. So I tugged his upper body into my lap, shielding him from view. Normally, he'd make an absurd remark, but he only laid on my thighs, his face an ashen gray.

The cable car lurched into motion.

"Thanks for keeping me safe, Knuckles." Kent managed to straighten in his seat, but his features contorted in anguish. "Looks like we're in the clear."

I bent down and examined the gash in his leg. My stomach dropped. Kent was wrong. He may have escaped LeRaffa's goons, but he wasn't in the clear.

Chapter 13 ───

A SHAKY CABLE CAR WASN'T the ideal place to examine a stab wound. But I had no choice.

I freed the accent belt from my frock and slipped it around Kent's leg. With a jerk, I cinched it tight.

He sucked in a breath, his jaw hard.

"Sorry," I whispered. "I have to stop the flow." But my makeshift tourniquet wouldn't do any good if the blade had sliced an artery. If so, Kent could bleed out in less than five minutes. Rosalie Adams's ominous words about him dropping dead resurfaced. My gut clenched. Though now was not the time to dawdle. "I need to look at it."

He gave a tight nod, and with quick but precise movements, I ripped the tear in his trouser leg larger. The blood-soaked fabric gave way to my demand as I leaned in for a better glimpse.

The cabin lights were weak at best. Even in the dimness, I could see the gash was significant. Thankfully there were no telltale signs of any major vessels being severed. Relief trickled through me, but it was no match for the flooding dread. I'd once embraced premature hope, only to be crushed with loss. I shoved away the pressing guilt and examined the wound again. The area needed cleaning. Until then, I couldn't quite gauge the cut's depth.

A million questions rolled through my mind. Why had Kent been at the Terminal? Same reason as me? How had he gotten inside? What had gone wrong? But nothing took hold as much as the very real fact that he needed medical attention. I stole a quick glance out the window. "Bond Street's ahead. The hospital—"

"No." His dark lashes fluttered open, and he peered at me through the haze of pain. "My flat's closer."

My brows edged higher. Given our current location, if we got off at the next stop, we'd be less than two blocks away. Yet that wasn't what surprised me. I hadn't realized he still lived in that studio apartment above a cigar shop. The one he'd taken me to on our wedding night. I almost pressed a hand to the searing ache in my chest. I thought I'd buried these feelings in the graveyard of my memories. Dead. Nothing left but the skeletal wisps of forgotten dreams. But the idea of returning to the very place we'd sealed our union had pulsed everything back to life. "You need to see a doctor."

His eyes clenched shut. "Can't."

I nearly growled in frustration. But I couldn't be angry. Because I knew. I fully understood his reasoning. LeRaffa's goons must know they'd injured him. By now they'd alerted their enormous underground network to be on the lookout for any man admitted into a hospital with a stab wound. Moreover, knife and gun injuries had to be reported. With the majority of policemen accepting graft money, the odds of the dispatched officer being on LeRaffa's payroll was high. Going to the hospital could prove just as dangerous as his wound. I hated the corruptness, but I hated being forced into this position even more. I couldn't attend to Kent. He had no idea what I'd gone through more than a year ago.

By the time the cable car approached the next stop, Kent was already clambering to his feet. With a resigned sigh, I supported his weight, and we managed to exit into the crisp night air. His arm draping my shoulder and mine circling his waist, we hobbled toward his flat.

"Sorry for the imposition." Kent's words were conversational, breezy even, but his voice rasped with pain.

What would've happened had I not been there? LeRaffa's men would've caught him. I didn't want to imagine what they would've done to him.

As if listening to my thoughts, Kent squeezed my shoulder. "I owe you one."

I said nothing. I didn't want anything from him. Not anymore. Long ago I'd desired more from him than he'd been willing to give. It had been a foolish whim of a silly girl who didn't exist anymore.

After a challenging block-and-a-half trek, the flight of steps leading to Kent's door nearly did us in. Sweat dotting my brow, I skimmed Kent's trouser pocket for his key. Stumbling into his apartment at two in the morning with his arm curling around me wouldn't exactly be good for my reputation, but I recalled he'd chosen this flat because of its discreet location. Probably the reason he still lived here. I, above anyone else, knew how much the man prized his privacy.

One step inside, and nostalgia hit. The last time I'd crossed this threshold I'd been leaving with no hope of ever returning. My life had been in shambles. My heart even more so. I shoved aside the taunting thoughts and helped Kent to his bed, still situated on the left side of the room.

I ripped the torn trouser the rest of the way, exposing his entire lower leg. His skin was crusted red. The bleeding had slowed but still oozed from the wound. He needed stitched up. And I'd be the one to do that. My fingers curled into a fist, as if refusing to take on the task that had gone so utterly wrong back in Pittsburgh.

"Look at you, wife." His eyelids drifted shut. "Throwing me in bed and ripping my clothes off."

Despite myself, I breathed a laugh. His remark was beyond ridiculous, but his playful words tugged me back from the dark recesses of my mind. Away from my failings. "Let's take your shoes and socks off, then I'll clean—"

"No."

"No what?" I reached for his foot, but like a toddler, he jerked away. "I have to clean your leg."

"Take off the shoes, but leave the socks on," he snapped, before adding, softer, "Please."

His adamancy surprised me. I realized I'd never glimpsed his bare feet. Even during our only intimate time, the room had been dark. What was so awful he didn't want me to see? Or maybe the pain was getting to him, making him more delirious? Either way, I couldn't waste any more time than I already had. "I need to clean your leg." And find something to numb the pain. Because while he seemed lucid, the second I drove a needle through his skin, he'd be begging for relief. That was, if I could even locate a needle and thread.

Cleaning the wound was top priority. And sadly what I needed, I couldn't get. Alcohol would work to both sterilize the cut and numb his sensitivities, but that was nearly impossible. Sure, I could visit one of New York's thousands of gin joints. I'd just been in one! But even the Terminal no doubt watered down their alcohol. And I needed something potent to fight off infection.

My gut clenched, but I wouldn't acknowledge the pressing fear. I glanced over to find Kent watching me.

"There's a medical kit in the closet." He opened his mouth, then shut it, as if debating his words. "Our wedding gift's there too."

I shot to my feet and rushed to the corner of his studio flat. I slid open the pocket door, and my gaze connected not only with the metal medical kit on the floor but a jug of moonshine. Kent had kept it all this time? The elderly farmer who'd given us a ride in his wagon to the train station after our ceremony had also been a backwoods moonshiner. As a wedding present, he'd gifted us a generous sample of his latest batch. Even during those rash moments four years ago, Kent and I hadn't been brave enough to try it, both of us aware of the dangers of guzzling bad liquor. But I couldn't question it now.

I set the moonshine on the floor by the bed. Cracking open the kit, I browsed its meager contents. There were a couple of rolls of bandages. A pair of scissors. Tweezers. And the bluntest needle known to humankind. No thread. I darted to the bathroom and opened his medicine cabinet. Okay, no help here. The shelves held his shaving kit, extra soap, and a few combs. My gaze landed on a small tin canister.

Dentotape Flat Dental Floss Silk.

That could work. The lid specified twelve yards. If this dental floss was truly made of silk, it could possibly hold better than regular thread. I grabbed it, as well as the shaving kit, and returned to my patient.

"Kent." I lifted the moonshine. "I'm going to pour this on your leg. But first you need to drink as much as you can."

His gaze flicked between me and the alcohol. "That might kill me."

"Possibly." I tugged the cork free and sniffed the open jug. Strong indeed. "Which is why I think we should risk taking you to a clinic."

"No."

Stubborn man. "Fine." I held it to his lips. "Then drink up."

He took a swig and started coughing. No doubt it tasted like turpentine. But this moonshine was a jug of mercy. Without the alcohol, it'd be nothing short of torture pouring the rest of its contents on his gaping wound, then digging through his skin with a dull needle.

After he drank a good amount, I rearranged the pillows behind him so he could rest easier. I focused on keeping everything as sterile as I could, starting with the needle. Once satisfied, I picked up the jug. Kent braced himself, clutching the sides of the mattress. I inhaled, tilted the jug, and . . . froze.

The emotion I'd been struggling to avoid pressed into me with a vengeful force. My hands trembled. My breath darted in and out of my chest in quick spurts. This situation proved too similar to the one that'd haunted me for so long. My vision grayed. At once I was back in the sickly glow of that mildewed basement, crimson stains burning into the cracks of my fingers. And those eyes—so like my own—blinking up at me in agony.

I now pressed a hand to my thundering heart, unable to shake the suffocating failure.

My mind knew I was overreacting. Kent's wound wasn't nearly as critical as my birth father's, but still . . . there was a risk. And fear had a way of stretching long shadows over my reasoning, keeping me from the clarity I desperately needed.

I slid my eyes shut. A hot tear leaked out. I dashed it away, only for my fingers to be caught in a warm hand.

Kent's.

I'd thought he'd be halfway into oblivion by now, but his gaze locked on mine, his eyes saying more than words could, offering comfort in those tender gray depths. He didn't know what had happened back in Pittsburgh. Only two people knew the full truth, and one was now dead. Because of me. I gently squeezed Kent's hand and released. Before I emptied the entire container on his leg, I exhaled a shuddered breath. My heart longed to pour itself out in prayer, to ask the Almighty for help. I'd counted on my own strength and ability for as long as I could remember, but now I feared my stubbornness might also become my ruin.

Because I already had the blood of one man staining my soul.

I couldn't bear Kent's too.

● ● ●

I gave Kent a folded cloth to chomp down on and emptied the moonshine on his wound.

His anguished groan tore into me. I hated adding to his pain, but I refused to take any chances that could encourage infection.

With most of the blood cleared away, I inspected the cut. Though deep, it wasn't as long as I'd first thought, less than two inches or so. I shaved the surrounding area, not entirely certain if necessary, but again, would rather err on the side of caution.

Kent had mercifully passed out, leaving me with the care of his body. His leg was as toned and muscled as I remembered. It matched the rest of him. Strong. Capable. Yet as I now looked at him, I frowned at his pale complexion. Just how much blood had he lost?

I threaded the needle with the floss and gave it a good tug, testing its strength. For the next half hour, I concentrated on stitching him up. By the time I finished, I was trembling all over. Be it adrenaline, nerves, or the overwhelming relief that the bleeding had stopped, I couldn't be certain. But I was certain I was an utter mess. My arms, hands, beneath my fingernails were all speckled red. My frock had been stained as well.

I had no choice but to wash up and change. Though into what? My chemise and bloomers were probably okay, but I didn't want Kent to awaken and find me half-naked. It didn't matter that we were legally still married—I refused to open that closed door. After snatching a soft shirt from his closet, I filled the tub and sank into the warm water. My muscles practically screamed with relief. I soaked in the moment's peace, until I realized I had to use Kent's soap. It astounded me that even while asleep in the other room, awareness of him surrounded me. His scent now on my skin, tangling my senses. Soon his shirt would be wrapping my body. Thoughts of him bombarded my mind. It was like some sort of alluring siege. An all-out invasion. How long before Kent Brisbane scaled the walls of my heart as well?

I almost sank beneath the water, if only to drown out the murmurs of longing coming to life within me. But I couldn't dawdle. I needed to rest. Perhaps my defenses would be stronger come morning.

I dried off and pulled his shirt over me. The hem hit about four inches above my knee. Scandalous by society's standard, but it couldn't be helped. Besides, Kent had seen my legs . . . and much more.

With that unhelpful thought spiraling through me, I rinsed out my frock in the remaining bathwater, then reentered the main room. Kent was still out cold. I checked my stitching job, wishing there was more I could do, my frail fortitude wanting more reassurance he'd be okay. Which for some reason poked my frayed nerves. This entire situation was unfair. Unfair to be in a circumstance ghostly similar to the one that had nearly broken me. Unfair to be so depleted when I needed every scrap of strength. And unfair to force me to tend to the man who'd dashed my heart in the very room he'd once cradled it so intimately.

But what else could've been done?

With a heavy sigh, I exchanged the cloth beneath his leg with a fresh one, checked his wound again, then crawled up in bed beside him.

SOMEONE TOUCHED ME.

I jolted awake and reached for the gun beneath my pillow. Only I wasn't in my bed, and my reflexive lurching put me in a terrible position—sprawled across a man's chest.

Kent's.

Last night's events flashed. The Terminal. Finding Kent. His injury. The stitches. I'd slept light at first, rising every hour to check the bleeding. I didn't know when I'd fallen into a heavy slumber, but I wished I hadn't. If only to avoid this current circumstance with my body currently draping Kent's.

"Morning, Vinny." His low drawl held the gruff residue of sleep. "I didn't mean to wake you, but your hand started to get . . . curious."

I flushed, because, sure enough, my fingers had slipped beneath his shirt, a warm abdomen beneath my palm. "Sorry," I mumbled, and peeled my traitorous hand, along with the rest of me, off my husband's torso. Over the years, I'd found myself in dangerous situations, but this was a different kind of threat altogether. Because Kent's tousled hair, rumpled shirt, and slow-building smile held a lethal appeal that had me scooting to the far edge of the bed opposite him.

"How do you feel?" Needing more distance, I stood and trained my gaze on a blank spot on the wall, my back to him. I needed to examine his leg, but I gathered a few extra breaths to clear my riotous head.

When he didn't answer, I turned and found his hot gaze sweeping over me.

My hand went to my collar and pinched it shut, as if I'd exposed more flesh than just my lower neck. "I had to borrow your shirt."

His lips hitched into a roguish smile. "I'm not complaining." He pushed up with his palms, as if to rise, but I darted to him.

"Don't move." I pinned him with my glare. "You need to keep still."

"I only wanted to sit up more, Knuckles." He glanced at my hand, which I'd unknowingly curled into a fist. "I know better than to cross you."

"Let me help then." I propped up the pillows behind his back, then looked at his leg. The floss had held. The bleeding stopped. The flesh was swollen around the stitches, but that was to be expected. My hand went to his forehead to check for a fever, which would indicate the onset of infection. His skin was cool. I understood infection usually would develop within the first week, so he wasn't exactly in the clear. My eyes slid shut with a relieved exhale nonetheless.

His fingers swept over mine, and he tugged them to his chest, keeping them captive. I shot him a glare, a scold dancing on my lips, but his face held a tenderness that stalled my pulse.

He gently squeezed my fingers. "Thank you. For everything."

I nodded. He didn't know what this had cost me, which was why I needed away from here. From him. "I understand why you didn't want to go to the medic centers, but you really need a doctor to make certain this heals right." I kept my voice from trembling, which I counted a success. If my birth father had been treated, would things have gone differently?

But Kent was already shaking his head. "Can't."

I tugged my hand from his. "Surely there's a doctor who won't rat you out to LeRaffa." Hundreds of physicians worked in the city—all we needed was one who was honest. But how to find them?

His head tilted. "Is this your way of saying you don't want be my nurse?"

"I can't." For so many reasons. "I can't stay here. It's not proper."

"You're my wife."

"Which no one knows."

"They could," he challenged.

Did he even realize what he was saying? Perhaps his remark could be blamed on the lingering moonshine in his system. "Listen, what about Dr. Ewing? You just met him at Hemswick, but I've known him for years."

"You trust him?"

Did I? The older man had never given me reason to question him. I couldn't imagine a principled man like Otis Ewing stuffing his pockets with mobster money. He was wealthy on his own accord. "Do you truly think LeRaffa's men would still be after you? Tell me what happened."

He shifted, and I almost pressed my hand on his shoulder to still him, only to realize he'd tugged something from his trouser pocket. He needed out of his clothes, which by now must be stiff from dried blood. That was the only part still unsanitary. But I wasn't about to change the man's pants. For that reason alone he needed Dr. Ewing.

"What's that?" I nodded at the paper in his hand.

"I scouted the area of the Terminal all day yesterday. That was how I found the second entrance. Not nearly as guarded as the main one. I got in undetected and found LeRaffa's office down a stretch from the gin joint. Apparently his men didn't appreciate me searching their boss's headquarters. Throwing knives is a lot quieter than shooting bullets." He held out the paper to me. "But I got the prize. See for yourself."

I took the paper from his warm fingers and opened it up. It was a handwritten receipt stating an exorbitant sum, no doubt what Adele Thayer had owed LeRaffa. They'd both signed it. "This is what LeRaffa took from her flat. He didn't want the police to know she was mixed up with him."

"How do you know this?"

"I was searching Miss Thayer's bedroom when LeRaffa walked in." I relayed the story of my hiding in the closet and seeing the cigarette case. "I confronted him about it last night, and he told me he only wanted the receipt."

Kent's gaze darkened on me. Perhaps he wasn't keen on my being in a strange bedroom with a notorious lecher. But it wasn't as if LeRaffa had known I was there. Any objection Kent might have, he decided not to voice it.

"But why would he take the receipt?" he said. "Especially if her death was ruled a suicide. It makes his actions more suspicious."

"I agree." I lowered onto the mattress, careful not to brush his leg. "One would think he would want the authorities to find it. Because if the ruling would happen to shift to murder, this receipt removes any motive from LeRaffa. He got his money, so there's no reason to kill her." I set the paper on the bedside table.

"Maybe, like you said, he didn't want any traces linked back to him."

I considered all the scenarios. "I don't think they were lovers. He didn't speak like a man besotted by her charms. Though he *did* mention she came from a family associated with the Galleanists. I think that's the best lead to go on. He implied her old connections are important."

"Really?" His voice lowered, something hinting in his tone. "The man seemed to confide in you. A legendary crime boss known for his formidable ways, yet he speaks so candidly with you. Makes me wonder if he was besotted by *your* charms."

I folded my arms. "Doubt that had anything to do with it."

He shrugged, unconvinced.

"How did you know about the Terminal to begin with?" His gaze darted away, and my suspicions rose. "Out with it."

"Just one of my sources."

"Is your *source* of the female variety?" Then it hit me. "The secretary at Wallace Stratton's modeling agency." That haughty woman had been the one who'd first mentioned the subway with a knowing look in her eyes. I didn't need Kent's confirmation to know I'd guessed correctly. I bet that was the appointment he'd rushed off to the day I'd visited his office. "Speaking of others being besotted by charm."

"I didn't charm her," he grumbled. "She volunteered the information."

"Same with LeRaffa." I met his challenge, then nearly laughed. "We're being ridiculous."

"It usually happens when I'm around you. You have this maddening way of robbing my sanity." He winced then, and I didn't think it had anything to do with our squabble.

"You're in pain."

"It's not my leg." He draped an arm over his forehead. "It's the blasted moonshine. A sledgehammer hitting my temples is preferable to this."

I moved to the bathroom and pulled out the headache wafers I'd found last night in the medicine cabinet. "Here. Take this." A pitcher of water and a glass sat on the bedside table. I poured and handed the glass to him, along with some wafers. "You guzzled a lot last night. I'm surprised you can even think clearly."

"Strongest stuff I'd ever tasted. I wasn't a hundred percent sure I'd wake up again." He took a long swig of water and popped the wafer into his mouth.

"I'm glad you did" was all I could say. Because I'd certainly been nervous he wouldn't. I had no idea how much blood he'd lost. His complexion hadn't returned to its normal coloring. He needed more rest. "I'll contact Dr. Ewing and ask him to visit. You don't have to explain you were stabbed. Just say you got injured and I tried to sew you up."

He handed me back the glass, his fingers brushing mine. "I can manage, Vinny. You've done more than I could ask."

"Do you have someone who can stay with you? What about Warren Hayes?" Weren't they more like brothers than friends? Surely the newspaper tycoon could spare a couple of days to help Kent.

"He's at his country home." He laid his head back against the pillow. "Don't worry about me. I've been in worse scrapes than this."

Indecision swept through me as I escaped to the bathroom. My frock, which I'd draped over the tub, was still slightly damp from my quick soaking. The blood hadn't entirely washed out. But it would have to do. I dressed and folded Kent's shirt. My tired eyes met me in the mirror's reflection. I'd revisited a nightmare last night, and everything in me screamed to run out the door and not look back. Kent had basically told me I could leave. Dismissal marked his tone. Though could I go? Caging in a sigh, I returned to the main room, hoping Kent might have dozed off. He hadn't. His solemn gaze was fixed on the ceiling.

As if sensing my presence, he lolled his head to the side, peering at me beneath hooded lids. My hesitation must've been easily read, for he gave a soft smile. "I'm fine, Vinny. Really. I shouldn't have put you in this position in the first place."

But who else did he have? Warren was out of town. He didn't have any other relatives. Though I suppose . . . I was his family.

The thought sobered me. I could easily telephone Dr. Ewing, but who was to say if I arranged for him to come that Kent wouldn't turn him away. Or even answer the door. My husband wasn't one for relying on others. Even last night, he'd initially told me to leave. Mostly because LeRaffa's men were chasing him. But even if the goons weren't an issue, I doubted he'd have asked for my help with his injury had I not forced him to accept it.

I glanced at his leg. These first few days of healing were crucial. Infection was presently a bigger threat than the stab wound. An unexpected sting of tears made me turn away. Secrets billowed between us like enormous flames, threatening to consume us. But as with all fires, there were also sparks. And right now those little flickers of heat terrified me. I couldn't deny my attraction to him, just as I couldn't leave his side.

So for better or for worse, I would stay.

● ● ●

Around noon, I did have to leave, though only with the intention of returning quickly.

I stopped by my flat to discreetly gather some clothes and other needed items. While there, I asked Paulo to keep an eye on my apartment. When I exited Park Towers, a ghostly sensation crawled over me. I was being watched. I tossed a glance over my shoulder in time to see a shadowy form disappear behind the corner of the complex. No question I was being tailed. With swift but casual strides, I moved toward the area my car had been parked. My arms were burdened with my belongings to take to Kent's, but if necessary, I'd drop it all to retrieve my weapon from my purse. I dumped my things onto the passenger seat of my car, started the engine, and took off.

My next stop was to be Hemswick. I endeavored to snatch a medical encyclopedia from Father's library—a true sign of my desperation— and to ensure Mother was faring well. I'd intended to spend the entire day with her, but as things were with Kent, I couldn't risk being away for long. However, since I was being watched, I decided to be extra cautious and take the longer, more complicated route to see Mother.

Once confident I was no longer being followed, I pulled into Hemswick's drive and rushed inside. I needn't be concerned about Mother craving my company, because her parlor was crammed with people. Some were friends from church. Others were those she played cards with. My gaze caught on Dr. Ewing. I was tempted to beg him to accompany me back to Kent's flat, but refrained. Kent wouldn't appreciate a roomful of strangers knowing he'd been injured. Though I highly doubted any person here had connections to LeRaffa.

I claimed the space between Mother and the minister's wife on the scroll-legged sofa. I wasn't fully seated when Mother dove into conversation. "I was hoping you'd stop by today." Despite her bland tone, she had that familiar gleam in her eyes, putting me on my guard. "I invited our new neighbor for tea, but he was currently busy."

I didn't miss her subtle emphasis on the word *he*. She didn't seem to expect a response, and I certainly didn't want to encourage the conversation.

Yet she continued anyway. "Mr. Dashell inherited the home from his uncle." She sipped her tea, regarding me over the brim of her dainty cup. "He came by this morning to meet me. I discovered he's only a couple of years older than you. He's quite handsome."

I kept my expression placid, but my mind scrambled for a way to stop the inevitable.

"Since he couldn't come to tea, I invited him to the Palace Theater on Friday."

"Mother, we only have two tickets." And I wasn't entirely certain I could attend with her at all. It depended on how Kent's leg was healing. Hopefully, by that time he'd be past the threat of danger.

"I know." A small, mischievous smile graced her face. "I'm giving him mine."

No, not good. As if the past twelve hours hadn't been emotionally draining, dealing with a wounded-yet-stubborn husband, I could now add a scheming mother to the mix. It wasn't like I could explain to Mother that I refused to step out with a gentleman because I legally belonged to another. I still needed to have that conversation with Kent. "I'm not going with a stranger. Just give Mr. Dashell both tickets." Despite my aggravation, I kissed her cheek. "I need to leave."

"So soon? Are you working on a case?"

"Yes." Not exactly a lie. "I'll check back soon."

"But what about Friday?"

"Sorry, Mother. I can't."

"Delvina." Disapproval marked her tone, as if I were seven and she'd caught me filching scones from the kitchen. "I know you aren't keen on my matchmaking but—"

Mrs. Ida Elliot approached, and I'd never been so relieved for her interruption. I secretly wished Mother would play the role of cupid with Ida, matching her friend with some eligible mister. Though Ida was only in her forties, she might not wish to marry again, considering her late husband wasn't an attentive one. I shook off the thought and gladly surrendered my seat. Within seconds Ida had fully commanded Mother's attention, discussing plans for an upcoming bridge game. I said my goodbyes. The path to the exit brought me past Dr. Ewing, giving me an idea. If Kent refused care from doctors, I could still get help indirectly.

The doctor perched on the chair by the door, his fingers curled around a cigarette. His gaze went to mine, then lowered to the book I was holding. He nodded his approval. "That's a good volume."

"I'm trying to expand my knowledge, but I'm curious on the proper care for wounds. This edition says open air is the best healer." I made that up. I hadn't even cracked open the book yet. "But I always heard it's best to keep injuries covered. Funny how the same topic can have contradictory remedies."

Mother eyed me suspiciously. She knew I didn't voluntarily read anything. But I ignored her sneaking glances and determined to listen to every word Dr. Ewing said.

"No open air. Too prone for infection." He blew out a stream of smoke and stubbed out the rest of his cigarette on the ashtray on the side table. "Antiseptic plaster. That's the way to go."

My heart sank. I'd used the antiseptic plaster before, and it hadn't been strong enough.

"Or . . ." Ida piped up from her place beside Mother. "You can use honey. It fights bacteria and promotes healing."

Dr. Ewing sniffed. "An old wives' tale, that one. Modern medicine has progressed past such."

She notched her chin higher. "I'm an expert in the ancient practice of medicine. Almost from the earliest times, honey has been the best form of treatment because it provides a natural barrier and keeps the wound moist. Modern medicine shouldn't negate the tried and true."

So as Ida predictably waxed on about her family being a credit to the medical world, I made my escape. Though her suggestion made me retrace my route to the library and exchange the medical encyclopedia for the one on natural remedies and herbal cures. While the woman exasperated me, I trusted her judgment. During a stretch of my youth, she'd tutored me on ancient treatments and even tribal surgeries. It had been fascinating until she'd started testing me on the material as if I'd intended to open my own practice at the ripe age of fifteen.

Though I was grateful for her knowledge because I now recognized the error in wanting Dr. Ewing to treat Kent. The man would've no doubt used plasters, and the very idea churned my stomach.

I returned to Kent's flat and nearly jumped out of my skin at him standing up and hobbling away from his dresser. "What are you doing?" I barely refrained from yelling. But seriously, the man had been stabbed less than twenty-four hours ago.

"Ah." He sighed happily. "I've missed you and your scolding."

"Lie back down. Now." I gently placed my items on the ground and rushed to him. "Put your weight on me." He obeyed because he had no choice.

Thankfully, it was only a few steps to the bed. He settled on the mattress.

"Let me have another look. Hopefully, the wound didn't reopen." I didn't try to keep the annoyance from my tone.

"I was only changing." His grin unleashed. "Perhaps I should've waited and let you do the honors."

Despite his maddening remark, guilt tugged. I probably should've assisted him into a fresh set of clothes before I'd left. But there was nothing I could do now. I assessed the stitches. Thankfully, they held. "Stay put." I lightly jabbed a finger into his chest. "I'm going to put a salve on your cut."

I moved to my bags and grabbed the jar of honey I'd swiped from Mother's pantry. After washing my hands, I poured a good amount of the fragrant, oozing liquid onto his wound. I hoped I made the right choice in choosing the honey over the plasters.

Kent huffed a laugh. "Now if we only had some tea and biscuits."

My gaze narrowed at his amused eyes. "Don't mock."

His face quickly sobered. "I was trying to lighten everything. I feel so silly, you having to tend to me like a child."

"Don't thank me yet," I snapped, then regretted it. But I couldn't bear any gratitude. I didn't deserve it.

His hand cupped mine. "What's the matter?"

"Nothing."

"That doesn't sound like nothing."

"Forget it." I fumbled putting the lid back on the honey, then nearly dropped the jar. With a low growl, I set the jar on the bed and finally met Kent's concerned gaze. "Last night stirred up some bad memories. I had to stitch my birth father's wound." Regret pooled in the base of my stomach. "He died because of me."

His brow furrowed. "I thought Big Dante shot him."

He referred to the rival gangster and the falling out that had ended my birth father's life. "He did." I nodded. "But my birth father wasn't long for the world, and I'm to blame."

He didn't say anything, but his grip strengthened on my hand, offering comfort. That was what he'd do. If words failed him, he'd show his support through touch. And it nearly unraveled me.

"Big Dante shot him on two occasions." I tried to strip the emotion from my tone, yet failed. "The first time sent him into hiding because he was wanted for murder." Though my birth father had been innocent, there'd been a nationwide manhunt. "He couldn't go to the hospital. So I dug the bullet from his shoulder and sewed him up." I bit my lip, keeping it from quivering. "But then he struggled with infection. It had made him weak and . . ." I shook my head. "If Big Dante's second bullet didn't kill him, the infection would've."

"Which is why you're taking my wound seriously."

"Yes." I huffed a humorless laugh. "But you never take anything seriously, so what's the point?"

His thumb brushed my knuckles in rhythmic strokes, drawing my gaze to his. "I take things more seriously than you realize."

"Like what?" I scoffed. "Name one thing."

He didn't hesitate. "Like us."

"What about us?"

"I think we should give things another try."

Chapter 15 ———————————————————————

MY HEART BEAT AN UNTAMED song in my chest as I waited for Kent's teasing grin to unleash. Or for his eyes to dance with laughter. But those silver flecks flashed among the stormy gray hues, deepening with intensity the longer he watched me.

"Are you serious, Kent?" Ironic, since I'd just accused him only seconds ago of being incapable of it.

"I am."

The deep rumble of his voice sent chills along my skin.

"I want to prove I can be the husband you deserve." The determination in his set jaw coupled with the smooth delivery of his words almost convinced me. But there were things a woman just didn't forget. Judging by the way Kent's eyes touched my face almost in tender fascination, it seemed he had no memory of the failings between us.

I waited until I was certain my voice wouldn't shake, then asked, "Do you need reminding how things went the first time?"

"It depends." His brows raised in a curious bend. "Which part would you like to remind me of?"

To my satisfaction I didn't flush, which had probably been his motive, given the husky insinuation in his voice. I was about to scold him, but he surprised me by cupping my face.

"I remember, Vinny." His knuckle trailed the line of my throat and skimmed my birthmark. For some unknown reason, he'd once adored my biggest blemish. Given the way his eyes tracked the brush of his hand, perhaps he still did. "Will you give me another chance?" he murmured. "Give us a chance?"

I shouldn't let him touch me like this. The gentle graze of his fingers was only on the base of my neck, but it felt intimate. Like a secret between lovers. "What will change?" I rallied my defenses. I couldn't fall under his charming trance. "You completely shut me out."

He dropped his hand to his lap. "I know."

I expected a mountain of excuses or complete silence on the matter, but instead he owned his mistake. Could he have changed? "Does this mean you'll tell me?" I leveled my gaze on him. "Everything?"

He glanced away. "Let's discuss us first."

"This is discussing us," I countered. "You won't ever be faithful to me when you're committed to your secrets."

He opened his mouth, then slammed it shut.

I waited for his explanation, but he suddenly seemed more interested in a spot on his bedside table than continuing this discussion. "You're proving my point." I gestured at his mute face. "You ask for a chance? I'm sorry, but I can't. How can you expect to work things out when you give me nothing to *work* with?" I launched to my feet, glad I'd left my things by the door, because I wouldn't be staying here any longer than necessary. In fact, I could leave the honey for Kent to apply himself and repeatedly check on him throughout the following days, allowing me to return to my flat. Whatever Kent had in his mind about rekindling our relationship obviously wasn't going to happen. Not unless he offered more than he'd been holding back. And he was nowhere close.

"Vinny, wait." He looked as if to stand, but at my glare, he thought better of it and held up a hand. "If we divorce through proper channels this time, it will be public."

Yes, it would. I wasn't thrilled about filing or appearing in court, but there was no way around it. The entire process would be tedious and lengthy. We could go to Reno, but even in the divorce capital of America, it would take six months.

"If it was anyone but you, things might go quietly." He paused, as if considering his words. "But you've been a popular topic for the press lately."

He was right. Ever since word had leaked that I was Hugo Salvastano's daughter, I'd been under public scrutiny. I'd grown tired of hearing my name on the radio gossip hour, seeing my grainy face in news columns. It was like my life had become a broadcast serial drama, society awaiting the next installment. *Just what would Delvina Salvastano Kline do next?* The entire thing disgusted me and had taken a toll on Mother. Journalists knocking on her door at all hours. The unending ring of the telephone.

There'd been a time she couldn't leave the house. Mother hadn't been able to attend her husband's funeral without getting bombarded by the press. It'd pained me she couldn't grieve in peace. Things had swayed somewhat in my favor since Marianne VanKirk's rescue, but I could easily predict the scandalous rumors to renew if Kent and I divorced.

Could I put Mother through that again? I sat on the edge of the mattress, doubt sinking into me. "I usually don't care if the newshounds bite, but Mother endured a lot of heartache recently. I'm afraid this would break her." A weary sigh escaped my lips. "I can't do that to her again. Only that would mean . . ."

"Remaining married."

A thrill ran down my spine, but I attributed it to nerves. And *only* nerves. I worried about Mother. She'd be hurt I'd kept this secret from her, though she couldn't exactly fault me since she'd withheld the truth about my birth parents for two decades. "I suspect Mother would rather see my name in the paper for being quietly married than publicly divorced. But then again, no matter what we do, I'm going to disappoint her. Since I was a girl, she's always envisioned my wedding ceremony." Something I hadn't considered during those rash moments of our elopement. At that time I'd been blinded by the hurt my parents' secrecy had caused. Though now I could see clearly. "She'll be crushed knowing there will be no wedding."

"Then we have one."

"Pardon?"

"Your mother wants you to have a ceremony, then let's do it."

Just like that? My head had been spinning nonstop since Kent had announced he'd like to remain married, yet he reclined on his bed all casual and unfazed, as if he'd had ages to think this through. "It's not that simple."

"Yes, it is. If we're going to try to fix our marriage, we have to make it public somehow, right? The best thing to do is control our own publicity."

A derisive laugh ripped from my lips. "I've never had a say in anything." From years ago with those dumb articles rating me as a debutante, to when news broke about the Klines not being my natural parents, to recently with the slander about my being a mobster's daughter, I'd had no influence regarding what was printed about me.

Kent's face softened, as if reading my thoughts. "You just need to know the right people. So happens, my best friend owns one of the leading presses. We invite his paper to our small ceremony and let the power of the press announce our marriage."

"I can't let Mother think we're just *now* marrying. I'm done with that lie."

"No, we'll tell her the truth. As soon as my commanding officer gives me orders that I can march again like a good soldier, we'll go speak with her. Then like I said, we'll have a wedding."

He was right. We needed a way to announce our relationship, but this was all happening at a dizzying pace. I pressed a finger to my pounding temple. "Kent, let's stop and think this through. Are we actually considering staying married only to avoid divorce? Avoid scandal? That's madness, isn't it?"

He shrugged, as if we debated on what we should eat for dinner instead of a decision that would determine the rest of our lives. "Marriages have been built on less."

"That's not helpful."

"What about this?" He gently swept up my hand in his. "Do you despise me?"

I considered his question, sorting through all the emotions. Hurt by him? Yes. Angry at his behavior? Certainly. But hate? "No. I don't."

"That's something." He brushed a kiss across my fingers, as if I'd just declared my undying affection for him rather than confessing I didn't loathe his soul.

I rolled my eyes, ignoring the rush of heat beneath his lingering touch. "Me not hating you isn't the issue. It's everything else. I don't know if I can do this again. Because if history repeats itself, so help me, Kent—"

"I'll tell you."

My pulse leaped. "Everything?"

"Yes." His Adam's apple bobbed, as if this conversation was physically painful. "One question a night. I'm going to hate this, but I hate even more that I've let secrets come between us in the first place."

His tone was apologetic. While I appreciated he accepted fault in our ruined marriage, I didn't miss the sly way he proposed this little arrangement. "You just said *each night* I can ask a question, which makes me assume I'm to stay here to get my answers?" I figured after his wound healed, I'd return to my flat until this supposed wedding ceremony. Leave it to Kent to angle for more with the perfect bait. Answers. I could finally pluck the truth from the shadows of our past. But at what cost? Would Kent confirm what I'd seen that afternoon at Penn Station? Did I truly want to know?

"Yes." His voice broke into my thoughts. "I want you with me, Vinny."

My stomach fluttered. "As a married couple."

"Because we are."

"What will I have to do to earn these answers?"

His smile grew slowly. "Why, Knuckles, what ever could you mean?"

"You know exactly what I mean. What do you demand of me physically?"

All teasing dropped from his face. "I demand nothing. If there's to be any sort of touching . . ." He stacked his palms behind his head as he relaxed against the pillows. "From now on, you initiate it. I'll only

155

touch you where you touch me first. So if you grab my hand, I can hold yours. If you plant one on my lips, I have that same liberty."

"That's the rule then?" I eyed him skeptically. "You won't touch me unless I touch you first?"

"Easy as that." He nodded, and there it was, that wicked smile that sent fire up my spine. "Unless you feel you won't be able to keep your hands off me."

"I think I'll manage." According to him, I set the boundaries. I asked the questions. Yet there was a catch. I had to remain with him. I'd only planned to stay until his wound had healed, but this new agreement placed me within his reach indefinitely. Not to mention, there was also to be a wedding ceremony in my near future.

"What do you say, Vinny? Should we give it a go?" He tossed back the question he'd so flippantly asked at Mother's dinner party.

I could imagine a thousand ways this venture could go wrong, but my heart dared me to hope. And I was never one to refuse a dare. "Okay, Kent. I accept your terms."

Surprised pleasure sparked in his eyes. "Then it's a deal, Mrs. Brisbane."

"Don't get too comfortable. I'm ready to cash in on my allotted question." I shouldn't take enjoyment at his dropped smile. He needed to realize I intended to test this little arrangement. If he truly resented allowing secrets to come between us, he needed to prove it. "What happened the morning of our wedding day?" I'd burst into his office with a shattered heart, but he'd been noticeably distressed even before he'd met my tear-stricken eyes. I believed whatever had occurred had been significant.

He raked a hand over his face, gaze averted.

"Already planning to back out of our agreement?"

"Not at all." He exhaled. "It's just that after I tell you, you're going to have more questions. I promise I'll get through it all, but . . ."

"You want to go slow."

"Please, love."

He hadn't called me *love* since our wedding night. I knew my husband was a man of many secrets, and I could be patient if it meant uncovering them all. "I understand what you're asking. I'll respect it. But this has gone on unanswered long enough. What happened, Kent?"

Chapter 16

Kent
1920

THIS LOOKED LIKE THE PLACE.

I was familiar with this area of Manhattan. I'd once been hired to trail a local attorney who had an office on this very street. The man's father-in-law had been convinced the lawyer was a cheating scoundrel, only to discover he had needed a second job to keep up with his new wife's extravagant spending habits. Across the street from this fellow's practice stood a quaint café—the place I was expected to meet Kit Mason, my mother.

I paused at the door beneath a dark green awning trembling in the early fall breeze. In a few moments, I could have answers to lifelong questions. My earliest memories hadn't been spent in a mother's arms, but on a damp floor. No soothing lullabies had met my young ears, but the cries of hungry mouths. I was never a child. I was a number. One of the hundreds of thousands who'd been abandoned at birth. And all I wanted to know was why.

With a shake of my head, I entered the café, the strong scents of bacon and coffee greeting me. I wasn't the sort to get nervous. I'd deadened that sense shortly after I'd worked up the courage to leave the children's home for a life on the streets. Those days had served to numb any sensitivities. It had proven a survival instinct necessary for the time, but lately those calluses seemed to have softened and left me vulnerable. I blamed Delvina Kline. Her teasing smile, her entrancing wit. It wasn't charm as much as it was her essence. There was an innocence about her that contrasted her reckless streak. She was gentle yet wild. It didn't make sense. But it was a fascinating combination that lured me.

Even now I lingered on the fringe of the most significant appointment of my life, and she continued to steal my thoughts. The little thief didn't know the power she wielded.

I scanned the area, searching for a middle-aged woman. A few older gentlemen gathered around the long counter, sipping coffee and complaining about the dip in temperature. A table of women sat by the window. A line of booths along the back wall was filled with couples of various ages. But in the corner booth sat a lady I'd guess to be in her forties. A furrowed brow hovered above a taut expression.

My gut told me she was Kit Mason. The woman who'd answered Warren's ad. The woman who'd given me up.

I took an extra second to observe her. Her small hands fidgeted with a napkin. Her shoulders hunched against the wall, as if to make herself smaller, her countenance tight with nervous energy. As far as resemblance went, there wasn't any. Her pale yellow hair poked out from beneath a purple hat. From my standpoint, her eyes were also light. Her features were opposite mine in almost every way.

But that didn't mean anything. Perhaps I took after my father. It was strange to think I could discover more about him as well. If I'd bothered to hope for some kind of connection to the woman across the room, I would've been disappointed. I could be staring at the very woman who'd brought me into this world, and I felt nothing. My heartbeat was a routine thud in my chest. I wound my way through the maze of tables and approached.

Her eyes widened upon seeing me, almost like an animal caught in a trap.

"Ms. Mason?" I offered a friendly smile.

She nodded. "That would be how you'd know me" was all she replied. As a boy, I'd imagined her voice a thousand times, dreaming up soft tones and a gentle lilt. It seemed a perfect match to Ms. Mason's.

She didn't stand and embrace me. Her eyes didn't gloss with tears. Nothing to indicate she was relieved or emotional about meeting her son.

I gestured to the bench opposite hers. "May I join you?"

"Of course. Of course." She dropped the napkin into her lap, only to reclaim it and fuss with the edges.

"Thank you for agreeing to meet me." I sat and tried not to dwell on the enormity of the moment. This was the first time I had ever conversed with a family member. My mother. If I were the sentimental type, I'd wonder how often she'd thought of me over the years. Did she regret letting me go?

She offered a sad—sad?—smile. "It's the least I can do. You should know what happened." Something hinted in her tone.

I hadn't expected my birth story to be a joyous one, but the dread weighing her words put me on my guard. "Would you like to order first? I'd be honored if you'd allow me to purchase your meal."

She shook her head. "I'd only like a coffee, if that's okay."

"Certainly." I waved the waiter over and ordered us both coffees. Hopefully it was strong.

Her soft gaze roamed my face, and a gentle smile budded. "You grew up well."

There was a significant gap between the time she'd seen me last and now, consisting of numerous moments when I was certainly not well, but I was thankful to have survived the worst of days. I'd witnessed many who hadn't. "Thank you."

"I'm sure you have a lot of questions for me." Her heavy exhale stirred the strands of hair framing her narrow face. "Perhaps let me relay my side of things and why I did . . . what I did."

I could only nod.

"First of all, my name is not Kit Mason."

The waiter returned with two steaming mugs. Once he walked away, I gave her an encouraging smile. "I gathered as much."

She moved to pick up the cream pitcher and fumbled it, splashing some onto the table. "I'm a bit nervous."

"Nothing to be nervous about." I swiped up the spill with a napkin. "I know this is a bit awkward for us, but I'm thankful for this chance to reunite. You can imagine as a boy I always wondered if I'd get to meet my mother."

She blanched. "I think there's a misunderstanding."

"How so?"

"I'm not your mother."

I stared at her. I'd endeavored not to fully hope for a happy ending regarding my mother, but the searing ache in my chest proved I hadn't succeeded. "Then who exactly are you?"

"The one who took you from her."

"Wha—"

"I did so to keep you safe." Her hands fluttered, as if she was scared I'd accuse her of kidnapping. Which to be fair, wasn't out of the question. She leaned over her coffee, lowering her voice. "You were in danger, or else I wouldn't have acted so rash."

"What sort of danger? From my mother?" If I thought I had questions before, it was nothing compared to the ones stacking in my brain.

"I should start at the beginning." She stirred sugar into her coffee in fast swirls. "My name is Judith Long. When your mother knew me, my last name was Powell. You see, I was a nurse at an asylum for unwed mothers."

So that brought light to one shadowed matter. My mother hadn't been married.

"I was new at the asylum and eager to help, but I soon found out things weren't as they seemed."

I took a sip, barely tasting anything. "Meaning?"

"Have you heard of the San Francisco foundling asylum?"

"Yes." I set my coffee down, suddenly sick to my stomach. "It was shut down because infants were disappearing." My gaze sharpened on hers. "I was born there?" That place was completely across the country.

"No, but this one was run similarly." Sadness tinged her voice. "I didn't know. Most didn't. Especially the young mothers. Your mother admitted herself to the asylum when she was in advanced stages of expectancy. I'd taken care of her. She was young. Quiet." Her eyes met mine. "And terrified."

My chest squeezed. For so long my mother had been just some blurry image in my imagination, almost make-believe. Of course I knew I had a mother, considering the natural order of things, but she'd always been some distant figment of my mind. So while this woman hadn't been the one who'd borne me, she knew the one who had. It was a different sort of feeling.

"Your time was very near, and I'd run to get some fresh towels from storage." Her jaw tightened. "That was when I'd heard them."

"Who?"

"I don't rightly know. But it was a man. An angry, cruel man." Her gaze darkened, as if reliving the memory. "He was speaking with the asylum owners, and they were arranging . . ."

"Arranging what?"

"Your death."

My brows raised, but I said nothing. How could I? I hadn't a rational thought in my brain after what she'd just revealed. So I sat blinking at her, trying to grasp it all.

"You can imagine how shocked I was," she continued. "I thought the asylum was a respectable place, only to find out the truth. It frightened me, but more so, it angered me. Who could hurt an innocent babe? You see, your mother signed the register as May Freemont, but us nurses assumed it to be a false name. We suspected she was running from someone. Somehow this man had found her. So I ran to tell her about what I overheard."

I studied her mannerisms and listened intently for any signs of deceit. Though why would she lie about this? What would she gain by it?

"She begged me to take you. Told me to take the little money she had in her bag and take you far from there." Her eyes glossed over. "She said she planned to take you to the children's home in the city because she didn't have the means to care for you. So after the quick delivery, I took you to safety."

It was difficult to imagine the Rose Grove Children's Home as a haven, but considering what I'd just heard, perhaps it wasn't too far of a stretch. Though why would anyone want to harm me? Was this cruel man she'd spoken of my father? Someone else?

"She never had the chance to name you. I've always felt awful about that. A mother should name her child. Though she did get to hold you briefly before I ran away. I followed her instructions and gave you up at the children's home using the name Kit Mason."

I had known the children's home had named me. For that reason, I'd been acutely aware that if my mother had been searching for me, it would prove more difficult since she hadn't my name. I at least had Kit Mason. Which only turned out to be the woman across from me.

I reached into my pocket, withdrawing the brittle tag. "I have a piece of paper written by the person who turned me over to the home. Do you happen to know what it says?"

She recited it word for word. At least in that regard, she'd been truthful.

Surprise lingered in the lines of her face. "You kept that paper." Her hand went to her cheek. "You've thought all along I was your mother. I'm sorry. I only did what I did to protect you and honor your mother's wishes."

"You say she went by the name May Freemont?"

"Yes." She gave a sad smile. "But among her things was a hand-kerchief embroidered *VR*. I think her real name might be Violet since there was a purple flower above her initials."

I opened my cigarette case and jotted it down—*VR. Violet?* Though the scribbled notes were unnecessary. I doubted I'd forget anything from this meeting. "Is there anything else you can remember? What did she look like?" A description of her would help my search, but I wasn't kidding myself—I wanted to know all I could about her.

"It's been so long." Her gaze drifted toward the ceiling, as if trying to search the archives of her mind. "But I remember her eyes were a remarkable shade of gray. Dark, just like storm clouds. I'd never met someone with that eye color before." She peered at me. "Yours are like that too. Did you know that gray eyes are rare?" She posed the words with notes of esteem, as if I'd personally had a say-so in the shade of my eyes.

"I've heard that a time or two." Though to know I shared the trait with my mother made me appreciate it more.

"Other than that, I can't recall anything else. Oh, and—" Her mouth crimped shut.

"What?"

"It's nothing."

"If you have any other information, I'd like to know."

She sighed. "It's just, I remember wondering if she was a kept mistress." Her cheeks reddened. "She was beautiful and carried herself with poise. Her hands weren't rough or callused, like ones in manual labor. Her clothes were high quality and expensive."

"Perhaps she was from the upper class?"

Skepticism dimmed her eyes, but she shrugged. "It's possible, but usually when someone's from the upper class, it's not as easy to disappear."

Which was true. The elites were the talk of the society pages. The gossip columns lived for news of that caliber—a socialite's disappearance—if only to suspect scandal. No, this woman was probably correct. Which only made my birth that much lower. A son of a prostitute? I shouldn't be surprised. I was a calculated thinker, always prepared for the worst while fighting with everything within me to prevent failure. But I couldn't prevent this. I was conceived and unwanted, a burden from the beginning. It wasn't self-pity, just the plain facts.

A part of me could envision my hands, small and grubby, scrambling through garbage bins for food, keeping my eyes on the sidewalk in case *she* was looking for me. It was a deluded dream that always clung to me, like the sweat in the summer or the prick of chill in the winter. Though I'd suppressed it over time, I could never quite shake that fanciful hope.

Now it shriveled up. Dead.

Still, it wouldn't hurt to ask around. Someone might have heard of a kept mistress with the initials VR. Or maybe the name of Violet.

Time to switch perspectives. "What can you tell me about the man you overheard?"

She sat silent for a moment. "I never got a good glimpse of him. But his voice was deep and harsh. He was very clear about his intentions and what he wanted. He told them to make your death appear as an accident. I assumed he had power."

"Why?"

"Because he told them you had to die or else there'd be repercussions with the asylum. He vowed to shut it down." Fire flashed in her eyes. "But I saw to *that*. After handing you over to the home, I told the authorities about the missing babies. They closed the place and arrested the owners."

Ah, a new lead. "What were the owners' names?" If still locked up, I could speak with them. The conversation wouldn't be pleasant, but they would know the man who'd supposedly threatened my life.

"Dudley and Betty Hopkins. They both died in jail."

There went that. "Do you know if my mother left the asylum unharmed?"

"I hope so." She grimaced. "They didn't seem to care about harming her. Only you."

Perhaps the man was my father and my mother had been his mistress. She could've used her expectancy as leverage over him. Or maybe she'd blackmailed him. The scenarios were endless.

"I'm sorry there isn't more I can give you."

Disappointment cut through me, but I offered a warm smile. "Thank you for risking your life to save mine."

After we said our goodbyes, I exited the café with more questions than when I'd come in. My lifelong case had just become more complicated.

Chapter 17 ───────────────────────────────

Delvina
1924

TRUE TO MY PROMISE, I hadn't asked Kent anything else about his past that night . . . or the following two days. His confession had seemed to fatigue him. I didn't want the extra stress affecting his recovery. So despite my curiosity, I'd kept quiet. But to know that he'd discovered that horrific truth behind his birth the very morning we'd eloped? Well, it explained his desperate need for family. It seemed we both hadn't been thinking clearly that day.

Not only had I not learned anything more about my husband's past beyond my one question, I also hadn't made any progress with Adele Thayer's case. Yesterday, when Kent had been resting, I'd gone to the library and browsed past newspapers, searching for articles about the Galleanists. But I didn't get any significant names or leads tracing to Miss Thayer. It'd been a failed effort from the start, considering I hadn't her true surname.

Despite things being slow with the case, I was pleased with how Kent's leg was healing. I wasn't certain which had been the biggest factor in his quick recovery—the properties in the honey, his resting, or maybe the cut not being as deep as I'd thought. Perhaps a combination of all three. The fear of infection was behind us. And while I didn't want the man sprinting down city streets, I believed he could walk without alarm of reopening the wound.

I was also fairly certain Kent was grateful I no longer hovered over him like a mother hen. Though now my nerves were thin for an entirely different reason. It was Friday—the day Mother had set me up to attend a play with a complete stranger. I'd emphatically told her no, but I understood enough about Mother's stubbornness to know she forged ahead with the arrangements nonetheless. I needed to speak with her.

I poked my dozing husband.

He stirred but kept his eyes closed.

I tapped him again, then opened the curtains. "Wake up, Kent."

"Vinny." He squinted, as if the gentle morning light gouged his vision, and draped his arm over his eyes. "You poked my shoulder. Twice."

I smoothed a hand down my beige dress. I'd taken to rising before him so I could ready for the day in privacy. "You'll live. You just survived a stabbing—I'm pretty sure you'll make it through the puny press of my fingertip."

"No, I'm thinking about our rule." His voice was rusty with the residue of sleep. "Your right shoulder is all mine."

"You're ridiculous." I turned so he wouldn't see my smile. Since we'd agreed that he had allowance to the areas I touched him first, the only contact had been his leg while applying the honey salve.

"Just abiding by our terms, wife." He adjusted against the pillows and lay there patiently as I inspected his wound, per our routine these past few days.

"Looks good." I stood from my crouched position. "I believe it would be okay for you to . . . venture out."

His brows jumped high on his forehead. "Really?"

It was no wonder I'd caught him off guard, considering all this week I'd demanded he remain in bed, still as possible. "We need to visit Hemswick today and tell Mother. I'll drive." The traffic would take us nearly three times as long than taking the cable car. But driving would reduce the amount of walking to the stops. That was top priority. "I think if you put most of your weight on your left leg and your walking stick—" I caught his stunned gaze. "What? Why are you looking at me like that?"

He shook his head with a huff of surprised laughter. "I thought I'd have to nudge you to speak with your mother. The other day you dreaded it."

And the dread hadn't left. "It's for the best we tell her about our marriage, especially since she arranged for her single neighbor to take me to the theater this evening."

Something flickered across his expression, but he kept unusually quiet.

I folded my arms. "What, no objections?" I thought for certain he'd have some sarcastic quip about the setup.

"About you gallivanting around the city with other men?" He'd spoken so casually, as if this was a conversation every marriage experienced.

I took the honey jar and pried open the lid. "Not that I'm baiting you to adopt the jealous-husband role, but a little effort would be nice." I shot him a teasing glance, then poured honey over the stitches.

"I can't win with you." He let out a good-natured groan and sank back against the pillows, his posture relaxed. "It took some *effort* to persuade you to remain married to me, and now you're complaining I'm not behaving like the leering lover. The past few days you've scolded me for standing up. So that rules out my plan of challenging the gentleman to a duel."

"A duel?"

He gave a decisive nod. "Pistols at dawn."

I rolled my eyes, but somehow my smile poked through my feigned irritation. "I hope there are less violent ways to win my affection."

His gaze took on a sudden interest. "Such as?"

I put the lid on the jar with a shake of my head. "If I tell you, it doesn't count."

"So I have to figure that out?"

"If it's worth it to you, you would."

His voice dipped low, his gentle timbre almost a caress across my skin. "You're worth it."

The moment shifted. It didn't slip my notice how he'd swapped the pronoun *it* with *you*. As if I was worth figuring out. Was I? I hadn't been four years ago. But I couldn't hold those transgressions against him. At least until I knew the full story. "Well, don't put a duel on your schedule because . . ." *Schedule.* A chill pricked my neck. That was it. What had been feathering my brain about Miss Thayer. Her schedule.

When I'd met with Wallace Stratton at his agency, he'd said he and Adele had argued about an appointment. I'd been so focused on catching him in one lie that I'd missed the other. "He said it never left his office," I quietly mused. "Was he deceiving me there as well or—"

"Can I be included in this conversation?" Kent lifted a hand, as if trying to snatch my attention.

"I visited Wallace Stratton at his agency. He showed me Miss Thayer's planner. He told me the book never left his office."

Kent nodded. "He told me that, too, when I looked through it. As if her appointment book was some sort of treasure. I couldn't find anything significant about it."

"Me either." I stood and paced the small area rug in front of his bed. "But here's the interesting part. Before I left his office, I confronted him about the argument he had with Miss Thayer the day she died."

Kent's eyes slightly widened, as if their disagreement was news to him. It seemed his client hadn't been entirely up front.

"Stratton fumbled his words. But one thing he did say was Miss Thayer was going over the planner in her apartment."

He caught on to my logic. "The planner that supposedly never left his office."

"Exactly. So Stratton was either lying about keeping the planner solely at the agency, or Miss Thayer stole it from his office, or—"

"She had *another* planner altogether."

"Yes." I stopped pacing. "I searched her flat for a personal schedule but couldn't find one."

He tapped his cigarette case on the bedside table. The one that housed all his notes. "Maybe she kept her planner in something more discreet."

"Brilliant." I clapped my hands in a rare burst of excitement, prompting his smile. "And *maybe* she kept her schedule on her person, carrying it close because she didn't want people to see." Just like my husband. Which meant I needed to pay someone a visit. A jolt of energy swept through me. "Kent, you need to get ready while I'm gone, but take your time. Be careful about your stitches. We'll go to Mother's when I return."

He watched as I grabbed my purse and slipped into my heels, his downturned mouth and folded arms showing how unamused he was in being left behind. "And where are you off to?"

I reached for the door. "The morgue."

Kent's eyes shadowed with suspicion. "Her body isn't there anymore."

"That's not what I'm looking for."

• • •

The lowest level of Bellevue Hospital had been home to the city's mortuary since after the Civil War. Though the morgue wasn't exactly my destination, but the archives room. The click of my heels echoed off the stone walls as I made my way through the maze of hallways.

"Delvina Kline."

I stopped at the familiar voice behind me. Just the man I'd come to see. I turned in time to catch Laurence Calloway's mustache twitch with his smile. "Hello, Laurie. It's been a while."

"Almost a decade." He nodded with another warm grin. "Have you come for another lesson? I warn you though—this job cuts more than just hair." He gestured down the side hall leading to the mortuary. His jovial face held more wrinkles since I'd last seen him, but the light in his brown eyes remained youthful. He made a show of studying my hairstyle. "Looks even. You're doing well." This man hadn't always been an assistant to the chief medical examiner. Back when I'd known him, he'd been a barber working at the mortuary on the side. I'd completely forgotten, until this morning, that he'd landed a full position here. "The Castle bob was made for you."

The year of my debut, I'd met Irene Castle. The famous ballroom dancer had cut off her dark tresses in a bold move, and in a major show of support—and perhaps a minor bit of defiance against society—I'd done so too. This had happened five years before the bobbed style had truly caught on. Father had hated it, but Mother only encouraged me to embrace what I loved. And I'd *loved* having shorn hair. After I'd sliced off my locks, I'd struggled to find someone to trim my hair evenly. Which had been how I'd stumbled upon Laurie. I'd paid him to teach me how to cut my own hair.

"Well, I didn't come here to learn the process of embalming, but I am curious about Miss Adele Thayer."

His face went blank. No doubt the number of bodies that passed through here was staggering.

"She died on Tuesday, a week and a half ago. It was ruled a suicide by gunshot wound."

"Ah yes. I remember her." His tone was hesitant, and I was unsure if the reluctance stemmed from my prying or . . . something else. "Sad way to go."

Miss Thayer's distraught face flashed in my mind. She'd been so upset about Maude Welch's passing at Mother's dinner party. Did she have any loved ones distressed over *her* death? The truth needed to prevail, and a renewed sense of purpose pushed my chin up. "Do you recall if she had powder marks on her right hand? Or anything unusual? Maybe signs of a struggle?"

His mouth pressed together. "I'm unauthorized to say."

"What about her report?" I switched my approach, but the slight uptick of his brow clearly revealed he wasn't buying my feigned ignorance. "Aren't those public records?"

He chuckled with a shake of his head. "Nice try, Delvina. You know those are only released to kin or authorized persons." He seemed to favor the word *authorized*, but I found it constricting.

"All I need is a quick glance."

"The files are confidential."

"I certainly wouldn't want to risk your job. I know how hard you worked for it." I glanced around at the doors lining the hallway. "What if you went to lunch?" So I could freely browse.

He gave a rueful smile. "It's a bit early."

"Coffee break?"

The corners of his mouth lifted. "Never touch the stuff."

"Then maybe you need some fresh air. You can't get in trouble for taking a quick break. If something happens while you're away, you can't be blamed, right?" He began to shake his head, but I put my hand to his shoulder. "She was murdered, Laurie. I went through the proper channels first, but the police refused to listen. Miss Thayer deserves justice. You won't be doing this for me, but for her."

He blew out a breath. "Five minutes. That's it." His voice lowered, "But I can't let you in."

"Not a problem. I'll figure it out." I smiled. "Just point me in the right direction."

"I'm not allowed to tell you that the classified files are two doors down on the left. So don't even ask." He scowled, but there was a twinkle in his eyes I could hug him for. "If you get caught, I can't help you."

"Thank you."

He shrugged. "Nothing to thank me for. Like I said, I can't help you." With that, he walked away whistling.

I waited for him to turn the corner, then hustled to the door he'd indicated and withdrew my ring of various picks from my purse. Thankfully, the hall remained empty as I fussed with the lock. It finally gave way. Within seconds I was inside and shutting the door behind me. The room was long and narrow, with floor-to-ceiling shelves. Sunshine streamed in through the high windows on the back wall. I skimmed the shelves, each labeled by year. I quickly found 1924 and searched the alphabetized files.

Thayer, Adele.

I snatched the folder and moved toward the window for better light. Heart pumping, I scanned the first page listing her personal information. A lot of the lines were blank. The next page held the details about her death. My gaze landed on the fourth paragraph. No powder marks on her hands. According to this report, the chief medical examiner had relayed his findings to police, but the ruling of suicide remained.

Fire sluiced my veins.

Never mind her being left-handed—Adele Thayer hadn't pulled the trigger at all. If so, gunpowder would be on her skin. The police hadn't wanted to be bothered or . . . they'd been paid off. Men like Wallace Stratton and Angelo LeRaffa could certainly afford to bribe the authorities.

From the report, there wasn't any sign of struggle. No bruising or cuts. I returned the paper to the file. The final page listed her belongings, everything on her person when she'd entered the mortuary. My pulse leaped. Would the planner be named among her dress and stockings? Or perhaps a compact that held the names of her exclusive clients? I read the cataloged items. Besides her clothing, shoes, and undergarments, the final thing listed was fifteen bobby pins.

Another failed lead.

My eyes drifted to the bottom of the page, freezing on the final line. A Norman Young had signed for her things. Next to the name was the relation—her brother—followed by an address.

I'd found a family member.

Chapter 18 ———————————————————————————————

"THIS IS AN INTERESTING SURPRISE." Mother's tone rang with delight upon seeing that Kent accompanied me to Hemswick, her thin face brightening with a smile.

Guilt poked my heart with an accusing finger. During the ride here, I'd kept the dread of this impending conversation at bay by relaying to Kent what I'd discovered at the city mortuary. He'd recognized the address as a shoddy apartment complex in a bad area of the city. Tomorrow we'd visit Adele Thayer's brother. Postponing to the following day had taken some persuading, since Kent had long grown tired of lying about his flat, but I didn't want him overdoing. So when I bargained to also wait until tomorrow to ask him another question about his past, he readily agreed to my deal.

Mother's parlor was decorated in tranquil blues and creams, a glaring contrast to my riotous heart. I hated the idea of hurting her with the truth about my marriage, but she'd be devastated even more should the news break from another source.

"It's good to see you again, Mr. Brisbane," she said upon sitting.

I had the sudden fear of Kent doing something ridiculous, like calling her *Mother*. Thankfully, he only graced her with one of his charming smiles. He'd taken extra care in his appearance today. His dark waves were tamed into submission. His jaw, which had been lined with almost a week's worth of stubble, was shaved smooth. He'd worn the suit I'd picked out, highlighting his tall, broad form. Beyond his physical features, I appreciated his confident air, especially since I seemed to have lost my courage somewhere between the front door and here. Which was ridiculous. Earlier this week I hadn't flinched when confronting Angelo LeRaffa, a ruthless gangster, yet before my petite mother, I couldn't keep my heart from racing.

"Likewise, Mrs. Kline. I apologize for coming unannounced." Kent waited for me to sit on the sofa beside Mother before claiming the adjacent armchair, taking extra care with his leg.

I'd grown so accustomed to his flirty mannerisms and somewhat absurd remarks that I'd forgotten the man could behave himself when he put his mind to it. Though a part of me wished for one of his witty comments, because the room settled into a silence that made me twitchy.

I knew what needed said, but my lips seemed fused together. My gaze strayed to Kent, whose cool composure became my lifeline. He offered an encouraging nod, and my chest warmed. For so long, things had been just me. I'd never had the luxury of support. We were in this together, and that assurance gave me fresh boldness. "Mother, I don't know how to say this any other way, so I'll be direct."

She was hardly ruffled. "You always are."

"Kent and I are married." And just like that, the secret I'd chained to the shadows was out in the light.

Confusion crimped her mouth, soon giving way to a beaming grin. "And you thought I'd be upset about that? I'm overjoyed!" She pressed her hands together in a show of exuberance. "Though I'm mildly disappointed not to see you as a bride. When did this happen?" She looked between Kent and me. "Why so secret?" Her gaze dipped to my stomach. "Are you expecting?"

My mouth parted, and a strangled squeak escaped my throat. It was natural for her to suspect such a thing, but my scalp prickled with heat nonetheless. And I would *not* venture a glance at Kent. No doubt he was amused by her probing question. "No. Nothing like that."

Her head tilted as she awaited my explanation.

I dug my nails into the edge of the sofa cushion. "We got married four years ago."

"Four . . . years?" Her bright eyes dimmed with disappointment. "You've been married all this time?"

My gut churned. "We married in secret, and then . . . we divorced."

Her hand flew to her open mouth. I'd known Mother's feelings on the subject of divorce, but I'd rather endure her endless scolding than wither beneath her stunned silence.

"I'm sorry," I whispered.

"The divorce never went through." Kent had graciously omitted the part that I'd tried to be sneaky about the whole ordeal. "Delvina and I are still married."

Despite the temptation to let the story rest, I couldn't remain captive to guilt any longer. I explained everything about the fraudulent scam I'd fallen prey to.

"Well." She fussed with the lace on her sleeve. "That is unexpected." Her hesitant eyes met mine. "What are you going to do now?" There was an underlying plead in her tone. What she truly wanted to know was if we intended to pursue a legal divorce.

I covered her hand with mine. "We decided to remain married."

Stark relief melted her taut features. "Oh, Delvina. I'm so glad to hear it."

Kent leaned forward, securing our attention. "I want to give your daughter a wedding." A rare solemness weighted his tone. "Soon, if possible, but I'd like her to have everything she wants."

Our gazes locked and held. Confessing this old secret brought a new sense of grounding, as if we'd finally given our relationship something solid to anchor to. Kent seemed to be aware as well, for his gray eyes deepened with a serious smolder I'd yet to witness before and now couldn't turn away from.

"A wedding?" Mother's gleeful voice broke the moment. "Really?"

"Yes, so we can announce our marriage to the public." Kent repeated what we'd discussed the other day. I still wasn't sure we could control our own publicity, but he seemed confident.

"That's a wonderful idea." Mother was practically glowing.

I needed to take command of this conversation before she had me married in the center of Times Square in a hot air balloon. A slight exaggeration, but Mother tended to lean on the extravagant side. "I want to keep things small."

"Of course," Mother surprisingly agreed. "A smaller wedding will be easier for short notice. How soon are you thinking?"

"Wednesday." Kent offered that day as if it were no big deal to coordinate a ceremony and reception. Although, we *had* gotten our license and married within in a matter of several hours the first go-around.

Her silver brows lifted, then sank in determination, as if accepting the challenge. "We'll get it done."

"Mother, please keep this a secret until afterward. We can't have anyone knowing until the press covers it, not even Mrs. Elliot."

She readily agreed.

"For now, we can do all that you want to—shopping for a dress, picking out flowers."

She lit up like Rockefeller Center on Christmas Day. "I'd love that. Are you free after dinner, Delvina? We can look for a gown." During the entire debacle with the invasive press, Mother had taken to visiting the dress shop after closing hours. She paid enough for the privilege.

I smiled. "Needless to say, I must decline the theater tonight with your neighbor. Kent's not in favor of sharing me," I teased, breathing deeper with the boulder of shame lifted from my chest.

"Well, of course he's not." Mother hopped—hopped?—up from the sofa and moved beside Kent, pressing a maternal hand to his shoulder. "It seems long overdue, but welcome to our family."

Kent had given me his name, and I'd given him my family. Seeing Mother dote on him and Kent responding so graciously tugged at the tender edges of my heart. Kent had a mother again, with an addition of a sister.

Kate!

I needed to speak with my sister in Pittsburgh. We hadn't had much time to catch up since discovering each other's existence several months ago. I doubted she'd be able to travel to New York by Wednesday, but she should be told. I could add that to the growing list of things I needed to confess to her.

Mother waved me over, and I obliged. A blissful sigh parted her smiling lips. "If only your father were here for this." She wrapped her arm around my waist, keeping her other hand clasped on Kent's shoulder. "We have a daughter, and now a son." Pride laced her voice. "And perhaps some more to add in time." Her glossy eyes met mine, and—to my horror—she rubbed a hand over my stomach.

I made the error of glancing at my husband. The mischievous glint in Kent's eyes set my skin on fire.

● ● ●

"At least that's over." My breath seeped out as I pulled away from the Kline estate, leaving the ritzy area of Manhattan. The plan was to drop Kent off at his flat, then later meet Mother at her dressmaker's. I could've chosen to remain at Hemswick and let Kent drive my Duesenberg, but I wasn't certain if maneuvering the pedals would aggravate his leg. Better to err on the side of caution regarding his wound. "Thank you for being on your best behavior."

He grinned. "I'm always on my best behavior."

"That's debatable."

"And yet I wasn't the one traipsing around the city mortuary this morning. You still haven't explained how you got the information about Miss Thayer's brother. You broke in, didn't you?"

"It wasn't dangerous."

"But was it legal?" He turned a knowing glance my direction. "You've got a habit of believing something's legal only to find out it's not." He, of course, referenced our marital status.

"You don't seem upset about it." I fixed my eyes on the upcoming traffic, though I was tempted to look at him. "Our botched divorce, I mean."

"Not at all." He was quick to reply, his deep timbre making my stomach flip. "I've never been more appreciative of fraudulent schemes."

"It took away your bachelorhood."

"I'll give up anything to have you."

I wasn't prepared for the impact those words had on my defenses. I tensed, my heart begging to believe them, but my mind reminding me of the hurt I'd once endured. Pretty speeches only went so far. I remained quiet for most of the way back to his flat, until finally breaking the silence. "Will you be okay while I'm gone today?"

He nodded. "Warren's back in town. I invited him over."

"When did you arrange this?"

"This morning while my wife was committing felonies."

"In the name of justice."

"Good thing you're in good graces with Judge VanKirk. He'd probably let you go free," he continued, as if I were on the verge of getting my mugshot taken. "If not, I promise to write you every day."

I snorted.

"I'll put in a good word for you when the judge visits later."

I eyed him warily. "I thought you told me Warren was coming over?" Had I just caught him in a lie?

"I invited them both. I plan on asking the judge to perform the ceremony. I'll let him know about our situation. He seems the decent sort. I trust him to be discreet." His lips lifted in a smile. "After all, didn't he say officiating our wedding would be 'the least he could do' for us?"

Judge VanKirk had indeed told us that. His daughter had practically begged me and Kent to wed, nominating His Honor to preside over the nuptials. That night seemed so long ago, and yet it'd been about two weeks.

"Warren's arriving later, after the judge," Kent continued, "so I can discuss the coverage for our wedding." He shook his head. "Maybe you should stay with me, Knuckles. I might need your right hook."

"Why?"

"I never told him about our marriage. He might sock me."

"He wouldn't." And had Kent truly not confided in his best friend?

"Probably won't." Kent sighed, his brows knotting. "But I'd rather take a punch in the gut than disappoint him. We've been through a lot together."

I pulled into the lot behind Kent's flat and put the car in neutral, pulling the brake. "That's how I felt telling my mother." I glanced at him. "We sure made a mess of things, didn't we?"

He shrugged. "Depends how you look at it, I guess." His demeanor had shifted, and I could tell his upcoming conversation with Warren weighed on him.

I curled my fingers around his hand, resting on the bench between us. "Warren will understand." I hoped. I hardly knew my husband's best friend, but from everything Kent had told me, the newspaper mogul seemed like a reasonable person.

Kent nodded. "Thank you, Vinny." He held my gaze for a heart-pounding second, then dropped it to my hand, still wrapping his. "You know what this means, right?"

I pulled my fingers away with a light scoff. "Yes, per our rule, I touched your hand, so you can freely touch mine. So scandalous."

A wolfish smile lifted his lips. "I'm gaining access to you part by part."

I wrinkled my nose. "You sound like an ax murderer."

"Or a determined husband."

"You're enjoying this far more than you should." This morning it had been my shoulder, now my fingers, but Kent grinned, as if he'd bet on the winning horse at the Belmont Stakes.

"There's one part of you I want most of all."

I braced myself for something . . . well . . . a husband would say.

He leaned close, not touching my face, of course, since I hadn't his. "You know what that is?"

"I've a pretty good guess."

"Your heart."

Chapter 19 ───────────────────────────────────

A LONG-STANDING TRAIT OF ELIZABETH Kline was her undeniable sense of loyalty, a distinction that even extended to her dressmaker. While high society crammed Fifth Avenue boutiques and salons, Mother remained a staunch supporter of T. Ellerman, a quaint shop on an offshoot street of the popular thoroughfare. Tabitha Ellerman had sewn my debut gown when other designers had claimed they'd been overbooked. Mother and I had known the truth. Dressmakers could rise or fall solely based on *who* wore their creations. I'd been a risk they hadn't wanted to take. Tabitha had been more than happy to sew my gown, and she'd acquired a lifelong client in Mother.

And now it appeared the older woman with fiery-red hair and an eagle eye for fashion would be outfitting me for my wedding. Tabitha brought out a rack of dress "shells" that she would embellish to my liking. I was usually picky about my wardrobe, but I wanted nothing more than for Mother to have an input in this experience.

"What do you think of this one?" Mother held up a lilac taffeta covered in large flouncy bows.

The dress was painful to look at, but I probably deserved to wear it. It was clever on Mother's part to visit the dressmaker so quickly after my confession. The residue of guilt still squeezed my breath like a whalebone corset. So if she wanted to punish me by making me look like an enormous powder puff, so be it.

"Who's the groom?"

"Mr. Kent Brisbane," Mother proudly announced, as if he were the king of England.

Tabitha's face slacked. "I haven't heard that name in ages."

My hand stilled on a velvet frock. "You know him?" I hadn't specified the exact dress shop to Kent, and now I wished I had. How would he be acquainted with Tabitha Ellerman? Had he done some sleuthing for her?

With a nervous giggle, she opened a drawer full of fabric swatches, then abruptly closed it. "I'm sure we're not speaking of the same person. The one I knew was my neighbor in a way."

I could tell she was careful in her phrasing, testing her words before spilling them. Was her hesitancy because of the marked class difference between us? Kent had always been the first to claim he'd never belonged among our sort. That actually had been a point in his favor for me. And judging by what he'd told me the other day, he'd been orphaned, left to be raised in a children's home. I hadn't asked which institution he'd grown up in. Though I was aware some of those establishments were deplorable. What had it been like for Kent? My curiosity spiked, and I purposed to get answers from Tabitha.

"He lived near Vandever Heights?" This from Mother, whose arms were full of ribbons and lace. "That's such a lovely area of town."

"Not exactly." Her gaze flitted about the room. "He worked near me."

Kent's first office was nowhere near this place. Perhaps he had another location between then and now. "His detective agency?"

"No, I only knew him as a boy." She busied herself adjusting a sash on one of the gowns and seemed content to let the subject rest.

"Tabitha." It appeared Mother was through with her dressmaker's minced words.

"He worked at a shoeshine station." She pointed outside. "In front of the barbershop for a couple of years." Her eyes turned sad. "And slept behind my store."

My breath hollowed. Kent. My Kent. Had lived . . . on the streets? Behind this very shop? My mind scrambled. What had happened at the children's shelter? Had he run away? Or perhaps he'd been turned out. I tried to think back to our conversations. He hadn't let it slip once that he'd made his home on the spit-stained cement. Now all I wanted to know was why. Why hadn't he told me?

Tabitha shook her head. "Here he was shining shoes for the swells while he hadn't any on his own feet. Even in the winter."

His feet.

My gut sank, recalling the other night. How adamant he'd been about leaving his socks on. Had he suffered from frostbite? Something else? I struggled piecing it all together.

Tabitha misread my silence. "I'm sorry. I shouldn't have mentioned it." She gestured toward the line of wedding gowns. "I hope this doesn't change things." As if I'd refuse to marry him because of his misfortunes.

I was certain there were plenty of gentlemen who'd posed as high-society toffs to trick a naive heiress into marrying them, but that wasn't how things had gone with us. I'd been the one to rush Kent into marriage. He'd never pretended to be someone he wasn't. He'd revealed he wasn't among the upper crust on our first encounter. Though he hadn't explained much else. "No." I shook my head and forced a smile. "It changes nothing."

I could feel Mother's gaze on me, but I refused to glance over. I barely held my emotions in check as it was. For the next few hours, I went through the motions, my mind spinning. I deferred to Mother for everything, which she enjoyed, acting as if it were my debutante ball all over again.

We decided on a dress. My measurements were taken. What felt like a hundred veils had passed through my hands before Mother had mercy on me and picked one. After a few more details were discussed, Tabitha assured us everything would be finished by Tuesday evening.

Soon our coats were on, and we exited onto the walk, the sun having descended this past hour. My gaze strayed to the spot Tabitha had specified in front of the barbershop. There wasn't a shoeshine stand anymore, but I could easily picture it.

Mother's hand pressed my arm. "Are you okay?"

No. Not even a little bit. I only nodded to where Charles, her chauffeur, waited by the parked car. "It's dark now. You should get home."

Her smile was gentle. "So should you."

"Do you think it's strange we're living together?" I'd refrained from telling her I'd been sleeping on the sofa the past few nights. It was the most uncomfortable piece of furniture in existence, but after waking up that first morning sprawled across Kent's chest, I'd kept far away from his bed as possible.

She laughed. "He's your husband, isn't he?"

"Yes."

"Husbands and wives are supposed to live together."

"But—"

"This wedding is something you should've had long ago." Her expression turned wistful. "Your dress is going to be stunning. Thank you for going with pink."

I hated pink. But I loved Mother. And love considered the other person over oneself. Right now all I seemed to consider was Kent. After seeing Mother off, I started toward my Duesenberg, then paused. I couldn't return to the flat. Not yet. With slow steps I walked behind the dress shop, taking in the narrow alley. Moonlight slid along the cobblestones. I wrinkled my nose at the odor of musty rot from the nearby garbage bins. There were shadowed slots between each shop. Had Kent slept in one of those nooks, away from the bitter wind?

An ache yawned within me, and I no longer just wanted to see this place—I wanted to feel it. I tugged my hat off my head and shrugged free of my coat. Ignoring the pressing chill, I slipped off my heels, and the sting of cold stone sliced into my soles.

Then I sat.

The night air bit into my skin, but I welcomed it. I knew it was foolish to linger in the dark, but I could hardly bring myself to care. Because all my mind's eye could see was a little boy in threadbare clothes and no shoes. Perhaps digging through the garbage, hoping for a discarded meal. Or shivering against the building, using an old newspaper as a blanket.

I skimmed my hand along the ground, the grit scraping my palm. Had Kent been frightened? Had he been bitter at the world for carrying on around him even as he fought to stay alive? I thought about my childhood, how I'd run about Hemswick utterly carefree. I'd never had to worry about my next meal or if the temperature would dip below freezing. I'd been fed and sheltered.

Kent had been robbed of that comfort. It was no wonder he'd shied away from speaking of his past. I understood him more in this moment, sitting among the filth, than from the hundreds of words we'd exchanged.

Scratching noises by a stack of discarded boxes made me jump. I caught a glimpse of dark fur and shuddered.

Rats.

Had this alley been littered with rodents when Kent was here? It was almost too much. I stepped into my heels and returned to my car. The haze in my mind refused to lift as I drove to Kent's flat and climbed the stairs to the door. With quiet movements, I entered the apartment, unsure if he still had company. My question was answered with silence.

Had Kent gone out? He'd promised to stay and rest.

My pulse leaped, but one glance to the left side of the room, and I relaxed. Kent was already asleep in bed. It was only a little after nine o'clock, but the man was out.

I knew I should change, but I found myself walking toward him, my gaze transfixed on his dozing form. His dark lashes fanned against his upper cheeks, his full lips slightly parted. I'd always thought him handsome, but tonight he was breathtaking. Because now I knew.

Over the past week, he'd slowly been giving me pages from the volume of his life. Tonight I'd come across the missing chapters. Now I wanted to read all of it, all of him. I'd never been one for physical books, but this proverbial edition, I longed to devour every word. To run my fingers across the lines and paragraphs that detailed Kent Brisbane. To memorize those quiet passages hidden from the rest of the world but that had defined the man with whom I shared a name. I felt more connected to him now than those intimate moments on our wedding night.

A rush of affection swelled within me, and I climbed onto the bed. I needed to be close. He didn't stir as I nestled beside him, not exactly touching but near enough to watch him breathe, savor his warmth.

I glanced down at his feet, covered by socks. Kent had once encouraged me to flaunt my birthmark, my blemish, yet I suspected he was ashamed of his own flaws. Perhaps his scars served as painful reminders of that awful time. But to me . . . I wanted to pull those socks off and celebrate the marks of endurance. According to what he'd shared the other day, death had been chasing him since the day he'd been born. From my discovery at the dress shop, it hadn't stopped there but pursued him throughout his youth. My husband had cheated death no doubt a thousand times over.

He'd done so all on his own. Or . . . perhaps he'd had some help. Divine help. My gaze snagged on his left hand. It clutched a small New Testament. The Bible nearly escaped my notice because half of it was obscured beneath a fold of the blanket. Kent had never talked to me about his faith before. Perhaps it was a conversation we needed to have. But first . . . I felt the nudge to surrender my own heart, broken and tattered as it was. Tonight had shattered me, and it was time to place my life in more capable hands than my own.

A prayer on my lips, I closed my eyes. When I reopened them, I shifted my watery focus to my husband. It wasn't Kent against the world any longer. We were connected. My gaze traced the angles and planes of his face as a tear slipped down my cheek, followed by another. I was to say vows in less than three days' time, but I quietly said one within me. I hadn't yet the answer to the most pressing question about that day at Penn Station, but I promised to stay this time. I'd fight for this. For us.

● ● ●

I woke the following morning to find my husband staring at me in befuddlement.

His cloudy gaze ran the line of my form, a knot puckering between his brows. "Is everything okay?"

I smiled at him, which seemed to confuse him more. Last night's events came flooding back. "Yes, why?"

He dragged a hand over his face, bringing to my attention a crease on his cheek from his pillow. "You're still in your dress."

"Oh, I forgot." I stretched, and something popped in my lower neck. It appeared one night in the bed wasn't enough to straighten out the cricks in my body from the previous days on the world's worst sofa.

"Also, you're in bed," he said with a lazy curl to his lips. "Not that I'm complaining." He turned on his side toward me, and his smile dropped. "You've been crying."

My chest squeezed as my fingers swiped beneath my eyes. I'd been so disoriented when I'd returned from Tabitha's that I hadn't cleaned up. I was certain my tears, mixed with my kohl mascara, had carved black tracks down my face. Lovely.

When I didn't answer, he studied me more closely. "Did something happen last night?"

Yes—my heart had been shattered, and the fragments were now embedded in the narrow alley behind the dress shop. "I got fitted for my wedding gown."

"And that's why you cried? I've heard of a blushing bride but not a sobbing one. That does wonders for my ego, by the way."

He teased, but I couldn't join in his amusement, because all I could think of was what I'd discovered about his past.

When I gave no reaction, his brow dipped. "Listen, Vinny. If this is too much, you don't have to go through with it. I don't want you to be miserable with me."

"No, I want this. Really, I do." I slid my eyes shut, wishing for my head to clear. After a few deep breaths, I met his gaze. Should I discuss what Tabitha had said? Would he be annoyed that I'd pried her for answers? Maybe this conversation should wait. Besides, I hadn't yet explained why I was still fully clothed and in his bed. "I hope you appreciate the lengths I went to for my gown. Mother made me try on nearly every dress in stock. When I came back, you were already asleep. I didn't want to wake you by flitting about."

He gave me a look. We both knew the man slept soundly. "You're acting strange."

"You're full of compliments this morning."

His smile quirked. "Oh, now you want my flattery?"

I ran my fingers through my hair, tugging free the tangles. "No, not until I've had coffee."

"How about some eggs and hotcakes with that? Maybe some bacon."

He was wooing me with the lure of breakfast, and it was working. After hardly eating anything yesterday, my stomach nearly begged for sustenance.

"There's a great café a block down from here."

My eyes fell on the bedside table, where his New Testament now sat. "Kent, you never told me you're religious." I nodded at his Bible.

He ran a thumb over the leather binding. "I'm just a guy who knows where his help comes from."

His soft words confirmed my wonderings from last night. "Me too." I could now say that with confidence. "Well, except for the guy part."

He chuckled, but the gentleness in his eyes latched on to my heart. "I'm glad for it."

I nodded, then slowly rolled out of bed, needing an extra second to collect my emotions. Self-reliance was second nature to me. It was still necessary in some aspects, but regarding who had absolute control over my life? The ownership had shifted. I smiled at Kent, a peace settling over me. "Let's check your wound."

He complied, propping a pillow under his leg on the mattress. His skin was nearly healed, but I applied a few dabs of honey just to be on the safe side.

I returned the honey jar to his nightstand and stood. "How did your meetings go last night with Warren and Judge VanKirk?"

"The judge agreed to officiate." He scratched the stubble on his chin, a smile forming. "You should've seen the unabashed grin on His Honor's face."

I believed it. He and Mother seemed cut from the same cloth in regard to the role of matchmaker. "How did Warren take the news?"

"Surprisingly well." He took his time standing up, and I knew he was being careful on my account. "He knows I don't confide much about private matters. But he did say if I acted stupid like that again, he'd pummel me. So there's a nice incentive."

"I like him." I flashed a saucy smile as I pulled a dress from the closet. It was mildly weird having my frocks hung beside his shirts. It was the picture of domestic harmony. Different, yes, but I didn't exactly hate it.

"Don't get any ideas. You're married to *me*."

It seemed we'd found our conversational footing once more, which only pushed my mouth into a teasing smirk. "As if I need the reminder."

He moved into my space. Probably because I still hovered near the closet and he needed clothes for the day, but the heated look on his face told me his mind wasn't on waistcoats and trousers. "Say the word, and I'll help you to never forget."

"I'm sure you would"—I batted my lashes at him—"but you promised me breakfast."

"You little minx." He chuckled low. "After that are we heading to visit Adele Thayer's brother?"

"I'd like to."

He nodded. "I say the earlier, the better. That area's not the safest, but most of the troublemakers don't stir until nightfall."

"Sounds good to me." I pointed at his leg. "As long as it's not too much walking."

"I'll let you carry me if I get taxed."

I moved closer, giving him my most intimidating look. "I'm serious. We need to be careful about your leg. It's practically healed, but I need to remove the stitches soon, and we can't take this lightly."

He mimicked me by drawing nearer so that our faces were only inches apart, but instead of returning my scowl, he was all self-satisfied smiles. "I find it sweet how obsessed you are with my body." He swept his hand down the length of him in a haughty manner.

I reached out, aiming to swat his smug fingers, but at the last second he turned, and my hand smacked . . . his backside.

Oh no. I quickly tucked my hand behind me, feigning an innocent expression, praying he'd realize it was an accident.

No such luck.

He pivoted on his heel almost reflexively, his eyes a mixture of surprise and barely concealed glee. "You know the rule, Vinny."

"I-I didn't mean it." I backpedaled, and he matched me step for step. "You turned. I was supposed to swat your hand."

"So it's my fault?"

"It always is," I shot back.

He playfully darted for me, but I evaded him, dropping my frock and scurrying the few steps needed to make it to the wall. I pressed my rear flush against the cold plaster, protecting my hindquarters. "You're not supposed to chase me." My rebuke was flimsy, given my breathlessness.

He approached with slow, even strides, a grin curving his mouth and his eyes hot on mine. He remained quiet. A silent Kent was far more dangerous to my defenses than a playful one. I refused to peel my gaze from his, until he was before me. He pressed his palms on either side of my head, bracketing me with his arms.

He was close. Too close. "Thank you, Vinny."

I watched him carefully. "For what?"

"Proving my point."

"Which one?" I adopted a bored tone, not wanting him to know how his nearness affected me, and made a show of studying my nails. "You attempt so many."

His head dipped, his face nearly skimming mine. "You really can't keep your hands off me."

"Ridiculous." I gently shoved his chest—no, his chest!—then nearly smacked my skull against the wall in frustration. What was wrong with me? That absurd rule messed with my mind. But it wasn't our agreement as much as it was him. My husband flustered me on so many levels. When his brow spiked at my touch, I gave him a pointed look. "No."

His deep laughter surrounded me as I tried to gather my wits.

"You know, Knuckles, I'm thinking this marriage of ours is looking quite promising."

"Of course you do, but maybe do me a favor?"

He held out his hands. "Anything."

"Try not to be drunk for the ceremony this time around."

His head reared back. He stared at me for a long minute, his jaw working. "What are you talking about? I wasn't drunk that day."

I folded my arms.

"Whatever gave you that idea?"

"Hmm. I don't know," I said sarcastically. "Maybe because when I came into your office that day, you reeked of alcohol." I'd been in a state, yes. But even in my distress, I could tell the man had been drinking.

He leaned in close. "So this is what you've thought these past four years? That I didn't know what I was doing when I married you?"

"Not at first." I'd been too blinded by emotion. However, after he'd boarded the train, my mind tauntingly presented the blatant clues I'd overlooked. "Looking back, I thought I'd talked you into it and the alcohol only encouraged things."

He mumbled something I couldn't catch. Then, "You thought you had to talk me into it?"

The incredulous note in his voice made my stomach dip. Had I judged it all wrong? No, I knew what I'd seen.

"Let me set the record straight." He ran a hand through his hair and stepped back. "This is what happened the day we married."

Chapter 20

Kent
1920

I COLLAPSED ONTO MY CHAIR in my office, my mind sifting through what I'd been told at the café. Kit Mason had not been my mother but my mother's nurse who'd taken me to supposed safety. I tipped my head back, staring blankly at the ceiling. Of all the scenarios that had run rampant regarding this morning's meeting, I'd never imagined this. It seemed far-fetched. Why would someone want to kill me? Could the nurse have been lying? If so, she deserved the leading role at the Plaza. There wasn't anything suspicious about her mannerisms. Besides, what benefit could she possibly have in relaying such a wild tale?

Snippets from our conversation sailed through my mind. Had I missed something? An important clue?

Time to investigate.

I cracked open my cigarette case and read my scribblings.

> *Mother's initials VR. Violet? Purple flower on handkerchief.*
> *Unwed mother asylum in country. Man wanted me dead. Nurse*
> *Kit Mason—real name Judith Powell Long—escaped with me.*
> *Turned me over to the children's home.*

Oh, and let's not forget the *kept mistress* theory. I begrudgingly added that.

I stared at the two letters—VR.

Who are you, Mother? Why the secrets?

Had she truly been a fallen woman who'd been shunned by her married lover? Was she still alive?

An idea sparked. I'd accumulated a sizable network of informants, consisting of a slew of folks who owed me favors. I could put feelers out for a kept mistress who'd disappeared from the city around 1898. Or maybe I could—

A derisive scoff ripped through my lips. Who was I kidding? I snapped my cigarette case shut and tossed it onto my desk, my vision blurring around the edges.

The chances of any leads coming from such vague information were beyond slim, practically impossible. I needed more. Once again this was out of my reach. The very crux of my existence—everything so far out of my grasp. Yet like a sap, I kindled the flickering belief that I could snatch what I wanted. A family. A home.

Delvina's face flashed unbidden. I pressed the heels of my hands into my eyes, as if I could physically scrub her from my memory. If I'd entertained any idea of a relationship, I could now torch it, brush away the ashes of hope, and forget about her. Because if I'd felt unworthy of her before, what I'd learned today only widened the chasm between us. I'd guessed I was born on the wrong side of the blanket, but now it was fact.

I launched to stand, my chair skidding back into the wall, that all-too-familiar impulse slithering over me. I'd learned as a boy never to approach shadows, which were usually in the form of vagrancy officers or gang leaders. I could hear the slap of my bare feet on the cobblestones as I escaped my pursuers. Now years later, here I was, still being chased, but this time by my failures. I couldn't outrun them.

Perhaps I shouldn't have dismissed Warren so easily. I'd agreed to meet him at his club after the meeting, only to change my mind once I'd gotten there. The gentlemen's lounge held more gossips than an old biddies' bridge night. Besides, I'd already been in a foul mood made worse by Jack Larson bumping into me as soon as I entered, spilling his drink all over me. Which was most decidedly liquor and not near beer, like the joint allegedly served.

So I'd told Warren I'd catch up with him later and came here to sulk. How manly.

The door burst open.

Delvina dashed into the room, her movements clumsy, her hand clutching a paper. "I'm sorry. I'm sorry." Her eyes were swollen with tears.

I stepped out from behind my desk in time for her to launch into my arms. Her chest heaving against mine, she clung to me with a fierce grip, still whispering apologies for intruding.

"Delvina, what's wrong?" A surge of protectiveness had me pressing her even closer. My mind went back to our first encounter, to the gentleman who'd dared tried to assault her. "Did someone hurt you?" So help me, I'd tear him limb from limb.

She nodded against my chest.

My jaw screwed tight. "Who is it? I'll take care him."

Her head popped up, nearly grazing my chin. "No, it's nothing like that. It's just . . ." Her face crumpled, and she nestled against me. "I can't stay in this city a second longer. I only came here to say goodbye."

Wait. Goodbye? I eased back, my hands sliding to anchor her shoulders. "Delvina, please start from the beginning. What happened?"

Her chin sank. "It's awful."

"You can trust me. Whatever it is, I won't breathe a word." As a man of my own secrets, I could easily collect hers and lock them safe with mine.

She sniffed once. Twice. I wasn't certain if her nose dripped from all the crying or if she had, unfortunately, caught whiff of my liquor-soaked lapel. Either way, I dug out my handkerchief. "Here." I pressed the cloth into her palm.

A ghost of a smile touched her lips. "I'm slowly bankrupting you of these."

I'd given her one the first night we'd met, but I'd surrender all my handkerchiefs if only to bring back the light in her eyes.

She turned away to dab her face. "Mother was already downstairs for breakfast, but I went to her bedroom to return the sapphire earrings I borrowed. I saw a secret drawer in her box. I wasn't trying to snoop—it just stuck out to me."

"So you opened it."

She nodded. "I found this." She held out a paper, a slight tremor to her fingers. "It's hard to read because . . . well, you'll see."

The page had been creased in several spots, and the ink had faded. I glanced at the sloppy scrawl. The letter had been addressed, *To our daughter Delvina Salvastano.*

Not Kline. Had Delvina's suspicions been correct? She had been adopted? Something feathered my brain. Salvastano. Where had I heard that name?

"They lied to me." Her arms dropped to her sides, her hands clenching. "All this time they could've told me *why* I was such a misfit. Now I know. This"—she flicked the corner of the letter—"is a farewell note from my birth parents in Italy. It's hard to read because their English isn't good. But it's clear enough."

Her voice broke, and it was all I could do not to pull her to me and crush her close. "Did you confront them?" I returned the paper.

"I did. Mother cried. She said she wanted to wait until I was old enough to understand, then by that time, she couldn't bring herself to tell me."

"I see." I gently took her free hand and led her to the chair. "And your father?"

She scoffed. "Oh, he apologized but then went on to say I need to keep quiet about the whole ordeal. He doesn't want it blown up into a scandal." Her finger traced the edge of my cigarette case.

I'd forgotten I'd tossed it on my desk. Stupid. The last thing I wanted was Delvina opening it up and discovering the truth about me.

But this moment wasn't about me. I leaned on the desk beside her. "Maybe he wants to protect you."

"Doubt it. Even if that's true, their influence has never been able to make that wretched sphere accept me." She sat back in the chair, abandoning the cigarette case. "But it's too late anyway."

"What is?"

"The news is going to break." Her eyes welled with fresh tears. "Someone overheard my conversation with my parents. I don't know if it was a servant or the company. Mother invited—"

"You confronted your parents in front of their guests?"

She stared at me as if I were an imbecile. "Of course not. We were in Father's study, but anyone could've listened at the door. I wasn't exactly quiet." She strangled the handkerchief. "This story will be smeared over the papers tonight, and all of New York will be laughing at me. Not that I should care, but I hate that they were right."

I reached for the telephone.

She jolted. "What are you doing?"

"Putting in a call to Warren Hayes. I'll convince him not to print that kind of rubbish."

She swiped her red-rimmed eyes. "You would do that?"

"I'll do anything to keep you from hurting."

Her lips parted at my declaration. I hadn't intended for it to come out so adamant, but I wouldn't take it back. I meant it. I'd rather cut off my right arm than glimpse her pain-pinched face.

She placed her hand atop mine on the candlestick base. "I appreciate it, Kent. But it's no good. Father was the one who fed the news to the press. Once he discovered we'd been overheard, he telephoned the papers—I think he felt he could control what would be said." A humorless laugh escaped her lips. "He lied. Told them I knew about it all along and we'd kept this private because it was no one's business."

I gave a solemn nod, hating she was going through this. "What can I do to help?"

"Nothing. From what I gathered, my birth parents just handed me over to strangers."

Our pasts were oddly similar in that respect. "Maybe it was for a good reason."

She shrugged. "Mother mentioned a famine in Italy, and they were scared I wouldn't survive."

A frightened mother concerned for her child. Another strange resemblance to my own story. "I've heard people will do drastic things for those they love."

"Was it love though?" she countered. "Because I would move heaven and earth to provide for my child before giving them up."

She didn't understand the ways of the world. She'd grown up in luxury, not having once to scavenge for food or worry if the next meal would be the last. Hunger was a cruel beast, and I'd seen many become its prey. Although now was not the time to lecture on the woes of humanity. She needed a listening ear.

"What if they didn't think I was worth the effort, so they rejected me? Why is this a reoccurring theme in my life? Why am I unwanted? By my birth parents, by society? What's wrong with me?"

I could show her just how much she was wanted, but good sense made me restrain. Her fragile tone coupled with the vulnerability in her eyes had me treading carefully. She didn't realize, but I understood her pain, having been an outsider all my life. Alone. But she had the added sting of betrayal. Good intentions or not, the Klines' secrecy had hurt her, only to have that anguish soon rubbed in her face by the press. "Nothing's wrong with you."

Her gaze turned inward, quietly calculating.

"Talk to me, Vinny. What can I do?"

She rose to her feet, her eyes sparking with defiance. "I'm leaving town."

My heart slammed into my ribs. "Where will you go?"

"Away from Manhattan." She set her shoulders back, as if to storm out of my office and leave the world behind, but instead of rushing toward the door, she closed the distance between us. Gaze on mine, she laid her fingertips to my jaw. "I only wanted to come and thank you for your help these past two months." She lifted on her toes and kissed my cheek, her body soft against mine. "I'm glad I met you, Kent Brisbane." She stepped away, the finality in her words like a punch in the gut.

Only seconds before she'd rushed in, I'd decided to let her go, and now I wanted to hold on to her forever. Which was foolish, since my circumstance hadn't changed. It was better for her sake to have nothing to do with me, but I disliked her leaving the city by herself. "Can you go with a friend? I hate the idea of you being alone right now."

"You do?"

"Yes. Very much." I realized she had the meddle to handle anything thrown at her, but the waves of sorrow rolling off her matched with her rash streak could lead to trouble.

"So I should go with a friend?"

"It's probably for the best."

She peered up. "Then where are you taking me?"

I nearly choked. What? She meant me? And then it struck. I was her only friend. My pulse pounded and chest ached in tandem. What was I to say? If I rejected her in any form, it would only add to her heart-ache—confirm her belief that no one wanted her. "Vinny." I waited un-til we locked gazes. "I am your friend. But I don't think you realize what you're suggesting."

"Yes I do." She reached up and smoothed my collar, her thumb graz-ing my neck, awareness of her igniting my blood. "You don't want me to be alone. And I want to be with you."

"You want to be with me?"

"Yes. Very much." She tossed back my words, and my resolve with-ered.

I locked my jaw against the primal instinct that'd once been as natu-ral to me as breathing. The city streets had taught me to never miss an opportunity, like a penny on the sidewalk or an abandoned glove on a park bench. It'd sometimes been a race to snatch it up. If I didn't fight for it, another chance might not come.

But Delvina wasn't a shiny coin. "Perhaps we should think this through some more. The Klines should have been up front about your adoption, but they do love you."

"My mind is made. I'm going. I can't stay with them another min-ute." She fixed her gaze on me with determination, but there was also a fragileness to it. Like a house stacked of steel cards. The deck might be solid, but one light shove and it would fall to pieces. "Tell me you don't want me, and I'll go."

How could I? How could I reject her when she already felt forsaken by everyone else? Did she realize the position she placed me in? If I told her I didn't want her, not only would I be lying, but I'd be piling on more hurt. If I told the truth—how badly I desired her—I'd be taking advantage of her sensitive state. Besides, after what I'd discovered this morning, I was hardly the man she deserved. "There are things you don't know about me. I grew up in an entirely different world than you." I shoved a hand through my hair, hating the sour taste of my own words but knowing they needed said. "I'm not worthy of a person like you."

"I'm not truly from that world either, remember? I wasn't born into it, and I certainly wasn't embraced by it." She moved closer, as if sensing my weakening. "Tell me you don't want me," she repeated, her voice lowering with challenge.

I matched her almost inch for inch, until near enough to count the amber flecks in her eyes. "Listen, Knuckles, I'm just a man. But I'd like to think I'm a principled one. If you want me to be with you, the only way is to get married." If she wanted to twirl the temptation around like a flaming baton, she needed to understand the burning magnitude of her stunt. "Do you want to make a life-altering decision on a whim? When you're not yourself?"

Instead of retreating, she tipped her head up, lips hovering dangerously close to mine. "If anything, what happened today only encouraged me to take my life into my own hands. I've admired you since we danced in the garden. So for me, I'm not acting rash. I'm acting on my heart."

"If you don't want kissed, I suggest—"

She silenced me with the press of her mouth against mine. Her delivery wasn't chaste but adamant, the pressure like a fiery dare, coaxing me to claim her heart in exchange for mine. She didn't realize she'd stolen it long ago. The little thief. And now she robbed me of all reason as her hands tangled my lapels, pulling me flush against her.

This was absolute madness, and her teasing touch only lured me deeper. She tugged my lower lip, demanding a response. My arms closed around her, anchoring her to me. She sucked in a breath, and

I clenched the advantage, taking over the kiss, upping the intensity. I guided her backward against the wall for support without breaking our connection.

"Kent," she whispered against my lips, a soft, feathering touch compared to the demand of the moment. "Be my family."

And that was all it took for me to cave. Family. It was always what others had that I hadn't. She couldn't have said a more tantalizing word because that was what I hungered for most.

So I pressed her close, her form melting into mine, as if it were supposed to be this way for the ages.

I was getting lost in her, and I needed a clear head, my conscience screaming for a say. "Are you certain you want to do this? To marry me? Because there's no going back." I dropped my hands from her body so as not to persuade her, but she whisked them back up and pressed them to her cheek.

"There's nothing I want more. Please marry me." She ran her lips across my knuckles, kissing each one slow and hot. "Kent, take me to Elkton."

I couldn't speak for some silly fear that any word would ruin it all. So I nodded and crushed her close as my answer. With her in my arms, I realized I'd do her every bidding to make her happy. Even whisk her away to a marriage mill in Maryland. Because people did drastic things for those they loved.

• • •

It was almost alarming how quickly one could get hitched. A quick train ride south, a walk-up license booth, followed by a no-wait ceremony, and Delvina exchanged her last name for Brisbane.

Throughout that day, her hand had gripped mine, as if afraid I'd back out. While I held reservations about the hastiness of it, I held no regrets about making her mine. No, my fear was she'd wake up tomorrow and resent the decision, which was why I'd determined to never give her reason to.

"What now, husband?" Delvina's bright smile overtook her face, a contrast to her distressed expression only hours earlier.

"As I see it, we have a couple of options." I tucked her hand in mine and pressed close as we strolled down the sidewalk toward a café. "We can spend some time here in Maryland. This being the marriage capital of the East Coast, there are plenty of places to stay. Though we might not be assured of privacy. Or we can return to New York. There's a train leaving at seven."

"I don't want to go back." She stopped. "I know the news will be out soon. I'm not ready to face it yet."

I hated to inform her that she was more likely to be discovered here in Elkton than Manhattan. This town's claim to fame was quick weddings. From what Warren had once said, journalists hung about in hotel lobbies, trying to sniff out a scandal. "But you're not alone. I'll be with you." I squeezed her hand. "I won't let anything happen."

Her face softened. "Thank you. But I don't want the beginning of our marriage to be filled with pestering newshounds."

"Ah, but my flat is hidden."

Her nose scrunched. "What do you mean?"

"I rent the room above Hal's Cigar Shop off an obscure street in midtown. Most assume the space is used for storage, and Hal keeps it that way. The city doesn't know it exists because I use my office address for everything. I probably pay more rent than I should, but it's worth it to be invisible."

"Invisible." Her smile was wistful. "That sounds lovely."

I didn't know any other way. But I could see how she'd value being away from the public eye. The only other option was my hunting cabin, but it wasn't wired for electricity. I'd won the place last year in a grueling round of poker. It was, in a word, simple. I couldn't take her there to spend our wedding night. Not when she could probably have picked a man who could've afforded the Ritz-Carlton. "I honestly think you'll be more concealed at my flat than anywhere else. A hotel around here might be too risky."

"So we'll spend our first night together at your place." She seemed as if she was trying to talk herself into it. No doubt the weight of everything—the finality of it all—was settling in. For her cheeks reddened, and her gaze touched everywhere but my face.

I couldn't have that. "Hey." I slid my thumb beneath her chin, gently lifting until bashful eyes met mine. "I may be your husband, but I'm your friend. No expectations from me, okay?"

Confusion marred her brow. "But it's our wedding night."

"Yes, but it's also been an emotional day for you." And for me. "I want nothing more than for you to be comfortable with me." I raised her right hand and kissed the inside of her wrist. "Besides, I'm still terrified of you and your wicked right hook."

"No you're not." She swatted me, but something remained in her eyes that I couldn't quite decipher.

We grabbed a quick meal, and a local farmer offered us a ride to the station. When he discovered we'd just been married, he gifted us a jug of moonshine. Apparently he had a still in the backwoods. We accepted the liquor, but it had a menacing look to it, as if it would scorch the lining of your stomach. Suffice to say, we hadn't drunk any.

When we reached New York Penn Station, I successfully steered my wife away from the rows of newsstands, and I made two calls. One to a cabbie who owed me a favor and would keep Delvina's identity and destination a secret. The second was to Warren. He informed me that Delvina's story had leaked but was overshadowed by the tragic death of a Broadway actress who'd succumbed to the sleeping sickness. I didn't tell him of my sudden marriage. It wasn't the sort of thing you blurted out on a public pay phone in the middle of a terminal. Besides, I wanted things kept between me and her for a while.

I returned the speaker and faced an awaiting Delvina. "It's not as bad as you imagined." I relayed what Warren had said.

She shook her head. "Here I was concerned about my name being bandied about, and this young woman lost her life. It certainly puts things into perspective."

"You have nothing to be ashamed about. Your feelings were valid."

She gave a small smile.

"Our car should be here soon." I only knew our driver by one name—Davidson. A bit of a mysterious fellow, but he was a great guy to have like you. He ran a cab company, but also owed me several favors.

It was nearly eleven o'clock by the time we reached my area of the city. Delvina had fallen asleep on me and hadn't stirred when Davidson slowed the automobile to a stop. I gently lifted her and carried her to the door.

She was still dozing when I unlocked the flat and entered. I gently placed her on my bed, setting the ridiculous jug of moonshine on the floor beside her. Most men would be disappointed for their bride to conk out on their wedding night, but I was relieved.

Sure, the idea of having a beautiful woman in my bed was enough to make my blood hot. But she'd been through enough today without having to be concerned about my advances. Besides, I was half expecting her to wake up and regret the entire thing. But what I could offer? A safe place. I lifted a blanket and tugged it over her.

Wait. I should remove her shoes, but a low mumble pulled my gaze to my wife's face.

Her lashes fluttered open, revealing her pretty eyes, dark brown pools that a man could drown himself in. "Are we home?"

That word. Home. It was softly muttered from her lips, but it rolled within me like a peal of thunder. The woman had lived in a house that could pass as a palace, and she considered this little flat her home?

"You carried me?" She turned on her side, facing me. "All the way here?"

"I did."

Her gaze flicked to the door, then back to me. "We crossed over the threshold, and like a dolt, I slept right through it."

With a shrug, I held out my arms. "We can step over it again. I'm nothing if not obliging." My body practically hummed to get her in my arms once again. Which, despite my teasing, was why I remained fixed to this spot on the rug. Because after this morning's heated kiss in my office, I knew the level of passion Delvina Brisbane was capable of.

Her laughter was melodic, somehow making the room warmer. With her palms, she pushed herself to sitting. "Did we really get married?"

"I've got a paper to prove it. Any regrets?"

She stretched with a low moan that did absolutely nothing to help my weak resistance. Her hooded gaze on me, her lips tugged into a playful curl. "I regret that I didn't run off with you that day we roller-skated at the Hayeses' place. Then I could've been an old married woman of three weeks rather than just hours." Her gaze narrowed. "Why are you standing over there as if I have something you might catch?"

"I . . . uh . . . thought you might want some space."

She tossed back the cover and patted the space beside her on the bed. "And here I thought it was the bride who was supposed to be nervous on the wedding night."

I hooked my thumbs on my pockets, keeping me from reaching for her. Did she have to look so alluring? It really wasn't fair to an honest guy trying to keep a promise. "I wouldn't say I'm nervous."

The light in her eyes faded, her expression much like the one this afternoon when I'd suggested taking things slow. "Then what are you, Kent?"

Then I understood. She hadn't been bashful earlier, as I'd thought. In my office she'd lamented about being unwanted. Could she perhaps feel that *I* didn't want her? It was so beyond ridiculous that I nearly laughed. But in the span of seconds, the vulnerability had returned to her eyes. If she believed I could be in any way repulsed by her, I was going to enjoy proving her otherwise. I approached the bed. "What am I, love?" I palmed the mattress, dipping close to her with a low murmur. "I'm very much enamored with my wife."

Her lips parted in surprise before stretching into a smile I hope she'd only ever use for me. "In that case, Mr. Brisbane, come show me how enamored you are."

That was all the invitation I needed.

Chapter 21 ————————————————————————————

Delvina
1924

"So you see, Vinny?" Kent picked up the dress I'd dropped, his gaze never straying from mine. "The only thing that spiked my blood that day was thoughts of you." He handed it to me, and his thumb grazed mine. "That hasn't changed."

With the wall behind me and my husband in front, I had nowhere to escape. I held the dress in front of me like a tweed shield. Because his words were like spears of fire, setting my heart aflame. So I clung to the one memory that could douse it. "Hmm. A flattering account but not sure I trust it."

"Why not?" He looked mildly affronted. "I told you that dandy Jack Larson spilled his drink—"

"Yes." I held up my free hand. "I believe that. It's the latter part of your pretty speech that remains questionable. Because if you were so infatuated with me as you say, then—"

"Why did I leave the next day?"

I nodded.

"I'll tell you. I promise. But can it wait until this evening? Because if we're heading to a sketchy area of town, we need to go soon."

He was right. With it being late October, daylight was scarce. There were parts of the city one just didn't dare venture into close to sundown. Plus we both needed to get ready, then grab food.

While Kent had a valid reason for delaying the conversation, I couldn't help but suspect he was stalling.

Because Kent certainly had left the day after our wedding, and he didn't go alone.

• • •

"Are we going to come up with a plan to visit Norman Young? Or just make things up as we go?" Kent sat behind the wheel of his Model T, me on the passenger side. After we'd eaten breakfast, he'd suggested we take his car, since my posh carriage—his words—would attract attention.

I'd surprised him by relenting and allowing him to drive. He seemed so grateful with the small gesture that I could swear he'd been about to kiss me, but he hadn't, no doubt respecting our rule. I wasn't sure if I'd made a mistake by agreeing to those terms. Because as things were, I'd rather him pursue me than the other way around. I'd tried that before, and it hadn't gone well.

"You realize this person could be Miss Thayer's killer?" Kent's deep voice sliced into my wonderings.

"If Norman Young murdered his own sister, then why would he sign his name and address on the morgue receipt?"

"Why wouldn't he?" Kent shrugged. "It only makes him appear more innocent, like he's got nothing to hide."

"My source said her family is tied to the Galleanists. So I doubt we're about to encounter a gentle fellow who snuggles kittens."

Kent huffed a laugh, either derisive, since we both knew my source had been Angelo LeRaffa, or amused by my absurd fictional description of Mr. Young. "But if you ask me," he said with a quick glance my way, "the name Young doesn't exactly sound native to Italy."

I had to agree. I was a true Italian, having birth parents hail from the country as well as being born there. It saddened me that a handful of extremists committed horrific acts, subsequently casting all immigrants in a negative light. It was unfair.

As we drove farther from the heart of Manhattan, the scenery shifted from sleek skyscrapers to soot-layered buildings, similar to the area where we'd discovered Marianne VanKirk, only more dilapidated.

Kent parked a block down from the intended apartment complex. Having no idea what we were walking into, we'd both ensured we had our weapons at the ready. The complex was nowhere near like Park Towers. The dark gray stucco building—which may have been light tan at one point—stood five floors high, boasting rows of grimy windows and a rusty fire escape.

There was no one about, and the light wind whistled through bare branches of a maple tree, lending an eeriness to the air. Kent and I seemed to move as one, our casual gaits belying the alertness in our gazes, until we reached the front entrance of Greenwich Village Apartments.

"I don't want to split up." Kent scowled at the paint-stripped door. "But I think that might be the best strategy. I'll get the front-desk clerk away from their post, and you look through the ledger. I'll go in first."

Couldn't we just bribe the person to tell us Norman Young's room number? Letting a wad of cash speak for us seemed easier than maneuvering someone away. But before I could offer my suggestion, Kent squeezed my hand, said "Please be safe," and slipped inside. I gave him about a minute, then followed. The interior wasn't much more of an improvement over the outside. The faded lobby furniture huddled around an area rug as frayed as it was stained.

The counter ran along the back wall, and behind it stood a tall man with a jaw as hard as granite and an even stonier glint in his eyes. Though sporting a severe expression, he couldn't be much older than Kent and was outfitted just as sharp. More so, actually, because Kent had purposefully dressed a bit disheveled, having left his tie in the Model T and unbuttoned his collar, to match the scruffy environment.

Kent leaned against the counter, unfazed by the fellow's glower. "You the manager here?" He scraped every trace of refinement from his voice, a rough lilt deepening his tone.

"Yeah." The man crossed his arms in a tight fold and took in Kent's measure. "What do ya need?"

He shrugged. "I want to look at an apartment."

The manager picked up a stack of letters, flipped through at a leisurely pace, then tossed it aside. "Not sure if I have any vacancy."

Kent's gaze fell to the discarded mail, then to the manager. "Tully Crivillo says otherwise."

I pressed my lips tight against a gasp. Because my husband had just casually thrown out the name of a leading Galleanist. What was Kent doing? We suspected that Norman Young had ties to the anarchists, but that didn't mean everyone in his building was of the same group. Unless . . . Kent knew something I didn't.

"Never heard of her." The manager shrugged with a bored grimace. "And next time, tell the dame to mind her business. If I wanted word out about this place, I'd put an ad in the papers."

Tully Crivillo was definitely not a *dame* but a middle-aged man suspected of sending bombs through the mail. So this fellow's response clearly revealed he no idea about the Galleanists. He'd passed a test he hadn't known Kent had given.

"Speaking of dames." The manager spotted me over Kent's shoulder. "That one with you?"

Kent turned, and his gaze swept over my form appreciatively, as if this were the first time he'd ever set eyes on me. "No, she's not." His lips ticked up in a flirty smile. "Though I wish she was."

I dipped my chin, as if hiding a blush, which was so unlike me that I almost laughed. "I'm waiting for someone." I made a show of glancing at my watch pin. "He's to meet me here any minute."

The man's dark glare fixed on me. "This lobby ain't for social events, lady."

A smart retort burned on my lips, but I forced a tight smile. "Once he's down here, we're going out."

"As much as I'm enjoying your delightful exchange"—Kent rapped his knuckles on the counter—"I want to know if you've rooms to let." He withdrew several bills from his pocket. "If not, I can look elsewhere."

The manager went to reach for the money, but Kent drew back. "I want to see an apartment first. Then we'll chat."

"Follow me." He grabbed a couple of keys from the row of hooks and pointed to the steps. "I've two empty on the third floor."

I wasn't thrilled about my husband climbing flights of stairs, but I could hardly object. Within seconds they disappeared. The lobby now vacant, I rushed back to the counter.

I quickly found an account book with leasing agreements. My gaze scanned the pages for Norman Young's name. Not a thing. What if Miss Thayer's brother had jotted down a random address when signing for her belongings? Then we'd be back to where we'd started. I shoved away the pressing disappointment.

I skimmed the desk, and my eyes fell on the pile of letters the manager had sifted through. The envelopes had been addressed to . . . Norman Young. My pulse thudded. The manager was Miss Thayer's brother?

Of course. Why hadn't I spotted the resemblance? Not that I'd known Miss Thayer well enough to memorize her features, but I could see a faint similarity. Now it all made sense why Kent had tossed out Tully Crivillo's name. Because Kent had glimpsed the letters as well.

Now to find his place. The Park Towers' manager lived on-site. Was that the same situation here? If so, where would Mr. Young's apartment be? Hopefully, Kent would keep the man busy long enough for me to find it.

I could see which rooms were occupied, and perhaps by process of elimination I could find Mr. Young's. I flipped back a few pages and checked the renters' names again. Only this time I paused.

Winnie Baron.

I recalled the single conversation Miss Thayer and I shared regarding a play we'd both seen last year—*The Widow's Triumph*. We'd both agreed it was a stunning portrayal of a woman overcoming hardship, and one of the lesser-known characters was named Winifred Baron. Winnie? Could it be? It didn't hurt to check. I snatched the extra key to the designated apartment and went in search of Kent.

As if my thoughts had summoned him, he sauntered down the stairs, his wound obviously not an issue.

I rushed over. "You knew the manager is Norman Young."

"I suspected as much from his mail." He notched his chin toward the desk. "But then a tenant confirmed it by yelling Young's name . . . among a few curses. There's currently a small mishap in the hall."

By the scent of smoke clinging to him, I eyed him warily. "You didn't purposefully start a fire to get Young's attention away from you, did you?"

He smiled. "I'm flattered you find me so crafty. But I think this place, with its shoddy wiring, has enough gumption to pull it off without my assistance."

"Wonderful. Because we need to go check apartment 2A."

"Is that Young's room?"

"I don't think so."

"And I don't think Young's a violent anarchist." He tugged his waist-coat and followed me. "Did you see his response when I brought up Tully Crivillo?"

"I did. He was completely oblivious." Which only brought more questions.

Shouts rang from above, hurrying our steps. Hopefully, the fire was easily contained and the building wouldn't go up in flames. That would most certainly put a crimp in our search.

We located 2A. If my guess was right, the room would be vacant, but I knocked anyway. After a few seconds, I shoved the key into the lock and opened the door.

The apartment was small, tidy, and thankfully empty. A chair with pilled cushions stood next to a three-legged table. The bed centered the room, its solid-wood frame with four ornate posts standing out in such a humble space.

Kent closed the door behind us. "And this place belongs to?"

"Miss Thayer, I think."

"Interesting" was all he said as he strode to the closet.

I moved to the vanity at the foot of the bed. The tray was cluttered with cosmetics and a well-used grooming set. While I'd discovered the Terminal subway ticket in her jewelry box at Park Towers, this one here held nothing but paste necklaces and tarnished rings.

"Ah . . ." Kent held up a lacy handkerchief and brought it to me. "Recognize this?" He waved it in front of my face.

By sight no, but by scent? I sniffed the highly fragranced cloth. "Miss Thayer's."

He nodded, and I tried not to get irked that my husband was familiar with another woman's perfume. Kent returned to the closet as I reached behind the mirror for any secret nooks. "Why do you think she has two residences?"

"Don't know. Maybe she needed two places."

"LeRaffa made it sound like Miss Thayer was desperate to separate from her family." I kept my voice low, though I could still hear the commotion upstairs. "This doesn't look like distance to me."

He quit rummaging through her closet and moved behind me. He met my eyes in the mirror's reflection. "Sorry to disillusion you, darling, but I don't exactly see a notorious crime boss as the pillar of honesty."

I scowled. He was right, of course. The man wasn't moral, but why would he invent such a story? Unless that had been the one Adele had fed him? I moved to her bed and lifted the pillow. Nothing. I stooped and slid my hand beneath her mattress, coming up empty. "I know something's in here. I can feel it. Why else would she keep this residence?"

Kent's gaze drifted past me, eyes squinting. Quick as a wink, he moved to the edge of the bed. "This post." He tapped the decorative wood. "The varnish is duller than the others. It's been handled more." He twisted the knob at the top, and it popped off.

I scurried to peek, but he dipped his fingers inside, retrieving a slim leather planner, bent from being stuffed into the small crevice.

"We'll look at it once we're safely away." He tucked the book inside his coat pocket and returned the knob. "I'll make sure it's clear. We'll go down the back staircase and use the side exit I spotted earlier."

Kent cracked open the door, then quickly closed it. He snatched the key I'd placed on the table earlier and locked it. "Can't go out." He wedged the chair beneath the knob. "This should buy us some time."

"Why?"

"Because our friend Norman's heading this way," he said with minimal urgency.

We moved toward the only other exit, the window. I pushed back the lacy curtain. "A fire escape would be nice."

"That would make things too easy."

"We can't jump. We're two stories high."

Kent hoisted the sash and peered out. "The escape's two windows over." He straightened to full height, and his gaze dropped to my shoes. "How's your balance in those things?"

"Good enough."

"There's a ledge leading to the escape. It's somewhat narrow." A struggle deepened the grays of his eyes. "Maybe we can wait it out." He reached for his weapon.

"No, I can do it." I pressed a reassuring hand to his arm. "How about your leg?"

"Well enough, but I might need a thorough massage—"

The doorknob jiggled, followed by a loud cuss.

Before Kent could protest, I climbed out the rickety window and maneuvered onto the ledge, which was about a foot wide. If anyone happened to be out back hanging their laundry, they'd easily spot me. I forced one step at a time, more like scooting than walking, making room for Kent.

He eased out, and I said a quick prayer for our safety. I pressed my chest to the stucco, the coarse surface snagging the trim of my coat. Kent was close behind, whispering words of encouragement. It was sweet, if not a bit distracting. When I risked a peek back at him, he had one hand against the building and the other pressed on . . . his trouser pocket. Only Kent would be concerned about dropping his pocketknife rather than harbor any fear for his own safety. I reached the fire escape and forewent modesty by swinging my leg over the railing and climbing onto the landing.

Within seconds Kent was beside me. We hustled down the steps and darted around the building. Uncertain if Norman would appear, we withdrew our weapons as we dashed to the car.

No one followed.

We remained watchful while starting the car, Kent behind the wheel again. Soon we were back on the road, leaving the area in a fit of dust.

Kent's hand slid inside his coat pocket. "If this book's only a bunch of shopping lists, I'm going to be slightly annoyed."

"Only slightly?" I huffed a laugh, still trying to catch my breath from all the running. "We just risked our lives."

"There's no one I'd rather almost die with than you, Vinny." He extended his arm along the back of the seat bench, his fingers skimming my right shoulder.

My nerve endings awakened beneath his touch, humming to life with his slow mesmeric strokes.

"We're a good team. What do you say I put a *D* in front of my agency sign?"

I stiffened. "Don't tease me, Brisbane." If it were any other subject, I could endure his jesting. If he only knew how badly I wanted my own office space. "I've been goaded enough by pompous men lately, refusing to—"

"Wait." He held up his hand. "I meant no offense. I know you've worked hard to build clients. I wouldn't take that away from you. I just thought we could be partners. But if you want our agencies to remain separate, I won't mention it again."

"Are you serious?"

He nodded. "I won't bring it up if it bothers you."

"No, I meant about joining our agencies. Sharing an office."

He took a left onto an alley and turned down another, until we were on the back streets, away from traffic. He shoved the gear into neutral. "I want to share every part of my life with you." He shifted on the bench, facing me, Miss Thayer's planner resting on his lap. "Vinny, you're a top-notch detective. Anyone with brains can see that. The way you solved the Big Dante case, but even early on with the Davis investigation. That was good sleuthing."

I sucked in a sharp breath. "How'd you know about the Davis case?"

Charlotte Davis had been one of my first clients. She was the wife of a leading department store owner in lower Manhattan. A former employee had taken Charlotte's daughter, and in a vengeful ploy had almost sent the child away on an orphan train. I'd recovered her. "That was entirely confidential."

He shrugged. "People talk."

Why wouldn't he meet my gaze? "Kent?" There was no way that word had leaked. We'd been extremely cautious. Which only meant one thing. "She went to you first. You sent her to me."

His eyes flicked to mine, but he said nothing.

Looking back, I'd only placed one ad, but clients had just appeared in Hemswick's parlor. "Just how many cases did you turn over to me?"

"It doesn't matter, does it? You proved yourself. You deserve—"

"How many?"

He blew out a breath. "Several dozen."

I could only gape at him. Not a couple or even a few, but *several* dozen. How had his agency survived after shoving away that much business? I became a private investigator only weeks after we'd been granted a divorce. Well, fake divorce. But still, it'd been out of spite at first. My heart had been shattered, and all I wanted to do was prove to Kent Brisbane that I didn't need him. I'd planned to steal all his clients, yet all the while he'd been turning them over to me. Question after question rolled in, but all I wanted to know was . . . "Why?"

"I never meant for you to find out." He kneaded his brows, gaze abashed. "Believe me, it wasn't because you needed my help or that I didn't think you'd succeed on your own."

"Why?" I demanded softly.

A beat of silence. "Vinny, I don't think you realize how much you meant to me." His smoky gray eyes burned an entrancing smolder, sending waves of heat between us. "Still mean to me."

Words fell short. I should be angry at his high-handedness, but I wasn't. Because I knew what it must've cost him. Growing up as he had—living in abject poverty—it must've pained him to pass on those opportunities. Business wasn't guaranteed. Detective agencies threaded the city, all scavenging for clients. And he'd freely given them up. For me.

I leaned over and wrapped my hands around his neck. His eyes widened. He probably thought I planned to strangle him for invading my affairs, but I had another idea. With my thumbs, I grazed the strong line of his jaw, savoring the scrape of stubble. My palms slid along his throat, trailing downward to where his pulse pounded in the masculine dip at the base. I felt his rugged swallow. "Thank you," I whispered.

His voice rumbled low against my skin. "I'd do anything for you."

Because people do drastic things for those they love. Words from years past stirred my soul. He'd helped me without anything in return. Without me even knowing.

Hoping to make my motive clear, I ran a knuckle along his collar, identical to the area of my birthmark.

His eyes darkened with intent, but I wasn't finished.

Our gazes knotting, I pressed my finger on the corner of his lower lip and dragged it across, a slow, languid sweep. I repeated the motion on his upper, ensuring my touch had whispered over the entirety of his mouth, stopping on that alluring scar. Watching my own ministrations, my skin flushed warm. I leaned closer, the edge of my nose nuzzling his cheek. "You know the rule, Brisbane."

In one fiery second, he erased four years of separation, closing the distance between us with the burning press of his kiss. His arms wrapped around me, hauling me closer as his mouth worked over mine with delicious execution.

Our first kiss the morning of our wedding day had been utterly reckless—two young hearts tangled in chaotic passion. Not so now. His touch was deliberate, the crushing way he held me, the dizzying delivery of his kiss, even the expertly timed sips of breath. As if he'd envisioned this one moment a thousand times.

Maybe he had.

I responded by twining my arms around his neck, endeavoring to contribute as much as I received. His mouth explored my neck, ending its fiery journey at my birthmark. He pressed a lingering kiss there, as if branding me with his ardent devotion.

Too soon he eased away. His hands went to my face, a gentle clasp, as his eyes roamed over me in tender fascination. Affection welled in those charcoal depths, sweeping away the last remnants of my reservation.

Then he kissed me again, like a husband who adored his wife.

Chapter 22

"WHAT DO YOU THINK WE'LL find?" I asked Kent, nodding to Miss Thayer's planner resting between us on the bench. We were still in his automobile, reveling in the delightful aftermath of our reunion. While I was certain Kent was keen on continuing our romantic reacquainting, I suggested we examine the pages, if only to calm my racing heart.

His thumb brushed over my knuckles, sweet and gentle. "Only one way to find out. Would you care to do the honors?"

I hadn't expected that courtesy, considering Kent had been the one who'd found the book. But my curious nature wasn't about to pass up the opportunity. With a gracious smile, I opened the small leather-bound planner. The first few pages weren't anything of consequence. Miss Thayer had jotted routine errands, such as visits to the post office and market. Kent's earlier complaint about this being her grocery lists weren't too far from the mark. "Nothing much," I said on a sigh, leafing through. I found entries from the previous two months and paused. She'd scribbled down styling appointments, but . . . "Look." I held the planner between us. "These don't match the fashion sessions she had listed for Stratton's agency."

He peered at me with questioning eyes.

"Like right here. Mrs. Babcock's listed." I pointed to the inky scrawl. I'd known Mrs. Priscilla Babcock for years, and I would've remembered the entry in the book held captive in Wallace's office.

Kent scratched his cheek. "Do you suppose Miss Thayer took extra appointments without letting Stratton in on it? Maybe that was the cause for their squabble."

"I think that's a great possibility. Perhaps he thought she was trying to steal business away from the agency and stepping out on her own." I ran my finger down the page and nearly jolted at Miss Thayer's words. They were notes about her time with Mrs. Babcock. Though instead of ramblings about the society woman's complexion or which cut of gown would suit her rounded figure best, Miss Thayer had written something else entirely.

Husband visits gambling den. Bankrupted the family. They're selling properties to cover debts.

Kent's low "hmm" told me he'd caught it as well.

I glanced over. "This changes things."

"She was blackmailing her clients." He tapped the page. "Or at least intended to."

My gaze fell over the inky letters, so femininely scripted, but venom dripped from each word. "No wonder she was able to repay LeRaffa so quickly."

"Or LeRaffa could've been one of her victims. If she had dirt on him and forced him to cough up dough to keep quiet, he could've easily silenced her for good."

A shudder rolled down my spine. It seemed logical, but then . . . "You found that receipt written in Miss Thayer's own handwriting."

"I found a piece of paper with a dollar amount and their signatures. LeRaffa was the one who called it a receipt. For all we know, instead of her paying him back, it could easily be mistaken as him giving her hush money."

He had a point. I wasn't naive enough to think LeRaffa had been honest with me. He could've conjured up that entire story about her family's involvement with the Galleanists to throw me off his trail. Because it certainly appeared that Norman Young hadn't any ties to the known anarchists. "I thought it was strange that LeRaffa broke into the apartment to steal a receipt that—if his story was true—would clear him of any possible motive. But if he was the one to pay her off—"

"It puts the motive back on him. He may have paid her off once, but who was to say she wouldn't try to weasel even more cash out of him."

I nodded. Each of my cases had been like solving a puzzle, every new piece bringing me closer to the final picture. While I'd always savored the thrill of the mystery, there was something comforting about working alongside Kent. We made a good team. My mind went back to that silly nickname the press had forced upon us—Sleuthing Sweethearts. Perhaps it wasn't a bad thing after all.

Kent's shoulder playfully nudged mine, bringing me back to the moment. "As much as my now-healed leg tells me LeRaffa's no good, my gut says keep checking. Because we now have a book of new suspects."

That we did.

I flipped the page, finding more salacious entries. This time about Mrs. Henderson, known for having elaborate parties in order to flaunt her wealth. According to Miss Thayer, the woman's husband had a fling with the nanny. I dropped the book onto my lap, my stomach churning. "It seems like Miss Thayer gained entrance to these people's houses and somehow dug up scandalous information."

"But how?" He scooped up the planner and browsed it.

I rubbed my temples, subduing a headache. Interesting how only moments ago I'd been practically in a euphoric state, caught up in the arms of my husband, and now those sordid notes tugged me to the ground of reality—exposing marriages that were in shambles, reminding me of a crucial secret I needed uncovered about Kent's past before I fully handed him my heart.

Kent continued, unaware of my internal struggle, "I doubt these ladies spilled their dark truths to her." He flipped the page, and his jaw tightened.

I leaned over to read what caused his tense reaction, my eyes landing on a familiar name—*Geneva Hayes.*

Warren's wife.

"There's nothing else on that page." No notes of any kind. But there was a faint strikethrough of pencil, as if Miss Thayer had gone back and crossed Geneva off. "It looks like Miss Thayer scratched out her name." I wasn't certain what to make of that. Either Miss Thayer hadn't felt like Geneva harbored anything worth blackmailing, or maybe the appointment had gotten canceled, or—

He tossed the book onto the bench between us. "Let's go." The gruff edge of his voice matched the engine's growl as he shoved the Model T into gear and peeled out.

I wanted to examine the rest of the planner, but Kent's aggravated mood prevented me from reaching for it. "I'm assuming we're going to Hayeses'?"

His chin dipped in a tight nod. "Warren will want to know."

I'd often wondered about their friendship. Warren Hayes had once been the matrimonial prize of our circles. Every mother had hoped their daughter would catch his eye. Because not only was the man a millionaire, he also had influence, being the publisher of one of New York's leading papers. So how did a high-class swell become like a brother to Kent? How had they even met?

Kent's agitation seemed to lighten by the time we reached the Hayeses' town house. "This should prove interesting" was all he said before taking my arm, tucking it in the crook of his, and leading me toward the large, stately home. But instead of approaching the gated front entrance, he led me around a side path to the back. The entire property was hemmed in by a masonry fence.

Without hesitation, Kent tugged a brick loose from the mortar and withdrew a hidden key. He held it up. "I kept forgetting mine when I'd visit, so Warren, ever the tinkerer, set this up so I wouldn't scale his fence anymore." He gave a sheepish smile. "I may have accidentally trampled his mother's rosebushes upon my last climb."

I shook my head, but I could see it all too clearly. "Well, we've scaled enough structures for one day. Which reminds me." All amusement dropped from my face, and I eased near enough so he could glimpse the vehemence in my expression. "I want you to take it easy with your leg."

He angled away.

Insufferable man. "If you're rolling your eyes—"

"I'm not."

"Then why did you give me the cold shoulder?"

He turned back to me, his smile slowly building. "Because I didn't think you'd appreciate me kissing you senseless out here in the open."

His words swept any rebuke off my tongue.

"That look you get when you're trying to be stern is awfully tempting to a fella like me."

"You're talking nonsense." And I would not let my thoughts trip over themselves at his remark about kissing. So I cut him my most severe glare, which only made him draw closer.

"Like now." His thumb traced my jawline, stopping just under my chin. "Why do you think I enjoy getting you riled up all the time?"

"Because of our rule," I said, unusually winded. "You're trying to touch my every last nerve."

His grin sparked, even as he inched closer. "Because you press your lips so tight together that when you relax them, they're slightly swollen, making me want to keep them that way." His gaze fell to my mouth.

"Behave." My feeble warning was breathy and pathetic, even to my own ears.

"It's challenging when you're around." He hooked his arm around my waist and kissed me anyway. Or maybe I kissed him. It happened too fast for me to dissect, but it was over almost as quickly as it started.

Soon Kent was opening the back gate, and we went up the path to the rear entrance of the house.

He gave a quick knock, and within seconds the butler appeared.

"Good morning, Mr. Brisbane."

"Jenkins." He squeezed past the butler, clapping the man on the shoulder. "We don't need announced." He held his hand out to me, and the butler didn't even arch a brow.

Kent's fingers twining mine, he guided me through the kitchen into the hall. "Warren," he called. "You have company."

"If that's you, Kent Brisbane . . ." An exasperated female voice sounded from a few doors down. "I'm mad at you."

"Geneva," he whispered to me by way of explanation, not even breaking his stride. "I can't think of any reason why," he answered louder, in his signature breezy fashion.

"You're married! For four years! And you didn't breathe a word, you dirty sneak." The woman herself appeared in the hallway, hands firmly on her hips, eyes narrowed in daggers. Though I couldn't exactly call her intimidating, not with her adorably rounded stomach revealing her expecting state. Her large blue eyes caught sight of me, and her mouth softened to an O.

It was evident she wasn't anticipating my presence. She waddled toward us, the front hem of her dress slightly higher than the back, heightening her cuteness. "I do apologize." She cut a sharp look to Kent. "Not to you. I'm still angry with you." She took my other hand and pulled me into a hug. "I'm apologizing to you, Delvina. Normally I behave better than this. But I just learned that Brisbane has been keeping secrets."

"He likes to do that." I ignored Kent's light scoff. Not that I could say much else, with Geneva embracing me tightly as if we were old friends. Out of the socialites, she had been the nicest. She hadn't attended a lot of public events, but when she had, she'd always gone out of her way to speak with me.

"Well, of all the people Brisbane could be secretly married to, I'm glad it's you. You're probably the only woman who can keep him in line."

"Or I can tug her out of line with me." He smiled broadly. "It's much more fun that way."

My mind traveled back to the day he'd taken me roller skating and the words he'd said to convince me to put the skates on. *"Haven't you heard? The misfits have all the fun."* As if coaxed, my gaze sought his, only to find him watching me intently. Had he been thinking of the same thing?

A tiny smile played on Geneva's lips, and I realized she'd witnessed our exchange. "Are you two hungry? I'll request some scones to be brought out with our coffee. They're heavenly."

Heavy footsteps sounded on the back staircase, and Warren Hayes appeared. His gaze fell on us, even as he wrapped an arm around Geneva. "Ah, the not-so-newlyweds are here." A grin split his face, and Geneva lightly swatted his arm.

"We're making the worst impression," she said with a resigned sigh. "Again, I apologize, Delvina. We usually have better manners than this."

"We do?" Warren playfully goaded his wife, and it was difficult not to smile.

"Yes." Her eyes narrowed in a mock glare. "We do." She angled toward me. "So let me make this up to you, dear, by plying you with raspberry scones and every savory thing from our kitchen."

"Am I invited?" Kent asked good-naturedly.

"I suppose. But if you pull this kind of malarkey again"—she smiled sweetly—"you'll be forced to sit by my mother at every dinner party from here to eternity."

I held in a snicker. Mrs. Ashcroft had a reputation for being demanding. The woman thrived on being the center of attention for every conversation. Kent, as her seat companion, would be stuck catering to her every whim.

The threat made him stand taller and raise his right hand, as if repeating a solemn swear. "I promise. Besides, I'm too busy to pull any stunts. My hands are full convincing Delvina of what a great catch I am."

I wrinkled my nose at him, and his low chuckle surrounded me as we migrated to the parlor. Geneva swiftly spoke to the maid and then rejoined us. Once we were all seated, Kent leaned forward. The crease between his brows and lowering of his tone transitioned us from our light welcome to the reason of our visit. "We've been working on a case."

Warren leaned forward, giving his friend his full focus. Kent explained about Adele Thayer's death and the events leading to the discovery of her planner.

"She wrote your name, Geneva." My husband opened the book and showed it to her. "Have you met with her?"

"Yes and no." She exchanged a significant look with her husband, then added, "My mother tried to arrange an appointment with her for me. But when Miss Thayer explained over the telephone the price and everything involved, I politely declined."

"What do you mean *involved*?" I found myself asking.

"She told me that to get a clear picture of my style, she'd like to see my closet, inspect my current wardrobe. Only then could she offer tips on improvement. Having recently dealt with a snoop, I'm overly reluctant to let people sift through my things."

I wondered if the mishap she'd referred to had anything to do with the near scandal that had arisen last year regarding this couple.

Kent shifted. "Intelligent move, Geneva, considering she was blackmailing socialites." Warren's brows rose, but Kent cut him off with a raised hand. "Not just yet, old man. I know this is a good scoop for your paper, but there are too many things we need to wrap up before this can go public."

"Understood." His friend nodded. "Any way I can help?"

Kent sat back and stroked his chin. "I'm thinking Miss Thayer got her information by searching the bedrooms of her clients with the intention of blackmail. Someone must've had enough and silenced her."

It appeared the likely scenario.

"Can I see the book?" Geneva asked. "Are the other women people I know?"

"I recognized a couple of names," I said as Kent handed her the planner. Though I knew for certain one woman was out of the country during Miss Thayer's death, which counted her out. There was Mrs. Babcock, of course. Mother had mentioned visiting her greenhouse for my bridal bouquet, so I could easily work in a conversation about Miss Thayer into my visit. "While blackmail's a great motive, there are more suspects who have just as strong a reason for killing Miss Thayer." Wallace Stratton, for one. And LeRaffa was another. And now I supposed we could put her brother down. Though uncertain of his particular motive, he certainly had acted suspicious.

"So you're sure it wasn't suicide?" This from Warren.

Kent nodded. "Positive."

"And the police?"

"They refuse to listen," I answered, unable to keep the frustration from bleeding into my words.

Warren's gaze bounced between us. "Think they'd been bought out to turn a blind eye?"

Kent opened his mouth to respond, but Geneva spoke first. "This is strange." She studied one of the pages. "Miss Thayer listed Maude Welch."

"Mrs. Welch was one of her clients," I explained, as Miss Thayer had mentioned her at my mother's dinner party. "She'd seemed sad about her death."

Kent gave a disbelieving laugh. "Or maybe Miss Thayer felt sorry she lost the chance to blackmail the woman."

"But wait." I sat forward. "That appointment—the one with Maude Welch—was booked with Stratton's agency. Remember? Wallace remarked that she was *their* client. So why would she be listed in Miss Thayer's personal one?"

"Maybe she poached her away from Stratton?" Warren seemed just as involved as we were.

Geneva waved the planner, nabbing our attention. "That's not what I'm trying to point out." Her eyes fell upon the page, then to us. "Maude's name is listed recently." She tapped her finger on the inky words, and I moved so I could see.

I locked eyes with Kent. "This date is well after Mrs. Welch's passing. At least four weeks later."

But that wasn't all. Her name was listed on the very day Miss Thayer was murdered.

Chapter 23 —————————————————————————————

MY PLACE HAD BEEN RANSACKED.

After visiting the Hayeses, we'd swung by Park Towers so I could grab more things and check in with the manager for any messages. Nothing had been left at the front desk, but as I'd opened my flat door, I discovered someone had left me a very personal message.

Fast as a blink, we drew our weapons. As if one unit, we entered the foyer, our footfalls quiet. No noise met my ears, but the disarray seemed to scream at me. Anger boiled in my chest as I stepped over the Chippendale cushion, removed from the chair and thrashed to shreds.

The parlor was in upheaval. Paintings ripped, frames disjointed. Vases shattered. The floor was a mosaic of broken things. My breath thinned. Who could've done this? It didn't seem like the intruder was still here, but that didn't prevent Kent from checking my bedroom, ensuring all was clear.

I stood there, as if my rapid blinks would somehow change the scene before me. But no, it was chaos. I understood they were only things, all easily replaced. Well, maybe not the Chippendale piece, though still. It went beyond slashed fabric and fragmented glass. Someone had invaded my space with the intent to destroy. Why? Had they purposed to harm me as well?

"No one's here." Kent reentered the parlor, holstering his gun.

I tucked my revolver away seconds before he wrapped me in a hug I didn't realize I needed. It seemed he craved the contact too, judging by the way his hand stroked the back of my head, as if reassuring himself as much as me. My eyes burned with the sting of tears, whether from sadness or fury, I couldn't determine—both waged strong within me. We embraced in the center of the rubble for several moments.

I eased back first. "How'd they get in?" Needing to focus on a task, I disentangled from Kent's arms and checked the lock. With a meticulous eye, I inspected the doorframe, swiping my hand across the smooth wood. No signs of forced entry.

Kent studied the windows and faced me with a shake of his head. "All the sashes are closed and locked. The one in your bedroom is too." Of course he'd already investigated that.

"What about the servants' entrance?"

"You got one of those?"

Though I hadn't a personal maid, my flat was equipped for extra domestic help. "Third door on the right." Kent was already striding down the hall before I could finish. I called after him, "The key is hanging on a hook by the jamb." At least it should've been. If that was gone, then I supposed the intruder would have free access to my apartment. Not a comforting thought.

Within seconds he returned. "It's locked. The key was where you said it was." He swept a hand over the debris, a grimace tugging at his scar. "Can you tell if anything's missing?"

I motioned him to follow me, and I picked my way to the bedroom. Its disheveled state was similar to the parlor's. Clothes strewn everywhere. My dresser drawers had been emptied and tossed about. My jewelry box had been smashed, all its previous contents in an untidy pile on my vanity tray. It wasn't as if I'd taken inventory of every single belonging, so it would prove challenging to determine if anything had been stolen. I picked up a diamond bracelet I'd received from my Kline parents. "Look at this."

Kent let out a low whistle. "That alone's worth a hefty sum. A burglar would filch that in a heartbeat if given the chance."

And yet they hadn't. Nor had they taken my sapphire earrings or opal pendant. After sifting through the tangled pile of chains and trinkets, it seemed my jewelry was accounted for. If the intruder hadn't broken in to steal expensive baubles, what had they been after?

I couldn't even judge when this had occurred, since I'd been staying with Kent. Or . . . maybe I could. I crouched beside a taupe stain on my cream carpet. My perfume. I pressed a finger there. The spot was dry. If the break-in had been recent, the fragrance would've been much stronger and perhaps still damp. I looked over at Kent, who'd been sweetly hanging up my gowns. Never mind that the toe of his shoe was barely inches from a pair of lacy bloomers.

I stood and joined him by my closet. "Did you tell anyone I'm working the Thayer case?"

His brow darkened. "No. Of course not."

I smiled at his adamance. "Just wanted to be sure. I feel whoever did this is linked to Miss Thayer's death." With my heel, I tried to subtly scoot the bloomers near the heap of sweaters, but the movement only pulled Kent's gaze to my infernal undergarments.

His lips twitched. "Would you like me to pick that up for you?"

"No thank you." I snatched them from the floor and shoved them into one of the discarded carpenter bags. "All I'm saying is"—I pushed my hair from my face, determined to get the conversation where it needed to be . . . off my bloomers and onto the case—"Wallace Stratton knows I live in this building." Thanks to my foolish admission at his office. "That's why I needed to be certain you didn't tell him about my investigating her death." Though he probably could have deduced such a thing on his own.

"What about that Paulo character?"

I swiped wayward locks of hair from my forehead. "What about him?"

"He knows you're looking into Miss Thayer's death." He glanced at the door, as if the large maintenance man would appear any moment. "You said he once lived on the wrong side of the law."

I waved him off. "I trust Paulo. He owes me too much to do this." My gaze skipped over the wreckage that had once been my pristine flat.

"Although the intruder could be the person who followed me the other day. I'm still furious I didn't get a good look at—"

"Someone followed you?"

Oh, I hadn't mentioned that little detail? "It was no big deal. It was the day after the mishap at the Terminal, when I came here to get my clothes. I saw I was being tailed, but I lost them pretty quickly." Because I wasn't about to let whoever it was trail me to Hemswick.

He cupped my face with his hand, his tender gesture at odds with his furrowed brow. "Why didn't you tell me?"

"Honestly, I don't know. It happened the day we discussed our relationship. That conversation seemed to wipe everything else out of my mind."

He nodded. "I can see that." Now his thumb stroked along my cheekbone, igniting the skin beneath. "What do you say I give this place a thorough search, see if our prowler left anything behind, while you gather some of your stuff to bring home? Then I want to take you somewhere to get your mind off everything." There was a hopefulness in his expression he usually masked, but this time he let me see.

Whatever he'd planned seemed to be important. If I were able to salvage any resistance after his candidness, him referring to his flat as our home would've bankrupted my defenses.

Although I did have one hesitation. "How's your leg?"

"At ease, commander. My leg's doing great. Besides, where we're going doesn't require much physical activity." He slung his arm around me and waggled his brows. "Unless you want it to."

"Go be a detective." I shoved his chuckling self toward the door. Only when I was certain he was out of earshot did my own laughter emerge.

●　●　●

The intruder had left no trace. Unsurprising but disappointing. So after I'd gathered my things, I'd sought out Paulo, letting him know what had happened, asking him to keep an eye on the place. Now in Kent's automobile, I huddled into my coat, the outside temperature having dipped while inside Park Towers.

"Sorry I couldn't find anything helpful," Kent said after a few minutes of driving. He'd been cutting looks over his shoulder, ensuring we weren't being tailed. My car had been equipped with mirrors, but Kent's was . . . basic, to say the least.

"We still had a productive day." I rallied a smile, trying not to think about my flat in shambles. "I'm wondering if Adele Thayer's planner holds the key to all this." We hadn't much time to discuss what we'd discovered within those bent pages. "What about the double-booking of Maude Welch? As far as I can remember, she was in both books—the one for Stratton's agency and her personal one."

His hands flexed against the steering wheel, then curled around it tightly. "Maybe Miss Thayer found something interesting while on her visit for Stratton and decided to revisit Mrs. Welch later. No, never mind." He blew out a frustrated breath. "That can't work. Mrs. Welch's name was listed after her death."

More specifically, her name had been jotted down the day Miss Thayer had been killed. That was significant—I could feel it in my bones. "Let's go over all that we know about Mrs. Welch."

He shrugged. "We don't know much."

"Humor me."

That earned a full smile. "Always, love."

"It was mentioned at Mother's dinner party that Mrs. Welch lived in Guam for a while. Then we know she returned to the States and lived in Manhattan until she passed from the sleeping sickness."

"Why did she live in Guam?"

"I don't know. Next time I see Mother, I'll ask her about Mrs. Welch's past. Maybe there's a clue there." I waited for Kent's nod, then continued. "How about this. Let's dissect the connection between Miss Thayer and Mrs. Welch. We know Miss Thayer consulted Mrs. Welch through Wallace Stratton's agency. She and Wallace had been surprised to learn about Mrs. Welch's death."

"Miss Thayer more so than Stratton." He slowed to a stop at the sign, waving pedestrians to cross. "I would venture to say Miss Thayer was agitated."

"I agree." I could still envision the young woman's horrified expression. How she'd bobbled her silverware, nearly spilling her drink. "She was distressed. I know you said earlier that she could've been upset about losing Mrs. Welch as a potential blackmail target, but I don't think that's it. Something is off about this entire case."

Kent grew quiet, allowing me to process.

"Why *did* Miss Thayer react so strongly about Mrs. Welch's death?" It didn't make sense. "I understand if she was sorrowful, but nervous shock? Mrs. Welch passed from sleeping sickness. It wasn't as if *she* was murdered."

"Unless she was."

"And Miss Thayer knew it." The spiked hair on my arms had nothing to do with the chill. "Wait." I shook my head, grabbing hold of reason rather than fanciful assumptions. "Sleeping sickness isn't covered up that easily."

I knew a great deal about sleeping sickness from researching it on Mother's behalf. If there'd been foul play, I imagine it would've been obvious. Most poisons carried a telltale sign. Like arsenic and cyanide convulsing the body, causing vomiting, showing marks of agony. Sleeping sickness was just . . . sleeping with the chance of never waking up. "Think she was drugged with barbiturates?"

Kent was pensive, more so than I'd ever seen. "They're easy enough to obtain. But I doubt it. That kind of stuff stays in someone's system long after postmortem. Unless whoever examined her purposefully overlooked it."

We were silent for a couple of minutes, each lost in thought, when Kent suddenly said, "Blast."

I jumped, thinking something was wrong, like a stray cat running onto the road. "What?"

"It was Dr. Ewing." He nearly growled the name. "He attended Mrs. Welch. Remember he said so at the dinner party? He was even about to elaborate on the case but—"

"You cut him off for Mother's sake." I recalled that clearly, even my flush of emotion at witnessing Kent's attentiveness to my mother. "I'm glad you did."

"Even though we might have learned an interesting detail about her death?"

"Even though," I answered softly. "So now we think of a way to get information out of Dr. Ewing. Or I can always try to break into the morgue archives again."

"And here I thought you'd turned your back on your life of crime, darling." He shrugged, as if giving up trying to reform his lawless wife. "We'll sort things out later. Because for the next couple of hours, you're mine."

I rolled my lips inward, suppressing a smile, but given the flash of pleasure in Kent's eyes, he was aware of the effect he had on me. I cleared my throat. "That sounds quite territorial of you, Mr. Brisbane."

He drove onto a vacant lot. "In all fairness, I'm open to reciprocate. I am very much yours."

Warmed by his words, I peered out the window, immediately recognizing the industrial ghost town. "You brought me to the Hayes Publishing old building?" It was this same place Kent had taken me over four years ago.

"I thought I'd go for the sentimental route. How's that working for me?"

"Too early to tell," I teased back. "I'll let you know."

"I can live with that." He jumped out of the automobile and opened my door.

I was reluctant to move. "We're not roller skating again, are we?" As much as I'd enjoyed learning that day, I wasn't in the mood for zipping around on shoes with wheels.

"No, I had something else in mind."

The husky notes in his tone roused my curiosity. He took my hand and led me through the familiar passageways and staircases to the basement.

My hand went to my parted mouth. In the center of the space was a table arranged in elegance. An expensive centerpiece, fine china settings for two, and a basket off to the side. This formal arrangement was out of place in a dusty basement, and I absolutely adored it. "How did you manage this?" I'd been with the man all day.

"Seems my best friend is more of a romantic sap than I am. We talked about it earlier at his house."

"But"—my brows lifted in suspicion, even as I ran a finger along the luxurious tablecloth—"I'd only agreed to come with you an hour ago."

"I remember once telling you I'm not one for hedging my bets."

He'd said those words the night we'd met. I recalled that evening with perfect clarity, mostly because I'd replayed those moments in my head for days—weeks—following. I lifted the lid of the picnic basket, and my stomach rumbled at the scent of roasted chicken. The basket of bread appeared warm, indicating Warren must've recently left.

"There's another reason I brought you here." His head tipped back, his gaze on the ceiling for a heart-pounding second before settling on me. "I wanted to share a bit about my past. Perhaps it will explain some things."

A twinge of guilt niggled my chest. Maybe I should have confessed what Tabitha had told me last night. How I understood more than he realized.

"The other day I told you I was given over to the children's home by Kit Mason, the woman who was my mother's nurse."

I nodded.

"It wasn't a good place. There were days I went without food because there wasn't enough to go around. I slept on the cold floor. I ran away when I was nine." He looked away with a pained expression. "Then I lived on the streets."

I grabbed his hand and softly pleaded, "Tell me about it."

And he did. He told me about getting a shoeshine job outside the barbershop and sleeping behind the dress shop. He explained how before winter hit, he'd pooled his earnings along with other homeless kids to lease a flat not much larger than a closet to shelter them in the night hours. That expense prevented him from buying food and clothing, specifically shoes.

"I worked from sunup to sundown with nothing but parcel paper wrapping my feet." A somberness haunted his gaze. Kent wasn't just relaying his past—he seemed to be reliving it. "The tissue on my soles is dead from frostbite. I couldn't fight in the war because of it." Shame darkened his tone, and I hated it.

I grabbed both of his shoulders, anchoring him to the present. "That's because you had to fight your entire life. The odds were against you, Kent, and you survived."

"I'm no hero, Vinny."

"Then what's your definition? Because to me, a hero's someone who refuses to quit. You faced hard things. Only to wake up and do so again. Then again." I ran my hands down his arms to grasp his hands. "You're the bravest man I know."

He blinked away the moisture in his eyes. "I had a scrap of paper with the name Kit Mason on it and a pocketknife I found in a gutter. That was all I had to my name."

Ah, that was why he'd been protective of that knife. I felt awful now for calling it silly.

"I don't even know where I'd be if it wasn't for Geneva." He explained how she'd witnessed one of his high-society patrons box his ears for spilling shoe polish, and she took the issue to Warren's paper. A young Warren had found Kent and brought him to Warren's father, who offered Kent a job.

Kent pointed to the back left area of the basement. "I spent many nights right in that little room."

"Warren's father allowed you to stay here?"

He palmed the back of his neck. "No, it was all Warren's idea. Even way back then, he had an inventor's brain. He built a nook for me to sleep in, hidden from view." He glanced about—only this time there was a fondness in his expression. "Warren's mother caught him sneaking food, and she brought me into their home. She taught me how to read and write."

This morning I'd questioned the origins of his and Warren's friendship. Now I knew. They basically had grown up alongside each other. "I can see why this place is special to you."

"That's why I brought you here those years ago. I wanted to share this space with you." The vulnerability in his expression melted me more than a thousand suns. This was the side of Kent I'd begged to see, but he'd refused to draw back the curtain until now.

I ran my hand along his arm until our fingers twined. "Why didn't you tell me about this place back then?"

"I was never supposed to meet you, Vinny. I'm a kid from the streets. An orphan. I only attended those soirees and parties because Warren dragged me along, and nobody dared refuse him. I definitely didn't belong with someone like you." He brought our joined hands to his lips. "I should've told you, but—"

"You thought I'd see you differently if I knew?"

"Most would."

He was right. Most would've turned their noses up at him, unfair as it was. Our sphere hardly accepted anyone. Even those who supposedly belonged to it, such as me. "I don't see you differently, Kent. I see you better." With my free hand, I cupped his face, skimming my thumb over the scar beside his lip. "Is that how you got the scar? From your time on the streets?"

"I'd gotten into a fight with another kid who tried to steal my money while I was sleeping." His hand came over mine, still on his face. "I have a thousand stories from those days, none of which would impress a lady."

"I didn't need to be impressed. I needed a husband."

"I'm trying to fix what I broke between us." He shifted his weight, taking in a deep breath. "I have something for you."

"Are you giving me a key to this place too?" Before we'd left Park Towers, Kent had surprised me by giving me a key to his office, which he claimed was mine as well. Our office. Our detective agency. It all felt too much, but also right.

"Not exactly." He withdrew from his pocket a small velvet box that made my heart pound. "This place always meant hope to me. This was the first time I felt that things just might be okay. It represented a new life." His gaze turned tender. "This marriage didn't start out as we hoped, but maybe it's a new beginning for us too."

My vision blurred. "I feel that way too."

He opened the box, revealing a diamond ring surrounded by small rubies. "Before you get angry that I visited a jeweler with my bum leg, I'll have you know, I bought this last Friday."

I counted back in my head. "That was the day I came to your office to tell you we were still married." He'd purchased the ring then? That was even before we'd discussed our future.

"I knew in that moment, Vinny. I got a second chance that I didn't deserve but wouldn't squander. I wanted to do things the right way. So I bought you a ring. Sorry it's four years too late."

"Wait. Have you been carrying that around all day?" My eyes widened at his sheepish grin. "You walked the ledge with that on your person, didn't you?" Which now explained his awkward shifting, with one hand against his trouser pocket as he'd balanced on that narrow stone to the fire escape.

"In my defense, I kept the ring with me so you wouldn't accidentally stumble upon it at the flat." His smile couldn't get any wider. "Though you nearly came close this morning with your affectionate tap on my backside."

I snorted. "It was unintentional."

"Not how I saw it, but whatever you say." He glanced down at the box, his expression sobering. "All joking aside, in a few days we're going to stand before a judge, but I want to promise you now . . ." He started to lower to one knee.

I threw my hands out. "Don't kneel. Your leg."

He gave me an impatient look. "Are you interfering with my proposal?"

"I'd rather you stand."

"I assure you my knee can withstand a minute of kneeling."

"Fine. Proceed."

"Ah, so romantic."

A smile tickled my lips, but it was more from the happiness springing through me than from Kent's teasing.

"Delvina Brisbane, God's given us this second chance, and with His help I'm determined to be the husband you need me to be. I've adored you since that evening in the garden. Things might have slipped away from us, but I still feel the same." He slipped the ring onto my finger and kissed my knuckles. "Will you remain married to me?"

I peered into his shining eyes, admiration welling within me. Down here in this humble basement, near the room my husband had once sheltered in, everything hit me differently. If our marriage was to survive, we had to fight for it. I remembered the silent vows I whispered only last night. Today I got to answer aloud. "Yes." Before I could get the word fully out, Kent was on his feet, pulling me to him.

He kissed me. His hands cradled my face as his mouth worked over mine in sweet devotion. I melted against him, savoring the moment, which tasted like forever. This morning in his car, there'd been an urgency in his kiss, as though trying to coax my heart more than my lips. But now his touch whispered assurance, every touch a promise.

● ● ●

We eventually ate our dinner, which was a tad on the cold side, but I didn't regret the delay. Kent and I were closer than we'd ever been, giving me hope for our future. My gaze fell to my ring. I was now an engaged and married woman, a rarity not many could claim. While I'd never wished for any of the heartbreak, I felt stronger and wiser than the young girl who'd tripped in her roller skates and fell heart first for the private detective.

"Thank you, Kent," I said softly. "For the ring. For taking me here." I reached across the table and grabbed his hand. "And for sharing about your past. I know that was difficult for you. I just wish you would've talked about it sooner."

His thumb swept across my wrist in rhythmic strokes. "The day we married, I had this sickening dread that you'd realize how far beneath you I was and . . . consider it all a mistake."

His words swirled around me, taking me longer than it should've to string together. But when I did, my gut sank. "You thought I left because of your status?"

"It doesn't matter now, love."

"Oh, but it does." I gently retracted my hand from his. "I left because I saw you."

His head tilted in question.

"I saw you at Penn Station that day." My heart, so buoyant with joy mere moments ago, deflated in my chest. I hadn't expected to tackle this subject so soon after Kent's proposal, but now that I'd opened the door, I might as well barge through it. "I followed you there and watched you board a train with another woman."

He flinched, something akin to anguish tightening his features. "No." He pressed the heel of his hand to his forehead. "No, Vinny. That was not what you think."

"I know what I saw."

He muttered under his breath, then leaned forward, gaze intent. "Let me explain."

Chapter 24 ————————————————————————————

Kent
1920

MY RIGHT ARM GREW NUMB, but I wasn't about to wake my wife. Delvina curled against me, her head pinning my shoulder to the mattress, her soft breaths slipping through parted lips. A view I hoped I never would lose the wonder of. Because even though this was my first morning as a married man, I already looked forward to decades with her in my arms.

Was it only yesterday I'd discovered the brutal truth surrounding my birth? Oddly, the same had happened to Delvina. We'd both found out significant details about our parents, and yet . . . we hadn't. My mother remained a mirage of my imagination, and Delvina's birth parents could be anywhere on the globe.

We'd both been shocked by revelations about our absent relatives, and then, as if in united defiance, we'd established a new family. Ours.

Drawn by our newly formed bond, I twisted to wrap my other arm around her, cradling her sleeping form.

Her dark lashes fluttered, then lifted, giving me another glimpse of something that never ceased to pull the air from my chest. Her gaze held the remnants of slumber, but the soft morning light filtering through the blinds touched her face, making those onyx hues sparkle.

"Kent." My name on her breathy sigh had me easing close and dropping a kiss on those heavy eyelids.

"Good morning, love." I smoothed the hair from her forehead, a slow sweep that made her body shiver. Was she cold? Or was that the effect of my touch?

She tugged the sheet to her neck and curled into me, only to grow quiet again. I guessed she'd fallen back asleep, and so it surprised me when she softly said, "I think I made a mistake."

My body tensed. That beast of dread that, only last evening, I'd locked away in the dark corners of my mind broke free from its brittle cell and charged with bared fangs. I'd feared she'd waken with a clear head and regretful heart. "How so?"

Her mouth opened then shut, as if uncertain whether to release the pressing words.

"You can tell me anything." No matter if it crushed me. After I'd left Warren's residence, setting off on my own again at seventeen, I vowed I'd never put myself in a position where I'd be forced to beg or plead. I never wanted to return to the pathetic kid who hated handouts but desperately needed them. Vow or no, I'd do anything to make her stay.

"It's just"—she blinked up at me, her fingers toying with the edge of the sheet—"I haven't brought any clothes. I know we didn't plan on marrying, but I feel kind of foolish not having anything to wear."

Relief as sweet as her kiss swept through me, and I didn't even try to bite back my smile. "I fail to see the problem here."

"Kent." Her rebuke was more amused exasperation than cutting scold.

I'd happily endure any reprimanding if that meant keeping her with me. "I'm only teasing." I met her eyes. "Slightly."

Her foot connected with my shin. Not forceful enough to bring any pain, but just enough contact to spur playful retaliation. Beneath the sheet, my hand found her waist and my fingers danced along her ribs.

She gasped. "Unfair! No tickling!"

"Not my fault if you're unprepared to finish what you start."

She tried to roll away, but I hauled her back to me, her laughter warming me just as much as her skin against mine.

"Truce!" she exclaimed between scrapes of breath. "And here's my peace offering." She kissed me with enough fire in her delivery that I could only offer my own treaty, matching her passion and furthering our negotiations.

After some time, we finally returned to her dilemma. "Here you go, Knuckles." I handed her the softest shirt I could find in my closet. "Yours until we can get you some clothes." I wasn't sure whether she intended to retrieve her wardrobe from Hemswick or send me to purchase what she needed. If the former, then she'd need to speak with her parents. If the latter, then I'd have to visit a pawn shop along the way to afford everything. I glanced at my watch chain on the bedside table. The solid gold should fetch a nice price. Perhaps I could manage a modest ring for her.

"This is perfect." Delvina's voice pulled my attention to her. She nuzzled against the collar of my shirt, inhaling deeply. "It even smells like you."

Every intelligent thought disappeared. Gone. Who was the current president? No idea. What year was it? Nineteen something. My entire brain emptied of all knowledge except how alluring she looked wearing only my shirt.

She caught me staring and smiled. "I'm fully covered." Her fingers brushed the hem that skirted her thighs. "This is far better than the dowry box my mother had stockpiled for me. Can you imagine . . . an entire cedar chest full of frilly things, and most of them pink." She shuddered dramatically, as if that specific color was the equivalent of some sort of awful disease.

"Ah, is that why you declined the flowers yesterday?" The walk-up wedding booth had offered a sad assortment of slightly dead pink roses. If I couldn't get her an engagement ring, I'd at least wanted her to have a bouquet, but she'd dismissed the idea entirely.

"I already have everything I wanted." She caught my hand in hers and gave me a sultry smile. "Besides, when Mother finally finds out about us, I didn't want to have to explain why I had roses." She rolled her eyes. "I'd never hear the end of it."

Delvina made it sound like the most shocking question her mother would ask regarding our rushed marriage would be about a bridal bouquet. "Does Mrs. Kline dislike flowers?"

"Oh no, she loves them." Delvina picked up her discarded dress from the floor, distracting my thoughts about how it had first landed there last night. "But she's mentioned a thousand times how she wanted me to have daylilies and veronicas for my wedding, as she did."

I stilled, giving her my full attention. A flower that began with *v*. "I'd never heard of veronicas before. What color are they?" Yesterday's conversation at the café leaped out at me. The woman had mentioned my mother had a handkerchief with the initials VR, along with an embroidered flower. She'd suspected her name was Violet, but now I wasn't certain.

She shrugged. "Like roses, they can be different colors."

"Purple?"

"Certainly."

There it was. That distinct feathering in my gut, reminding me to take action. What most referred to an intuition, I'd named my survival guide, the gentle nudging that had led me since I'd been a boy. Because of it, I'd dodged innumerable scrapes. It appeared I should follow once again, starting with a telephone call.

• • •

While Delvina spot-cleaned her dress in the bathroom, I slipped downstairs and contacted the one person who had a fingertip on the pulse of New York City—Margaret James. We'd met as children, both living on the streets. Once a brilliant pickpocket, Mags had been taken in by a middle-class family with upper-crust connections. She'd married a high-society gent but had never forgotten her roots. Mags made it her life's mission to rescue the homeless and give them a decent education, while also teaching them useful skills.

Needless to say, she heard not only the gossip of the swells but also the murmurs of the city's underworld. After the operator made the exchange, I shared with Mags what I knew, specifically asking her to check into someone named Veronica, or possibly Violet, who'd disappeared in 1898.

Mags couldn't guarantee results. Not that I could blame her, given the few details I provided.

I returned only seconds before Delvina emerged from the bathroom, and I ignored the press of guilt climbing my spine. The less Delvina knew about my past, the better. She was naturally inquisitive, and I was innately guarded. I wasn't too concerned though. We needn't solve everything in a day's worth of marriage. An entire lifetime stretched before us.

We enjoyed our time in the flat, hidden away from the rest of the world. I stepped out briefly to snag us some lunch from the diner down the block. The owners hadn't even raised a brow when I'd asked for an extra portion. Good folks.

After we'd eaten, Delvina excused herself to take a bath, while I browsed the notes about my mother, adding the new possibility of her name.

"Brisbane," young Billy called through the door. The kid had a set of megaphones for lungs. "Telephone for you."

With a quick check at the closed bathroom, I shot up from the sofa and welcomed my freckle-faced secretary. "They say who it was, Billy?"

He waggled his orange brows like a half-pint rascal. "Some dame."

Mags? Already? She'd never gotten back to me this fast. I found a penny in my pocket, which Billy's grubby hands swiftly snatched from my palm. "Hurry down and tell her to wait."

"Got it." And then he took off, his footfalls sounding like a legion of soldiers rather than a ten-year-old kid.

My gaze bounced back to the bathroom door. How long did women take to bathe? A half hour? An hour? I had no clue. I doubted Mags had enough information to keep me on the line too long. I probably could be downstairs and back before Delvina finished. With that plan, I flew down the steps, much quieter than Billy but a whole lot faster.

In the back room, among crates of cheap cigars that reeked like tar, a telephone sat out of place on the shelf. I grabbed the candlestick base, the receiver pressed to my lips. "What you got for me, Mags?"

"Fine. Hello to you too, Brisbane." I could practically see her rolling her eyes at me, like when we were young. "I found her."

Three words, and my heart stopped cold. While I'd considered myself decently skilled when it came to sleuthing, I'd repeatedly failed to find my mother. It'd taken Mags less than five hours. Though I couldn't get ahead of myself. I'd foolishly thought Kit Mason had been my mother. This woman Mags had dug up could be a false lead as well. "You sure it's her?"

"Meet me at Penn Station in an hour."

I glanced at my pocket watch. It was nearly two o'clock. "Can't you tell me now?"

"I'm taking the three thirty-five to Delchester. Find me beneath the clock. We can talk until I have to board." With that, she disconnected.

With a heavy exhale, I returned the speaker to the base. I kneaded my brows, as if the movement would somehow slow the spinning thoughts. I had to go to the Penn. There was no question. But what was I going to say to—

"Who was that?"

I jolted.

Delvina leaned against the bottom of the stairway banister, a single brow arching. When had she come down? I tried to recall what I'd said to Mags. Had I mentioned my mother? No. I hadn't revealed to Mags who the person of interest was.

I smiled. "Just someone from a case I'm working on." Not exactly a lie. I reached for her, and she hesitantly let me pull her into my arms, a familiar fragrance meeting me. Sweet mercy, she'd used my soap. My scent in her hair, on her skin, stirred some primal reflex within me, making me hold her tighter. I didn't want to leave her. Not even for an hour.

But I had to.

"I thought you said . . . you're invisible here." She eased back to look at me. "That's why you have a telephone at your office. You know, for your cases."

My jaw locked. I *had* said that. Because it was mostly true. Though given the wary glint in her eyes, she believed she'd caught me in a lie. "You're right. But some of my informants have this exchange number." My fingers bunched the fabric at her waist, and I realized she was wearing her dress from yesterday. It must've dried from her spot-cleaning this morning. "Listen, Vinny—"

Noise from the front of the shop interrupted me.

I dropped my hands from her sides in exchange for her hand. With a nod up the steps, I led her back to my flat.

Once inside she looked at me expectantly. What could I say? I couldn't tell her. Not this. Not yet. I'd wanted to savor these moments with her before bringing up the ugly facts about my birth. She'd known I wasn't from her class, but she wasn't aware of how beneath her I was. Besides, I wasn't even certain if Mags had found my mother. So what would be the point in baring the sordid truth if I didn't have to?

"I'm sorry." I kept her hand in mine, lightly squeezing her fingers, willing her to understand through my touch. "Something important arose about a long-standing case. It needs my urgent attention."

Instead of being dejected, she brightened. "Okay, let me get my purse." She reached for the black bag on the end table. "Maybe I can use the knowledge you taught me to help. Two heads are better than one, right?"

The eagerness in her voice nearly did me in. "I'm sorry, Delvina, but I need to attend this one alone. I'm uncertain what I'll discover." I implied there could be danger. There were definite risks, but the kind that could inflict pain on my heart. What if I went to the station only for Mags to reveal my mother had passed away? All that searching, that hoping for a reunion, would be gone.

"I see." Delvina's arms wilted to her sides, her fingers slipping from mine. "When will you be back?"

"As soon as I can." I kissed her goodbye. "I promise." I grabbed my hat and was out the door before I could change my mind.

• • •

Since its opening over a decade ago, Penn Station had been a hub of activity. Millions of New Yorkers had huddled beneath grand skylights, awaiting adventure.

Several clocks hung throughout the large hall, but I assumed Mags had meant the enormous one suspended from the ceiling. And there she was. Margaret James, with her tall frame and fiery-red hair, was easy to spot. She was browsing the evening paper, but I knew she was taking in her surroundings more than catching up on the latest society gossip.

"Good evening, Mrs. James." I nodded politely, as if this were a random encounter rather than a planned meeting. "Fine weather this afternoon."

"Indeed." She folded the newspaper in unhurried movements. "I found her."

Though she repeated the words from the telephone call, my heart clenched so tightly my chest ached. "She's still alive?"

"Yes." She offered a warm smile. "But I don't know for how long."

My initial relief spiraled into unease. Mags held on to her pleasant expression like a seasoned actress, employing a familiar private detective tactic. Drama attracted attention, so it was crucial to relay information with a positive or neutral demeanor. To any onlooker it appeared Mags and I were having a friendly conversation, not discussing something of a serious nature.

I adopted the same strategy, forcing the tension from my limbs and leaning a shoulder against a nearby pillar. "Is she ill?"

"No. There's danger involved." She spread open the newspaper with a flourish and nodded at an article.

I moved closer, my gaze on the paper but not really seeing anything but black on white.

With the paper acting as our shield, she spoke freely. "The reason I was able to locate Veronica Ridgeway is because someone else has been searching for her."

Ridgeway. I finally had a last name. As for the other bit of information . . . "Who's looking for her?" Had I another sibling? Relative? Or what about that hostile man from the asylum who had wanted me dead? I shook my head. It'd been over two decades—doubtful he'd continued the search this long.

"She wasn't a kept mistress as you suspected."

My pulse leaped.

"In 1897, a year before the date you gave, Veronica Ridgeway was having her debut season."

A debutante? "She was . . ."

"The niece of Dorian Ridgeway. Known bachelor. Veronica's parents died from influenza, and he'd taken her in as a ward. He was her guardian until she disappeared."

That could mean I might have a great-uncle still alive. That was one thought of a million scenarios rolling through my mind. What if Dorian Ridgeway had been a beast and my mother had run away? What if he felt disgraced about her being with child and had ordered my death? "Your source said she disappeared. Was it willingly or by force?"

"I'm uncertain. My contact was hesitant to tell me even this much." She tilted her head toward the tracks. "As we speak, my contact is on a train out of the city, for fear of their life. I sent them to one of my safe houses."

"I'm not following, Mags. Someone's after both Veronica Ridgeway *and* your contact?"

"Somebody paid my contact an enormous sum to locate Ms. Ridgeway." She rattled off a staggering number that would've made my mouth slack if I were anywhere but a public place. "My contact, in turn, gave me this information. If their mystery client finds out my contact betrayed them, it could be ugly."

I knew Mags wouldn't disclose the name of her contact, but I appreciated them risking everything to help me. "This mystery man that hired your contact, is it the uncle? I'm sure he has the wealth to spend in hopes of finding her."

"Dorian Ridgeway is long dead." She shot down my theory.

"Whoever this person is, they're extremely clever. They hired my contact through an ad in the paper, then communicated with a series of letters. It was all done anonymously."

Surely there was a trail. "Where did your contact send their replies? What address?"

"A letter box from the Eighth Avenue post office."

Well, there went that. Anyone with enough money and forged papers could rent a postal slot.

"The box belonged to an A. Punire." She closed the newspaper. "Which I bet is a false name."

"But it's a clue." Not a very pleasant one. I recalled the huge volumes of books Warren's mother had propped in front of me, one being dead languages. "In Latin, *punire* is the core word for *punish*." More specifically, to take vengeance. Or to cause to have pain for an offense.

A bolt of dread cut through me.

"Like I said, this Ridgeway woman is in danger. Here." She handed me a slip of paper. "It's the address my contact gave Punire just this morning."

"'Greenford,'" I read aloud, then again in my head because it seemed too much of a coincidence. I didn't believe in those. "I-I know this town." It was near my hunting cabin.

"I suggest you find her before Punire does."

I dragged a hand over my face, the weight of it all crashing into me with bullying force. I'd just gotten married. I couldn't leave Delvina. But could I let this threat to my mother go unchecked? This Punire person already had several hours head start. I might already be too late. My gut twisted. Delvina was at my flat, safe. My mother was in danger. "Thank you, Mags. I owe you."

"This should save you time." She opened her satin purse and withdrew a ticket. "My train takes you as far as Delchester. The connecting one will drop you off not far from Greenford."

Seemed Mags was familiar with the area as well. "I need to make a telephone call."

"Make it quick." She gave a pointed look at the terminal. "Should be boarding soon."

I quickly located a public telephone. A fleeting thought told me to take Delvina with me, but I dismissed it. Delvina needed to be kept safe at all costs. If that meant keeping her in the dark about this case, then so be it. I couldn't let anything happen to her.

I waited for the exchange, my heart beating a wild tattoo in my chest. Finally my landlord answered. "Hey, Roger, can you send Billy upstairs and fetch the woman there? I need to speak with her."

There was a pause. "Sure."

Let the man think whatever he wanted. I wouldn't tell a soul we were married until Delvina confessed it to her parents.

After several long seconds, Roger mumbled, "Billy says there ain't no woman up there."

I rubbed my forehead, knocking my hat askew. Where was Delvina? "Okay, jot a note and have Billy slip it under the door. Write down that I had to leave town for an urgent case." I only prayed she'd understand and not question the little I could relay.

As a detective I always strove to have the upper hand, but now it seemed like everything was slipping through my fingers. Scrambling, playing catch-up to a possible killer, wasn't how I preferred to conduct an investigation. I had to think. What could give me the advantage?

I boarded the train with Mags, only to step back off a couple of minutes later.

Because why take twice as long traveling by locomotive when I could get there in half the time by airplane?

• • •

"What are you hunting?" Having already discarded his goggles, Warren tugged his leather flight helmet from his head. He'd been all too eager to fly me to Greenford in his Curtiss biplane. One could never predict the weather, but we'd had clear skies from start to finish.

We'd landed only minutes ago on a flat stretch of grassland on the adjacent property. I'd apologize to Farmer Erickson for the wheel ruts in his field later. For now I needed to find Veronica Ridgeway, my mother.

"What am I hunting?" *A man named Punire.* "I'm actually thinking of setting a trap this time." Indeed I was. Once I located my mother, I planned to send her to my cabin while I waited for Punire.

Inside my small A-frame, I pumped Warren a glass of water, hoping he didn't want to linger. I hadn't told him anything. No mention of being married. Not a single word about the possible danger I was about to step into. Thankfully, Warren was accustomed to my secrecy and never badgered me.

"Are you sure you don't need help?" His assessing gaze swept over my dusty cabin. "I will take any excuse to get out of tomorrow morning's conferences." He rolled his eyes, but I knew the man loved his job.

"I'm good, old man." I clapped his shoulder. "In fact, I'm going to head into town before things close. I appreciate the lift."

Warren downed the rest of his drink, then swiped the extra gasoline from my shed before taking off again. I wasted no time locating my map of the area and searching for the exact address on the slip of paper Mags had given me. *428 Pine Lake Road.* I couldn't find it. So I cranked the engine of my 1912 roadster, which was nothing but a glorified buggy with a rickety engine, and headed toward the rumor room.

Visiting Greenford as many times as I had over the past two years, it was only a given that I'd become acquainted with the townsfolk, including Amelia McGregor. She had an ear to the entire town, literally, since the middle-aged widow was the local switchboard operator.

Once parked, I strolled into the general store, and after a wave to the aged proprietor, I slid to the back where Amelia sat in front of her switchboard.

"Kent Brisbane, is that you?" Holding the earpiece to her head with one hand and a sandwich with the other, she motioned with her chin to enter the room.

"Pleasure to see you again, Mrs. McGregor." I took the stool beside hers. "I need to get in touch with Veronica Ridgeway."

"Who?" A piece of tomato slipped from her sandwich, flopping onto her plate. "I don't think I know that name. Not anyone in Greenford, anyway."

Rookie mistake. If my mother was truly hiding away, she'd use an alias. However, it did make me wonder once again who Mags's contact was. How had they been able to track my mother if she was living under a different name? "I might have it wrong." I fished the piece of paper Mags had given me from my pocket. "Know who lives at this address?"

Since her hands were still full, she nudged her glasses up the bridge of her nose with the back of her wrist. "Sure." She gave a definite nod. "That's Dori Flowers's place."

Dori Flowers.

"Ah, that's her," I rattled off conversationally, though my every muscle seemed to hum, ready to dash away to find her. She'd taken a variation of her uncle's name—Dorian—and since Veronica was a flower, she'd used that for her last. Clever, while also remaining somewhat familiar to her. "Can you patch a call to her?" I gestured to the giant switchboard. "It's rather urgent."

She pressed her lips together. "Sweet Dori lives in a cottage outside of town. She doesn't have a phone."

My gut sank.

"But her neighbor does." She brightened, as if just remembering. "She usually swings by Dori's place to get her mail. I can have her relay a message if it's as important as you say."

That could work. I would have to phrase my words so that my mother would understand the urgency, but no one else. I didn't know who Punire was or where he was lurking. But this way I could forewarn her and then pick her up before any harm came to her. "I would appreciate that," I said over my pounding heart.

She handed me a piece of paper, and I wrote my message:

Dori, my name's Kent Brisbane. I met you long ago with our mutual friend Judith Powell.

*The situation today is as serious as back then. I'm going to
pick you up soon. It's dark out, so be careful.*

While the sun hadn't tucked beneath the horizon just yet, there was
another form of darkness invading Greenford. I prayed she'd grasp the
underlying message, especially when I'd coupled it with the name of
the nurse from the asylum. With a deep breath, I slid the note toward
Mrs. McGregor. "It's important this is relayed exactly." I dug into my
pocket, withdrawing the few dollars I had left. "Please keep this confidential."

Her eyes widened as she read my words. "That crucial, huh?"

"Afraid it is."

"Noted." She put the patch cord into the slot. "But keep your money,
Kent, for when you lose it playing me in poker." Her smile peeked
through before she resumed the business of connecting the line to my
mother's neighbor.

I wasn't about to correct her regarding my gambling resolution, but
listened as, with skilled efficiency, she communicated my entire message to a Mrs. Lockwood. After she disconnected, the kind operator
gave me detailed directions to the cottage. I tipped my hat with a "thank
you" and was out the door.

The lane leading out of town altered to narrower and bumpier. I
prayed my tires would hold up under the forced speed as I flew past
farmland and massive barns. According to Mrs. McGregor, I was to
head west for five miles until I reached a Y, then go right.

A part of me should be anxious about finally, after all this time, meeting my mother. But my protective edge needed to remain razor sharp,
disallowing any soft tug of sentiment. I'd even shoved away thoughts of
Delvina right now because focus was key.

The roadster lurched forward with a loud pop. Smoke billowed.
The engine sputtered. I pumped the brakes until everything just . . .
stopped. Dead.

No.

I slammed my hands on the wheel. Of all times to fail. I jumped out and assessed the damage. I had no idea what was broken. Hadn't my wife once said she knew how to fix an engine? A frustrated laugh broke through my lips.

I turned a slow circle, taking in my surroundings. I was in the middle of nowhere. There wasn't another automobile, home, or even a horse in sight. I'd only gone about three miles, which meant I had several more to reach my mother.

My mind spun with options. I could run back to town and hire someone to drive me there. But that could take more time than I could spare. Ensuring my gun was still holstered, I took off down the road, fueled by agitation and adrenaline.

Nighttime slowly pressed into the sky, mocking my efforts. By the time I reached the Y, the backs of my legs burned like fire, but I had to keep going.

The distinct growl of an approaching vehicle had me swirling around, my hand discreetly on my hip. I held my gaze on the driver as he slowed to a stop.

A pudgy face poked out the side window. "That your Model T back there?"

"Yes." I kept my tone friendly but stayed alert. For all I knew this man could be Punire. "Broke down on my way up yonder." I pointed down the road.

"Where you headed?"

My fingers grazing my weapon, I tossed all my proverbial cards on the table. "Dori Flowers's place."

He pushed his hat up to scratch his forehead. "You a friend of hers?"

"You can say that."

"I'm Dr. Evans. I was heading to the Lockwood house." He nodded at the passenger seat. "I'll drop you off."

I hesitated. It could all be a ploy. But what other option did I have? I accepted his offer and prayed I made the right choice. Once inside his Ford Touring, I checked my pocket watch. What should've taken me thirty minutes was now pushing over an hour. And if I had any misgivings about this man beside me being anything but a small-town physician, his in-depth account of his last patient's oozing rash would clear all doubt.

By the time we reached a tiny house nestled among a grove of trees, it was fully dark. A lantern in the window was the only indication anyone was home. Dr. Evans walked with me to the front porch, probably more skeptical of me than I was of him. I'd yet to give the man my name.

He knocked on the door. Once. Twice. "Ms. Flowers, you home?" Another pound, but louder. "A young gentleman here to see you."

My breathing shallowed as I awaited to meet face to face the only person who shared the same blood. After several long seconds, the doctor gave me a quizzical look.

Hadn't she gotten my message? Or worse, had she gotten my message and taken off?

Without waiting for approval, I turned the knob and moved inside, the doctor calling after me.

I skidded to a halt. I'd found my mother.

She was dead.

Chapter 25

Delvina
1924

"SLEEPING SICKNESS." KENT'S BLANK STARE was enough to pull me from my chair to his side. "Dr. Evans, the man who drove me to the cottage, he said she died of sleeping sickness." His words were void of any emotion, but the stormy grays of his eyes revealed his inner turmoil.

Four years ago the mysterious disease had been in its infancy, growing more prevalent with each passing month. I was ashamed to admit that while I'd felt sympathetic to those who'd lost loved ones to this unknown epidemic, I hadn't the flooding compassion that coursed through me as I'd listened to Kent's recounting of that sorrowful day. For what I'd been mostly numb to, I now had a yawning ache for the widespread loss.

I lowered to crouch beside my husband, but he surprised me by tugging me onto his lap. His arms encircled my waist, though not tight enough to where I couldn't twist to face him.

I cupped his face, and a muscle in his jaw pulsed against my palm. "I'm sorry, Kent."

He leaned into my touch. "I failed." His face was hard lines and anguish. "I failed her."

"There was nothing you could do." My tone was gently adamant. "The doctor said—"

"She was murdered."

I blinked. He'd said that without any hesitation whatsoever, making my own thoughts hiccup. "Murdered? How do you know this?"

"My investigations." He held me even closer, as if needing the contact. "Dr. Evans quickly diagnosed sleeping sickness because it *looked* like it. There weren't any signs of foul play. Her body was lying on the sofa, as if she'd drifted off and never woke up. I knew the moment I saw her that she was dead."

"Then why don't you believe the doctor?"

"Because of Mrs. Lockwood."

I thought back to what he'd told me. His mother had a neighbor who checked in on her. "She was the one the operator gave your message to, right?"

"Yes, that's her." He nodded. "She delivered my message. My mother was alive two hours before I showed up at her door. And according to Mrs. Lockwood, she was perfectly well, nothing amiss."

My eyes stung. I understood the point Kent conveyed. It was bizarre for his mother to be fully healthy one moment, then dead the next. But my heart latched on to something else entirely. "She knew." My voice was barely above a whisper. "Mrs. Lockwood did deliver the message, so your mother knew *you* were coming for her."

His Adam's apple bobbed. "Yes."

"Did Mrs. Lockwood tell you her reaction to your message?"

He pressed his mouth together, and I could almost sense that wall building between us. As if, for each hidden part of his soul he revealed, his mind wanted to raise the protective hedge. Thought by thought, brick by brick until he sealed himself away from the world, from me.

I shifted closer and wound my arms around his neck. "Tell me, Kent. Let me in."

His gaze linked mine. "Mrs. Lockwood didn't see her read the note. She left it on the table and went to check the supply of firewood. When she returned to the house, she said Mother was flitting about the cottage. Then handed Mrs. Lockwood her letters to post. That was it."

Kent recited the account as if reading a page from someone else's story. Detached. But I knew better. He numbed himself to the pain. His mother hadn't sobbed at the reality of her long-lost son finding her. It appeared she'd had no response whatsoever. That seemed difficult to believe, but the hardened glint in Kent's eyes kept me from pressing further. I didn't want him to shut me out. "Wait. What if she never read it?" I could see how that might've happened.

"No, she read it. Mrs. Lockwood said the message was moved. It wasn't on the table when she came back into the house."

Well, there went that theory. "Did Mrs. Lockwood tell you anything else?"

He nodded. "When she left, she passed another automobile on the lane." He gave me a significant look. "Because of my note, she figured it was me, so she hardly paid notice."

"It wasn't you though." I processed aloud. "So someone visited your mother in that short time between Mrs. Lockwood leaving and you arriving."

"The murderer."

An icy chill slid across the base of my neck, raising the hair. "Did you speak to the police about this mysterious visitor?"

"I did." The silver in his eyes was like crackling slate. "I didn't tell them I was Dori Flowers's son, just that I was a private detective. Dr. Evans stayed true to his diagnosis, and the local deputy wouldn't investigate any further."

That sounded overly familiar to Miss Thayer's case. "If your mother was killed, how did they do it?" My shoulders collapsed with my sigh, my mind shifting to Maude Welch. "Remember what we talked about yesterday? That Mrs. Welch's death could be murder under the guise of sleeping sickness?"

His thumb grazed the top of my thigh. "We're not even certain there's anything suspicious about Mrs. Welch's passing. We only know that Adele Thayer was shocked by it."

"I'm visiting Dr. Ewing tomorrow. I'll get answers."

"I'm sure you will." He mustered a smile, but it wasn't his signature one, which brightened every part of his face. "We should probably pack up and leave soon. I don't want to be in this part of the city near dark." He squeezed my leg, as if signaling me to get up, but I had one more thing I wanted to ask.

"I know why you left." I understood about his informant Mags. Kent hadn't run off with another woman, as I'd originally thought. He'd only acted on a lead to find his mother. I got that now. "But why didn't you contact me?"

"I couldn't."

"A simple telephone call."

"No. There's nothing simple about it." An urgent pleading invaded his gaze. "I didn't know who this Punire person was. He could've been lurking around Greenford, watching me as I investigated." He exhaled. "Most likely he'd fled town, but I couldn't risk it. That's why I didn't telephone or send a wireless. I didn't want anything connecting back to you. If the killer trailed me and caused you harm . . ." His voice deepened to a raw brokenness. "I already lost her. I couldn't . . . lose you too."

Only he had for a while. Because I hadn't understood.

He rested his forehead against mine. "I wasn't in a good state, Vinny. What if my roadster hadn't broken down? What if I'd gotten there sooner? I rushed to Greenford to save her and ended up burying her." He shook his head. "Earlier that day I'd planned to hock my gold watch chain to buy you a wedding ring. You know what happened to that chain? I had to sell it in Greenford to afford a small headstone for my dead mother. Then I stayed an extra week at my hunting cabin just to be sure no one would follow me back to you."

I knew the rest of the story. "And when you came home, I was gone." I eased back to peer into his handsome face. "You never chased after me."

"You don't think I wanted to?" He shifted in his seat, keeping me steady on his lap, but his foot knocked the table leg, making the dishes shiver. "Want to know why I didn't? Because your husband was a coward." He scoffed. "I grew up on the streets. I fought for each day. I knew every dirty trick to stay alive. What good is all that knowledge if I couldn't help anyone? I couldn't help my mother. When you left, I thought you were better off. Cutting ties with you kept you safe."

"I can handle myself. I'm capable."

"You are." His gaze softened. "But like I said this morning, you don't know how much you mean to me. I vowed to find my mother's killer, and I didn't know what that would involve. What danger I'd bring home. I couldn't let . . ." He shook his head, squeezing his eyes shut. "I couldn't let anything happen to you."

The more he spoke, the less tense he became. I remained quiet, hoping my open expression encouraged him to continue.

"But over the past years, when I didn't find Punire, I realized what I'd truly given up. I'd lost my mother. Lost my wife." His dark lashes lifted, his gaze holding mine. "So when I got the chance to have you again, I wasn't going to bungle it a second time." He nuzzled my cheek. "I never meant to hurt you. I'm sorry about what happened."

My fingers skimmed the back of his collar, the tips of his hair. "I waited a long time for that apology."

"Was that a good enough delivery? Or shall I try again?" His tone was lighter, making me believe he needed a reprieve from the previous heavy topic.

"You can try," I teased, feeling his smile against my jaw. "But that one was pretty effective. I'm not sure you could top it."

He tipped his head back. "Sounds like a challenge." His gaze burned hotter with each passing second, tempting me to fan the sparks. "But please remember, while I do owe excessive groveling, you haven't been entirely blameless."

"Me?" I drew close, brushing my nose with his, only to pull away before he could kiss me. "I'm the soul of innocence."

"Want me to rattle off your infractions?"

"Enlighten me."

He pressed his lips to my jaw, his touch lingering. "The first time I saw you, you stole my breath. The day you left, you robbed me of my sanity." His murmuring was a slow crawl along my cheekbone to my ear. "And I hate to tell you, but you've raided every part of me. Thoughts of you overtake my mind." A kiss to my neck, followed by several more. "This heart no longer beats for me, but for you. You, Delvina Brisbane, are a thief to the highest degree." He now peered fully into my face. "Will you please accept my apology? If I can't have any dignity, I at least want your forgiveness."

"I accept," I said breathlessly, and Kent spent the next several minutes proving his ardent gratitude.

Chapter 26 ——————————————————————————————

AFTER SPENDING MOST OF THE following morning cleaning my flat with Kent, I strolled into Dr. Ewing's office, while Kent met with Warren to discuss the final details of the ceremony. Since I was later attending an appointment with my mother to pick out flowers at Mrs. Babcock's greenhouse, I wouldn't see Kent until tonight at Hemswick for dinner. But I was determined to find answers at both my meetings today.

The secretary had ushered me into one of the examining rooms, which resembled more of an upper-class parlor than anything clinical. Born to great wealth, Dr. Ewing had defied convention by electing a profession in the medical field rather than squandering his family's money. I'd always admired him for that. While most of our sphere would normally shun him for such a move, the upper crust actually embraced his decision because they had an ally, someone to deliver their children, tend to their scrapes and ailments, without fear of anything going public. Dr. Ewing was reputed for his discretion, which only made my mission all the more challenging.

"Good afternoon, Ms. Kline." He entered the room. "My secretary said you telephoned because you need clarification on symptoms?" His brows raised to his salt-and-pepper hairline. "I'm hoping everything is well at Hemswick?"

"Oh yes. Everyone is well." Had I imagined it, or had relief flickered across his features? "But I was hoping you may be able to help me. Mother's been quite distressed about the rising numbers of sleeping sickness. I was wondering if there's been any progress on a cure. Or if there are any precautions we can take."

"I could probably speak for hours on the subject and still not give you anything conclusive." He rubbed his neck. "You see, every case is different with encephalitis lethargica. That's the scientific name for sleeping sickness," he needlessly clarified. "There's been no underlying connections between those who succumb to it, which has us in the medical profession stumped."

Even though I was aware of all that, I nodded slowly, making a show of processing what he said. "I only know of a few who passed from it. Like Maude Welch. Her death really upset Mother, since Mrs. Welch visited for tea not long before her passing." It was only yesterday we'd uncovered that Mrs. Welch's death might be significant, and I hadn't yet the chance to speak with Mother on it. I'd rectify that today. "Would you happen to know what symptoms Mrs. Welch had? Like I said, any precautions you can recommend?"

He considered me, as if being selective about what to say.

"Please, Dr. Ewing. My mother was anxious about it. Any relief you can offer would be appreciated." I wasn't lying. The sleeping sickness epidemic bothered Mother. And while I had ulterior motives in finding out more about Maude Welch, it wouldn't hurt to pick his brain on the subject.

At mentioning Mother, his expression softened. I knew the doctor and my mother had known each other for decades, but the traces of tenderness in his hazel gaze went beyond the parameters of friendship. Interesting.

"Anything I can do to help your mother's nerves, I'll oblige. She's been through a lot over the past several years." As far as subtlety went, he had none. The scolding in his tone, coupled with the narrowing of his gaze, revealed he judged me at fault for Mother's collective stress. Fair enough. During my youth, I'd certainly had a rebellious streak, and lately the exposure of my birth father's scandals had made us walking bull's-eyes for the press.

But Mother and Father had their share of fault as well. If they'd been open from the beginning about my adoption, then we could've been spared the brunt of discovery. Though Dr. Ewing wouldn't know, because once the news had broken about my parentage, per Father's orders, we'd acted as if it were public knowledge the entire time. I was ashamed to confess I'd lied about it all, spinning fanciful stories as an act of defiance. I'd even deceived my birth sister, Kate, when I'd met her. I'd rattled off tales that I could recall my birth mother's lullaby and my journey to the States. I hadn't. I *did* know the lullaby, but only because my birth mother had taught it to Mother so I would have a part of her to remember. But of course, Mother hadn't revealed this to me until later in life.

"Maude Welch's case was probably the quickest I've seen." Dr. Ewing brought me back to the present. "So fast that her servants were unaware she succumbed until it was too late."

My mind flashed to Kent's account of his mother. If what Dr. Ewing said was true, then it seemed plausible that Veronica Ridgeway could've died of sleeping sickness. But there was also the issue of the mysterious visitor. "Is that unusual?"

He shook his head. "There are cases that progress faster than others. Some have mild bouts and recover, while others never wake up. No two are alike, which keeps us guessing."

"I see." This wasn't helping.

"Is there any other way I can be of assistance?"

"No. Mother will be appreciative that you've done your best to educate us."

His grin flashed, almost too brightly. Then as if realizing his sudden show of emotion, he tampered it down. "Yes, well . . . happy to help."

"I do have one last question. Blame it on my curious nature or my profession, but is there any chance sleeping sickness can be a cover-up for something else?"

"Such as?"

"Murder."

He laughed. "I think you might read too many mystery novels."

I'd never read a detective story in my life, but I'd let him think that was the basis of my nosiness.

"The answer is no," he continued. "I can see how passing from natural causes, such as the elderly dying in their sleep, can be misjudged for the encephalitis lethargica epidemic. But not murder. Foul play is simple to spot. Most poisons cause violent reactions, and other drugs will dilate pupils or leave behind definite signs. No." He shook his head adamantly. "You can't pass a murder off as sleeping sickness."

● ● ●

"Oh, these are so lovely!" Mother walked through the aisles of the greenhouse, fawning over each bloom she passed.

Mrs. Babcock's butler had brought us here to browse the greenery with a promise his mistress would join us soon. Knowing I only had a window of time, I'd been quizzing Mother about the Ridgeway family since we'd left Hemswick. She hadn't met Veronica Ridgeway, since she and Father had been overseas during the time of Veronica's short stint in Manhattan. Mother had only known Dorian Ridgeway by name. According to her, the man had been more of a recluse due to declining health and had been confined to a wheelchair. That alone made me doubt he'd been the one demanding Kent's death at the unwed mothers' asylum.

If Mother had been suspicious about my persistent questions, she hadn't shown it. Her demeanor had been open and pleasant, her mood chipper. Though I expected that to change as I broached my next topic.

"Mother, how well did you know Mrs. Welch?"

She paused, bent halfway to sniff a gardenia. "Not overly so, but I liked to consider her my friend all the same." To her credit, she kept a neutral face. "Such a shame about dear Maude."

"I don't recall ever meeting her."

She gave a sad smile. "No, it's unlikely. Maude married a naval officer shortly after her debut. He was assigned to Guam after America took possession of it."

"What brought her back to the States?"

"Her husband passed. They lived on a naval base there, I think." She shuddered. "I couldn't imagine living there, but Maude loved it."

"She told you so?"

"When she visited for tea. She asked if we could stroll the garden because she missed the outdoors. If she was disappointed by our grounds, she was kind enough not to say so."

Hemswick's garden wasn't much but manicured shrubbery and statues. While Mother adored botany, she hadn't the patience for it. "Though she did seem interested in Ida's courtyard, I doubt she saw much over the stone wall."

The stone wall. I rolled my eyes. When I was ten, I'd brought home a stray dog who seemed to prefer Ida Elliot's lawn for doing his business. She'd made a statement by building a wall to shut him out. Unfortunately, the new stone barrier included a gate, which sadly hadn't shut *her* in.

"What did you and Mrs. Welch talk about?"

She bit her thin lip. "It was mostly Maude reminiscing about her youth." Her tone wavered, and I thought maybe she was upset about Mrs. Welch's passing. So she surprised me by saying, "I have a confession to make. When Maude visited, I was having one of my grief spells over your father. I didn't want to turn her away, but I hardly remember a word she said. She talked of people and places, but I can't recall a single thing. That's awful, isn't it?" To Mother there was nothing more shameful than a neglectful hostess.

"Your husband passed away only a couple of months ago." I linked my arm in hers as we walked down one of the fern-lined aisles. "I'm certain Mrs. Welch understood, especially having gone through the same situation."

Just then, Mrs. Priscilla Babcock joined us, putting an end to our conversation. As the tall woman approached, a gracious smile brightening her round face, I was reminded this appointment had dual purposes. One was to get flowers for my bouquet, and the other was to find out if Mrs. Babcock had been blackmailed, since her name was in Miss

Thayer's planner. How to do so tactfully remained uncertain. The two older women engaged in small talk until our hostess asked what the flowers were for.

"I know of a young lady in need of a bouquet, and I told her your flowers are best in all of the state." Mother preened but kept her gaze rigidly on Mrs. Babcock, as if a glance at me would give away the secret.

Mrs. Babcock glowed under the praise. "You know, I do this as a hobby. Gardening is my delight."

"Everything is so vibrant." I gestured to the rows of petunias. "It will be difficult to decide. But I read somewhere that calla lilies are the recent fashionable flower."

Mrs. Babcock tapped her lips. "They are lovely, but I confess I'm not much into modern trends."

"Not at all?" I casually asked, deliberately stepping to the side so Mother wouldn't be between me and the older woman. I needed to gauge her reaction. "I thought I'd heard you once hired Adele Thayer to brush up on the latest fashion."

Mrs. Babcock inhaled so deeply that I feared she wouldn't leave any air for her plants. "I had a horrible experience with that woman. It's truly shocking."

"Really?" I feigned interest in an orchid, not wanting to appear too eager. "What happened?"

"I had an important event coming up and, of course, wanted to look my best. So I asked Miss Thayer for advice. And do you know what she did? I found her snooping in my bureau drawers."

Mother gasped.

I widened my eyes for show, but I was hardly shocked. "What did she say when you caught her?"

"Oh, some foolishness about wanting to examine the pieces I had so she could familiarize herself with my tastes." She sniffed in disgust. "But those weren't my clothing drawers. It was where I kept my papers." She gave me a pointed look. "More like my husband's debts."

"Why would she do that?" I glanced at Mother, as if confused. "Did she intend to blackmail you?"

At this, Mother pressed a hand to her cheek. "Surely not."

Mrs. Babcock shrugged. "Maybe, but it wouldn't do any good. Everyone knows about Harold's gambling."

Miss Thayer must've arrived at that conclusion and hadn't followed through with any blackmail. "I'm sure it came as a shock to read about her death in the papers."

"Oh no, dear, I knew about it before it hit the *Times*." Her hand flopped in a dismissive wave. "Maria told me. She rooms with the lady who cleaned Miss Thayer's flat. Rosamond? Rosemary? No, that's not it."

"Rosalie?" I supplied. "Rosalie Adams?"

She snapped her fingers with a decisive nod. "That's it. Rosalie. Poor thing must think she's the death angel, considering this happened twice. In such short time."

My forehead scrunched. "What do you mean?"

"Rosalie Adams also tidied Maude Welch's flat. The dear found Mrs. Welch's body, just as she found Miss Thayer. Though Maude succumbed to sleeping sickness. But still, death is death."

Mother grew pale, so I directed her to the veronicas as a distraction while my mind absorbed this new information.

Rosalie Adams cleaned house for Maude Welch and Adele Thayer. Two women who'd died within six weeks of each other. I recalled Ms. Adams's chilling response in my flat when I'd mentioned the possibility of Kent hiring her. *"I just be having rotten luck with clients lately. I don't want Mr. Brisbane to drop dead."* She'd also linked it to superstition, but perhaps there was an actual connection. Perhaps Rosalie might not be all too innocent.

I needed to speak with her.

Chapter 27 ───────────────────────────────────────

THANKFULLY, I'D HAD THE PRESENCE of mind to collect Rosalie Adams's contact information the last time we'd met. While she hadn't a telephone in her apartment, I'd sent over a telegram requesting she come to my flat in the morning. I would have rather spoken to her that evening, but I'd promised Mother I'd oversee the decorating of the reception hall for after our ceremony. Kent offered to help, which made the task more bearable. Especially when he'd tug me behind a pillar to remind me what a catch he was. His words.

We'd returned to his flat a little before midnight, which meant Kent wasn't too appreciative of me dragging him to Park Towers early this morning. He'd poured out all his charms trying to keep me beside him in bed. We'd yet to return to the initial intimacy we'd shared our first night of marriage, and I suspected Kent wanted to wait until after the ceremony, on account of me. Though I could tell by his heated touch, his gentlemanly restraint was wearing thin. Thank goodness the wedding was tomorrow. But that only meant we had a full day of preparation.

After almost a half hour of waiting at my flat, Kent looked up from the book he was reading. He'd brought with him the natural cures and ancient practices edition I'd borrowed from Hemswick library the day Mrs. Elliot had told me about honey being excellent for wounds. "This is interesting." He tapped the page. "Did you know this has a section on poisons?"

My brow scrunched. "In a book about remedies?"

He set the huge volume on the end table and joined me on the sofa, his hand on my thigh, a wolfish smile tugging his scar. "Maybe the cure becomes the poison."

"I'm not sure how that would be helpful," I said dryly, even as Kent kissed my jaw.

"Maybe it's the reverse." He breathed against my neck. "The poison can be the cure."

There was actual merit in that. I thought about deadly nightshade. Adding a few drops of serum from the plant onto the eyes could help with vision, but eating the berries or leaves would kill. However, in Maude Welch's case, the killer couldn't have used nightshade. The reaction from the poison would have been too violent. But Kent's other remark niggled within me, making me jolt upright, nearly knocking his chin with my shoulder. "You're brilliant."

"Glad you think so, darling." His lips resumed their ministrations, this time on the soft flesh behind my ear. "But I'm just getting started."

"No." I swatted him, albeit weakly, because the man really was good at rendering me dizzy. "You said 'maybe it's the reverse.'"

He eased back, confusion marking his brow. Clearly his mind wasn't on the case.

"We've been viewing Miss Thayer's death as the focal point, with Mrs. Welch's passing being a secondary link. But what if it's the reverse? What if Miss Thayer died because she knew something about Mrs. Welch? We should be digging into Maude Welch's history."

"That's possible." He tucked his arm around me. "But from what you said, Mrs. Welch had been out of the States for more than two decades and just recently returned. What possible trouble could she have gotten into in such a short amount of time?"

"I don't know. Plus there's so much in Miss Thayer's past we can't overlook. Her ties with LeRaffa, and of course, this blackmail business. But it's worth looking into."

"I agree. And it might help to look into the facts a bit more." His voice lowered in that rumbly way when in deep thought. "We know Miss Thayer was a snoop. We also know she'd consulted Mrs. Welch.

No doubt Miss Thayer searched through her things. Perhaps she found something among Mrs. Welch's belongings that she shouldn't have."

I shifted to peer up at him. "So when Mrs. Welch turned up dead, Miss Thayer knew why."

He nodded. "Which would account for her nervous reaction about Maude Welch's passing."

"I just can't get away from her response. Miss Thayer *was* distressed." I rested my head on his shoulder. It was like trying to untie a dozen tangled knots and not knowing if the string you tugged helped loosen or jumbled things worse. "Miss Thayer wrote down Mrs. Welch's name in that planner we found. Her name was on that Tuesday's page. Which was also the same day that Rosalie Adams said Miss Thayer had a mysterious appointment. That has to be connected."

"That turns out to be the day Miss Thayer gets shot."

"Exactly. Which leads me to wonder. What if . . ." I glanced up at my husband. "Suppose at this mysterious appointment, Miss Thayer confronted Mrs. Welch's killer? Blackmailed them?"

"It's a sound theory. The best we have so far."

I agreed. It was the only one that seemed logical. "But what could Mrs. Welch have been hiding? What secret? She hadn't been in the States long. Plus, Dr. Ewing said there's no way a person could pass murder off as sleeping sickness."

He scoffed. "There's a way. We just haven't found it yet."

I gave his arm a gentle squeeze. I knew he was thinking of his mother. Two unrelated deaths that seemed too similar. Just how many killers were out there taking advantage of this epidemic? They disposed of their victims only to blame it on a mysterious disease. It was disgustingly clever.

"Do you think Rosalie Adams has any part in this?"

A knock sounded.

Kent nodded at the door. "We'll soon find out."

After ushering her in, I introduced her to Kent. My husband had a way of putting most people at ease, and Ms. Adams was no different. Though his charming smile and dark good looks probably helped.

"Thank you for coming." I gestured for her to sit, then lowered onto the sofa. Once we women were seated, Kent claimed the spot beside me. "I just recently found out that you used to clean Maude Welch's flat."

She nodded. "That be right. Mrs. Babcock got me the position. I room with her maid."

At least Rosalie was telling the truth there. "Did Miss Thayer know you cleaned house for Maude Welch?"

She considered this for a moment. "No, I don't think so. I don't be gossiping about my employers." She said this with adamant conviction, and I wondered if this was more for Kent's benefit, in case he had any question about hiring her.

"I understand you were the one who found Mrs. Welch after she passed."

Her shoulders nearly spiked to her earlobes. "I did." As if realizing her tense state, she exhaled slow, relaxing against the cushion. "I found her, and the next month I be finding Miss Thayer. I must be cursed."

"I doubt it," I said gently, while still watching her every move. She seemed sincere enough. "This might be uncomfortable for you, but I need you to think back to the time of her passing. Mrs. Welch's, I mean. Was there anything unusual? How did she appear when you found her?"

She gripped both armrests. "What do you mean?"

"Did it look like there was a struggle? Any anguish on her face? Any signs of other forms of sickness, like vomit?"

"No. Nothing like that. It was all peaceful like. I thought Mrs. Welch be asleep, but I couldn't wake her. The doctor said it was the sleeping sickness."

Dr. Ewing. He certainly held to that diagnosis. Maybe it was. Only moments ago I'd felt confident we should be investigating Mrs. Welch, but what if I was wrong? Was I jumping to unfounded conclusions? "What about Mrs. Welch's behavior the days before? Was she acting odd at all? Or did she have any suspicious visitors?"

Ms. Adams sucked in a breath.

"The information you give would only help," I added. "I wouldn't use anything you say to besmirch her character."

"It's just . . ." She shook her head. "I'd nearly forgotten."

"Forgotten what?" I sent a sidelong glance to Kent. He'd been quiet, letting me handle all the questions, but I knew he listened intently.

"She said she be having someone over and didn't want 'em to see the box. She asked me to take it home with me."

"Did you?"

She nodded.

"What's in the box?"

"It's not open." She pressed a hand to her cheek. "I remember somethin' else. She handed it to me—the box—and said her visitor can't be knowing about 'Veronica Mystery.' Whatever that means."

Veronica? *Our* Veronica? My gaze swung to Kent, but he was already standing.

He met my eyes briefly before nodding at Ms. Adams. "Pardon me a moment." Then he disappeared into the bedroom.

It took a second for my brain to catch up. I'd thought for certain Kent would question Ms. Adams about Veronica. Instead he'd all but rushed out of the room. Why? I'd never had great success on guessing what transpired within the confines of Kent's mind, and I doubted I would now. Trapping the sigh in my chest, I returned my attention to Ms. Adams. "Did Mrs. Welch speak of this Veronica often?"

She shook her head. "Not around me. That be the first time I be hearing that name." She fussed with one sleeve, then the other. "Are we done, Miss Kline? I need to run to my flat before headin' to work."

I glanced at the bedroom. Whatever it was that had drawn Kent away must have been important. "I'll walk you to the lobby." I stood, and she followed suit.

"You be asking a lot of questions about Mrs. Welch," she said as we moved down the stairs. "Is that important to Miss Thayer's death?"

"Possibly." I slid my hand along the wooden rail, trying to rearrange my scattered thoughts. "I would like to see that box Mrs. Welch gave you."

She grimaced. "I forgot my key at my flat or else I be headin' straight to work. I got double shifts at the theater. Won't be back until late."

We reached the lobby, and my eyes landed on Paulo. "Can you wait a moment, Ms. Adams? I won't be long." At her nod, I rushed to my favorite janitor. "How would you like to make a quick hundred bucks?"

"Nope." He shook his head. "I'm not burying any more bodies. Not even for you."

A laugh ripped from my lips. "Well, that's unfair." I spotted the glimmer of his tease and pressed on. "I need you to accompany Ms. Adams back to her place and retrieve a box for me. All you have to do is set it in my flat." If my day hadn't already been planned down to the minute, I'd retrieve it myself. But Kent and I were supposed to meet Mother to go over the final details of the catering, followed by more wedding reception preparations, then I needed to pick up my gown. I probably should eat at some point as well.

He glanced at his watch. "I can swing it."

"Great! Be sure to relock my door when you leave." I patted his shoulder. "By the way, I would offer you three times that to bury a body," I said cheerily, hearing his husky chuckle as I returned to Ms. Adams. "Would you mind if Paulo went with you to get the box?"

"Not at all," she answered readily, and I wondered if her overly chipper smile was due to her guilt about tricking him with her fainting stunt.

I watched them leave and returned to my flat, reaching the door just as Kent opened it. "Okay, what was that about?" I asked once inside. "Why the vanishing act into the bedroom?"

"I've a hunch." He caught my hand in his. "Don't hate me."

"With an opening like that, it's almost a guarantee. Question is, how much am I going to hate you?" I teased, then I noticed the glimmer of . . . something in his eyes. "Kent, what's going on?" I practically pulled him to the sofa.

"Remember my hunting cabin?"

"The one you swindled from an unsuspecting poker player?"

"Not the phrasing I would've picked, but we can go with it." He held on to my hand, his fingers practically twitching against mine. "I find it interesting that Ms. Adams said the very name of the man the cabin once belonged to."

"Hold on." I shook my head, trying to recall Rosalie Adams's precise words. "She said the name Veronica."

"Yes, but after that she said—"

"Mystery. As in solving a mystery."

"No, she said *Mr. E.*" He ignored my skeptical look. "Back to the hunting cabin. It belonged to a fellow named Mr. E. Don't you think it's strange that I won it from him? A cabin that happens to be located in the same town my mother lived and . . ."

Died. "Greenford."

He nodded.

That was a bizarre coincidence. "We're not even certain that was what Ms. Adams said. Nor are we certain she was talking about Veronica Ridgeway."

"I am." That confident glimmer in his eyes, like a dart of fire in a swirl of smoke, all but confirmed it. "I think with the similarities between her and Mrs. Welch's suspicious deaths, it's worth considering." He hesitated a moment, then said, "This is going to sound crazy. But this man, Mr. E, he only ever sat at my table. No matter if I trounced him the month before, he returned. He never broke a sweat about losing hundreds to me."

"Did he talk to you?"

"Not really. His mustache drooped on his upper lip once. So I'm pretty sure the man wore a disguise. Toffs that visit dice joints and gambling dens are known to do that."

Did he even realize that there must be thousands of Mr. E's in Manhattan alone? "Then why do you think it connects—"

"What if he's my father?"

My jaw unhinged, but I soon shook off my surprise. Kent could be grasping at things, as I felt I'd been earlier. We both wanted this case solved and behind us, but I wondered if we were being too hasty. "Why would you think that?"

"Why else would he sit at my table every month, even though he never won? Why would he hand over hundreds as if it were no big deal? Why would he own a cabin in the same speck of a town as my mother's cottage?"

When broken down that way, I could see why Kent was intrigued. "Okay, what are you planning? You said 'don't hate me.' Which makes me think you're going to do something stupid."

"I appreciate your confidence in me, Knuckles."

"You're stalling. Out with it."

He squeezed my hand. "I'm going to the gambling den. I want to ask around."

But that wasn't all. For having a formidable poker face, I could see right through it. "And where exactly is this place?"

He released my hand to palm his neck. "Kingston Avenue."

No wonder he'd thought I'd be upset. This city had as many gambling dens and dice joints as it had speakeasies, but even I recognized the significance of Kingston Avenue. Despite its regal name, the street was in the worst section of Manhattan. Never mind the places we'd recently visited. Because Norman Young's apartment complex would be considered prime real estate compared to anything on Kingston Avenue. Crime lords. Rumrunners. Probably a handful of murderers. Those were the kinds of residents who made up that street. "You want to stroll into gangster territory the night before our wedding?" Dust didn't stir in those kinds of places until dark, meaning Kent could be gone all evening and possibly morning. I couldn't even accompany him. That poker pit was men only. I might have been bold at Spider's pool hall, but only because he was my friend. I'd be attracting trouble if I tagged along.

"I telephoned Denny just now," Kent went on, as if he hadn't just frozen my world with this glacial news. "He owns the laundry service downstairs. He tells me the joint's running tonight. And more so, Randall's in town. He owns the gambling den. No doubt he'll be there. If anyone knows who Mr. E is, it's Randall."

"But will he tell you?"

His thumb paused mid-swipe across my hand. "Maybe."

I wasn't entirely certain that Rosalie Adams had said Mr. E, but I wasn't about to argue. If Kent had heard right and this man was, in fact, Kent's father, could I deny Kent the chance to find out? On the flip side, Mr. E could quite possibly be a killer. He could be the fellow who'd attempted to arrange Kent's death the very day he was born. But then . . . if that was the truth, then why would Mr. E seek Kent out at the gambling den? If indeed that was what transpired.

There were too many ifs and maybes for my comfort. This could all be nonsense and an entire waste of time, not to mention an unnecessary risk of danger. Though again, could I rob Kent of this opportunity to find out? He'd already lost his mother. "If you go, I want you to be careful." I was aware Kent had grown up around ruffians and could handle dangerous situations better than most, but I wanted reassurance.

His gaze slowly slid over my face until finally locking on my eyes. "I promise."

I could think of a million ways this could go wrong. The most pressing one would be Kent encountering a murderer. Another problem I could foresee? My husband getting caught up in the thrill of the search for his parent and leaving me behind. Again. Not to mention missing an important detail, such as a wedding. Our wedding. "Make another promise to me."

He stroked my cheek. "Anything."

"You better promise to stand before the judge with me tomorrow. So help me, Kent, I want this marriage to last more than a day after the ceremony. But even that won't happen unless the groom's present." Yes, we'd been married all this time, but my heart needed him to show up, to prove he cared.

His gaze hooked mine. "I'll be back as soon as I can. I promise."

My eyes slid shut of their own volition. "I recall you saying this to me before. That didn't work out too well." He'd told me those exact words four years ago prior to going to Penn Station.

"Which I regret." There was an ache in his voice that pulled me closer. "But I regret even more the words I held back so long."

"Which are?"

"I love you."

I stilled. I'd expected him to rattle off something absurd. Or maybe even confess he should've taken me with him. My emotions weren't prepared for that kind of declaration. But he was right. He hadn't said it until now. And those three words were soaked in such tenderness, making me want to dip my heart in and let it steep in his affection. I didn't get a chance to respond before he was tugging at my waist, hauling me against his solid frame.

He lowered his head to peer into my face. "I think that's something my wife should know."

"Thank you." I kissed him. I knew he wasn't leaving for the dice joint until later, but that didn't stop me from demanding, "Come back to me, Brisbane."

"I will."

"You better. Because I love you too." My words barely escaped before his mouth captured mine in a declaration all its own.

Chapter 28 ————————————————————————————————

KENT STAYED BY MY SIDE the rest of the day as we added the last touches to the reception hall, sampled the cake and refreshments that would be served tomorrow, and helped Flossie arrange the table center-pieces. Everything was coming together nicely, but I couldn't shake the uneasiness in the pit of my stomach. It could be mildly blamed on the press being invited to not only city hall the following day but also to Hemswick for the reception. After spending years begrudging the very sight of them, we'd be welcoming newshounds into our family home. Though Kent had assured me Warren had handpicked the journalists and the coverage would be favorable, I still felt the need to pray he was right. For Mother's sake, if nothing else. But I knew the press wasn't the real reason for my tattered nerves. After we finished decorating and then dinner, I'd be accompanying Mother to Tabitha's to retrieve my gown, while my husband would be going to a seedy gambling den in the worst area of the city.

I'd offered money to bribe Randall for the information, but Kent declined, claiming it would appear too suspicious. I didn't know how he intended to get the details behind Mr. E's identity, but I did know that asking questions in that place was never a good idea. I'd heard too many sordid tales of broken bones and battered bodies all because pa-trons had gotten nosy.

As the time drew near to separate, my restlessness increased, and I struggled leaving Kent's side. Literally. I stuck close to him like a barna-cle to a boat. My husband seemed amused but had enough good sense not to tease. I wasn't myself. Any other time I'd be lured by the danger and devise a way to disguise myself as a man so I could tag along. But not today. I hoped this rare bout of clinginess could be blamed on the added strain of tomorrow's events and not a foreboding of something awful.

"I'll be fine, love," he said as he kissed me goodbye.

"You're armed, right?"

He tapped his temple. "Only with my intellect."

"Not funny." I skimmed my hands over his waist. No holster. "Where's your Colt?"

"No guns or blades allowed. They have big men stationed at the door that'll rough you up if you bring any in." He smiled, as if he hadn't just spiked my blood pressure. "Besides, I think this undertaking calls more for wit than weapon."

I didn't like this. Not at all. But I needed to trust Kent, that he knew what he was doing. "I'll be praying for you."

My remark made him pull me tight against him, and he locked those smoky eyes on mine. "Thank you."

And then he was gone. Him to the roughest part of Manhattan and me to T. Ellerman's Dress Shop with Mother. I had decided to leave my Duesenberg at Hemswick and have Mother's chauffeur, Charles, drive us across town. Tabitha was waiting at the door, my gown in hand, when we arrived a half hour after closing.

"What do you think?" She raised the dress high, more for Mother's approval than for mine.

My gaze ran down the satin frock, my smile budding. Yes, I hated pink, but what she'd done to the dress was subtle yet eye-catching. The satin had been trimmed in just enough ivory lace to enhance rather than detract. The neckline was fashionable without scooping too low, and the dropped waistline flowed with gentle layers.

I disappeared behind the dressing screen and slipped on the gown, the soft fabric whispering over my body. Tabitha buttoned me up and shooed me in front of Mother, who cried and laughed simultaneously.

"I told you!" Mother clasped her hands together, her aged face radiating delight. "That color looks divine on you. The fit is perfect." With a blissful sigh, she twirled her finger, signaling me to turn. "Kent is going to lose his mind when he sees you."

Meanwhile, I counted the minutes until *I* saw *him*.

Tabitha set the veil on my head and tugged at the ivory netting. "You truly are stunning, dear. Look for yourself." She pointed at the floor-to-ceiling mirror.

I did as Tabitha bade and nearly had to lift the veil to ensure what I was seeing. Mother was right. The pink complemented my olive complexion, and the dress fit well. The trending style was straight lines and no curves, but hints of my figure were visible. I looked like . . . a bride. And while I understood that was the entire point, the realization of everything hit me afresh. Yes, I'd been married to Kent all this while, but tomorrow we were finally letting the world in on our secret.

Although I needed my groom present to make that happen. Worry sank its claws into me. Kent was capable of handling himself, but I hated that he could be in danger. And while there was a decent chance of him meeting me before Judge VanKirk entirely covered in scrapes and bruises, I was aware there stood a risk of him never showing up at all.

Mother's hand rested on my arm. "You're doing the right thing. He's a good man." She must've misinterpreted my rigid posture as reluctance about tomorrow.

"I know, Mother." I lifted the veil and kissed her cheek. "The best I've ever known."

Tabitha left the room, giving us some privacy.

"I wish your father were here to see you." Her voice was gentle, her eyes glossy. "And the Salvastanos as well. They all would be so proud." She grabbed my hands and stepped back, taking me in again. "You look like her, you know."

Emotion washed over me again, but this time for an entirely different reason. My birth mother. I'd known from Hugo that she had passed away in Italy, but recently discovered from Kate that Amelia Salvastano had died in the Calabria earthquake, which had struck Southern Italy a few years after I'd sailed to America. Despite my fib to Kate, I had no memory of my birth mother. What she'd looked like. The sound of her voice. But my adopted mother had known her and was now offering me this gift. "Truly?"

She nodded, her fingers gently squeezing mine. "She was shorter than you, but in your face, I can see her. You're beautiful, just as she was. I'm grateful she shared you with us."

Mother didn't mention my birth mother often. Over these past years, she'd answered my questions but hadn't gone into much detail, and so I'd stopped asking. But she must've known I needed this moment. "Thank you."

She pressed our folded hands to her cheek. "I'm sorry I haven't spoken of her. Truth is, I didn't know her well, but . . ." She took in a delicate breath. "She was the one who nicknamed you Vinny."

I blinked. This was new.

"I allowed you to think that was our doing—that we first called you that, but we didn't. Her last words to you were 'I love you, my Vinny.' And while I haven't told you, we kept the nickname to honor her."

A tear ran down my cheek, but my heart was full. It was like a mending of sorts. A blending of both sets of my parents. "Thank you, Mother. For telling me."

Her eyes glossed with a soft smile. "You actually have Maude Welch to thank for that."

"Mrs. Welch?"

She dropped my hands to pick a loose thread from my shoulder. "Our conversation about her yesterday reminded me. Her father doted on her, always calling her his sweet Ettie."

I tensed. "You say Maude was called Ettie?"

"Her given name is Maudette," Mother continued, completely oblivious that she'd handed me a new lead. "As she grew older, most just took to calling her Maude."

My heart kicked even as my mind recalled a certain letter.

● ● ●

Several names had been tossed at me over these past weeks. Adele Thayer, Wallace Stratton, Angelo LeRaffa, Rosalie Adams, Norman Young, Maude Welch, Veronica Ridgeway, Dori Flowers, Mr. E. Not including all the names listed in both appointment books.

But I remembered Ettie specifically because I'd initially suspected she'd been one of Kent's lovers when I'd come across her letter that day in his office. And with that letter, she'd included a key. Several questions rolled through my mind. If Maude Welch and Ettie were indeed the same person, why had she contacted Kent? Had she needed him to investigate something for her? Or had she written him for an entirely different reason?

After seeing Mother and my gown safely to the awaiting car, I took the trolley to midtown, where Kent's office was located. I opened the door with the key he'd given me and bolted it behind me. Feeling my way through the dark, I found a lamp, illuminating the space. The letter still sat on the edge of his desk. I read over the words, albeit more carefully this time.

> Kent Brisbane
> *I missed you today. So I left this key here. When I return, I'll explain.*
> Ettie

I wondered why she hadn't just signed *Maude Welch*. Why her childhood moniker? Unless that served as a clue. Of course I couldn't be absolutely certain the Ettie from this letter was indeed Maude Welch.

I picked up the accompanying key, examining it. Corrosion spotted its brass body. This wasn't recently made. Initially, I'd thought it went to a flat, but Kent had pointed out its smaller size. This key might not unlock an apartment, but it could perhaps open a box. Coincidentally, Maude Welch had entrusted Rosalie Adams with a box, one that hopefully was now at Park Towers.

If this key opened Maude Welch's locked box, it would confirm that she had been the one who'd written Kent the letter.

I telephoned Kent's flat, but he wasn't home yet. I left a message with his landlord to have him meet me at my place, though I suspected Kent would be out most the night. I tucked the key and letter into my purse, then dashed out.

The evening chill followed me into Park Towers, making me wish I'd worn a thicker coat. I opened my flat, realizing Paulo had left the light on, but all was forgiven at the sight of a box on my end table, beside the remedy book Kent had left here earlier. I ditched my shoes and wasted no time withdrawing the key.

The rectangular container rivaled the size of a jewelry box. The wood, cedar probably, was nicely varnished, with dovetailed sides, but the row of large, silver-plated studs along the bottom ruined the elegant simplicity of the piece. It appeared Maude Welch's tastes were a tad gauche.

I swiped my finger over the metal keyhole on the front. As far as locks went, this one was simple. I could easily open it with my picks. But it was important to ensure the key from the letter belonged to this box. It would prove Maude Welch had tried to contact Kent before her death. And if indeed she had, then what was so significant about the contents that she'd separated the box from its key?

Only one way to find out.

I poised the key in front of the slot, and . . . it didn't fit.

My heart sank. I tried again, but no. This key went to a smaller lock.

So where did that leave this case? Was I wrong in assuming Maude—Maudette—Welch was the Ettie from Kent's letter? Was I conducting this case as hastily as I was with this key and lock? Jamming clues, forcing vital components into wrong slots, hoping something would magically open? Only to discover nothing fit together in the first place?

Before this case, I would've considered myself a skilled investigator. But now? I wondered if I should tell Kent to not even bother putting my initial beside his on his office door. Speaking of Kent, I sure hoped he was having more success than I.

At least I could still open the box.

I retrieved my picks from my drawer. Within a minute I had it open and lifted the lid, only to find an assortment of knickknacks. I ran my finger over a cameo pin with a bent hinge. An envelope contained a few photographs. By the back descriptions, the pictures were of Maude and her husband. A few dried flowers had been pressed in a small poetry book. Last, I picked up a wad of tangled ribbons.

That was all.

If there wasn't anything here of importance, why had Mrs. Welch committed this box to Rosalie Adams's care?

I emptied the contents onto the end table and inspected the inside, running my fingers along the velvet lining. Aside from a small tear in the corner, there was nothing amiss. I blew out a breath. Closed the lid.

Just to be thorough, I skimmed my thumb across the decorative studs.

One of them shifted.

My pulse leaped. The second rivet from the left wobbled beneath my finger. I slid it upward and exposed . . . a hidden keyhole.

Trying to tamp down my billowing hope, I snagged the key from Ettie's letter, and this time it worked.

Click.

In a flash the base separated from the box, dropping to the carpet, paper scattering. There had been a false bottom. I set the rest of the container aside, and lowered onto my knees, surveying what had fallen. Letters. There had to be at least a dozen. Perhaps more. I picked up the closest envelope and gasped.

It was from Dori Flowers, otherwise known as Veronica Ridgeway. I opened it up to read its entirety.

My Dear Ettie,

I paused. Veronica had known Maude Welch as Ettie. That explained why Mrs. Welch had signed her letter to Kent as such. Little by little things were falling into place. I read on,

I hope you are well and the island weather is being kind.

I realize you won't get this letter for what seems like ages, but I must tell you. If only to organize my thoughts.

I saw R today. He found me. After all these years, he showed up at my door here in Greenford. R told me his father had died. I know the proper feeling at such news should be sympathy, but I could not summon anything but relief. For so long I lived in fear that his father would find out the truth and come after me. I barely managed to save my son from his wrath. And now I'm free too. Now to escape the memories. Seeing R brought them back again.

Oh, Ettie. How did he even find me? He apologized. Said he was sorry for choosing his inheritance over me, riches over love. He'd tossed me aside when his father threatened to disinherit him. I never understood how he could reject me so easily. Maybe I shouldn't have run off like I had. But sadness has a way of dislodging reason.

I explained my side of the story. R didn't know his father followed me to the asylum. To his credit, he was horrified when I told him about his father's plan to have our child killed. R never told anyone, especially his father, that we eloped. If his father would've known, he would've tried to kill me too.

R seemed genuine in his regret, but it's not as though we can be together again. He belongs to another. But then, does he? We never divorced. We've separated in heart but not in truth. I could expose him. I have proof. But again, what good would that do? It's not Ida's fault. She couldn't know that I was Mrs. Elliot before she was.

I lowered the paper. "Veronica Ridgeway was married to Mr. Elliot."

"And it ruined my life."

I jumped at the familiar voice of my mother's neighbor. Ida Elliot stood in my bedroom doorway.

Chapter 29 ———————————————————————————

HALF OF IDA'S PROFILE WAS engulfed in shadows. She'd stepped into the parlor from the hall, meaning she had to have been in the back rooms, not just entering my flat. Paulo hadn't left the light on, Ida had. "What's going on?" I demanded. "Why are you here? And how did you get in here?"

Her face was pale, tears in the corners of her eyes. "I'm sorry. You weren't supposed to know."

"Know what?" Though I could venture a guess. I glanced at the letter in my hand. "That your husband was first married to another?"

"He never knew he told me. He confessed everything during one of his drunken stupors." Her jaw locked, as if she were reliving the moment, anguish tearing into her soft features. "How could he do that to me, Delvina? To Edward?"

Edward. I hadn't thought about that. If Reginald—R!—was truly Veronica's husband, Edward was illegitimate. Kent would be heir to the vast family fortune. My gut seized. Kent! To think the surly Reginald Elliot was his father. "I'm sorry, Ida. I feel for you, but . . ." I took in all the letters on the ground. Each inky scrawl penned in a feminine script—Veronica's. "I'm going to ask you again—how did you get in here?"

She took a step toward me, and I caught a flash of something in her hand, hidden mostly by her sleeve. "Same as before. I took Elizabeth's key."

"Before?" It hit me. "You were the one. You destroyed my flat." And she'd stolen my mother's key to get in. That was why there hadn't been any signs of forced entry—Ida had waltzed right in. "Why?" Moreover, *what* was tucked inside her sleeve. The way her hand crimped the hem made me think the object wasn't large. A knife? A derringer?

"To frighten you off." A tear rolled down her cheek. "Believe me—I didn't want to, Delvina. But you were getting too close. You were investigating Adele Thayer's death. I've been following you to see what you knew." She nodded at the letter in my hand. "But now you know it all. I can't have that. No matter how much I like you."

My heart pumped fast. My gaze skipped to my purse with my gun tucked inside. I'd have to go by Ida to reach it. I didn't exactly know *all*, as Ida had said. Just that Mr. Elliot was a bigamist. He'd married Kent's mother and had never divorced, making his second marriage void. Obviously, Maude Welch had been aware. The truth twisted into me, making my voice hard. "You killed Maude Welch."

"I had to. She was blabbing. I heard her rambling to your mother about Veronica Ridgeway."

Mother. She and Maude had been by the stone wall. Ida must've been outside as well and overheard. My blood burned. If Ida targeted my mother I . . . I didn't know what I'd do. Mother was my only parent left. "Ida, my mother doesn't know. She wasn't paying attention to anything Maude said."

"Maude didn't tell her. She just hinted here and there." She took another step toward me, and I shifted back. "So I visited Maude to find out *all* she knew. Which was too much."

Then she'd killed her. "Dr. Ewing said it's impossible to murder someone and pass it off as sleeping sickness."

"Doctors these days." She gave a sorrowful shake of her head, as if they deserved pity. "So narrow-minded. They don't see beyond their university textbooks. No, dear. It was simple. I've done it before."

My eyes snapped to hers. "Veronica Ridgeway."

"I couldn't let her live," Ida pleaded, as if she were the victim. "She could've exposed Reginald and then what would happen to me? To Edward?"

Ida was Punire! She had been the mysterious visitor, the one spotted leaving Veronica's cabin just before Kent had arrived. Ida had killed his mother. All because Reginald Elliot was a coward. If the man would've stood up to his father, none of this would've happened. Ida would've been married to someone else, and Kent could've established a relationship with his mother. Ida had stolen so much.

She sniffled like a pitiful villain. "I have to get rid of everyone who knew about Veronica and her child."

Wait. Ida knew about Kent? If she even tried to—

"Veronica had a child. You didn't know? Neither did I, until Maude advised me to give Reginald's fortune to the *true heir*. Maude told me she contacted the child. Can't you see why I had to keep her quiet?" A madness entered her tone, and I kept my gaze on her left arm, trying to catch a glimpse of what she hid. "Maude wouldn't tell me the child's name. But it was obvious when Adele Thayer telephoned me, asking if we could meet. When I asked her what about, she said she wanted to discuss 'Maude Welch and her discovery.' See? Maude told Adele Thayer that she had a right to Edward's fortune! I had to do it."

Oh. Ida thought Miss Thayer was Reginald and Veronica's child.

This was a tangled web of tragedy. Miss Thayer must've snooped around Maude's place and somehow found the letters. She'd intended to blackmail Ida Elliot, not knowing Ida believed Adele was Veronica's child. So Ida killed Adele, thinking she was eliminating the heir. But Kent was the heir. Something Maude Welch had figured out, considering the letter she'd left at his office. But how? How did Maude know who Kent was?

"What are you hiding?" I pointed at her left arm, and she reflexively tucked it to her side. "Turn yourself in, Ida." I inched toward her. "Make a clean breast of it."

"I'm too far into it." Her voice broke. "You're all that's left who knows."

A knock sounded at the door. "Vinny, it's me."

Kent.

Panic entered Ida's eyes. "Get rid of him. Or I'll be forced to." She backed toward the door, forbidding me to open it.

I weighed my options. I could charge at her, but I wasn't certain what was up her sleeve, be it gun or knife. I didn't want to act rashly until I knew. I took a step forward, placing me near the hall, but still too far from my purse. "You can't come in," I called to Kent.

"Why not? You messaged for me to meet you." Confusion marked his tone. "I thought you'd want to hear about—"

"No." I cut him off. I had no clue what he'd discovered at the poker pit. Had he discovered that the mysterious Mr. E had been Reginald Elliot? If so, I didn't want to risk him blurting it. Ida couldn't know he was Veronica's son. She would put a bull's-eye on his back too. Here I'd worried about him visiting the sordid haunt, while all the while the true danger was here in my flat. "It's bad luck to see the bride on her wedding day."

His deep timbre floated through the door. "It's not even midnight."

"It feels like midnight to me," I said as natural as possible over my rushing heartbeat. "It's what I need right now, Kenny."

A pause. "If that's how you want it."

I released my pent-up breath, unsure if I'd done the right thing.

Ida pressed her ear to the door, listening. After a few minutes of silence, she was satisfied he'd left, and she moved from the foyer. Her gaze fastened on me, the air between us charged with sinister intent. "I'm sorry, Delvina. I wish it didn't have to end this way." She tugged a tube from the inside of her coat sleeve.

A blowgun.

The poison can be the cure.

Kent's remark from earlier came back with a sting.

The cure . . . cure . . . cure . . . curare. Of course. That was it. How Ida had done it. "Curare."

"You remembered." Her voice was a chilling blend of approval and sadness. "I truly enjoyed those times I tutored you. You should've pursued medicine rather than being a detective." She said my profession with a bitter undertone. "Then we wouldn't be here."

"You can't kill me, Ida." I eased another step toward her, my mind grappling to remember the properties of the poison while endeavoring to stall as much as I could. "I visited Dr. Ewing only this morning and asked if murder can be posed as sleeping sickness. If I wind up dead so soon from supposedly that very thing, he's going to be suspicious." I took another step toward her. "And of course if you have a gun hidden on your person, you can't pull that staged suicide stunt again. Suspicious as well. By the way, Adele Thayer was left-handed. You put the gun in her right. That clued me in that she was murdered." But it would only take a single breath to hit me with a dart. Then I'd be paralyzed in seconds.

Her chin quivered. "I was rushed. I didn't want to do any of this."

"Then don't." I felt like we were going around in circles, but for now I'd keep spinning the wheel because I needed to think of a plan. I could dodge the dart. It would have to hit skin for it to work. My gun was out of reach. "Let me live. I won't tell a soul that Veronica Ridgeway was married to Reginald." I absolutely would, but this was survival.

She caught my bluff. "I can't trust you." She regarded the wooden tube with a dark glimmer in her eyes. "But I promise you it won't hurt. You won't feel a thing."

"You're right—she won't." Kent's voice boomed from behind me in the hall. "Because you aren't going to hurt her."

Kent!

He'd understood my signal. *Kenny.* He'd dryly told me to only call him that when I desperately needed him. At the time, I'd never imagined this scenario. He'd used the servants' entrance. Must've pocketed the key yesterday, and I'd never been more thankful for his thievery. But then . . . I remembered he wasn't armed.

My eyes ran over him. No bloodied lip. Or swollen eye. He'd emerged from the gambling den reeking like cigarette smoke but unscathed. Only to step into this mess.

Ida's gaze widened. "You shouldn't be here."

"Neither should you." His tone was low and lethal.

As it stood, Kent was behind me and Ida in front, me in the middle. "You have no weapon." Her voice cracked. "You can't protect her."

"On the contrary. I have a powerful weapon." He jerked his head toward the servants' door and hollered. "Come on in, Edward."

"No!" She screeched. "You can't bring my son here!" Her hand fluttered to her mouth, and her cheeks puffed.

Kent's arm darted out, shoving me against the wall.

Something whirled past my head. I lunged toward Ida, crashing into her, the momentum taking us both down. Her skull smacked the metal corner of the end table, knocking her unconscious, the blowgun rolling out of her fingers.

I picked it up. The shaft was empty.

Kent groaned.

My gaze whipped to him.

My husband dropped to his knees, sagging against the wall, a dart poking from his neck.

Chapter 30

No!

No, no, no.

I rushed to Kent's side. Folding my sleeve over my hand, as a makeshift glove, I tugged the dart from his skin and pressed it into the wall, out of the way.

His limp body pitched forward, his shoulder knocking mine. He couldn't fall onto his stomach. That would only complicate things more. Using my weight against his, I guided him so his back was on the carpet.

Every part of me shook. I couldn't lose him. *Think, Vinny.* My mind shuffled back to Ida's long-winded lectures, but all was a shadowy haze. Curare. What about it? Each second I wasted, the poison ravaged his body.

God, help me. Please.

I didn't remember curare as a poison because . . . Ida had never taught it as such. It was a tool. A tool for early physicians. Used in surgical procedures. Why? Why did they use it?

Think! If I could only toss a leash around my brain and subdue the riotous thoughts. Wait.

Subdue!

Ida had taught me physicians from bygone eras would use curare to subdue their patients.

It was as if a dark veil had been lifted, the light of those lessons flooding in. The curare would relax the muscles but not numb them. The patients couldn't move, yet they could feel, hear, and understand. They needed assistance breathing . . . or else they'd die.

I looked at Kent.

His body was limp, eyes closed, but his pulse thudded hard in his throat. His heart would remain strong until the poison collapsed his lungs.

He needed breath. I'd give him mine.

With a prayer on my lips, I jerked his tie knot loose and undid the top buttons of his collar, wanting to rid any tightness around his throat. I tilted his head—face upward, neck straight—aligning with his spine. "Trust me, Kent." I pinched shut his nose and filled his chest with my air, placing my right hand lightly on his chest, ensuring it rose and fell. It did. I pushed another stream of air through his body. Then turned my head, keeping close, feeling his exhale against my cheek. It seemed to be—

Someone charged into the room.

I jolted.

Edward!

I'd thought Kent had only said Edward was in the hall to spook Ida. But no, the man stood before me with a horrified expression. His suit was rumpled, hair flopping over his forehead, and he stank of cigarette smoke, like Kent.

"What happened?" He gulped, his alarming gaze bouncing between his mother and Kent. Ida still lay unconscious several feet away. "Is . . . she? Is he? Are they . . . both?"

"They're both alive," I said between breaths. Fine time to ask questions. "I need you to fetch the janitor. Paulo. He'll help with Ida." And also ensure she didn't get away. Plus, I needed Edward gone so I could focus on Kent.

He nodded and dashed out the door.

It was easy to see why he'd thought Kent was dead. His body looked lifeless, but his steady pulse gave me courage. I didn't know how much poison was in his system. Or how long I'd have to breathe into him. With every puff of air, my throat grew drier, even while tears collected in my eyes. Because Kent had pushed me out of the way. He'd taken the dart meant for me.

"You promised." I crushed my mouth against his warm lips, forcing life into him. "You promised to meet me before the judge. Keep your vow, Brisbane. Fight. Fight for us." My tear dropped onto his cheek, pressing between our faces.

I'd fallen into a steady rhythm—breathe, lift my head, feel his exhale. Then repeat. It could've been minutes, hours, an eternity. I had no idea. But his lashes fluttered. His index finger twitched.

A fresh burst of energy surged through me. "Keep fighting," I commanded, even as Edward returned, Paulo in tow.

Edward breezed past, hurrying to attend to his mother.

I administered another bout of air and motioned Paulo near. "Carry her to the spare bedroom. Check her for more weapons and keep an eye on her."

I couldn't give him much more detail than that, but Paulo nodded, his eyes communicating he understood my full meaning. *Don't let her escape.* With Ida removed to the back room, I focused on giving my husband my full attention, ignoring the rising lightheadedness.

I would do this all night if need be. All day. I sank closer to him, giving my lower back a reprieve. The grandfather clock punctuated the silence, helping me time my exhales.

A low moan rattled Kent's throat. I felt it more than heard. I pulled back. His eyes were open, looking at me. Those silver depths were so full of . . . life.

A sob begged to be released, but I couldn't risk clogging my airways with emotion. He still needed me.

Kent's hand flexed at his side. Slowly he was regaining control. His chest wasn't rising fully, but he managed to scrape in some meager breaths on his own. I cupped his face. "Let me help you a little longer." So I did. His heartbeat synced with mine as I pressed against him. His thumb skimmed the side of my leg. Sweet signs of recovery.

After a while, his mouth moved, a slight pressure against my dry lips.

He kissed me.

Tears rushed. The spike of poison must've weakened, the effects fading. He wasn't full strength yet, judging by his raspy wheezes, but the worst part was behind him.

I whispered a prayer of thanks.

"Now you know." His voice was a low hum.

Know what? I had no idea, but all that mattered was he was here. Still here. With me. "You can talk my ear off later. For now, I need you to rest."

With Kent on his way to recovery, I should be calling the police or checking on Ida. But the fatigue of the past however many minutes clamped into me. I curled into Kent's side, savoring each rise and fall of his chest.

Once again my husband cheated death.

● ● ●

Ida had awakened not long after. With Edward present, her wild mood had all but vanished, leaving the broken woman refusing to speak.

I telephoned Detective Matthew Burkett and explained everything. He apologized for not listening before and promised I'd always have an ally on the police force. I hoped his word was true—rather than the humble officer being acutely concerned I'd approach his superior about his sloppy effort with this case.

Seeing all was under control, Paulo escaped out the servants' entrance the second Detective Burkett stepped foot into my flat. After collecting the blowgun and, with his handkerchief, carefully extracting the dart from the wall as evidence, Detective Burkett handcuffed Ida and led her out, a somber Edward following behind. I'd quickly briefed Kent on what I discovered—Veronica having married Reginald and never divorced. Ida had found out and had killed the three women who knew.

There was still a lot to explain and still be sorted out, but for now Kent and I could draw a full breath, figuratively and literally.

Kent reclined on my bed. He'd been drifting in and out of slumber, and I never thought I'd be grateful to hear a man snoring soundly.

"It's after midnight, my bride."

I glanced over, surprised to find him awake and staring at me. "It is." It was 2:00 a.m., to be exact.

He shifted and stretched his neck, cracking it to the left, then right. "I thought you said it's bad luck to see you on your wedding day."

"It was the first thought that came to my head. I had to rattle off something to use your nickname as a signal."

"That was a nice touch, by the way. Calling me Kenny like that." He patted the bed, and I climbed up beside him. "Considering the time, are you still okay with me staying with you?"

As long as it's forever. "After the scare you gave me . . ." My hand slipped across his chest. It was okay. He was okay. "You'll be lucky if I let you out of my sight."

"That's quite territorial of you, Mrs. Brisbane." He tossed back my words from the other day. "I like you this way."

I laughed. After the evening we'd had, I needed this light banter. Kent did too, considering the tightness around his eyes eased. Though as much as I wanted to nestle against him and forget this evening, I couldn't. "If you hadn't shoved me out of the way earlier, that dart would've hit me." I'd like to think I could've dodged it, but Kent was as agile as I, and he couldn't. The dart had left the shaft surprisingly fast. "You gave your life up. No hesitancy."

"Well, Knuckles, if that's not enough to convince you that I love you, I'm all out of ideas."

"Fine. I'm convinced."

"Glad that's settled."

I smiled and moved to retract my hand, but Kent's own claimed it, holding my palm against his heart.

"So are you going to explain how Edward came to be at my flat?"

"It seems the chap enjoys a bit of poker. He was at the Kingston Avenue. I offered to give him a ride home. Before we left, I called my flat to check in with you. Roger gave me the message about you being here."

"So you headed to Park Towers first, before taking Edward home." Which made sense because my flat was in between the two places. It would've been silly of Kent to backtrack, since Park Towers was on the way.

He nodded.

"I never imagined quiet Edward to have an affinity for gambling." But then I hadn't figured on his mother being a killer either.

"Must run in the family," he added dryly. "Only because the person—"

"Kent, you have a brother now." I hadn't truly thought of it until this moment.

"Indeed I do." He relaxed against the pillows so I could snuggle more easily. "But we'll see if he'll want to speak with me after tonight."

No doubt Edward was in shock. Probably would be for a considerable amount of time. He'd discovered his mother was a killer and he was no longer heir to a vast fortune, within the span of a few hours. But Edward was a decent man. I hoped he and Kent would be amicable to each other, even establish a relationship. "Tell me what happened."

He stretched his arm around me, tucking me against him. "I went to the place as planned. Randall was there, so I asked him about Mr. E."

"Just like that?" I'd thought for sure the gambling den owner would make Kent owe him a favor, or rough him up a little, or flatly refuse.

"Just like that." He smiled, and I noticed a bit of weariness in his expression. "Randall said it was no use harboring the secret anymore, since the man was dead."

"It was Reginald Elliot." He'd passed away a few years ago. Actually he'd died only a couple of months before Veronica Ridgeway. Had Ida killed her husband? Or had she grown desperate after his death to be certain Veronica wouldn't claim his fortune?

"No. Not Reginald."

"What do you mean?" I poked my head up. "It had to be."

"Mr. E was Frederick Elliot. Reginald's father. That's what I was trying to say about gambling running in the family, since Frederick is Edward's grandfather, and I suppose mine too."

I sat straight up. "Oh, Kent."

"What?"

"The letters." They were still scattered across the parlor floor. I'd been so caught up in the moment, first dealing with Ida, then Kent's recovery, I'd forgotten. "I'll be right back." I hustled to the other room and carefully scooped up Veronica's words, beginning with the letter I'd been reading when Ida happened upon me.

I rejoined Kent in my bedroom. "*Frederick Elliot* was the one who tried to kill you at birth." I handed him the paper.

His eyes quickly scanned the page, then darted to me. "This was written by my mother." The wonder in his tone nearly broke me.

"These all are, I believe." I lifted the stack of envelopes. "But in the one you have, she writes about Frederick's passing and how she lived in fear because of him."

He glanced up from reading. "So Frederick Elliot was the man at the asylum who wanted me dead." He huffed a disbelieving laugh. "And just so happened to be the same fellow I trounced repeatedly in poker."

"Do you think he knew it was you?"

"It seems too much of a coincidence to believe otherwise. Though reading this"—he waved the letter—"I'm not sure."

"Either way, I'm glad for it." I claimed the seat beside him on the mattress. "You know I don't condone gambling, but a part of me finds it gratifying that you emptied his coffers again and again."

"That I did." His eyes fell to the paper again, the tender scrutiny in his gaze making my heart flip. At least he had a token of hers to remember her by.

"Though . . ." I glanced at the remaining notes in my hand. "How did Frederick Elliot come to own a cabin in the same town as your mother?" I set the letters between us. "Maybe there's more."

He picked another one up from the top of the pile. "Shall we read the rest, then?"

"Absolutely." I kissed his cheek. "Your mother will tell us her story."

And she did. Veronica's life was that of sorrow and survival. Through her letters we discovered she'd met Reginald during her debut, and they'd fallen in love. But Frederick Elliot thought Veronica, an adopted child, was beneath his son. When Frederick had gone overseas on a business trip, Reginald eloped with Veronica. They stayed at his secluded country estate, keeping their marriage a secret. When Frederick returned to the States, he assumed his son had taken Veronica as a mistress, since it had been understood for years that Reginald was to marry Ida. Ida's father and Frederick wanted to venture into business together, merging their talents, and Ida's father would only do so after seeing Ida wed.

So Frederick evicted Veronica, who was already well along in her pregnancy. She fled to Greenford after delivering her child and remained there.

Anger boiled in my chest. "I can't believe Reginald let his father treat her so cruelly." I looked at Kent. "Though it shouldn't surprise me. I've seen many men who put their livelihoods over their own families." I set the last letter down. "Though I still don't understand why Frederick had that hunting cabin."

"Maybe he followed Veronica back to Greenford as well. He could've bought the cabin to keep an eye on her. Maybe to ensure she didn't go after his son again."

That seemed extreme. But so was arranging an infant's death so he wouldn't interfere with your son's future.

Kent grew quiet, staring at the heap of papers between us.

I nudged his shoulder. "Does this help you feel close to her?"

He shrugged. "In a way." His gaze tangled with mine, his arms reaching for me. "Though I don't think I'll feel connected to anyone as much as I do you." He moved the letters aside and tugged me to him. "It's my turn to say thank you." He kissed the top of my head. "You saved my life."

My mind reeled back to those moments in the hall. How terrified I was to lose him. How God helped sustain us both. "And we see irony yet again." I craned my neck to peer into his questioning face. "Remember how I told you I'd ask people from different fields to teach me."

"I remember." By his tender smile, no doubt he was thinking of the time he'd tutored me in the ways of investigating.

"At one point I was interested in medicine, so Ida took it upon herself to instruct me. I would've never known about curare if not for her. Doctors would inject it into their patients to relax their muscles, though it wasn't an act of mercy. It was more for the doctor's benefit than the patient's because it stopped the patient from thrashing about during surgery. But the patient would feel the sawing of their limbs, the scalpel digging into their organs." I shuddered. "They could feel everything."

"That's true," Kent said. "I felt everything." His thumb traced my lower lip. "I thought my lungs were shriveling up. But then you saved me with your kiss." And then he thanked me with one of his own.

I eased back. "When you first opened your eyes, you said, 'Now you know.' What does that mean?"

"Just what I've been trying to get through to you, but you finally saw it for yourself." His gaze roamed my face, taking me in slow and tender.

"Which is?"

"That I can't breathe without you." He kissed me again, his arms holding me close. His every touch exploding with affection for me, I collapsed into him.

We stayed up through the night, poring over Veronica's letters, talking about the past, dreaming about our future, all with several kisses sprinkled throughout. Considering the day ahead, we probably should've turned in long ago. But Kent and I didn't have a stellar record of making wise judgments.

"It's nearly eight o'clock." I glanced at the wall clock. "What should we do now?"

He shrugged. "Maybe think about getting married."

"Hmm. Sounds good to me," I teased back. But I really did need to head to Hemswick. I'd promised Flossie I'd let her help me dress. Plus, of course my gown was there. "As long as we don't encounter any more drama between here and city hall." Well, there was bound to be a little since I intended to break the news to Mother about Ida.

"I'll drive you over, then head to the flat to get dressed."

I grabbed what I needed for the day, retrieving my purse last. However, as I moved to retrieve it, something else caught my eye. I stooped to pick it up and gasped.

Within my hands lay the final answer to a long list of questions.

Chapter 31

WHEN I'D ARRIVED AT HEMSWICK, Mother had been waiting at the door, an eager expression lighting her face. She looked beautiful in her lilac dress, trimmed with pale pink flowers the same shade as my dress. I hated to be the cause for dimming her bright smile, but it couldn't be avoided.

I'd quickly informed her about Ida. She'd cried when I explained about Kent's mother and cried even harder when I told her how Kent risked his life for me.

"I couldn't ask for a better son," she'd said, wiping her eyes. "No more hiding, Delvina. Go let the world see your love for him."

I couldn't be more ready.

Kent's casual attitude and breezy nature was noticeably absent as he watched me join his side before Judge VanKirk. He stood tall and handsome in a tailored dark brown suit, but his eyes were what captured my attention—they were fixed on me with such adoration that I could hardly breathe.

At noon sharp Kent and I publicly pledged our lives to each other before our family and friends, not to mention a few of Warren Hayes's journalists. My sister, Kate, had surprised me by attending the ceremony with her husband, Rhett. Mother had orchestrated it all, paying for their train travel from Pittsburgh. I was grateful for the opportunity to finally ask Kate for forgiveness for my series of fibs about knowing our birth mother.

Kate hugged my neck. "She'd be so proud of the woman you've be-come." Her brown eyes were glossy. "And that we've been reunited."

Kate and I had been separated for over twenty years and at one time had lived on two different continents. God had brought us together. I glanced over at my husband, conversing with Rhett. Another reconcili-ation. Last month I'd believed I was a secretly divorced woman with a strong disgust for Kent Brisbane. Today I loved him more than words could say.

After the reception luncheon, Mother shooed Kent and I out of Hemswick. By the time we reached the door to Kent's flat, I was begin-ning to regret staying up all night.

I stifled a yawn and peered over at my husband. "No matter how tired I am, I refuse to be asleep again when you carry me over the threshold."

Kent's mouth hitched in a roguish grin. "I'm going to keep you awake for way more than that."

I laughed as he swept me up into his arms. He might talk like a starved male, but I knew if I truly cried exhaustion, he'd be the first to fluff the pillows and tuck me in. That was just how he was. Selfless. Protective. And all mine.

He dutifully carried me into the flat and kicked the door shut behind him. Given his previous remark, I expected him to be rather eager. So I was surprised when he gently deposited me on the bed and strode to the closet. He returned, clutching a slim rectangular box. "I'm fresh out of moonshine," he teased, about our very first wedding gift. "But I have something else for you." He handed me the gift, his expression unusually bashful.

I opened the lid, and my heart warmed at the sight of a silver-toned nameplate. *Delvina Brisbane P.I.* It matched the one I'd given him those years ago. "It's perfect."

"It's for your new desk, which you'll pick out because I'm awful at that sort of thing."

"Thank you." I tugged him down for a kiss. "I'm looking forward to besting you at every case that comes through our office door."

I felt his smile against my lips. "I wouldn't have it any other way."

"Now I've something for you." I gave him a quick peck. I sensed his reluctance at my pulling back, but he didn't know what was in my purse. It was the final piece to the puzzle—how Maude Welch knew Kent was Veronica's son. And subsequently, how Adele Thayer discovered the link. When rummaging Maude's things, Miss Thayer had no doubt come across the very item now in my possession, which was why the young model attempted to arrange an appointment with Kent. That also explained why Miss Thayer was so interested in Kent at Mother's dinner party. "I figured out how Maude Welch knew about you."

His head reared back in surprise. "How?"

"Remember what you told me about the day you happened upon your mother? You mentioned her neighbor—the one who gave her your message—collected Veronica's mail and left that night."

He nodded solemnly. "Yes."

"*This* was Veronica's mail. The very one she'd given to the neighbor to post." I opened my purse and withdrew the envelope. "I found it under the sofa. It must've gotten separated from the bunch when everything fell from Maude's box."

He gave me a quizzical look, then opened the letter. "'Dear Ettie,'" he read aloud. "'I can't write long because my son is coming to visit. You read that correctly. My son found me! I've searched for years. Prayed for years. His name's Kent Brisbane. He left a message with my neighbor. He's concerned about my safety, but with Frederick Elliot gone, so is any threat of harm. I'll tell him all is well when he arrives. I'm so happy, I could barely write! As you know, I only held him but a moment, but he's stayed all these years in my heart. My dearly loved son.'" His voice broke, and I grabbed his hand. "'He'll be here soon. I'll write again.'"

She hadn't gotten another chance to write Maude Welch because Ida had beaten Kent to her cottage door.

He studied the paper, as if absorbing her words, making them a part of him. After several minutes, he set the letter down, his handsome face filling with raw emotion. "She wasn't indifferent, as I'd thought."

"Not at all. It appears she looked for you just as you had for her." I brushed a tear from his cheek, placing a kiss there. "I know things were tragic, but Ida didn't win. You'll reunite with your mother in heaven and will have ages and ages together." I pressed a hand to his arm, easing him to lie beside me on the bed. He obeyed my guided touch. "She loved you your whole life. Now I get to."

He ran his hand down the line of my body in reverent wonder. "I don't deserve you." His voice was an intimate whisper. He levered over me, his supported weight on his elbows, his gaze tethering mine with a calming strength. "But know this, love—those years we were apart, my soul was bonded to yours."

I shivered under his mesmeric attention.

His mouth slanted over mine, hovering, our breaths tangling. "I would've waited an eternity for you."

"And now that I'm yours again?"

He nuzzled my cheek, sliding to my ear. "Now I refuse to lose another minute, another second."

"Prove it."

And he did.

Epilogue

Kent

November 27, 1924

"YOU PROMISED TO HAVE FUN," Delvina reminded, brushing away the snowflakes dotting my shoulder.

"I am." I summoned a smile, though not exactly difficult with her gazing up at me. I hated the cold, but I loved her, so we braved the frigid temperatures for me to experience yet another youthful lark.

Two days after our ceremony, Delvina announced she'd introduce me to all the childhood adventures I'd missed. It was endearing, really. My wife was determined, and I'd gone along with all her ideas with the exception that I'd choose the winner's prize for each game. Most could guess what a married man would suggest as a reward.

We'd played blindman's bluff in our flat, run around Hemswick in a cutthroat game of tag, endured multiple rounds of jacks, and so on. Delvina was brutally competitive, making my hard-fought victories all the sweeter. Though in the games she'd emerged as winner, she'd chosen the same prize.

So when she'd discovered there was a first-ever Christmas parade along Thirty-Fourth Street—complete with floats, animals from Central Park Zoo, and enough clowns to provoke nightmares—I'd happily agreed. Never mind that it was Thanksgiving morning and bitterly cold—I wouldn't deny her anything.

I'd guessed the parade's theme was nursery rhymes, given the float toddling past us consisted of three grown men in a giant bathtub. I raised a brow at Delvina, and she laughed.

"I bet with all your money you could buy Macy's." She waved a hand toward "The World's Largest Store," the very business putting on this spectacle.

"Doubtful." I adjusted her scarf around her neck and tapped her pink nose.

"You're richer than me now." She batted her lashes, looking up at me in exaggerated adoration. "Aren't you the least concerned that I married you for your fortune?" She took delight in teasing me that I was now a resident of the land of swells. I wasn't. Not really. I was just a fellow with a few more dollars in his bank account. After we'd discovered the true identity of my father, it wasn't difficult to track down their marriage license, erasing any doubt about my legitimacy.

I tugged the belt of her coat, bringing her closer to me. "No, you married me because of my dashing good looks."

"I won't deny it." Her playful smile slipped into one of tenderness. "As for the money, I think what you're doing for Edward is honorable."

I intended to go halves with him. It was only fair to divide the Elliot fortune with my half brother. Not long after his mother was taken into custody, he'd shown up at our office and apologized for his family's treatment toward my mother and me. It was still difficult to process that Ida Elliot was Punire. To think that the woman felt she'd needed to punish my mother simply because she'd fallen in love and married a man who had no backbone.

I sighed and returned my thought to the son. Edward seemed a decent sort. He and I had met up several times to play poker, no gambling, of course. Delvina would probably tug off all my fingernails if we'd played for real money. Not that I would.

"That reminds me." She lifted on her toes to watch a horde of acrobats tumbling down the street. "Edward's joining us at Hemswick for Thanksgiving dinner." She gave me a sidelong glance. "Mother's invited a few young ladies as well."

"She mentioned the other day about hiring our investigative services to search for an eligible bride for the poor man." Elizabeth Kline had taken Edward under her motherly wing. Though I wasn't sure if that was entirely a good thing, considering her penchant for matchmaking.

Delvina shook her head with a smile. "As if we need more work."

She was right. We had more cases than we knew what to do with. As promised, we'd given Warren's newspaper the exclusive on Adele Thayer's case, with the added information about Maude Welch and my mother. The story had attracted national attention. It was mildly absurd, the coverage we'd received. Journalists were one thing, but radio stations had asked to make our investigations a serial broadcast. The "Sleuthing Sweethearts" was now a running cartoon in the funny papers. Whoever the artist was always drew Delvina as a glamorous socialite and me a gangly bumble.

While a person suspiciously costumed as Humpty-Dumpty strutted past, I curled my arm around my wife's waist, and she leaned into me. These moments with her were gifts. Something I hoped I'd never take for granted.

Delvina whistled at the food vendor, waving him over. "Buttered popcorn's another thing on my list you need to experience."

I grinned at her, and she rewarded me with one of her own. I'd actually eaten popcorn before, but I hadn't the heart to tell her. In fact, I had everything I wanted. A family. A woman I'd cherish for as many days as God would grant me. My path hadn't been easy. From the beginning I'd fought for the right to walk this earth. But as Warren had so often pointed out, those dark moments enabled me to appreciate the light. With Delvina by my side, I vowed to embrace it fully.

Author's Note ————————————————————————————————

THANK YOU FOR READING THIS story. I hope you enjoyed Delvina and Kent's adventure. Some readers might recognize Kent from his side role in *Walking on Hidden Wings* and Delvina from her mysterious debut in *The Mobster's Daughter*. It was so much fun to feature these characters in a story of their own!

Now's the time to gush about the historical facts that were in the book. I always look forward to writing these author's notes. It's my little space that I can unleash my inner history enthusiast.

Divorce in the early 1900s was frowned upon, just as it was difficult to attain. Couples had to appear in court, and there had to be legal grounds for the divorce, such as abuse, desertion, adultery, and the like. The quickest one could get a divorce was in Reno, and it took about six months. In the 1930s Reno adjusted their laws and shortened the length to six weeks. So in the 1920s, if couples were desperate for a quiet divorce, they would turn to foreign avenues. The most popular was Paris, but other countries held a lot of appeal as well. So when I read this, I thought it would be interesting to play into the scam angle, since it most definitely occurred back then.

On the flip side, one could easily get married. The town of Elkton, Maryland, really was the marriage capital of the East Coast. They had walk-up booths where a couple could get both licensed and hitched in minutes.

In my research of 1920s New York, I found that John Powers opened the first modeling agencies in NYC in 1923. Before that the modeling industry didn't exist. But once the department stores found value in using live models rather than mannequins, the profession exploded outside the boundaries of NYC. The fashion-consultant service was also rising in popularity. Major department stores like Saks hired women with wardrobe expertise to consult customers.

While researching my previous book, I stumbled upon a 1920s newspaper clipping, and the article was rating that year's debutantes. The actual headline said "Classifying Debbies." The article had each debbie listed, and beneath their picture was a letter grade. I couldn't imagine how demoralizing that would be for a young woman to be rated as such. So I slipped that little bit into my story, which helped shape Delvina's character.

The sleeping sickness, or its medical term *encephalitis lethargica*, really occurred, starting in 1919 and peaking in about 1924. It's estimated over one million people were diagnosed. The epidemic was just as mysterious as portrayed in my story. Doctors were baffled about the unpredictable characteristics of the sleeping sickness. Even to this day, the epidemic remains a mystery, and there is no known cure. It led me to wonder how easily it would be for villains to kill under the guise of sleeping sickness. Which led to my search on how it could be done. Thankfully, my local library didn't blink an eye when I checked out stacks of books on poison. I needed a poison that didn't have visible effects. One that—on the outside—appeared as if someone was falling asleep.

I stumbled across curare, which is a plant in the jungles of South America. Tribes would use this poisonous alkaloid to paralyze and kill their prey via darts. Later physicians found merit in its properties. Curare would relax the muscles of their patients during surgery so they wouldn't thrash about on the table. Unfortunately, the poison did not numb or dull, so the patient would feel the excruciating surgeries—but wouldn't be able to move.

On top of that, curare would target the respiratory system, shutting down the lungs while the poison was active in the bloodstream.

So surgeons had to provide supplemental breathing for their patients. When used as a weapon, curare brought no pain and none of the violent reactions found in other poisons, such as hysteria, vomiting, or other intense responses. The heart would still beat strong and the mind would be clear—the only fatal trigger was the curare would shut down the lungs in a matter of minutes. When I discovered the way to rescue a person who'd been poisoned with curare was mouth to mouth, I immediately began configuring how I could work that into the story.

Other small facts in the story were fun to distribute throughout the book. John's Italian restaurant on Twelfth Street really was a notorious speakeasy, and the house special was the way patrons would order their in-house liquor. Also, the bit about the mob boss being gunned down just outside the restaurant doors is also true. Umberto Valenti had just finished a meal of chicken parmesan and emerged from John's restaurant, only to be gunned down by Lucky Luciano.

I was able to incorporate history into the fictional Terminal speakeasy. While the existence of the gin joint was completely my imagination, its location—just outside the Eighth Avenue line—was true. The city had abandoned the Fifty-Eighth terminal around the turn of the century, and just around the time of my story, the city sealed up the line, leaving that empty space. I thought it would be a perfect place for a speakeasy. While the gin joint was fabricated, the history behind the ticket was not. In 1920 the city discontinued paper tickets, using coin-operated turnstiles in their place.

The Galleanists were an actual anarchist group. The group was named after Luigi Galleani, an immigrant who promoted radical anarchism. Many of the members used violence, such as bombs, to encourage political agitation. Society credits the Galleanists for the tragic 1920 Wall Street bombing, which killed almost forty people and seriously injured over 140 bystanders.

The story about the lady pugilist, Helen Hildreth, is also true. Ms. Hildreth was winning the match against Johnny Atkinsson, when the police and boxing commissioner jumped into the ring and ordered the fight to stop.

Author's Note

One final note is on the epilogue, which took place at the first Macy's parade. Back then it was called the Christmas parade and occurred on Thanksgiving Day. The theme was nursery rhymes and included a handful of floats, like ones for the three men in a tub, Little Miss Muffet, and the old woman who lived in a shoe. The parade mostly featured Macy's employees dressed in vibrant costumes, but also incorporated animals from the Central Park Zoo. The parade was such a success that Macy's continued the tradition, and we now see what an enormous event it is today.

Acknowledgments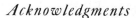

THE DREAMS WE KNEW IS my ninth book. It's surreal to think that I've written about a million words over the past few years. Though not even one word would've ever happened without the support of my family. My husband who first encouraged me to write. My daughter whose own daily courage inspires me to be brave and put my stories out there. My son whose artistic creativity encourages me to continue dreaming. I love you guys more than I could ever express.

Rebekah Millet, I'm so privileged to call you friend. Thank you for all the things. A special shout-out to Janine Rosche and Janyre Tromp— I'm so grateful for all our Marcos. Natalie Walters, the past five books wouldn't have been written if not for you. Thank you, friend.

Thank you to the Kregel team for all the hard work you've done for my past three books. My agent, Julie Gwinn, thank you for believing in me all those years ago.

Thank You, Jesus. My words may entertain, but Yours give life.

"A tangled web, a sleuthing adventure, a rekindled romance . . . *Walking on Hidden Wings* has it all."
—Rachel Fordham, author of *The Letter Tree*

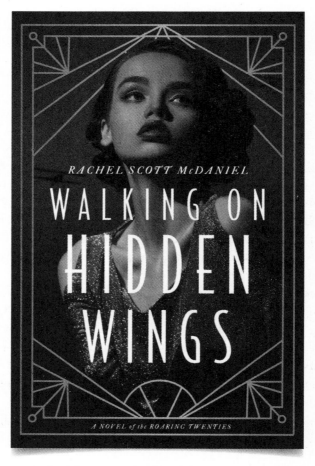

When Geneva Ashcroft Hayes's husband dies in a mysterious plane crash just months after their nuptials, authorities suspect murder. Trading her sparkling gowns for coveralls and pilot goggles, the New York socialite is armed with a new career as a wingwalker and barnstormer—and she's on a mission to find the killer.

KREGEL
PUBLICATIONS

"Each author's unique voice shines in this trio of novellas, each story rich in intriguing historical details, vividly drawn characters, and heart-stirring emotional resonance. A reading experience to treasure."
—AMANDA BARRATT, Christy Award–winning author of *Within These Walls of Sorrow*

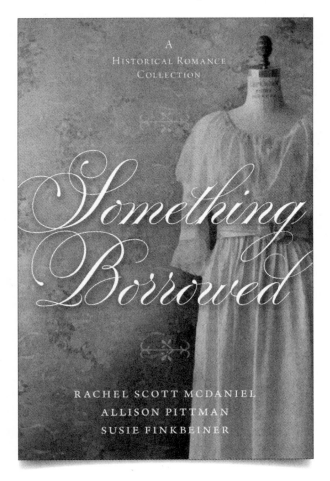

In this novella collection, three renowned Christian historical fiction authors trace generations of wartime romances through a wedding dress with love sewn into its seams.

KREGEL
PUBLICATIONS